The Oridian circling behi[...] [...]ing to avoid the horse's hooves to notice Alix closing in. She slammed into him from behind, running him through before he even realised she was there. His death cry was lost beneath the scream of his comrade as the king hacked into the shoulder of one of his foes, splitting him like firewood. But the move left him open, and his other attacker landed a hard blow to the king's ribs. The sword rang off Erik's armour, doubling him over just as an arrow hissed through the air where his head had been. The destrier skittered sideways. Alix flew at the king's attacker in a frantic attempt to drive him back.

Out of the corner of her eye, she saw the archer taking aim. Alix was on the opposite side of the horse; she knew she would never reach him in time. She did the only thing she could think of: She leapt at the king and tried to pull him down behind the horse's bulk. But the destrier was still off-balance, and with an outraged scream, the warhorse pitched sideways, crashing to the ground and pinning the king and his attacker both. The destrier struggled to stand. Alix dragged the king from the stirrups just as the animal righted itself and bolted away through the trees, leaving Erik exposed.

The archer nocked an arrow. Alix had only one course left to her. She charged.

The archer drew. A feral scream tore from Alix's throat as she bore down on him, sword flashing.

The man flinched. The arrow flew wild.

Alix drove into him blade-first, toppling them both to the ground with such force that the air was blasted from her lungs, and just for a moment, everything went black.

WITHDRAWN

THE
BLOODBOUND

Erin Lindsey

ACE BOOKS, NEW YORK

THE BERKLEY PUBLISHING GROUP
Published by the Penguin Group
Penguin Group (USA) LLC
375 Hudson Street, New York, New York 10014

USA • Canada • UK • Ireland • Australia • New Zealand • India • South Africa • China

penguin.com

A Penguin Random House Company

THE BLOODBOUND

An Ace Book / published by arrangement with the author

Ace Books are published by The Berkley Publishing Group.
ACE and the "A" design are trademarks of Penguin Group (USA) LLC.

For information, address: The Berkley Publishing Group,
a division of Penguin Group (USA) LLC,
375 Hudson Street, New York, New York 10014.

ISBN: 978-0-425-27268-8

PUBLISHING HISTORY
Ace mass-market edition / October 2014

PRINTED IN THE UNITED STATES OF AMERICA

10 9 8 7 6 5 4 3 2 1

Cover art by Lindsey Look.
Cover design by Lesley Worrell.
Interior text design by Kelly Lipovich.

For Don

ONE

†S moke crawled up the side of the bluff, carrying with it the screams of the dying. Alix strained her eyes, trying to pierce the swirling black folds, but all she could make out was the occasional gleam of metal or flicker of flame far below. It was impossible to tell how the battle fared. The cries of men mingled with the screams of horses and the baying of dogs, sounds of triumph and terror indistinguishable from one another.

The only thing Alix could see clearly was the neatly formed ranks of the White Wolves, holding their position on the western fringe.

"Why don't they attack?" She started to uncoil from her crouch.

A hand shot out and seized her wrist. "What are you doing? Get *down*!" Liam glared up at her, punctuating his words with a sharp tug.

"What does it matter who sees us now?" Without waiting for a reply, Alix twisted out of his grasp and started along the edge of the bluff. A muttered oath and the creak of leather told her that Liam was following.

She moved with more haste than care, springing between

the frost-slick stones and shooting the occasional harried glance at the Wolves. Their ranks remained unmoved—horses reined in, swords sheathed, bows lowered. Their standard flapped bravely at the lip of the bluff, the pole as straight and still as if it had been driven into the ground.

What in the gods are they waiting for? The enemy had long since moved into position. Arran Green had struck, leading his battalion down the eastern fringe to drive like a spear into the Oridian flank. The Wolves should have mirrored the attack from the west. Instead, Prince Tomald White simply sat astride his horse, immovable as a statue, looking on as his brother's army battled the enemy below.

A gust of wind nudged the curtain of smoke aside, offering the first clear view of the battlefield since the barricades were set alight. Alix lurched to a halt and sucked in a sharp breath. "They're falling back."

"Already?" Liam scrambled closer to the edge of the bluff, his eyes widening in horror. Beyond the writhing knot of men at the centre of the melee, the rear lines of the Kingswords had begun to blur, their ranks disintegrating under the pressure of the Oridian onslaught. They were outnumbered, but the Wolves were supposed to make up the difference.

Except they weren't.

Something cold and bitter rose at the back of Alix's throat, but she swallowed it down. "I'm going," she said, stepping toward the edge of the bluff.

"Alix . . ." Liam grabbed her arm again. "What do you think you're going to accomplish down there? You're a scout."

"What of it? You're a scout, and you're a better sword than half the king's knights. I can handle myself, Liam."

He hesitated. "Our orders were to stay here."

"And *their* orders were to attack." She stabbed a finger in the direction of the Wolves.

"What are you saying?" He knew the answer—Alix could see it in his eyes.

The king is betrayed. The words burned on her tongue, but for some reason, she couldn't bring herself to speak them. "Look," she said, "you can either regret not following orders, or regret standing up here watching our brothers get slaughtered. Your choice."

Liam paused another few precious seconds before his gaze hardened. "Let's go."

They threw themselves down the slope, skidding sideways to keep their footing as loose rock tumbled out from under them. They moved as fast as they dared; Alix had to lean into the hillside, her fingers brushing the dirt, just to keep from rolling an ankle. Even so, the descent seemed to take forever. Alix's thighs burned, and her breath came in short puffs of vapour. Still the slope went on and on. Gradually, however, the clamour of battle grew louder, the smoke thicker and blacker. And then they plunged into the dense wood at the base of the hill, and an eerie hush swallowed them.

Alix trailed Liam through the pines. A light snow had begun to fall, lending the scene a surreal aura of peace. Only the occasional cry or ring of metal reached back through the veil. Alix slowed to a jog, chain mail jingling, breath harsh in her ears. Liam bounded ahead.

A ghostly silhouette materialised through the trees. A horse, riderless, its white war paint spattered with blood. Liam faltered briefly as he watched it go by. Then another figure appeared, weaving erratically among the drifting snowflakes. A man this time, a soldier, both hands clamped against his neck as he tried in vain to staunch a gushing wound. Liam went for his sword, but the man staggered past without even registering his presence. Moments later, another soldier appeared, and another—Kingswords all, their faces taut with fear. Soon, the shadows swarmed with fleeing men.

Liam drew up short, throwing a grim look over his shoulder. It was worse than they'd thought. "Let's find Green," was all Alix could think to say.

Liam nodded and turned to go.

"Liam."

He looked back. Alix hesitated, the words dying on her lips.

A tense smile flickered across Liam's face, as though he understood. "Just be careful, all right?"

They pushed past the tree line, and hell erupted before them.

The valley surged like the sea under a storm. A riot of bodies heaved according to some unfathomable rhythm, steel and leather and blood and hide flowing around each other in dizzying tides of silver and crimson. Alix froze, momentarily overwhelmed under the assault of sound and motion. Then something crashed against her shoulder, knocking her to the ground, and she found herself lying amid a tangle of bodies. A young man with wide blue eyes stared vacantly in her direction. Shuddering, Alix scrambled to her feet.

She looked about wildly. Liam was nowhere to be seen. Hardly a glimpse of White heraldry anywhere. They had hoped to find Arran Green and the rest of their comrades, but instead Alix was adrift in a sea of Oridians. She needed to move; if she didn't regroup with the others, she was as good as dead. She backed up, keeping to the fringe of trees, her gaze raking the field for allies.

There!

A small island of Kingswords fought in a tight cluster nearby. Alix started toward them, but she didn't get far before an Oridian soldier blocked her path. He made straight for her, eyes glazed with battle lust. At his side dangled a massive sword stained with death. Alix gripped her own blade—light, but bloodforged—and gritted her teeth against the inevitable spike of fear.

He came at her with a sloppy swipe, his shoulder too low to get much force behind it, and Alix turned the stroke aside easily. It was then she noticed the blood darkening the man's leathers. The injury prevented him from raising his sword arm properly, and Alix took full advantage. She feinted, and when he committed himself to parry, she twisted out of the way and landed a solid blow to his flank, her blade biting neatly through boiled leather. The man cried out, folding over himself, and Alix came in again, driving the point of her sword under his armpit. She waited until his knees buckled before yanking the weapon free, the blade trailing a thick ribbon of gore.

She paused; she'd lost the knot of Kingswords in the commotion. Then she spied a flash of white in the corner of her eye and turned. A White banner mounted atop a golden spear pitched forward in the crowd, collapsing under an invisible assault. If the standard-bearer had fallen, his commander could not be far behind. Alix craned her neck to catch a glimpse of the coat of arms as it went down.

Gods preserve us, she prayed in horror.

It was the king's.

A horse screamed, and then Alix spotted him, just a flash of reddish-gold hair beneath a shining white half helm. His destrier reared, driving back the crowd with its reaching hooves. Alix could see him clearly now: surrounded, alone, his jaw set grimly as he swivelled his horse's head and pointed it toward the trees. The animal surged beneath him, and he broke away, half a dozen Oridians in pursuit. They were on foot, but even so, the king would not get far, not with the steep slope ahead. Horses were not meant for climbing, especially not heavy warhorses covered in plate. It would be hard enough just manoeuvring between the trees.

Alix felt herself running. She twisted and dove through the bodies, friend and foe alike, making for the spot where King Erik had disappeared into the trees. The snow fell more heavily now, flaying her cheeks with icy barbs as she veered back into the wood.

He wasn't hard to find. Alix could hear the cries of his attackers, high-pitched and jubilant, like a pack of coyotes harrying an injured stag. The clang of metal told her that the king lived yet.

Get there. Get there!

She burst through a dense copse of pines to find King Erik and his destrier beset by four Oridian soldiers. A fifth lay dead nearby. Erik alternated blows between a pair of attackers at his left flank, trying to keep them both at bay. A third was circling around the horse's rump, while an archer readied his bow a few feet away. An arrow already protruded from the destrier's unprotected foreleg, and its haunch bled from an invisible wound.

The Oridian circling behind the destrier was too busy trying to avoid the horse's hooves to notice Alix closing in. She slammed into him from behind, running him through before he even realised she was there. His death cry was lost beneath the scream of his comrade as the king hacked into the shoulder of one of his foes, splitting him like firewood. But the move left him open, and his other attacker landed a hard blow to the king's ribs. The sword rang off Erik's armour, doubling him over just as an arrow hissed through the air where his head had been. The destrier skittered sideways. Alix flew at the king's attacker in a frantic attempt to drive him back.

Out of the corner of her eye, she saw the archer taking aim. Alix was on the opposite side of the horse; she knew she would never reach him in time. She did the only thing she could think of: She leapt at the king and tried to pull him down behind the horse's bulk. But the destrier was still off balance, and with an outraged scream, the warhorse pitched sideways, crashing to the ground and pinning the king and his attacker both. Alix swore viciously even as she plunged her sword through the Oridian lying prone at her feet. Then she dropped to her knees to help her king. He lay unconscious, his helm knocked askew. The destrier struggled to stand. Alix dragged the king from the stirrups just as the animal righted itself and bolted away through the trees, leaving Erik exposed.

The archer nocked an arrow. Alix had only one course left to her. She charged.

The archer drew. A feral scream tore from Alix's throat as she bore down on him, sword flashing.

The man flinched. The arrow flew wild.

Alix drove into him blade-first, toppling them both to the ground with such force that the air was blasted from her lungs, and just for a moment, everything went black.

Erik White awoke to darkness and the smell of blood. Something was lying on top of him. A corpse. His head ached, and his left leg was a pulsing beacon of agony. He tried to move.

"Shh," a voice whispered in his ear. "Be still."

Erik froze. Shuffling sounded nearby, and low voices, speaking in a foreign tongue. Oridians.

He could feel warm breath on his neck. Whoever was lying on top of him was not dead after all. She was quite alive, though doing her best to pretend otherwise. She was covering his body with her own, so the Oridians would not notice him amid the clutter of anonymous dead. *Clever*, he thought.

He lay still, trying to ignore the pain in his leg. It was broken, if not worse. His ribs throbbed. He tried to piece together what had happened, but the last thing he remembered was being hunted down like wild game. And before that, the relentless tide of Oridians, and the sickening realisation that his army was losing. Something had gone terribly wrong.

A long time passed. Erik shivered with cold. Eventually, the weight on top of him shifted, and he squinted in the light. Hazel eyes stared down at him. A curtain of copper hair framed a lovely face etched with concern. He knew this face, but for a moment his sluggish mind would not surrender the information.

Black, he recalled finally. She was unbuckling his armour.

"Er," he began, but whatever he had intended to say dissolved into a gasp as a spasm of pain seized his ribs.

She removed his cuirass and cast it aside, then made short work of the smaller pieces. That done, she dropped to one knee, grabbed his arm, and slung him over her shoulder. She staggered to her feet, swaying a little, but managing to keep upright. She started to walk.

When his head quit swimming from the pain, Erik marvelled that she could bear his weight. *That's why she took off the armour.* Clever indeed.

Yet even so, she was clearly hard-pressed; each step was a lurch, painful to both of them. Erik wanted to say something, but he had to clench his teeth to keep from crying out. Eventually he gave up, letting himself slip in and out of consciousness. Each time he opened his eyes, he saw only the frozen ground passing slowly below.

After what seemed like an eternity, Erik heard voices.

"The king! Look to the king!" And then there were hands everywhere, and he was being lifted, gently but surely, away from his rescuer. Darkness began to take him again. The last thing he saw was Alix Black, standing unnoticed amid a gaggle of soldiers, her legs giving way beneath her.

TWO

Alix gasped and sat bolt upright. For a terrible moment, she saw only flame and shadow, her ears echoing with the screams of dying men. Slowly, the flames resolved into a single candle, and the shadows gathered into the shape of a tent. She was on a cot, something warm and heavy draped over her legs.

"*Gods' blood!* You scared the life out of me!"

The voice, only inches away, sent a bright arc of panic through her. Alix scrambled away from the sound. A silhouetted figure at her bedside raised a hand in a mollifying gesture. "It's all right, it's just me."

"Liam!" Alix threw her arms around his neck, clinging to him as though her life depended on it.

"Oh. Er . . . okay." After a moment of awkwardness, he relaxed, gathering her close. "It's all right," he repeated gently, "it's over now."

She drew away, embarrassed. "Sorry. I just . . . I didn't expect to see you alive."

Liam grinned. "At your service. Anytime, really." He leaned in and looked over her shoulder. "I just hope you didn't pull your stitches."

"I have stitches?" Alix twisted, and her question was answered by a sharp tug in her lower back. She hadn't even noticed the pain until now. When had she been wounded?

The memories flooded in like cold seawater into the hull of a sinking ship. Flashing steel. Vacant blue eyes. White war paint spattered with blood . . .

"The king!" she gasped. "Oh, gods, where is he?"

Liam's grin turned wry. "Don't tell me you've forgotten single-handedly rescuing the King of Alden?"

"I . . . that's not exactly how I remember it." Alix brought a hand to her forehead, willing the pounding to subside. Liam handed her a cup of water, and she downed it gratefully.

"You should take it easy. The healers say it's a miracle you made if off the field. I'm not even supposed to be here, pestering you." He lowered his voice, suddenly serious. "What happened out there, Allie?"

She smiled faintly. The only other person she had ever allowed to call her *Allie* was Rig. Liam had stumbled onto it, teasingly at first, and she hadn't objected. It was a small thing, but it comforted her somehow, a reminder of the brother she missed so terribly. *What I wouldn't give to have Rig here now.*

"If you don't want to talk about it . . ."

"No, it's all right." She paused, remembering. "After I lost you, all I could think was to fall back and regroup with the Kingswords. But I couldn't find more than a few pockets of them here and there. And then I saw the king. He was alone." She glanced up suddenly, something occurring to her for the first time. "Green. Is he . . . ?"

"Alive. Pretty banged up, but he's seen worse."

Alix nodded, relieved.

"How does a king end up alone on the battlefield?"

"I'm not sure. The enemy managed to take out his guard somehow. They drove him into the trees and cornered him. That's where I found him. We fought them off—barely—and then I had to carry him away. I walked for a long time before I found someone. I don't really remember what happened after that."

"Gods, Allie." Liam's eyes were round with awe. "That's . . . amazing."

She winced. "Not so amazing. I almost got him killed."

When Liam raised a questioning eyebrow, she explained, "I pulled his horse down right on top of him. A destrier in full plate. Knocked him out cold."

Liam stared. Then he burst out laughing. "I guess that explains the broken leg."

Oh, dear gods. Alix felt a flush creep into her cheeks. "It's not funny."

He only laughed harder. "What a dashing rescue! Why, it's like something out of a bard's tale! I can picture it now: the brave heroine . . ."

"Bugger off, Liam."

"The brave, *charming* heroine . . ."

"*Liam.*"

"What were you trying to do, anyway?"

She scowled. "There was an archer. I wanted to use the horse as cover, but I didn't count on the weight of the king's armour."

Liam shook his head and dabbed at his eyes. "Good old Alix. Act first, think later."

"I can't believe you're laughing about this. I broke the king's leg!"

"I'd say he's forgiven you." Liam gestured at their surroundings. "You haven't even noticed where you are yet. It might not be Blackhold, but it's the army equivalent."

Belatedly, Alix glanced around. The tent was huge, at least ten feet by twelve. A fur coverlet lay pooled at her waist, and she sat on a cot, a luxury she hadn't known since leaving the barracks months ago. "Generous of him." She shifted awkwardly under the blanket. "How is he, anyway?"

Liam sobered. "All right, considering. They say he's got a pretty nasty break, and some bruised ribs, but he's up and about. And mad as a hornet."

"The Kingswords . . ."

He dropped his gaze. "Massacred. Less than five thousand left, we think."

"Merciful gods." Tears welled in her eyes, but she blinked them back. *This is war*, she told herself sternly. Still . . . so many dead . . . "How could this happen?"

"The Raven betrayed us, that's how." Liam's eyes were steel, grey and hard and glinting with fury.

Alix blew out a long breath. Tomald White, commander of the Wolves and their prince—a traitor. He had left his own brother to die. "Why would he do that?"

"Maybe he's in league with the enemy. Or maybe he's just a coward. Does it really matter?"

His words barely registered. "And how could the Pack just stand by and watch?"

"They didn't. Not all of them, anyway. When the Raven ordered them off the field, hundreds deserted to join Green and the rest." Liam jerked a thumb over his shoulder. "Gwylim and Kerta are here in the camp somewhere. Ide too."

"The Blackswords . . . how many of them survived?"

Liam shook his head. "I don't know. I'm sorry. There hasn't been time to take stock. We've been on the run ever since the retreat sounded, just trying to put distance between ourselves and the Oridians."

"Where are we, anyway?"

"About fifty miles north of Teardrop Lake."

Alix started. "How is that possible? How long have I been out?"

"A couple of days. They gave you something to help you sleep. Said you needed it."

Her surprise quickly gave way to humiliation. A couple of days in the care of total strangers, being fed, tended, carted around, and gods knew what else . . . She paused, sniffing herself. Clean and fresh. Her eyes widened in horror. "Who's been bathing me?"

Liam laughed. "*This* is what you're worried about? Your modesty?"

"It wasn't you, was it?"

His laughter sputtered out instantly. "*What?* Don't be . . . of *course* not!" He rose quickly and cleared his throat. "Right, you should get some sleep. And I'll go and . . . not sleep. At all. Possibly ever again." He rubbed his eyes.

Alix smiled, despite herself. Every once in a while, it was possible to reduce Liam to the shy squire he'd once been. Tempting as it was to tease him, however, she could already feel her eyelids drooping. She would have thought two straight days of sleep would be enough, but apparently her body had other ideas.

"Thanks for staying with me." She yawned and slid down under the coverlet.

"No problem." He paused at the tent flap, looking back at her. "I'm glad you're all right, Alix."

"You too."

Sleep claimed her.

Alix peeled back the tent flap to reveal a brisk morning glittering with frost. A pale winter sun strained through the morning mist, washing the clearing in thin watercolours. The camp had not yet stirred; only a few soldiers milled about, carrying water, cleaning weapons, poking at the dying embers of cooking fires. It felt like any other morning, and for a moment, Alix just stood there, watching, some part of her praying that it had all been a bad dream. But of course she knew that wasn't true. She had woken up on a cot, in an unfamiliar tent, with a vile taste in her mouth and a subtle throb in the small of her back. The battle had been no nightmare—at least not the imaginary kind.

She let her gaze wander over the camp, taking a silent tally of the small canvas pyramids dotting the clearing. *So few*, she thought. Was this really all that remained of the king's army? They had been twenty thousand strong when they marched out of Erroman. Eight thousand of those had been Blackswords. Rig's men, and their father's before, men whose families had been loyal to the Blacks for generations. *Massacred*, Liam had said. Alix shuddered.

"Good to see you're up," said a voice, and Alix turned to find Gwylim beside her, a steaming cup in his hand. He looked haggard, his green eyes clouded over, his hair tousled into an ash-blond briar patch. "How do you feel?"

"I ache," Alix said, "inside and out." Inside, especially.

"Well, if it's any consolation, you look awful." He took a long pull of his tea.

"Thanks."

"That's it?" He made a small noise of disapproval. "Those Oridians must have knocked the vinegar out of you."

She looked at him askance. "You know, for such a short man, you're awfully brave."

"That's more like it."

Alix couldn't quite manage a smile. She gazed out over the tents. Gwylim drank his tea. Neither spoke for long moments. Alix longed to ask him about the battle, but she hesitated. Maybe he just wanted to forget. Gwylim and most of the other scouts had been sent with the Wolves, while Alix and Liam scouted for Green. Gwylim would have witnessed the horror up close, and it seemed unfair to make him relive it.

Yet in the end, she found she couldn't deny herself. "The Wolves," she said quietly. "What happened? Did Prince Tomald . . . did he not hear the horn?" Some part of her still refused to believe their prince would betray them.

"He heard it. We all did. He just didn't order the charge." Gwylim spoke matter-of-factly, but Alix didn't miss the way his fingers tensed around his cup, chasing the blood from his knuckles.

"What did you do?"

"Same as you. Ran down the hill and tried my best to get myself killed. Practically all the scouts did the same. Kerta and Ide and Nik."

"Nik's here?" Liam hadn't mentioned him.

"No," said Gwylim. He took another sip of tea.

It took Alix a moment to understand. When she did, her eyes squeezed shut. "Gods, I'm sorry. I know you were close."

"Lots of good men died out there." Gwylim avoided her gaze, continuing to stare out over the camp.

Something like nausea wrung Alix's stomach. How much of it was hunger, and how much horror, she couldn't tell. "So the White Wolves are disgraced," she said, more to herself than Gwylim. "Traitors to their own banner."

"The White Wolves don't exist." Gwylim's voice was quiet but fierce. "Half of them deserted. As for those who stayed with Prince Tomald, who stood by as he betrayed his king . . . They're *his* men. The Raven's men. They're not the Pack. There is no Pack, not anymore."

Alix had nothing to say to that, so she just nodded.

"The king named Arran Green commander general of his army," Gwylim said. "Such as it is."

Alix frowned. "What do you mean, such as it is? There's another twenty thousand swords in Erroman, and the Greyswords haven't even mustered yet."

"And who's to say where their loyalties lie?"

"I beg your pardon?"

Gwylim glanced at her out of the corner of his eye. "You're the noblewoman here, Alix. You know more about politics than a nameless sod like me. Think about it. Prince Tomald has powerful allies, to say nothing of the White Wolves and the tens of thousands of other soldiers he's commanded over the years. He's riding back to Erroman right now, convinced that King Erik is dead and the crown is his, and there's no one there to disagree with him."

"But the king *isn't* dead."

"Right. So the question is, what happens now?"

Alix grew cold as she processed the implication of his words. If Tomald wanted the crown, he would find plenty of supporters, especially among the army—enough to mount a credible challenge to his brother's rule. *As though one war isn't enough*, she thought bitterly. "Gods help us."

"The Virtues take no sides in the quarrels of men," Gwylim said.

"Spoken like an almost-priest." She gave him a wry look. "I'll bet you're asking yourself why you ever left."

"And here I was just thinking how familiar it all is. The treachery, the ruthless ambition . . . All we're missing is the temple."

A new voice spoke. "Merciful Nine, Gwylim, that's cynical, even for you."

Alix's nose wrinkled at the sound. It was far too early in the morning for a dose of Kerta Middlemarch. Alix made a point of avoiding Kerta until at least the midday meal, in much the same way she avoided imbibing heaps of sugar before breakfast. But she was careful to smooth her face into an expression of cool politeness as she turned to exchange greetings with her comrade. Her breeding demanded no less, and she would be damned if she shamed her late parents in front of a Middlemarch.

"How are you feeling?" Kerta asked, her big blue eyes gazing up at Alix through a veil of long lashes.

"I'm all right, thank you. And you?"

"Oh, I'm fine. I wasn't injured, fortunately."

Of course you weren't. Kerta didn't get injured. She also

didn't curse, drink, sweat, or allow a single perfect blond curl to stray from its proper place. She even fought primly. The second daughter of Byron Middlemarch, Kerta did everything in her power to live up to her family's ambitions. The only reason she lowered herself to serve as a scout was that she was too small—too bloody *dainty*—to do much of anything else. And anyway, that was only temporary; Kerta had bigger designs. Once her service with the Kingswords was through, she would no doubt marry well, perhaps even into one of the Banner Houses. The Browns, maybe, or the Greens. About the only house she *didn't* have a chance of marrying into was the Greys—and Alix's own, thank the Nine Virtues.

"Such a terrible day," Kerta said. "Each friend spared is a gift from above."

And just like that, Alix felt like a cretin. It was petty to indulge in ungenerous thoughts, especially now. Kerta had never been anything but amiable, and if her overtures were slightly overwrought, there were surely worse sins. Alix mustered something appropriate to say. "It must have been awful, being up there with the Wolves."

Kerta nodded sadly. "Bad enough to watch our comrades falling to the enemy, but to see Prince Tomald betray his own brother . . ." Her voice wavered, and she looked away. After a pause, she added, "At least King Erik survived, thanks to you. You're a true hero, Alix."

Alix squirmed even more. She cast about for a suitably gracious reply, but fortunately, Gwylim spared her the trouble. "Tell Alix what you told me—about the Trion."

"It's only a rumour," Kerta said.

That didn't bother Alix. Rumour fed an army as surely as dried meat and hardtack. "Tell me."

"Apparently, one of the Trions was spotted on the battlefield."

Alix's eyebrows flew up. "Which one?"

"The Priest."

Alix swore quietly. Of the three lords of Oridia, the Priest was the most feared. It was the Priest whose fervour drove the Trionate to conquer and convert. It was he who kept their army equipped with bloodforged weapons, who called down the favour of his gods before every battle. Rumour had it that he commanded other, darker magicks as well. Every child in Alden knew the name of Madan "the Madman," dark witch of the Trionate, haunter of shadows and nightmares.

Infamous as he was, however, Alix had never heard of the Priest being spied on a battlefield. "Who saw him?"

"One of the knights."

"How would an Aldenian knight know what the Priest looks like?"

Kerta shrugged. "As I said, it's only a rumour."

Alix started to ask another question, but that moment, Liam appeared, looking uncharacteristically serious. "Good," he said, "you're here. Green sent me to look for you. He wants to speak with us right away."

Alix winced. She'd been dreading this. "Just the two of us?"

"I'm afraid so. He's been saving it up until you were well enough."

"How considerate of him." Alix sighed and rolled her stiff shoulders, as though preparing for battle—which was not far off. "Oh, well. Better get it over with."

"Good luck," Gwylim called after them.

They would need it. A lecture from Arran Green was enough to make even the hardest man quail. From the moment she had stepped over the edge of that bluff and into battle, Alix had known she would be made to answer for it. Arran Green was not a man to take disobedience lightly, no matter how well intentioned.

They found Green near his tent, issuing orders to his squire. Alix and Liam paused at a respectful distance while they waited for him to finish. Alix watched Liam watching the squire. There was no resentment in his gaze, only interest. She hoped that meant Liam was finally getting over his anger at being replaced. More than once, she'd thought to ask him how he came to be banished to the scouts, but it was such a sore point that she didn't dare.

At length, Green sent the squire off and turned to his scouts, folding his hands behind his back as he looked them over. He held himself straight and proud as always, but Alix noticed that one shoulder hung slightly lower than the other. Dislocated, maybe. But if Green was in pain, he gave no sign;

his expression was inscrutable as always, pale eyes sharp beneath the thick brows, angular features hewn from granite, bearded jaw set in hard, unyielding lines.

"I am pleased to see you are feeling better," he told Alix. If he felt any real pleasure, his voice gave no hint of it.

"Thank you," she said with an awkward dip of her head. "And I was relieved to hear you were all right."

He grunted. "I should not be. Had I been at my king's side where I belonged, I would no doubt have perished along with the rest of his knights. Being assigned to lead the eastern charge was both a boon and a curse, it seems."

Alix and Liam nodded mutely.

"A hard-fought battle," Green continued. "It is a blessing that King Erik survived. You showed extraordinary courage, Alix."

But . . . She could feel the word bearing down on her.

"The fact remains, however, that you disobeyed a direct order. Both of you." His gaze shifted to Liam. "I explicitly told you to stay behind on the bluff. In defying me, you dishonoured yourselves and your commander. The king's army demands discipline above all else. Insubordination cannot be tolerated. I do not have to tell you that it is customarily punishable by death."

Alix felt the blood drain from her face. She had anticipated stern words, but this? Surely even Arran Green could not expect them to stand idle as their comrades were slaughtered, when even the White Wolves had deserted in droves? But a moment's glance was all it took to answer that question; Green's gaze was cold and unforgiving, his mouth pressed into a thin line of disapproval.

"I might have expected as much from a Black, but I am especially disappointed in you, Liam. You were my squire for almost seven years. You know better than to defy me."

Liam faced the rebuke with admirable composure. "I have no excuse, General," he said, raising his chin, "but surely Alix did right? She saved the king."

"She disobeyed a direct order."

"I'm rather glad she did, actually," came a voice over Alix's shoulder, and she turned to find King Erik hobbling toward them, leaning on a crutch. He winked at her discreetly as he passed. "Don't be too hard on them, Green. They have done their kingdom a great service."

Alix fought to suppress the blush spreading over her cheeks. Fortunately, all eyes were on the king.

Green's countenance betrayed no annoyance, but Alix knew it was there. "Of course, Your Majesty. Nevertheless, I wish to make certain that insubordination does not become a habit. We have just seen what becomes of an army when men take it into their heads to defy their orders."

Alix caught her breath, astounded by his lack of tact. Her gaze snapped instinctively to the king. A shadow of anger flickered through Erik's eyes, but it was gone as quickly as it appeared. "Indeed," he said, "and I don't wish to interfere, but I did want to thank my rescuer in person." He turned to Alix, smiling warmly. "The crown owes you a great debt, Lady Alix, and I owe you my life. You have my eternal gratitude. And may I add that you cut a very impressive figure on the battlefield."

"I . . . Thank you, Your Majesty."

"If only I had a hundred like you, we should have defeated the enemy even without the Wolves." The light drained from his eyes at these words, and he turned back to the commander general. "I would have a word, Green. We are at a safe distance from the Oridians now. It's time to talk strategy."

"Indeed, Your Majesty."

The king started to shuffle away on his crutch. "Bring your scouts. One can never have too many sensible voices."

Green's thick eyebrows gathered like a storm cloud, but he didn't protest. "As you say, sire."

Liam looked uncomfortable. "Why does he want us to come? It's not our place to—"

"Have you learned nothing today, boy?" Green snapped. "One does not question one's betters."

"Yes, General."

Exchanging a look, Alix and Liam trailed after Arran Green and the king.

THREE

Erik White perched on a field chair, trying his best to look dignified in spite of it. His leg hurt like a bastard, and though he had not admitted it to anyone, standing for too long made him dizzy. Not that he would be able to sit comfortably on this blasted chair. The thing was little more than a tripod of sticks saddled with canvas, and the edge pressed uncomfortably into the back of his thigh. Still, he ought to be grateful for it. Good men had died protecting the supply wagons during the flight from Boswyck Valley. Every spade, every blanket, every stick of furniture and wheel of cheese was a prize snatched from the Oridian horde. *You insisted you would have no trouble living like a soldier, Your Majesty*, he reminded himself ruefully. *Here is your chance to prove it.* He propped his left boot on a crate and waved for some water.

He watched Green making his way over, his charges in tow. Erik knew the old knight was irritated with him for inviting the scouts along, but so be it. Green deserved a little rankling after that outrageous lecture. To think he was actually *angry* with his men for their heroics. Absurd. The old knight had grown overprotective lately, and Erik meant to put a stop to it. Besides, he was curious about his fair young saviour. He had met

Alix Black once before, when she had been about fourteen, and he five years her senior. He did not recall much about that meeting, except how painfully awkward she had been. He could see even then that she would be a beauty, but Alix had been utterly oblivious to her own charms, blushing and fidgeting and avoiding the prince's eye. Erik could not recall for certain, but he did not think she had uttered a single word.

Watching her now, Erik decided that the years had been kind. Her features were more defined, and her copper hair was as beautiful as he remembered, falling past her shoulders in lazy waves. She had grown tall and strong—strong enough, apparently, to bear a grown man off the battlefield. Remarkable. Yet she was no ox; she moved with all the grace of her sex, and her figure, though fit, was unmistakably feminine. As for her fellow scout, he trailed behind her with obvious reluctance. A man of his size, good looks, and reputed skill with a blade ought to have carried himself with confidence. Instead he walked with his head down, and when they came to stand before Erik, he tucked himself behind Green, doing his best to remain inconspicuous. As though Erik might not notice him, and both of them would be happier for it.

Erik sipped his water, letting it clear his head. He needed to focus on the matter at hand. "Tell me, Green, what do you think my brother intends?" He kept his voice as neutral as possible, trying to disguise the hint of disbelief that still lingered foolishly in his breast. He could not doubt the testimony of his own eyes, and yet it was still so hard to fathom. *My brother. My own flesh and blood. How can it be true?*

"I cannot say, Your Majesty, though we can presume Prince Tomald means to claim the crown."

"That's absurd," Erik snapped.

Green gazed at him coolly. "As you say, Your Majesty."

He thinks you a fool. Erik could see it in the old knight's eyes. Perhaps he was not wrong. Erik cleared his throat. "Very well, suppose he does mean to take the crown. What then?"

"Most likely he will head for Erroman. He will need to gather more swords before he is ready to confront the Oridians again."

"But how will he explain himself to my court?"

"I doubt he will try. He will simply proclaim himself king."

Erik felt his whole body tense. "He would not dare, if he knew I was alive."

"But he does not," Green said, "and I recommend we keep it that way."

Erik pressed his lips together, momentarily at a loss. Rage was building inside him, the same rage that had overwhelmed him earlier, had caused him to lose his composure in front of the men. He could not let that happen again. He looked to Alix Black. "You agree?" he asked her, buying himself a moment to recover.

She started; she had apparently not realised she was nodding. Her eyes darted uncertainly to Green. The commander general took one look at his king and wisely decided to let her speak. He nodded stiffly.

"I do, Your Majesty," Black said.

"Why?"

She spared another glance at Green before replying. "We are weak right now, and vulnerable."

Erik scowled. "I'll not cower in the shadows. Besides, am I to allow my brother to entrench himself in the royal palace, telling the nobility any story he wishes?"

"Exactly." She flushed as soon as she had spoken, but Erik encouraged her with a brief incline of his head. She cleared her throat awkwardly. "Let him play his hand, sire. Bide your time while he explains what happened at Boswyck Valley. He'll spin so many lies that when the truth is finally revealed, he'll be hanged with his own rope."

"A risky strategy," Green said. "It will give him time to build alliances."

"I respectfully disagree, General," Black said, her eyes on her boots. "He won't trouble to build alliances if he believes himself unchallenged. Whereas if he knows King Erik lives, he'll scramble to fortify himself."

Green grunted and scratched the closely cropped fringe of his beard.

She had a point. No one would challenge Tom's right to the crown if they believed Erik dead, and Tom would not waste his time currying favour if there was no need. He had never had much taste for it, and he still had a war to contend with. All Tom needed to do was convince the nobility that he had no choice but to retreat. The mutterings of common soldiers would not be enough to gainsay him. "I see the wisdom in this," Erik said. *The wisdom in letting my brother think me dead.* He felt dizzy, as though it were all a dream.

"Strike your colours, Your Majesty," Black said, "and the royal pavilion as well."

"Prudent," Green agreed. "If the Raven sends scouts, he will find no evidence that the king lives."

Erik rose unsteadily. "Very well. I will do as you say. Put away anything that bears the royal crest." He took a deep breath, reaching inside himself and fetching his most charming smile. "And since Lady Alix helpfully relieved me of my armour, that's one less thing to worry about."

His words had the desired effect: a comely blush rose to her cheeks, diverting attention from her own discomfiture. "We make for Greenhold," he said. "I hope your cousin can lend us strength, General."

Green nodded. "I have no doubt of it, Your Majesty."

"Good. And now if you will excuse me, I have an appointment with the healers. They are most irritable when I'm late."

"You have a head for strategy, Alix," Arran Green said after the king had gone. "Perhaps I undervalued your input. The king has few left to advise him, and your family has ever been steady counsel to the Whites."

That might have been true when Alix's parents were alive, but she doubted many would say so now. Still, she accepted the compliment as graciously as she was able. "Thank you, General."

"Now pack your things, both of you. We break camp soon."

They started back for their tents. Alix could feel Liam's gaze on her, and when she glanced over, he was smirking. With the king well out of sight, Liam had relaxed, and the mischief returned to his eyes. "A head for strategy, huh? Is that just a nice way of saying you're sneaky?"

"Jealous?"

"I can be sneaky."

"I doubt that."

"Oh, I can. Believe me, I'm incredibly subtle. So subtle that you don't even see it. It's that subtle."

She laughed. "That *is* subtle."

He gave her an arch look. "For example, only yesterday I tricked you into my arms. You thought that was an accident, but it was actually a cunning trap."

Alix started to reply, but one glimpse of that crooked grin of his, and her wit deserted her. Again. When had *that* become a pattern? Flirting was a stock colour in any noblewoman's palette, and Alix had mastered it as well as any—or so she'd thought, until she met Liam. That she should find herself so discomposed by a no-name scout was an irony she could have lived without.

Mistaking her silence for annoyance, Liam touched her elbow, bringing her up short. "Allie, wait. I'm sorry, I shouldn't make light. What you said yesterday, about not expecting to see me again . . ."

The mischief was gone from his eyes, replaced by an earnest warmth. Alix tried to ignore the sudden flutter in her throat.

"I know exactly what you meant," Liam said. "When I lost you in the battle . . . I looked everywhere, but you'd just vanished. I thought . . ." He trailed off, his gaze roaming over her features, his hand tightening at her elbow. Alix found herself staring into his slate-grey eyes, pinned like a stunned rabbit. Slowly, his mouth curled back into a grin. "Are you blushing?"

She broke off from his gaze. "I'm always blushing. Don't get any ideas."

"Never had an idea in my life," he said solemnly.

Alix laughed, pushing her hair back from her face to hide her deepening colour.

"All right," he said with a mock bow, "I'm going to quit while I'm ahead. I'll see you in a while." He headed off to pack up his gear, looking well pleased with himself.

Alix kept walking until she reached the river's edge. A sharp wind swept over the water, bracingly cool against the warmth of her face. Not for the first time, she cursed her fair complexion for revealing her every emotion to the world.

Liam was going to be a problem.

She'd never become so close with anyone so quickly. In the few short months since she'd joined the Kingswords, Liam had become a central feature of her life—her scouting partner, her sparring mate, her closest confidant. And now he was becoming something else—something much, much more complicated.

She hadn't seen it coming. In the beginning, she'd simply clung to him out of necessity. She'd been alone and away from home for the first time, and she'd needed a friend. Liam had been there. He wasn't Rig, but he'd been there. He took care of her, and she let him, and it worked.

And then something changed. It seemed to happen overnight; she'd woken up one morning feeling more like a Kingsword than a lost little girl. She didn't *need* Liam anymore. But by then it was too late. By the time she noticed those beautiful grey eyes, that roguish grin, he had long since earned her trust. He'd slipped past her defences completely unnoticed. It was going to be a problem.

Because what I really need is another problem.

The sound of the rushing stream gradually pushed its way into her consciousness, bringing to mind an urgent need. Alix headed deeper into the trees to find a discreet place to relieve herself. She had just started back when a loud cooing drew her attention. Peering through the trees, she spied the king's messenger fussing with his bird, trying to stuff a scroll into the tiny leather case strapped to its leg. The pigeon fidgeted and pecked at him, frustrating his efforts and provoking a string of hot curses.

Alix paused.

She knew Berton, the king's messenger. All the scouts did; he often accompanied them on long-range patrols, using his pigeons to send reports back to their commanders. He was a gentle soul and loved his birds, and they seemed to love him. The man struggling inexpertly with his pigeon was definitely *not* Berton, she realised. It was possible that Berton had been slain in the battle, but what would the king's messenger be doing out here in the trees?

"Ho there."

The man started at the sound of her voice, sending the pigeon flapping and trilling. "Ho yourself. Be gone with you, girl, I'm busy."

"Mind your tongue. You address a lady."

The man blanched a little. He glanced nervously behind her, as though checking to see if she was alone, and his fingers brushed the hilt of his sword. His discomfiture left Alix little doubt she had stumbled across something he didn't want her to see. "Who are you?" She pitched her voice to carry through the trees. "What business do you have with that bird?"

"Who are you to demand my business?"

"I am a lady of a Banner House. I outrank you, and I have every right to demand your business. By whose authority do you send missives from the king's army?"

By now, her raised voice had summoned a pair of soldiers on watch. They picked their way through the trees cautiously, their swords unsheathed. Alix drew her own blade and pointed it at the stranger. "Take this man in hand. He is not the king's messenger, and I want to know who he reports to."

The watchmen exchanged a glance, unsure who Alix was and whether they should follow her orders. They must not have liked the look of the messenger, though, for they started in on him. The man tensed, his gaze snapping back and forth between Alix and the advancing soldiers. After a moment's hesitation, he bolted.

The watchmen gave chase. The pigeon burst into the air, its scroll case empty, its destination unknown. Alix started after the fleeing messenger, but she was in no condition to run anyone down; pain tugged sharply at her back, and she felt instantly dizzy. Fortunately, she didn't need to go far. The watchmen quickly overtook their prey, disarming him and wrenching his hands behind his back. Alix stopped to catch her breath as they dragged the messenger between them.

By now, the commotion had drawn even more attention. Someone had summoned Arran Green, and he stalked through the trees toward Alix, a forbidding scowl on his face. "What is the meaning of this? Speak quickly, Black, I've had my fill of you already today!"

The feeling is mutual, General. Aloud, she said, "I came upon this man in the woods, behaving suspiciously. He was attempting to send a message by pigeon. As you can see, he is not the king's messenger."

Green looked the captive over. "Bring him here."

"He had this on him, General," one of the watchmen said, handing Green a scrap of parchment.

Green scanned it, his face darkening. "Take this wretch to the prisoners' wagon!"

The watchmen hurried to obey. Green turned on his heel and stomped back through the undergrowth; all Alix could do was follow.

The king himself awaited them in the clearing. "I heard shouting. What's happened?"

"Black apprehended a spy, Your Majesty," Green said, handing over the parchment.

The king looked it over, but he only shook his head. "I can make nothing of it."

"It is in cipher, sire. That is how I know the man was a spy, though for whom, I cannot say."

The king gave an uneasy little laugh. "Why, it must be the Oridians. Who else?"

"Your brother comes to mind," Green said with only a hint of dryness.

A flash of emotion lit the king's eyes before he hid it by looking down at the parchment. "Tom never had much use for spies. He prefers to be more . . . direct."

"Agreed," said Green, "but these are strange times."

Strange times. That was putting it mildly. Half the continent at war, and Tomald White plotting to steal his brother's crown. *Plotting, but with whom? Could the Raven be working with the enemy?* It wouldn't do to ask the question aloud, not yet. The king was already struggling to accept what was happening. Conspiracy theories were unlikely to appeal to him just now.

"There may be other spies among us," Green said. "I suggest we take additional precautions."

"Such as?"

"You should assign yourself a personal guard, Your Majesty."

"I have a personal guard. You just appointed them yourself."

"Every one of them new and untested," Green said. "In any case, I do not speak of your knights. I refer to someone closer, someone who will accompany you night and day."

The king frowned. "A bodyguard? Is that really necessary?"

"Until we know more about your brother's plans, we

cannot rule out assassination attempts. And with your injuries, you are especially vulnerable."

The king's blue eyes turned to ice. "Are you suggesting that Tom would try to have me murdered? Stabbed in the back like some brigand in a bar brawl?"

Green returned his gaze evenly. "I do not know what to think anymore, sire, but we cannot afford to take chances."

The king shook his head, cursing quietly. "Very well. From henceforth, Alix Black will be captain of my knights, and my personal bodyguard."

Alix's mouth fell open. She had no words. She did not even have breath.

Arran Green had breath enough for both of them; he blew it out indignantly. "Your Majesty, she is a scout, not a knight. With due respect to her station, she—"

"She is quick-witted, observant, and skilled with a sword. Ideal qualifications in a bodyguard, wouldn't you say? She has already saved my life once, and rooted out a spy. Moreover, I can be sure of her loyalty, since her brother is a friend. Come now, Green, you have scouts enough. Surely you can spare this one."

"She is barely a fledgling, and wilful as an old mule."

Alix's face burned with shame, but the king only laughed. "So it is often said of me."

"Your Majesty, I strongly—"

"Your point is made," the king said coldly, "as is my choice. All that remains is to hear whether Lady Alix will accept the appointment." He turned to Alix, arching a redgold eyebrow.

Alix's mind whirred, and for a moment she feared she wouldn't be able to string anything sensible together. Thankfully, her breeding took over. "It will be my great honour, Your Majesty," she heard herself saying.

The king smiled. "Good. Come to my tent when you're ready, Captain. You will ride beside me."

Alix could only nod numbly, watching the king's receding back.

Four

Alix glowered her way between the tents, earning uncomfortable glances and a refreshingly wide berth from everyone she passed. She could practically hear her mother's voice scolding her for looking the gargoyle, but she didn't care. She'd had a *day*. Again.

"Ho there, sunshine," Liam called, with remarkable indifference to his health. Maybe he counted on safety in numbers. Gwylim and Kerta and Ide were all sitting by the fire, though from the worn look of them, they wouldn't last long.

"Did you bring us any wine?" Ide asked. That made three nights in a row. Ide seemed to be under the impression that attending the king gave Alix the right to pilfer his comforts.

"No." Alix plopped down near the fire. "But feel free to ask me again tomorrow."

If Ide noticed the sarcasm, she didn't let on; she merely sighed in disappointment. Alix had never met anyone who enjoyed her drink more than Ide. She had complained regularly about the Kingswords' paltry mug-a-day ration, and that was before the flight from Boswyck. Now, there was nothing at all. Ide considered it an incomprehensible failure of military planning that no one had thought to prioritise the wine barrels.

Alix shuffled closer to the fire, grateful for its warmth. "How are your new duties suiting you, Alix?" Kerta asked.

Like satin suits a sow. Alix felt constantly in the way, stumbled over by squires and healers and attendants and knights and sundry others who demanded their king's attention. She was trying to learn their faces, but they came and went like waves lapping the shore, and she couldn't keep them straight from one day to the next. Nor could she decide which of them she should trust and which to be wary of, for the king greeted them all with the same breezy warmth, clapping shoulders and trading jibes as though they were all the closest of confidants. How in the Nine Domains was she supposed to protect him when his tent was bloody *teeming* with strangers?

Aloud, she simply said, "I'm exhausted. I have no idea what I'm doing. Just the stress of not making a fool of myself is enough to do me in. And the king certainly doesn't make it easy. He's too busy being charming to be careful. He meets with anyone who asks for an audience, and if I try to impose a little distance, he just laughs and accuses me of being paranoid. What's the point of having a bodyguard if you won't let her do her job?" She shook her head in exasperation. "At least Green has stopped glaring at me all day, though I'm not naïve enough to think he's forgiven me yet."

Liam snorted. "As though it's your fault you were appointed. So much for not questioning one's betters."

"And the king?" Kerta asked, diplomatically brushing Liam's remark aside. "How are his spirits?"

"I wish I knew. For the most part he's as sunny as a summer day, but I can't tell how much of that is putting on a brave face. And every now and then he falls to brooding."

"Maybe he doesn't fancy bumping along in the back of a supply wagon like a sack of royal turnips," Liam said.

Kerta looked positively scandalised. "You oughtn't jest, Liam. The king has suffered a heavy blow." She laid a hand over her breast, mournfully. Alix resisted the urge to roll her eyes. "You should try to cheer him, Alix," Kerta suggested.

"No, she shouldn't," Liam said. "It's not her job, and anyway, the last thing she needs is to encourage him."

Alix frowned. "What's that supposed to mean?"

"Nothing." Liam picked up a stick and poked at the fire.

Kerta smiled knowingly and shook her head. "Now, Liam, you needn't worry about Alix. She can handle herself. Besides, you can't really believe those tawdry little whispers."

"I can't?"

"For pity's sake, Liam, the king is betrothed, remember?"

"Oh, I remember. He's been betrothed for how many years? If *that* doesn't tell you something . . ."

The scandalised look returned. Kerta sat up a little straighter. "Are you implying that the king is deliberately putting off his marriage?"

"Of course not. I'm sure he's eager to be rid of the dozens of beautiful women who follow him about."

A tiny line of disapproval appeared between Kerta's perfectly arched eyebrows. "If His Majesty hasn't found the right time, I'm sure there's a good reason."

"Maybe Sirin Grey is hatchet-faced," Ide said.

The king's intended was anything but hatchet-faced, but before Alix had a chance to say so, Gwylim yawned widely and got to his feet. "Fascinating as this subject is, it's late, and I'm tired."

"Me too," said Ide, rising.

They left behind an awkward silence. Liam continued to stir the embers, sending sparks swirling in the dark.

"It doesn't sound as though you're enjoying yourself much, Alix," Kerta said, trying to breathe some life back into the conversation.

"Not really."

"Then why do it?" Liam's gaze was still fixed on the fire.

"Because the king asked me to, Liam. It's my duty. If I'd said no, I would have brought shame on my family." Most of them might be dead, but that was all the more reason to conduct herself in a manner befitting their memory. She'd come late to that notion, as had Rig, but they embraced it now, and passionately. *Wayward children*, they'd been called, and maybe that was true, but they had time to set it right, and what better way to start than in the King's Service?

"I understand," said Kerta. She wasn't just being polite, Alix knew. Kerta had a name too. She was a Middlemarch. A lesser lord's name, to be sure, but a name nonetheless. Liam, though, had no family name. He wasn't nobility, lesser or otherwise.

Like Gwylim, like Ide, like all commoners, he inherited nothing; he had only the name he was given at birth. He had only *Liam*, only himself to honour and do right by. He couldn't understand what it meant to have a legacy to live up to.

Liam scratched around with his stick and said nothing. Kerta glanced from him to Alix and back. Then she brought a hand to her lips to cover an imaginary yawn. "I think I'll turn in too," she announced.

If her retreat was not exactly subtle, at least it was swift. Alix and Liam were left alone.

More silence. Alix waited in vain for Liam to break it. Eventually, she said, "If you're just going to sit there and sulk, I'm going to bed."

He looked up with a frown. "I'm not sulking."

"No?"

"I'm thinking. Hard to believe, I know, but it happens occasionally."

She sighed. There was no point in tiptoeing around it anymore. "You don't like it, do you? My being his bodyguard?"

"Don't be ridiculous. Why wouldn't I? Aside from the fact that I don't have to see you all day, I get to listen to Kerta go on and on and sodding *on* about how handsome and dashing His Majesty is, which I can assure you is a real treat."

Alix laughed. "That's aiming a little high, even for her." She shuffled over to sit beside Liam, bumping him with her shoulder. "If I didn't know better, I'd say you were jealous."

"Of course I am. I used to have you all to myself, and now I barely see you." The firelight played over his features, etching his profile in moving shadow. It gave him a strangely haunted look.

"That's not it, is it? Not all of it, anyway."

Liam sighed and tossed his stick into the flames. "Not really, no." He looked over at her. "I don't like the idea of you being his shield, Allie. There's no telling who might be out for his blood, and now it's your job to stand between him and his enemies. It makes me nervous."

Alix smiled. "That's sweet."

"I was going for gallant." He tried to muster a grin, but his heart wasn't in it. Instead he raked his fingers through his dark hair, a nervous habit that left it in a near-constant state of dishevelment.

"You're really worried, aren't you?"

"Of course I am. The gods only know who that spy was, or how many messages he sent before you caught him. We could be marching straight into an ambush. Or there could be assassins, or brigands, or, you know . . ." He gestured vaguely at the trees.

"Bears?" she offered wryly.

He flicked her a look, the glint returning to his eye. "Not to mention wolves and badgers and beavers."

"Beavers?"

"You laugh, but have you seen the fangs on those things?"

"Beavers don't have fangs."

"I know a few trees that would beg to differ. Keep your chain mail on, is all I'm saying."

She dropped her head on his shoulder, and they fell silent for a while, watching the fire rustle and snap. "None of us is safe," she said eventually.

"No."

"Things are going to get worse before they get better, too."

"You really are a ray of sunshine, you know that?"

"You started it."

Alix could feel his eyes on her. She twisted her head to look up at him, bringing her face within inches of his. His breath ghosted across her lips.

"Allie . . ."

She swallowed hard. Liam gazed at her with . . . *something* . . . in his eyes, something fragile and shifting. It was like watching a die tumble over itself, waiting for it to settle.

The die came up scratch. Liam looked away. "It's late."

Alix straightened, a little too quickly. "We'll reach the outskirts of the Greenlands tomorrow. Hopefully we can catch up on some rest once we get there."

"That would be nice." He gave her a thin smile. "Good night, Alix."

As she walked away, Alix looked back to find Liam staring into the fire, shaking his head.

"Where is everyone?" King Erik raised the visor of his helm to reveal a worried frown.

Good question, Alix thought. The village was completely deserted, save for a few stray dogs that snuffled hopefully around empty livestock pens and the closed doorways of stone-and-thatch hovels. No smoke curled from the chimneys, in spite of the morning chill. "It looks abandoned, sire, and recently."

"How can you tell?"

Alix inclined her head toward one of the huts as they passed. "The straw piled up at the side of that house is still fresh, and look at the animal pen."

"Muddy," the king said, "though the road is dry. You're right, it can't have been long." As he spoke, the wagon hit a rut, and he winced, his hand going to his thigh. Alix bit her lip in sympathy. They had done everything they could to make King Erik comfortable in the supply cart, but the wagon was of simple construction, designed for nothing more fragile than fresh apples. Even a thick layer of blankets under his leg wasn't enough to shield him from the painful jostling.

"Shall I fetch the healer, Your Majesty?"

"So he can dull my senses with his potions? I think not, Captain. I'm afraid there's nothing for it but to endure."

Arran Green appeared on the opposite side of the cart. "I do not like the look of this place, Your Majesty. I have sent riders ahead to scout the way, and to announce us at the castle."

The king frowned. "To announce *you*, I trust."

Green's countenance remained impassive, but his eyes hardened, as if to say, *Do you think me a fool?* "Indeed, sire. The men have all been informed of the need for secrecy. No man in this army will speak of you without my leave. Liam travels with word from Arran Green to his cousin, seeking shelter for himself and his men."

"Good." The king lowered his visor, and when he spoke again, his voice was muffled. "No one but Raibert himself must know. That includes his knights and servants."

Green nodded curtly. Then he squeezed his horse's flanks and rode back to the point. The king watched him go, his expression unreadable beneath the visor. "So dour," he said. "Even worse than Tom."

Alix wasn't sure whether the remark was meant for her, but it seemed safest to hold her tongue. As little as she cared for Arran Green's disposition, at least he was predictable. The Raven was anything but. One moment he was all smiles and jests, and the next he was sullen and waspish, or worse. Alix had seen him reduce grown men to quivering, stammering fools. How many times had she thanked the silent Nine that she had not chosen to join the White Wolves, as her rank entitled her? Not a day went by that she didn't congratulate herself for that decision, not least because it allowed her to avoid Tomald White.

He and his brother are night and day. Or maybe, sunshine and darkness.

"A crown for your thoughts, Captain."

Alix smiled nervously. "I think you will have overpaid, sire."

Thankfully, he didn't press her. Instead, he asked, "What do you suppose could have cleared out these villagers?"

"It must be the Oridians, or the rumour of them. Maybe we'll find the people within the walls of Greenhold."

"My thoughts also. Still, I'm surprised—the scouts say the Oridians are holding their position. We grow farther from them by the day."

"Fear spreads faster than a brushfire, my father used to say."

"Gossip."

"Sorry?"

"*Gossip spreads faster than a brushfire.* That's the saying." The king laughed, adding, "But it sounds very well with *fear.*"

"Oh." Alix felt the telltale beginnings of a blush, and she brought a hand to her face, pretending to brush away a stray lock of hair.

"Don't worry, Captain, the colour becomes you." Through the slat of his visor, Alix could see his wink.

Of course, that only set the blush aflame. *Gods, he's as bad as Liam*, she thought irritably. But she regretted herself moments later, when the king looked back over the empty village with a sigh. Who was she to begrudge him a few moments of humour amid all his troubles, even if it came at her expense?

"Olan is late today," he said absently.

Alix glanced up at the sky. Sure enough, the moon lurked, pale and round, behind a wisp of cloud. If Gwylim were here, he would call it an ill omen. Olan had prolonged his patrol into the day, when it ought to have been his twin brother's sole watch. Worse, his battered shield was in full view. Olan only raised his shield when the dragon was near; the rest of the time, it dangled casually at his side, showing only a slim silver arc.

"Do you believe, sire?" she found herself asking: An impertinent question, maybe, but she thought she knew the answer. Few noblemen would claim to be believers. Faith was for the common classes, quaint and unfashionable. Noblemen swore by the gods, and some even prayed, but it tended to be more out of habit than faith.

Still, the king seemed to consider his answer carefully, the horses' steady hoofbeats counting out a long pause before he spoke. "Do I believe the moon and sun are all that stands between us and destruction? Most assuredly. Do I think that literally means that the moon and sun are divine weapons wielded by gods to defend us from evil? I can't say that I do, but I would be very put out if you mentioned that to the priests."

She smiled. "Noted."

"And you?"

Now it was her turn to pause. "I don't know. Most of the time I think it's all nonsense, but every now and then something happens that I can't explain, and I wonder. Like the Priest. They say the Oridian army has never lost a battle when he rides with them." Hesitantly, she added, "The men say he was spotted at Boswyck."

"I'd heard that." The king's voice was unreadable.

"They say he knows magicks that can bend a man's will."

"I have heard that too." This time, the chill in his voice was unmistakable. He knew exactly where Alix was going with this, and he didn't like it. She swallowed and looked away.

The king fell into a sullen silence after that, and Alix knew she had only herself to blame.

Greenhold scowled down at them from under a darkening sky. A pair of towers flanked the gatehouse, their rough stone faces slashed with arrow slits that glowed faintly with torchlight, lending the impression of a great, many-eyed reptile. Alix could almost *feel* the archers watching them from above, as though they stretched her nerves for bowstrings. The gate stood firmly closed.

Arran Green turned to the knight riding beside him. "What are you waiting for, Commander? It grows darker by the moment."

The Greensword seemed to take the commander general's brusqueness in stride, as though it were nothing new. Perhaps he had met his master's cousin before. He was a blocky fellow with a broad, flat nose and a square jaw. Onnani, Alix guessed. She'd been staring since he rode out to meet them. It wasn't as if she'd never seen one before; there were plenty of easterners in the Kingswords, and even a few living as far west as the Blacklands. But an Onnani knight was something new. She wondered how a lowly fishman had managed to rise so high in the Greenswords—and what hint that might offer about the banner lord they rode to meet.

The knight called out to someone on the wall walk, and a face lit by torchlight appeared over the battlements. "Open the gate! It is indeed General Green and his host!"

Alix pursed her lips grimly. Apparently, the lord of Greenhold had not been prepared to take Liam's word for it. The Onnani knight wasn't an honour escort, but a scout sent to confirm the identity of the men at the gates. Such caution could only mean that Lord Green was expecting trouble.

A ponderous groan heralded the opening of the gate, and the great doors swung aside to reveal a scene of fear and disarray. Peasants crowded the bailey, along with their pigs and goats and such meagre belongings as they had been able to carry on their backs. Alix traded a look with the helmed knight at her side. King Erik had dismounted from the supply wagon just before they reached the bridge, not wanting to draw attention to himself. Now he and Alix stood behind Arran Green and his knights, only a handful of whom would ride into the compound. Even the vast bailey of Greenhold wasn't large enough to admit a host of five thousand, especially not now that it sheltered hundreds of peasants.

"It is as we feared," Erik murmured behind his visor.

"So it would seem, Your—" Alix caught herself in time. "Commander." From now on, she would have to be careful how she addressed him in public.

The king started forward, leaning heavily on his crutch.

"Let's make straight for the keep. I want to know everything, and quickly."

Arran Green had just dismounted when his cousin appeared, striding across the bailey with a greatsword strapped to his back. Alix knew him immediately by the long, thin face and dark brows that seemed to crowd his eyes. Raibert Green, Lord of the Greenlands, was younger than his cousin—in his midthirties, Alix judged—but he had the same permanently stern look that made him seem wise beyond his years. He had the same pale eyes too, though Raibert's were fringed with laugh lines that his kinsman's were entirely lacking.

"Cousin." Lord Green clasped arms with the commander general. "Thank the gods you're well. When I heard what happened at Boswyck, I feared the worst."

"What exactly did you hear?" Arran Green asked.

"Why, that the Kingswords were routed. The Raven and some of his men managed to escape, but most of the rest were slaughtered." Lord Green dropped his gaze. "Including the king, may he find peace in his Domain."

"I think he will have to wait awhile for peace," the helmed knight remarked.

Raibert Green didn't seem to know what to make of that, so he ignored it. To his cousin, he said, "Come inside, you and your knights. You must be hungry. The rest of your men should be safe outside, tonight at least."

"What do you mean, tonight at least?" asked the helmed knight. "Why do your people shelter at the castle?"

Lord Green regarded the disguised king bemusedly. Erik wore simple plate and mail, sturdy but unadorned, nothing that would signify him as anything more than an ordinary knight. Yet he spoke with authority, in a clear, crisp accent that suggested the highest breeding. Alix didn't blame Raibert Green for being puzzled. "The Oridians are all but upon us," he said. "We expect them in a day or two at the most."

"How can that be?" The helmed knight gestured vaguely to the south. "We left them far behind, and at last report, they were holding near the border."

Lord Green regarded the impudent knight coolly. "Do I know you, Commander?"

Alix was suddenly very conscious of the crowded bailey. "Pardon me, my lords, but may I suggest we discuss this somewhere private?"

Lord Green's gaze shifted to her, and he cocked his head slightly. "Now here is someone familiar," he said, a slow smile spreading over his face. "You're Riggard Black's sister, or my eyes deceive me."

She bowed. "Alix Black, at your service, my lord."

"You don't remember me, do you? I suppose I can't be offended—you were only five."

"I'm surprised you recognise me, my lord."

"Don't be. Not one girl in a thousand has those flaming locks, my lady, and I mean that as a compliment." He extended an arm toward the keep. "Please, allow me to escort you."

Alix glanced uncertainly at the king, but his eyes twinkled through the slats of his visor. He was enjoying this. He inclined his head discreetly, giving her leave. She took Raibert Green's proffered arm.

"The Oridians have divided their forces," Lord Green explained as they walked. "The main host remains near Boswyck, but a second crossed the Spearfish near Darton less than a week ago. Three thousand swords, I'm told." He sighed. "A small enough force, but with so many Greenswords lost at Boswyck, I fear we don't have enough to repel them. It will be a siege, and our stocks are already depleted this far into the winter."

"How many Greenswords are left?" Arran Green asked.

"Two thousand, camped just outside the walls on the far side."

"We have five."

Raibert whirled. "*Five?* By the Virtues, that's wonderful news!"

Arran Green permitted himself a thin smile. "If the enemy is wise, he'll turn back. If not, Greenhold will be the last stop on his journey."

Raibert closed his eyes in relief. "I'd thought the surviving Kingswords scattered over half the realm by now. This is . . . well, far more than I dared to hope for."

"Nor is that the whole of it," Arran Green said. "Take us to your study."

They ascended the steps into the keep, passing down long, echoing halls until they arrived at the study, a small but well-appointed room with a single window facing onto the bailey. Alix noticed the way King Erik's gaze lingered appreciatively over the well-stocked bookshelves, much as a stable master might examine fine horseflesh.

"Here we are," said Raibert when the four of them were alone. "And now, pray, who is this mysterious knight?"

"Have you not guessed it?" Without waiting for an answer, the king tore free his helm, grinning like a mischievous boy.

Raibert blanched. For a moment he just stood there, swaying a little, as though unsure whether to embrace his king or recoil from a ghost. "Your Majesty, is it really you?"

The mirth died in Erik's eyes. "It's true, then. You thought me dead."

"Everyone thinks you dead, sire, including your brother! I am overjoyed it isn't so!"

"My brother," the king echoed numbly, as though the word were foreign to him.

Raibert's gaze shifted to his cousin in a silent question. Slowly, dispassionately, Arran Green explained it all. Alix scarcely heard him. She was too busy watching King Erik as he leaned against Lord Green's desk, massaging his thigh with a flat expression. She saw no hint of denial in his eyes, no flicker of anger. He'd resigned himself to the harsh truth at last. Alix knew she should be glad of it, but instead she found herself fighting the impulse to put her arms around him.

"Gods' blood," Raibert said when his cousin had finished. "I can't believe it."

"Nevertheless," the king said, "it's the truth. My brother has shown himself a traitor, and what he lacks in legitimacy, he makes up for in strength. And that is only the beginning of our troubles, as you know too well. I need the Greenswords at my back, Lord Green, and more besides. Can I count on you?"

Raibert fell to one knee and bowed his head. "Unequivocally, sire. The Greenswords are yours, and whatever else is in my power to give."

"A bed, a warm fire, and something to eat," King Erik said with a smile. "Most of all, your counsel. If I may have that, I am content."

"At your humble service, sire. Once the enemy at our gates is defeated, we can rest here awhile, and then ride forth together."

Arran Green went to the mantel above the hearth and picked up a large ornamental timeglass. With great ceremony, he turned it over, watching as the sand began to trickle in a slow spiral into the empty vial at the bottom. "And so the countdown begins."

The king frowned. "I beg your pardon?"

"We cannot hope to keep the secret of your survival for long, sire. The Kingswords are loyal, but they are men. Sooner or later, someone's tongue will slip, and the Greenswords will know of your presence. Then the whole castle will know of it, and the town, and so on, until the Raven himself hears it. We must be prepared."

He's right, Alix thought. *It's only a matter of time.*

"That may be," the king said, "but every day we keep the secret is another day we rebuild our strength. We must be content to steal whatever time we can."

"And there are measures we can take here at the castle to conceal your identity," Lord Green added.

"Good. Now, let us repair to your solar and plan tomorrow's battle."

As they quit the study, Alix touched the king's arm, handing over his discarded helm. "Ah," he said, "thank you." He started to put it on but paused when he caught Alix's eye. "What is it?"

"I . . . Nothing, Your Majesty."

He smiled. "Not very convincing, Captain. Out with it."

After a moment's hesitation, she said, "I trust you aren't considering fighting tomorrow?"

His blue eyes clouded over. "I hadn't really thought about it. I suppose I can't."

"No, you can't." She avoided his gaze, uncomfortable with her own boldness. "Not even from the rear lines. Your leg is not yet healed, and we can't afford any setbacks."

"You're right, of course." Erik donned his helmet quickly, as though to hide his displeasure. "And what of you, Captain? Are we to deny Greenhold your sword as well?"

"My sword is yours, sire."

She'd meant it to sound resolute, but apparently she was more transparent than that. "At least we will be miserable together," the king said as he turned to go.

FIVE

† Alix stood on the ramparts of the gatehouse, watching as Arran Green addressed his men from astride his great grey warhorse. The commander general's words were lost to the wind, but every now and then, the men would raise their swords and pikes and give a rousing cry. Meanwhile, Raibert Green rode up and down the line, inspecting the ranks. Everywhere he paused, men tightened up or rearranged themselves while he gestured and pointed. At this distance, Alix could see little of the front lines—just the tips of their pikes glinting in the sun. She couldn't tell how deep the pikes ran, but the heavy cavalry at the flanks and the thick band of bowmen at the rear suggested that Arran Green expected to face mainly infantry.

"They look ready," the king said. He leaned so far out over the parapet that Alix's stomach squirmed.

"Yes, sire," she said, "and now that you've seen them, can I persuade you to join me inside the tower?"

"We're well out of range, and the view is much better from here."

Alix's sigh was too soft for him to hear. She turned back to the field, scanning the distant tree line. The Oridians could not be far. Any moment now, Arran Green would order the advance. The Kingswords would meet their foes on the open field, counting on their vastly superior numbers to make short work of the advancing host. They could fall back to the castle in case of need, but the Greens considered it so unlikely that barely two hundred archers remained on the ramparts.

Alix glanced down at them. They lined the wall walk, daughters of houses great and small, plus a few men who were either too weak or too talented with a bow to be placed elsewhere. She wondered how many wielded bloodbows. In the scramble to prepare for war, the Raven had ordered the royal bloodbinders to focus their efforts on equipping the archers, since the bloodbond conferred a far greater advantage on bows than blades. Cavell and Nevyn had worked night and day for weeks, drawing the blood of hundreds of archers to enchant their bows. But the Kingswords had marched before they could finish, and the gods only knew how many archers had fallen at Boswyck. Cavell had marched with them, but he'd been slain at Three Skulls. Only Nevyn remained, and he was back in the capital. It occurred to Alix that she might wield one of the few remaining bloodforged weapons in the king's army. It was not a comforting thought.

Below, Arran Green wheeled his horse about and started across the field. The destrier looked fearsome in its shining plate and stark white war paint, and the commander general sat as stiff and proud as the stone knights along the Gallery of Heroes. The men marched behind him in straight, disciplined ranks. Within moments, they had covered half the distance to the tree line, and there, Green held them. A wave of silver rolled in the distance as the pikes were set. The Kingswords were ready.

They did not have long to wait.

"Here they come," said the king.

Alix gripped the parapet and peered out at the dark mass of the tree line. Sure enough, flashes of light pierced the shadows where sunlight caught metal, and the breeze carried the distant whinny of a horse. For a moment, the forest itself seemed to advance, the trees marching forth as one, until gradually the forms of men took shape, marching behind the great golden trident of Oridia.

They had scarcely gained the field before a flock of arrows burst into the sky from the Kingsword ranks. The battle had begun.

"I should be there," the king growled as the missiles rained down on the enemy.

Alix felt the same way, but it would do no good to say so. *Liam can take care of himself,* she told herself firmly. *They all can.*

A shrill brass horn sounded the charge, and the enemy swarmed forward. The Kingswords answered; cavalry surged from either flank. The armies bled into each other, clotting into a single, dark mass on the field, and once again, Alix found herself standing at a distance, guessing at the fate of her friends and comrades.

The king started to pace, his crutch skidding precariously along the uneven stone. "Blast it, I can't see a thing!"

Alix had a sudden, sickening vision of King Erik plummeting to his death from the ramparts. Fate seemed to have a fondness for such irony. "Please, Your Majesty, there's loose rock here, and the parapet is low. Your crutch . . ."

He scowled, but he stopped pacing, and even moved away from the crenels. Alix dared to take her eyes off him long enough to glance at the battlefield—for all the good it did her. She could make nothing of the seething mass of metal and men.

The king sighed. "It's no use. They're too far away."

She started to answer, but suddenly he hissed in pain and sagged against the wall, his hand going to his thigh. "Bloody leg." He let himself slide down, armour scraping against stone, until he dropped onto his rear with a loud *clank*. "I need to rest."

"We could go inside," Alix suggested, but she knew what he would say.

"Not yet."

With a final glance at the inscrutable battlefield, she lowered herself down at his side. "I'll look again in a little while," she said in answer to his questioning gaze. "Staring at it will just drive me mad."

Instead they listened as the distant echo of battle drifted, dreamlike, over the walls of Greenhold. The sound drew bile to Alix's throat.

"I hate this," Erik said after a while. "A king belongs with his men."

"Does he?" Alix glanced at him shyly. "We almost lost you at Boswyck, Your Majesty."

He made a wry face. "I remember. That should not have happened, of course. I was supposed to be well behind the front lines." He closed his eyes and leaned his head back against the wall. "One of several deviations from the plan, as I recall."

Alix didn't know what to say to that, so she said nothing.

"Have you ever been betrayed, Alix?"

The question caught her off guard. She hesitated long enough that he opened his eyes and looked over at her expectantly. Swallowing, Alix said, "Not really, no. Small things, of course, but certainly nothing compared to . . ."

"Compared to my brother leaving me to die?"

The air left her lungs in a wordless gust. It wasn't the bitterness of the words, but the raw pain in the king's eyes that knocked the wind from her. This wasn't the Erik White she had ridden alongside this past week, the golden-haired king with the ready smile. She'd wondered how much of that was for show. Here, it seemed, was her answer. "I'm sorry," she said quietly. It felt ridiculously inadequate.

"I wonder, is that the worst of it? Has my brother betrayed his country as well? Has he sold us to the enemy?"

So it has occurred to him. It was the first he'd spoken of it, but Alix suspected it had been on his mind for some time. How not?

An aching silence fell. The king looked away, lost in his own thoughts. Alix couldn't help watching him, wishing she could think of something comforting, or at least wise, to say. If he noticed her staring, he didn't seem to care.

After a time, he said, "I keep asking myself how I failed to see it."

"See what, sire?"

"The hatred. How could I look into his eyes day after day and not see it? It must have been there. A hate that strong can't be invisible."

Alix felt compelled to say something, but what? She knew

nothing of the king's relationship with his brother. "Maybe it wasn't hate that made him do it."

"The Priest?" he said dryly.

She left that alone. "Ambition, maybe, or envy."

"Envy . . . Perhaps. But what is envy but a path to hatred? I should have seen that he was getting desperate. I should have acted sooner. I thought he would trust me, that my word would be enough . . ."

Alix didn't know what he was talking about, but it didn't matter. "You can't blame yourself," she said, all propriety forgotten. "Whatever happened between you, you couldn't have known he was capable of such treachery. What kind of man would suspect that of his own brother?"

"A wiser man than I, apparently."

If that was wisdom, Alix wanted no part of it. "That kind of distrust has a way of bearing itself out."

He looked over at her, his gaze shadowed and thoughtful. So much was going on behind those eyes, but it was a mystery to Alix, as inscrutable as the battlefield. Then, abruptly, he smiled. "Listen to me, brooding like an adolescent. Please forgive me."

Alix blinked, taken aback. "There's nothing to forgive, Your Majesty."

"You don't have to do that. Not when we're alone, anyway. You're a Black and a friend; we need no titles between us."

"As you wish . . ."

"Erik."

She dropped her gaze. "Erik."

"Good." He gave the ground a little thump. "I feel much better. You are an excellent bodyguard, Alix."

"Thank you, Your Majesty."

"But a slow learner," he laughed, winking. "Come, help me up. Let's have a look at how the battle fares."

Alix helped him to stand, feeling a little unsteady herself. Erik had vanished behind the royal mask as abruptly as if he had snapped down the visor of his helm. She wondered how long it would be until she saw him again, the man behind the king.

Just as they reached the parapet, a great cheer went up

from the walls below. The archers thrust their bows in the air, brandishing them in time with their shouts. Shading her eyes against the waning sun, Alix looked out over the battlefield.

The Oridian lines had broken. The banners were down, the men scattering as they fell back into the woods. The Kingswords had almost reached the tree line. Cavalry circled the enemy stragglers, cutting off their escape while the infantry bore down on them.

"It's over," Erik said. "The day is ours."

Alix knew she should be giving thanks to the gods, but she couldn't. Not until she knew Liam was safe.

As though he'd read her thoughts, Erik said, "Let's go down and meet them at the gate."

Smiling, Alix lent him her arm.

"Good morning," Alix said, her voice echoing in the vast emptiness of the chamber. Though the assembled royal guardsmen numbered more than twenty, the oratorium was designed to accommodate Lord Green's entire court, a gathering that could easily reach into the hundreds. Alix and her knights were swallowed by the space, a school of shiny silver minnows in the belly of a whale. They'd had little choice—they were too numerous for most of the other chambers in the castle, and they could not very well hold this gathering outside, not when there were so many pairs of ears about. At least this way, they could be sure of not being overheard.

"This meeting is long overdue," Alix said, "but it could not be helped. Nevertheless, I hope you have found occasion to meet one another in the course of your duties. You will need to rely on each other in the days ahead, and it's important that you know and trust your comrades."

The faces that stared back at her were impassive. They were men, mostly, and young. That wasn't surprising, Alix supposed. Female knights were few, and the older, more experienced knights who had once made up Erik's personal guard had all perished at Boswyck. The men standing before her had been appointed in the aftermath of the battle. Some of them might have even been knighted since then. Alix wondered how many battles they'd seen between them.

Not that you're in a position to throw stones . . .

She continued. "As you know, most of the kingdom believes that His Majesty King Erik fell at the Battle of Boswyck. For the moment, we cannot allow anyone to learn otherwise, and that includes our good hosts. Maintaining this secret is a matter of great strategic importance, and quite possibly a matter of life and death. That is a heavy responsibility, and it falls to you more than anyone, for you must go about your duties discreetly, without alerting the men and women of Greenhold to the situation. Needless to say, that will not be easy."

Still the faces before her remained blank. Was it just good discipline, or were her words really so uninspiring? She'd seen Rig address his men once or twice, and she'd stood with the rest of the Kingswords as Arran Green rallied them for battle. Alix had been struck by how much presence they had. They were no great orators, either of them, but they'd sounded . . . commanding. Alix didn't feel commanding. She felt like an impostor. *Barely a fledgling*, Arran Green had called her. Was that what her men saw when they looked at her? A fledgling, younger than most of them and just as inexperienced?

If they do, you'll only make it worse by worrying about it. They'll smell the doubt on you, and they'll never respect you. She cleared her throat. "Before we continue, are there any questions?"

Commander Kilby stepped forward. He was something of an elder among the guardsmen, the first to be appointed by Arran Green after Boswyck. He'd been in charge until Alix herself was named captain—a position lasting a total of three days. Alix was considering appointing him her second, but she hadn't seen enough of him yet to be sure.

"Speak, Commander Kilby."

"When will we begin drilling, my lady?"

"Captain." *My lady* was her rank by birth. *Captain* was her military rank, a title she'd actually earned—or so she kept telling herself.

He inclined his head. "Forgive me. When will we begin drilling, Captain?"

"As soon as I can determine an appropriate venue for it."

She meant to leave it at that and move on, but Kilby spoke up again.

"But, Captain, the men need to begin training as soon as possible. Guarding the king is a special skill."

"I'm aware of that, Commander, but we can't simply start drilling in the bailey, in full view of the entire castle. As you say, guarding the king is a special skill, and it would raise a few eyebrows if we started tackling each other in the yard."

A murmur of laughter rippled through the group. Kilby seemed to think it was at his expense, and he didn't like it. He coloured. "With all due respect, my lady—"

"Captain."

"With all due respect, *Captain*, we can afford no delay. Why keep our allies in the dark if it means risking the king's life? Why not simply tell them the truth and let us go about our duties? Greenhold might even tighten its defences."

"Greenhold's defences are as tight as they're going to get."

"Surely there is no question of Lord Green's loyalty?"

"What did you say?" Her voice reverberated in the sudden silence.

Kilby swallowed, his gaze dropping. "I'm sorry, my lady, I meant no disrespect. I simply don't understand—"

"You are not required to understand anything, Commander." She stalked over to him, boots ringing coldly against the stone floor. For the first time in her life, Alix thanked the gods for her height, for she would have felt ridiculous talking to the man's breastplate. As it was, she looked him right in the eye—or at least, she would have, had he not been studying his boots. "You are only required to follow orders. If that is too much for you, perhaps you would prefer lighter duties. There are always latrines that need digging." She ducked her head until she had trapped his gaze. "And if you ever call me *my lady* again, I'll have you doing laps round the bailey in nothing but your boots and your dignity, and we shall see which of them wears out first. Is that clear?"

He drew himself up and stared straight ahead. "Yes, Captain."

So much for making him my second.

"Is there anyone else who would like to register an opinion on how we do things?"

Silence. This time, she was grateful for the blank faces.

"Good. Now, it's time to go over the protocols during our stay at Greenhold. Listen carefully, because I will only say this once . . ."

An hour later, Alix went in search of the king, two royal guardsmen at her heels. As expected, she found him in the library. King Erik's fondness for books was well known, and she'd noticed him admiring the collection in Lord Green's study. While she was pleased to have found him so quickly, she couldn't help feeling uneasy that his habits were so easy to guess. Fortunately, she had a plan to mitigate that problem. "Your Majesty, I'd like to introduce you to your nighttime detail."

The king turned, an open book balanced in his hand. "I beg your pardon?"

"From now on, these men will be keeping an eye on things after you retire."

Erik frowned. "You mean to put guards on my door? Is that really necessary?"

"I believe it is, Your Majesty."

"Won't that draw too much attention? I thought the idea was to remain inconspicuous."

"Indeed, sire, so long as that does not come at the expense of your safety. But don't worry—I'm aware that putting guards on the door will look strange. For that reason, the commander general will also have a guard on his door, as will some of the higher-ranking officers. I've discussed the matter with Lord Green, and he'll explain to his people that it's merely a courtesy guard for his guests, given the recent troubles."

"Clever." The king smiled. "But altogether too much trouble to go to, Captain. I appreciate the thought, but I really don't need guards on my door."

Alix's jaw twitched. *First Kilby, now this.* "I think—"

"Nothing personal, chaps," Erik said, still smiling. Alix glanced behind her to find the guardsmen staring at her uncomfortably. They had no idea how to react. Alix couldn't blame them.

"As you say, Your Majesty."

There must have been more than a hint of frost in her voice, because the king cocked his head slightly. After a pause, he said, "Guards, will you excuse us a moment?" The two guardsmen beat a hasty retreat. Alix couldn't blame them for that, either. "You're angry with me," Erik said when they'd gone.

She gazed over his shoulder. "It's not my place to be angry, Your Majesty."

"Yet you very clearly are, so let's have it. What have I done?"

She met his eye. "You mean besides undermining my authority in front of my men?" It was beyond impudent, but she couldn't help it. She was still feeling raw after what had happened with Commander Kilby.

"My, my." The king closed his book. "That is a serious charge. Do you really believe that's what I did?"

Careful, Alix. It was too late to back down now, but she was on thin ice. For all his smiles and *Call me Erik*s, this was still the King of Alden, and she must never forget it. She took a deep breath. "If you had concerns with my proposal, Your Majesty, I would have preferred if you had taken them up with me in private."

She expected him to be angry, or at least amused, by this display of self-importance, but instead he gave a thoughtful grunt. "I suppose that's fair." He started to turn away.

"That being said . . ."

Erik turned back around, one eyebrow raised in mild disbelief.

"I don't want to have to justify the protections I put in place."

"I'm not to have a say?"

"If I am to be your bodyguard, I must be allowed to do my duty. I can't have you fighting me every time I propose a new security measure."

He frowned. "I hardly think I'm fighting you, Alix."

"Maybe *fighting* is too strong a word. But you haven't been very . . ." She'd been about to say *helpful*, but that was going too far, even for her. She dropped her gaze.

The king sighed. "I haven't been very cooperative, have I?"

Alix didn't trust herself to respond.

"Very well." Erik placed his book back on the shelf. "You're perfectly right, Captain. Of course you must have the freedom to execute your duties according to your judgement. I can't promise to stop getting in the way, but I do hope you'll tell me when I do." His smile returned. "Somehow, I don't think that will be a problem for you."

She flushed. "I'm sorry, Your Majesty."

"Don't be. If you didn't have any spine, you wouldn't make much of a bodyguard. Now . . . you were about to make some introductions, were you not?"

Alix bowed and withdrew to fetch her guardsmen. A smile tugged at the corner of her mouth, a small celebration of a small victory. She'd looked the king in the eye and said her piece, and he'd backed down—not because he hesitated to put her in her place, but because he agreed with her. She took another deep breath, and this time, it was in satisfaction.

Maybe I'm going to like this job after all.

SIX

†The following morning, the king stepped out of his chambers to find Alix waiting for him in the corridor. She must have been grinning, because he laughed and said, "Why, Captain, you're looking positively chipper this morning."

Alix couldn't deny it—she *was* chipper, and why not? The Kingswords were victorious, she was finally finding her feet as captain of the royal guardsmen, and she had spent the night in a warm, soft bed—her first decent night's sleep since leaving Blackhold to take up her King's Service four months ago. She could almost forget her country was at war. "It's a good morning, Your Majesty," she said.

Then they arrived at the solar, and one glance at Raibert Green was enough to banish that notion.

He and his cousin sat across from each other at the long table near the hearth, a bounty of breads and fruits and cheeses lying untouched between them. They stood as the king entered, Arran Green looking grave, his cousin worried.

Erik looked from one to the other, his own expression darkening. "What's happened?"

Arran Green's gaze slid to Alix. Raibert cleared his throat quietly and looked at the floor.

Oh, gods.

"A knight arrived at the gate just before dawn, Your Majesty," Raibert said. "A Blacksword."

Alix gripped the back of a chair, her heart stuttering in her chest.

"Blackhold has fallen."

Alix heard the words, though she wasn't sure who spoke them. Her breath suddenly sounded hollow in her ears, as though she had slipped underwater. She felt a steadying hand press discreetly at her back. Erik.

"When?" His voice cracked like a whip.

"Ten days ago, or thereabouts," said Raibert. "The knight—Commander Ellis, he's called—returned from an errand to find the village empty and the castle completely deserted."

The king's jaw twitched. "Oridians."

"A host of some thousands, according to the peasants," Arran Green said, "though reports from lay folk are notoriously unreliable."

"The good news is that Lord Black appears to have been warned in time to evacuate his household," Raibert said. "He met the enemy on the field, most likely in order to buy time for his people to flee. The Blackswords were defeated, but the peasants claim that Lord Black escaped with some of his men." Raibert strode around the table and took Alix by the shoulders. His pale eyes met hers steadily. "We believe your brother is safe, my lady. He was last seen heading east, toward the marshlands."

She nodded numbly.

Erik lunged away, pacing on his crutch. "How in the Nine Domains did an Oridian army reach the Blacklands without any warning? We have sentries all along the border!"

"All along the southern border," Arran Green corrected him. "My guess is they came through the mountains."

"From Harram? Don't tell me they've taken another of our allies?"

"Not that we know of," Raibert said. "They could have crossed through without the Harrami even knowing. The mountain passes are notoriously difficult to monitor, and the king's control over the tribal lands is minimal, to put it mildly."

"The mountain tribes would never suffer a foreign host to pass through their lands," Erik said. "Gods' blood, they don't even let their own king pass through!"

"Their king seeks to control their lands," Arran Green pointed out. "The Oridians do not—at least not yet."

"The Blacksword who brought the news," Erik said, "where is he now? I would speak with him . . ."

The conversation continued, but Alix had stopped listening. She was vaguely aware of King Erik pacing behind her, of Arran Green explaining patiently, of Raibert watching her with sympathetic eyes.

We believe your brother is safe. She focused on those words, willing her heart to settle. Rig *was* safe—she knew it in her bones. He was safe, and heading toward the marshlands, where the enemy would be loath to follow. He would be planning his next move, and Alix should be doing the same.

Drawing a deep, steadying breath, she said, "They're targeting the Banner Houses, Your Majesty."

The king paused in his pacing. "Sorry?"

"The enemy. They've already struck Greenhold and Blackhold. The Browns and Greys are probably next, and the Golds after that, if it's worth their while. They're trying to take out the Banner Houses before we can regroup with the Kingswords."

"I agree, Your Majesty," Arran Green said, "and it is a sound strategy. Had we not arrived when we did, Greenhold would be under siege and powerless to aid our cause."

"In that case," said the king, "the enemy's failure has exposed his strategy, and that presents us with an opportunity."

"It's not hard to guess where they will strike next," Raibert said.

"The Brownlands." The king resumed his pacing. "But it will take weeks for them to get there."

"Indeed, sire," said Arran Green, "which means we have time to prepare. We should send word to Lord Brown and Lady Grey immediately."

"And the Golds, surely?" Raibert Green said.

His kinsman shrugged. "As you like, but the Golds are militarily insignificant. I doubt the enemy will trouble himself."

"How many Blackswords do you think escaped?" the king asked.

"Impossible to know, but the peasants claimed several hundred."

"We need those men."

Arran Green grunted and scratched his beard. "What do you propose?"

"I propose that we find Riggard Black and his men and bring them here."

The commander general frowned. "No simple task, Your Majesty. It will take time."

The king gave a dismissive wave. "We planned to remain here awhile anyway, to restock and allow the men to recuperate. Let us make productive use of that time. Take your scouts and see if you can find Lord Black. If you do, we'll have gained hundreds of men. If not, we've lost nothing."

"Your Majesty, I know Riggard Black is a friend, but—"

"He's more than that. He is the lord of a Banner House, and in case you have forgotten, my brother means to usurp my crown. I need Lord Black's swords, and I need his loyalty."

Arran Green was visibly unconvinced, and even Alix could understand why. A few hundred men could hardly make a difference to their cause, not when the Oridians had fifty thousand at their border, and the Raven another twenty thousand in Erroman. Moreover, Rig's allegiance could not be in doubt—Erik had said so himself when he'd appointed Alix as his bodyguard. There was little to be gained by risking a search party. The king was making an emotional decision, not a pragmatic one. But the commander general would not dare say so aloud, so instead he fixed his disapproving gaze on Alix, as though she were responsible.

"It's only a few days, Green," Erik said.

Arran Green nodded gravely and said nothing.

The king turned to Alix. "If you wish to go, I won't deny you. He is your brother, after all."

Alix opened her mouth to thank him, but her conscience stole the words. She had sworn her service to the king. If she backed out now, she'd dishonour herself and her family. Rig would never forgive her for that. "I'm deeply grateful for the offer, Your Majesty, but my place is at your side."

Arran Green's gaze softened into something suspiciously like approval. Erik, for his part, merely nodded.

"Shall we eat, then?" Raibert asked, gesturing at the table.

The king graciously offered Alix a place, but she could not have eaten if her life depended on it. All she could think about was Rig, adrift and possibly wounded, wandering the Blacklands with gods-knew-what for supplies. If he had any sense, he would make for some minor lord's holdings, or seek out their uncle at Karringdon. But Alix knew better than that. Rig would be crouched by a fire somewhere, honing his blade and hatching his plans.

As bold as a Black, so the saying went, and it was truer of her brother than any of them. If Arran Green didn't find him, and soon, Rig would get himself killed.

"Are you sure you're all right?" Liam asked.

Alix realised she'd been quiet for a long time, staring absently into the flames as her thoughts churned over themselves. She hadn't even noticed the others go to bed. "Sorry," she said, running her hands over her face. "I'm fine, really."

He eyed her doubtfully. "Maybe you just want me to sod off and leave you alone?"

"It's your campfire."

"That's okay—I'll curl up in your nice bed in the castle and we'll call it even."

She laughed. "Nice try."

"Seriously," he said, his smile fading, "you should get some sleep. It's late, and you've had a rough day."

Alix glanced around at the slumbering camp. It must have been late indeed, for there were usually a few stragglers around until midnight, at least. Not only were she and Liam alone, most of the other fires had already dwindled to embers. Even so, Alix couldn't imagine going to sleep. "I'd just end up staring at the ceiling."

He nodded. Then, almost hesitantly, he said, "Still, you seem to be handling this pretty well, considering."

"I suppose that's because it could have been so much

worse. At least Rig managed to hold the enemy back while everyone escaped. If they took the castle after that, well—all they got was timber and stone. And we'll get it back."

Liam smiled and shook his head. "You're amazing, Allie, you know that?"

She was grateful for the glow of the fire, for it hid her blush. "Rig would box my ears if he found out that I sat around feeling sorry for myself."

"Tell me about him. What's he like?"

"You don't have to do that."

"No, really, I'm interested. Go on, then." He shifted on the log, as though settling in for a good tale.

She loved him for that. Liam always seemed to know just what she needed. "You and my brother would get on well, actually. You share a penchant for bad jokes."

He shook his head with mock sadness. "Hurtful, Alix."

"That's what he would say."

"A sensitive fellow."

"A complete brute, actually." She smiled fondly. "Impulsive, quick-tempered . . . A true child of Ardin."

"You don't say. Does he have red hair, by any chance?"

"Funny. And no—he's dark, like our father was, and shaggy most of the time. When I was little, he tried to convince me that he was part bear, and for a while I believed him."

"You were close."

"We still are. We've had our differences, of course, especially when we were younger. You know how it is with siblings."

"I really don't."

There was something in the way he said it that gave Alix pause. "You've never told me about your family." She hadn't really thought about it until now.

"That's because I haven't had one in a long time." He shrugged, but the gesture was too stiff to be convincing. "My mother died when I was eleven, in the Year of the Great Fever."

"Like my parents." *Along with half the kingdom.* To this day, the Blacklands were dotted with empty villages. Alix supposed it was the same everywhere.

"After that, I stayed with my mother's husband, but I think

it's fair to say we weren't great friends." His mouth tightened into something hard and bitter.

"Your mother's husband?" She realised her mistake as soon as she'd spoken. She would have given anything to take it back, but it was too late—she could tell by the colour flooding Liam's cheeks.

"That's right," he said. "I'm a bastard."

She'd guessed as much, but until now, she'd been tactful enough to avoid the issue. *Nicely done, Alix.* She wanted to tell him it didn't matter, that she didn't care, but it would only sound trite. So instead she held her tongue, cursed herself, and stared at her lap.

"Anyway," he continued, "I was squired to Arran Green when I was thirteen, and ever since then, he's been the closest thing I have to family."

Until he dismissed you without even making you a knight. Aloud, Alix said, "I'm sorry, Liam."

"Don't be. I was happy enough with Green. He always treated me well, and I appreciated that, especially after . . ." He trailed off, his gaze fixed on the fire. His whole body seemed to tense, to coil protectively over itself, and for a moment, Alix glimpsed him as a boy—a small, frightened boy. Suddenly, she understood.

Oh, Liam.

Impulsively, she reached out and brushed his face with her fingertips. He looked over at her, his features cast half in amber, half in shadow. "They healed a long time ago," he said quietly.

Alix wasn't so sure. "Have you seen him since then? Your stepfather?"

He started to answer, then made a disgusted sound and shook his head. "Gods, I'm a selfish *prat*." He leaned over and put his arms around her. "I'm sorry, Allie. I don't know how I made this about me all of a sudden. The last thing you need right now is to listen to somebody whining about family."

She let him fold her into his chest, just as he had done that night at the barracks, months before. That night, just that once, the loneliness had been too much for her, and she'd broken down. Liam had held her close. He'd stroked her hair and called her *Allie*. He'd felt like a brother.

He didn't feel like a brother now. Alix's insides swam with something warm and giddy and subtly terrifying. She closed her eyes, letting the feel of him surround her.

"Do you forgive me?" His voice sounded from his chest, rich and resonant against her ear.

Was it her imagination, or was he breathing faster? She looked up at him. He was watching her, his dark eyes shining in the firelight. This time, Alix didn't wait for him to decide. She stretched up and pressed her lips to his forehead.

His arms tightened around her. Alix kissed his forehead again, lingeringly this time.

His lips caught hers on the way down, glancing off her so gently that she barely felt the whisper of his skin. He hesitated, then brushed her lips again, fleetingly, like a question. She answered, fastening her mouth against his and grazing her tongue along his lip. She sensed his surprise. And then he was sighing into her, cradling her head as he leaned into the kiss. Alix drew him in in a rush of heat and raw nerves, and for a blissful moment she lost track of everything but the feel of his mouth, soft and warm and searching. When finally he broke off, she nearly whimpered in disappointment. Her skin was hot, and her breath came in short, shaky gulps.

Liam traced his thumb over her mouth. "Gods, I've wanted to do that for weeks."

"Only weeks?"

"I didn't say how many weeks." His gaze wandered slowly over her face, as if memorising every feature. "Do you have any notion of how beautiful you are?"

She couldn't think of anything sensible to say, so she turned her face into his hand and kissed his wrist.

"Allie . . ." He hesitated. "I'm not taking advantage of you, am I?"

"No more than I'm taking advantage of you."

He hummed sceptically, one eyebrow quirked. "I'm going to pretend that makes sense, but only because it's impolite to contradict a lady."

Alix laughed, but when he leaned in to kiss her again, her smile vanished, and her arms coiled around his neck. This time, his kiss was not a question, but a statement—an emphatic one. His confidence was new and intoxicating, and

Alix surrendered to it eagerly. The thrill of her blood chased everything else from her mind. She could do this all night. She could do this for the rest of her life.

He pulled away eventually. "I can't believe I'm saying this, but I have to be on the road at dawn. If Green catches me falling out of my saddle, it'll be my hide."

She groaned; she'd almost managed to forget about Arran Green and his search party. The anxiety came rushing back, along with something new—a pang of loss. "How long will you be gone?"

"About ten days, to be thorough. Green plans to split us up once we reach the marshlands." Liam stood and extended his hand, helping her to stand. "We'll find him, Allie." He squeezed her fingers.

"Please be careful."

She gave him a quick kiss on the cheek, and they went their separate ways, leaving the fire to slump into ashes.

SEVEN

Alix trailed after King Erik as he limped along the inner wall of the bailey. She carried his crutch in her hand, watching his ragged stride with growing unease. He was making his second pass of the barracks, but still he pushed on, stubbornly refusing to acknowledge that his leg was giving out beneath him. Alix had tried to return the crutch back at the stables, but he'd waved her off, claiming he felt fine. He seemed to think his pain was hidden beneath his helm, instead of written in every line of his body.

They were approaching the gatehouse. Alix scanned the battlements of the southwest tower, as she had on their first pass. The same pair of guards leaned against the parapet, looking bored. They took no interest in the anonymous knight passing below, though one of them waved to Alix in greeting. Satisfied that they were doing their jobs, if unenthusiastically, she returned her attention to the compound. The castle was surprisingly quiet, considering that its servants and trades-men were stretched to the limit providing for the army camped outside their walls. The forge rang out constantly, and the cistern drew a continuous stream of pilgrims from every corner of the bailey. A heady mix of lye, wood smoke, and horse dung brought water to Alix's eyes. Yet there was something subdued about it all, like a servant tiptoeing around a master he fears to wake.

As they reached the corner of the gatehouse, the king stopped and leaned against the wall, his hand going to his thigh. Alix cursed under her breath. He'd worn himself out, as she knew he would, and now they were on the far side of the bailey.

"Your crutch, Commander." She was careful to use the generic honorific of a knight. For now, the king's identity remained secret from most of the castle. There was still some sand left in their timeglass, though it was impossible to know how much.

Erik eyed the crutch balefully before tucking it under his arm with a sigh.

"Will you be able to make it back to the keep?" she asked him.

"I suppose I'll have to, unless you mean to carry me again." They started back toward the motte. "I don't do this for amusement, you know," the king said. "If I don't keep up my strength, it will never heal."

"But you overdo it."

She hadn't meant to say it aloud. She half expected a rebuke, but he only sighed again and said, "Perhaps."

Alix worried about how he would mount the steps to the keep, but he managed it, and soon enough they arrived at the solar. Her gaze drifted up, as it always did, to the massive beams crisscrossing the distant ceiling. She liked this room. Though windowless and dark, it was finely adorned, with carved wood panels and sumptuous tapestries lining the walls. The hearth stood ten feet tall, the mantelpiece flanked with hunting dogs sculpted of marble. A rich emerald-green banner hung in a billowing arc above the table, its colour wild and mysterious in the wavering light of the torches. Rough-spun silk, Alix thought, though it was hung too high to be sure. She wondered if it was the original banner conferred on Lord Green's ancestors when they were honoured with their name all those centuries ago, as reward for helping Aldrich the White stake his claim on what remained of a shattered empire. Its colour was echoed elsewhere in the décor, notably in the emerald-studded tableware. The only accent Alix didn't care for was the stuffed bear looming in the corner, which, in addition to being macabre and out of place, gave off a mildly unpleasant odour. There was a story there too, she felt sure, though she doubted it was quite as glorious as the founding of the Banner Houses.

The solar was empty as usual, cleared out for the king's use at the midday meal. A pair of royal guardsmen stood at the door, and as soon as the king crossed the threshold, he removed his helm and dropped it on the table with a heavy *clunk*.

"Gods, I hate that thing." He ran his hands through his red-gold hair before plunging them into a washbasin in the corner. He looked pale, even after he washed; he really had overdone it. He eased himself into a chair. "Will you eat with me?"

Alix's gaze dropped involuntarily to the food at the table. She was more tempted than she cared to admit. "I don't think I can stand guard and eat at the same time, Your Majesty."

"I appreciate the diligence, but we are safely ensconced in the keep of Greenhold, with two of my knights at the door." When she still hesitated, his mouth quirked. "Shall I command you?"

"Very well." She moved around the table to sit across from him. "Thank you, Your Majesty."

"Alix . . ."

She winced. "Sorry. I'm trying. It just . . . doesn't come naturally. Erik."

"Fair enough." He broke off a chunk of bread, then took up an emerald-encrusted knife and sawed off half a chicken. Alix waited until he'd loaded his plate before diving in, and she made sure to take only a little, just as her mother would have done.

"Strange, isn't it," Erik said, pouring some wine, "to sit here eating and drinking while the Oridians gnaw away at our lands. While your brother and Green and the others are out there, facing gods-know-what."

"It is."

"I feel like an ornamental fish, swimming around contentedly in a glass bowl, oblivious to the world beyond. I feel . . . *frivolous*."

Alix didn't feel like a fish. She felt like a sapling at the bottom of a hill, rooted helplessly to the spot as an avalanche thundered down the slope toward her. Aloud, she said, "There's nothing we can do right now. You need to recover, and we need General Green to return."

"I know. But I still feel frivolous." He took a long sip of his wine, and Alix sensed the royal mask snapping back into place. "So tell me, what's it like having Arran Green as a commander?"

Alix nearly choked on her water. What in the Domains was she supposed to say to *that*? "Sorry?" she spluttered, just to buy herself time.

The king laughed. "An intriguing start. Don't worry, it's just between us. You have my word. Besides, he won't be back for a few days yet. Chances are I will have forgotten by then."

Alix didn't believe that for a moment. "I only served under him for a few months," she said evasively.

"Come now, surely you have some sense of the man. Is he as hard as he seems?"

She considered. "He's certainly stern. He doesn't tolerate anyone questioning his orders."

"Even to save the king's life," he said dryly. "Yes, I'd noticed."

"But he applies the same standards to himself. It isn't his vanity that demands obedience, it's his principles."

Erik nodded thoughtfully. "I can respect that, I suppose."

"And he's fair-minded. He gives credit where it's due." *Mostly*, she amended inwardly. His treatment of Liam was still a mystery to her. How he could fail to make his squire a knight after so many years of faithful service . . . It just wasn't fair. Liam was a commoner, and a bastard at that, but he was the best sword Alix had ever seen, and he'd always conducted himself with honour. He'd *earned* knighthood, unlike the spoiled noblemen and women who were named Commander simply because of an accident of birth, as though blood alone could make a leader. And then, to add insult to injury, to banish Liam to the scouts, a service normally reserved for women, or men deemed unfit for the infantry . . . She would never understand it. Liam must have offended Green terribly to deserve such shaming.

"My father thought him the best of men," Erik said. *"You can trust Arran Green with anything,* he told me. I took that advice to heart." His gaze grew abstracted, as though clouded with memories. "But an honourable man is not necessarily an easy man to serve. It must be hard on . . . all of you."

"Sometimes." She wondered what it could possibly matter to him.

Erik sliced himself off a generous hunk of cheese. "And what of your fellow scouts, how are they to serve with? Your friend—Liam, is it? What's he like?"

Alix froze. *Don't blush. Don't you dare blush.* Fortunately, the king's gaze had dropped to his plate. "He's good," she said, stupidly.

Erik looked up, one eyebrow arched.

"Good with a sword, that is. And he's funny. It's nice to have someone funny around, you know, when things get difficult . . ." Merciful Nine, she was babbling. She fantasised briefly about crawling under the table. "I like all the scouts, really," she flailed.

"That's good, I suppose." He paused, his knife hovering over his plate. "I have to ask, Alix, why join the scouts? You're the daughter of a Banner House. You could have had a command of your own."

Only moments ago, this question would have embarrassed her. Now, it was a blessed relief. "Honestly, it's where I thought I could do the most good. I have a talent for"—*sneaking,* said a voice in her head that sounded suspiciously like Rig's—"stealth."

Erik's mouth twitched, as though he were suppressing a grin. "Is that so?"

"When I was a girl, I used to make a game of getting about without being seen. In the castle, in the woods, in the market . . ." She shrugged shyly. "I was good at it."

"A born thief," Erik said—quoting one of her brother's favourite jests. Alix's jaw dropped open, to the king's visible amusement. "Rig mentioned it once or twice. He appears to have had his hands full raising you. It seemed like every time he came to court, he would get at least one letter from home complaining of wild behaviour."

Alix's face burned. The fantasy about crawling under the

table was rapidly transforming into a fantasy about death by mysterious falling object. She scrutinised the grain of the oak table. "Are you torturing me on purpose, Your Majesty?"

"Perhaps." He buttered a piece of bread.

So glad we cleared that up.

The conversation wandered into safer territory after that, but the damage was done; Alix felt awkward for the rest of the afternoon. She fell asleep that night with thoughts of her brother. She couldn't wait for the triumphant return of the scouting party. She would fly across the yard and into Rig's arms.

And then she would kill him.

Alix was accompanying the king on his daily circuit round the bailey when the shouts went up from the ramparts: Arran Green had returned. She paused, her whole body tensing. *Please, gods, let Rig be with them.*

Erik glanced at her, his eyes glinting with anticipation. "Quickly, to the keep. I want this blasted helm off when we receive them."

They awaited Arran Green in the study. Raibert arrived first, still buttoning his doublet, and Alix caught a glimpse of the marriage chain at his throat: three gold links signifying man, woman, and child. It was only then she remembered that Raibert had been married almost a decade ago, before losing his wife and infant daughter in childbirth. He'd never remarried, and the fact that he still wore the chain hinted at why. He caught Alix looking, but offered no comment. Instead, he said, "I pray it's good news, my lady." Pray it he might, but Alix could tell from his eyes that he didn't believe it.

His doubt proved well founded: Arran Green entered the study alone. It was all Alix could do not to sag against the desk in disappointment.

"Greetings, Your Majesty," the commander general said, bowing.

Erik sighed. "You didn't find him."

"We did not." Arran Green's pale gaze shifted to Alix. "I am sorry, Captain."

"Did you find anything?" the king asked.

"Yes. I am convinced beyond any doubt that a host of Blackswords passed through the marshlands, and the fact that they remain together and in the field suggests that Lord Black is among them."

"That's wonderful news," Raibert said, mustering a smile for Alix's benefit. Bless the man, Farika was truly his sign.

"If you found evidence of their passing, why could you not track them?"

"We had not time, Your Majesty. As it was, we had to ride well out of our way to avoid the enemy. The host that attacked Blackhold is moving east, burning and pillaging along the way."

Alix fought down a wave of nausea. Those were Rig's people. Her people. *Gods-cursed Oridian swine.*

Erik swore quietly. "Meaning they're headed straight for the Brownlands. Did you send word, as I asked?"

"We did, sire," Raibert said, "but no matter how well prepared they are, the garrison at Brownhold will not be enough."

His cousin shook his head. "Not unless Lord Brown withheld more swords than the other Banner Houses, but that is unlikely. At best, they can survive a siege."

"And what of the main host, the army we faced at Boswyck?"

"Our scouts report they're still holding along the border," Raibert said, "and they have been reinforced."

"What are they waiting for?"

Alix wondered the same. With fifty thousand soldiers, they could smash Greenhold and Brownhold both, or at least besiege them into irrelevance.

"It is hard to say, Your Majesty," Raibert said. "My guess is they will wait until Brownhold falls, then regroup with the rest and make for the Greylands. The Greys have not yet mustered, so they'll be stronger than the rest of us."

"But not strong enough," said Arran Green. "The Greyswords number around ten thousand, but that is nothing compared to the host we faced at Boswyck. They will be little more than a nuisance, and once they are defeated, the enemy will be free to attack Erroman itself."

"Tom will never let the Greylands fall," Erik said with surprising conviction.

"Gods willing, Your Majesty," Arran Green said.

The king took up his customary pacing, this time without his crutch. "We cannot simply give the Brownlands over without a fight. That would allow the enemy free passage."

"I agree, Your Majesty," the commander general said.

"The force that took Blackhold—how many are they?"

"From what we saw, we judged them at five thousand. They appear to have picked up the remnants of the host we defeated here a fortnight ago."

"Very well. Then we will take five of ours, and keep them busy before they reach the Brownlands. The remaining two are more than enough to defend Greenhold in the event of a siege."

"As you command, Your Majesty. I can have the men re-equipped and ready by morning."

Erik paused in his pacing, his gaze dropping to his injured leg. Alix could read his thoughts as surely as if he'd spoken them. "Not yet, sire," she dared quietly.

His eyes iced over, and his mouth pressed into a thin line, but he did not argue.

"I will stay here with you, sire," Raibert said. "When you're well enough, we'll join my cousin and your men in the Blacklands."

"I believe I'll rest now." Erik's voice was tinged with bitterness. "I must build up my strength, after all."

The Greens bowed their heads as Erik turned and headed out of the study, Alix trailing behind.

"Your Majesty," she said as they neared his chambers, "if you would sleep, perhaps I might beg leave to say farewell to my comrades?" The idea of Liam going off to fight without her sat like a cold weight in her stomach, but somehow she'd known it would come to this. She wasn't a Kingsword anymore. She and Liam would never again be joined at the elbow. That hurt more than she cared to admit.

"Of course you must see your friends off," Erik said. "I admire your sense of solidarity, Alix."

She walked away from him wondering why those words should make her feel so guilty.

Alix found her friends sitting down to a meal of roast fowl and fresh bread—a luxury they'd earned for their service in searching for Lord Black. She felt a bizarre wave of shyness as she approached, and she couldn't quite decide where to rest her gaze. Inevitably, she fixed it on Liam, and was equal parts pleased and dismayed by the obvious hunger that crept into his eyes when he saw her. Fortunately, everyone else had turned to greet her; Liam's hungry look, and his crooked smile, were hers alone.

"Oh, Alix," Kerta said, "I'm so sorry we didn't find your brother. It was not for lack of trying."

Gwylim scooted over to make room for Alix on the log he was sitting on. "I don't know if Green told you, but I found clear signs of a small army crossing the marsh near Edin. Horses, riding in formation. Your brother rides at the head of that column, or I'm a fishmonger."

"You'd make a terrible fishmonger," Liam said.

"I do hate fish," Gwylim agreed.

Kerta ignored the banter. "We begged the general to keep looking. Liam especially."

"Pushed and pushed," Ide said. "Thought he was going to earn himself the whip for sure."

"Green doesn't believe in flogging," Liam said, his grey eyes still pinned on Alix.

Ide shrugged and bit into an apple. "Figure of speech." She'd cut her hair again, Alix noticed; it looped about her ears in ragged, boyish curls. Doubtless she'd done it herself, with or without a mirror. Ide didn't like "leaving 'em something to grab on to." She openly mocked Kerta for letting her hair flow about her face ("like blinders on a horse") and was only slightly less scathing of Alix's customary braid ("Give 'em a rope, why don't you?"). When Kerta had pointed out that Ide looked like a man, Ide had only shrugged and said, "Fight like one too." Judging by the scars crisscrossing her arms, that was Destan's own truth.

"Thank you all for trying," Alix said. "I know Rig is out there, and that's what counts. I'm just glad no one was hurt. Green says the enemy is deep in the Blacklands."

"Bold as you please," Ide said, "considering how few they are. The Raven will wallop 'em soon enough."

Liam's expression darkened. "Then what's he waiting for? The Oridians have put five villages to the torch. They've looted every pig and goat and bushel of grain, and left the farms in ashes. There'll be famine in the Blacklands if this keeps up."

"He must have a plan," Kerta said. "I'm *sure* he has a plan."

Gwylim nodded in agreement. "Traitor he may be, but Tomald White is no fool."

No one could deny that the Raven had a keen military mind, but Alix failed to see the strategy in letting the enemy weaken the Banner Houses. Unless . . . The familiar doubt surged back into her mind. "What if he's in league with the enemy?"

For a moment, no one spoke. They just looked at each other uncomfortably, wondering who would be the first to speak. *They've talked about this before*, Alix realised.

"I can't believe that," Kerta said.

"Why not?" Liam's exasperated tone left little doubt that they were going over familiar ground. "He left his own brother to die. On top of that, the Oridians are hanging around at the border, when they could have invaded in earnest weeks ago. How do you explain that, unless the Raven made a deal with them?"

"Maybe they don't really want to conquer us," Ide said.

"Just a bit of flirting?" Liam asked dryly.

Ide shrugged. "They're fighting us, sure, but we're the ones declared war on them."

"Because they annexed Andithyri!" Kerta said in her earnest, wide-eyed way. "King Erik was treaty-bound. We had no choice but to defend our ally."

"Not everyone feels that way," Gwylim said. "The Raven and Arran Green argued about it more than once in my hearing."

"The Treaty of Imran clearly states—"

"I know what it states," Gwylim said mildly. Kerta had the good grace to look embarrassed, caught giving a history lesson to an almost-priest. "I also know that scholars everywhere are still puzzled about what old King Osrik was thinking. It doesn't make sense to risk Alden's security for Andithyri, especially when the Trionate was already showing signs of expansionism. Andithyri could never protect us if the situation were reversed, so what did we get out of the deal? King Osrik should never have signed it."

"But he did sign it," Liam said. "Kerta's right—the king had no choice."

"Harram and Onnan are our allies," Gwylim said. "They don't seem to feel quite so obliged."

Kerta *tsk*ed. "Harram has always been aloof. They might be allies, but there is no treaty compelling them to come to our aid. We can't count on them. Besides, they haven't fought a real war for centuries. They wouldn't be much help."

"Onnan neither," Ide said.

Liam gave her an incredulous look. "They brought down the whole Erromanian Empire!"

Ide shrugged, unimpressed. "Fishmen might know how to be rebels, but that doesn't mean they know how to be soldiers."

Alix was only half listening, still stuck on the original question. The Raven *might* be in league with the enemy, but it wasn't a given. There could be a simpler explanation for his inaction. "The Raven would have to spend some time in the capital to secure his accession," she said, thinking aloud. "Maybe that's all it is. Maybe he's waiting to be crowned before riding out again."

"Better get on with it, then," Ide said. "Word of the king's survival will get out soon, especially now that the Kingswords are back to the road."

The image of a haemorrhaging timeglass flashed into Alix's mind. They might have a little sand left, or none at all. Her thoughts returned, as they had so often, to the spy they'd caught weeks ago. It seemed safe to assume he worked for the Raven. Had he managed to leak word of Erik's fate before they caught him? And if so, what would the traitorous prince do with that information? *Questions and more questions, but no answers.* She cursed and rubbed her eyes. "I just wish there were some way of knowing what he plans."

"Maybe you should hire a spy." Oddly, the suggestion came from Gwylim. Alix would not have thought an almost-priest would approve of such tactics.

As though reading her thoughts, the small man smirked. "The clergy make more use of spies than anyone. They keep close tabs on anyone with influence, including each other."

She regarded him sceptically. "Where would I find a spy?"

"If we were in Erroman, I could help. Out here . . ." He shook his head.

"Thanks for the suggestion, but I won't send some stable boy to spy on the Raven. That's as good as a death sentence." She rose, sighing. "I'd better go. The king will look for me when he wakes. I just wanted to bid you all farewell and . . . let Destan be your sign." Her throat tightened around the words. She should have invoked Rahl. Honour was well and good, but the Virtue that mattered most in warfare was strength.

Alix embraced each of them. When she came to Liam, he said, "Walk you back to the castle?"

"All right." She turned away, doing her best to ignore the knowing looks around the fire.

"I missed you," Liam said as they walked. "It's lonely out there on the road without you. I had Green, of course, but he's not nearly as cuddly as you, and he snores."

Alix laughed. "That's a mental picture I could have done without."

When they were out of sight of the camp, Liam put his hand on her back and started to steer her into the trees.

"The castle is that way," she said lamely, her blood already rushing in her ears.

"I'm aware. This way, please, watch your step . . . That's right. Here. That should do." He gathered her in and kissed her. Alix was vaguely appalled at how thoroughly she buckled in his arms—but she didn't let it dampen her enthusiasm. "You didn't think I was going to let you go with a simple fare-thee-well, did you?" he murmured in her ear. His breath on her neck made her shiver with gooseflesh.

"You're the one who's leaving."

"I don't want to, Allie. You know I don't."

"I know." She buried her face in his shoulder, seized with a wave of dread. The gods only knew what might befall Liam out there. The idea that she might never see him again was enough to make her feel physically ill. Even so, she didn't dare speak her fears aloud. Liam had enough to worry about.

He understood anyway. "One good thing about being a scout, it's easier to stay out of trouble. Unless Green is cross with me again, obviously, in which case he might just put me in the vanguard. Come to think of it, you'd better kiss me like you mean it, just in case."

She scowled up at him. "How can you joke about something like that?"

"I don't understand the question. Have we been properly introduced?" He pointed at his chest. "Liam."

She pushed him away. "You're impossible."

"Allie." He grabbed her hand.

She waited, but he didn't say anything; he just stared down at her, his thumb drifting over her knuckles. "When all this is over . . ." she started to say, but found she had no idea how to finish the sentence. *When all this is over, what then? Even if you both survive the war, you'll still be the king's bodyguard, and he'll still be a soldier. And a bastard.*

He read it all in her eyes. He didn't try to reassure her; there was no point. He just drew her in and kissed her.

They met Arran Green on the path back to the castle. "There you are, Captain," he said, his dark brows drawn into their customary frown. "The king is looking for you."

"Yes, General." She started to hurry her step, but Green held up a hand.

"Wait a moment. Liam, the captain can make it the rest of the way on her own. I would have a word with her in private."

Liam ducked his head. "As you say, General." With a last look at Alix, he turned and headed back down the path toward camp.

When he was out of earshot, Green said, "It is time you and I had a discussion. About Liam."

She felt the blood drain from her face.

"The two of you have become . . . close." It was not a question. "It has to stop. You know as well as I do that it cannot possibly go anywhere, and he is more vulnerable than you might imagine."

Alix couldn't believe she was having this conversation, and with Arran Green of all people. "I don't understand," she said, unable to prevent a shade of anger from tinting her voice.

"Of course you do. You are far more experienced than he is. You should know better."

Her whole body went rigid. "I beg your pardon, my lord?"

Her discipline fled as the noblewoman reared up inside her. "Exactly what are you implying?"

He sighed impatiently. "You mistake my meaning, *my lady*. I refer to your experience of the world, and the way in which it works. A woman of your station knows only too well what is possible, and what is not."

"And what business is it of yours?"

Arran Green leaned in close enough for her to see the flecks of jade in his pale eyes. "Do not test me, Alix. You may be a Black, but you are still a whelp, and you understand very little of what you meddle in. Whether you choose to believe it or not, what I say is as much for your benefit as his." With that, he shouldered past her and headed down the path, leaving her shaking with fury.

Alix stood there long enough for the shimmer of tears to drain from her eyes. Then she drew a deep, wavering breath and headed back to the castle.

EIGHT

†That night, Alix turned in early, as the king had done, but sleep eluded her. She stirred restlessly in bed, her conversation with Arran Green playing and replaying in her head. Swells of emotion rose and fell like waves crashing against the shore: rising anger, cresting outrage, waning guilt, quiet resignation. As much as she resented Green—his harshness, his condescension, and most of all, his bloody *presumption*—there was more than enough truth in his words.

I knew this was going to happen. Too late, but I knew.

No one would begrudge her a casual dalliance. It was common enough in the king's army—hells, it was practically obligatory. The two years of King's Service was a time for youthful adventure, for the hunting of prey and the sowing of seeds. Even Rig would half expect her to end up in the arms of some handsome soldier or another. As long as she was careful to avoid unwanted complications, she needn't worry about names or politics or rank. But Liam wasn't just some handsome soldier. Apart from Rig, he was her best friend.

And he was a bastard. A nobleman's bastard, if she were to

guess. His accent might be common, but his features were anything but: the strong jaw, the high cheekbones, the long, graceful fingers. A no-name he might be, but his father had a name, Alix was almost sure of it.

She frowned in the dark. Might his father's name be Green?

It would explain everything—how a bastard came to be squired to a banner knight, and why Arran Green would see fit to meddle in Liam's personal affairs . . .

Alix sat up suddenly, all pretence of sleep vanishing. If Arran Green was Liam's father, it would even explain why he'd banished Liam to the scouts the moment war was declared. "He's protecting his son," she whispered to the shadows. *That's why he was so angry with us at Boswyck! He feared for Liam's safety . . .*

The more she thought about it, the more convinced she became. Liam the bastard was actually Liam Green. Or at least he would have been, had his mother been Arran Green's wife. *I wonder if Melicent Green knows.*

Alix sighed loudly. Even if she was right, it didn't matter. A bastard was a bastard, however noble the sire. If she herself had been a lesser noble—a Middlemarch, say—she might have entertained some hope that she and Liam could be something more than a dalliance. But being the blood of a Banner House had obligations. When her King's Service was through, Alix would be expected to marry, and marry well. *That* was what Arran Green meant; *that* was why he interfered. *He's afraid I'll break his son's heart.* Maybe Liam feared the same. Maybe that was why he'd hesitated for so long.

Alix growled and dug the heels of her hands into her eyes. It was no use; she was never going to sleep. She needed to speak to Liam, tonight, now, or she would go mad.

She pulled a cloak on over the top of her nightgown and slipped down the corridor, nodding curtly to the guards. She felt silly, stealing away in nothing but a nightgown and a pair of boots, but fortunately the cloak covered enough that her scanty attire would not be apparent to anyone. She hurried through the bailey and under the portcullis, ignoring the curious glances of the Greenswords manning the gate. They knew her now, and she had every right to come and go, but it was an odd hour to be paying a visit to the Kingsword camp.

She met no one on the road, and as she neared the camp, she veered off into the trees. The scouts' fire always stood a little apart from the others. Scouts were obliged to rise earlier than their comrades, so they preferred to avoid the noise of the camp. That suited Alix's purpose well; she hoped to draw Liam away without anyone noticing.

The soft glow of firelight seeped through the trees. Alix picked her way through the undergrowth as silently as she knew how. She was far enough from the light that it didn't interfere with her night vision, and she moved patiently, in spite of the anxiety churning inside her.

He was still awake, thank the Virtues. Unsurprisingly, Kerta and Gwylim were there too. Alix had no idea how she was going to separate Liam from the others without being seen. He was too far to whisper, and anyway the others would hear. She thought about throwing something, but she wasn't confident enough of her aim. So she waited, shivering in her nightgown, cursing herself for an impulsive fool.

Liam was joking around, as usual. His crooked grin gave way to laughter, Gwylim and Kerta joining in. Alix watched him talking, laughing, ruffling his hair so that it stood even more of a mess than usual. Somehow, the careless look only made him more appealing. Her thoughts drifted back to the afternoon, to the warmth of his arms and the rich tones of his voice in her ear. Something like hunger stirred her insides.

She was nearly numb with cold when her opportunity finally came. Kerta rose to go to bed, and Gwylim followed soon after. Liam sat by himself on the log, looking thoughtful. It was now or never.

"Liam!"

He looked up with a frown. She called again, a harsh whisper that cut through the trees, and he stood hesitantly, making his way toward the sound. When he was close enough, she whispered, "In here!"

"Alix? What in the Domains are you doing?"

"Shh! Come away. Follow me."

She withdrew deeper into the wood, Liam blundering through the trees behind her. Under other circumstances, it would have been comical. She waited for him to catch up, with no clear idea what she was going to say. She'd made no decisions. She was totally unprepared, making it up as she went along. Her heart beat faster.

"Alix, what—"

She stopped his mouth with a kiss. Green's words burned in her mind, inspiring only defiance. She took Liam's face in her hands and kissed him with a determination she hadn't known she felt. He tensed, caught flat-footed by this sneak attack. Alix knew she should explain, but she couldn't stop herself. She slid her fingers inside his tunic.

He jumped, giving a little cry of surprise. "Allie, your hands are *freezing*! What are you wearing?"

In answer, she shrugged off her cloak.

Liam froze, staring at her in nothing but her thin, clinging nightgown. She let him look her over. The heat of his gaze banished her chill; she could have stood there all night but for the storm of impatience building inside her. She stepped into him, slipping her hands back under his shirt. He started slightly, and for a moment she thought he would pull away. But instead he bent his head into her kiss and pulled her against him, his hand pressed into the curve of her back so that she could feel every firm line of him. The cold receded into memory. Instead she was consumed with a flush so intense that it made her dizzy.

She pulled him down into the leaves. He hesitated, holding himself off her. "Allie . . ."

"Shut up, Liam. Please."

She saw indecision in his eyes, but then fire burned through, consuming everything else, and his mouth was on her neck, his hands roaming over her curves. The weight of him on top of her felt like craving.

Alix couldn't think straight. There was a roaring in her ears that drowned out even the sound of her own ragged breathing. Her hands were moving of their own accord, her mind overthrown by a longing so powerful she thought she might burst. She reached inside his clothing, down past his stomach, and grabbed him.

His whole body jerked. He pulled his head back, staring down at her. His eyes were molten glass. Alix shimmied beneath him, moving her nightgown above her waist.

He hovered over her for a moment, chest heaving, desire and doubt warring openly on his face. Alix pulled at the laces of his breeches. And then he was inside her, and she arched into him, and everything else dissolved.

Alix's hair was matted with sweat, even as she shivered. Liam trembled too. "Are you cold?" she whispered.

The dark pools of his eyes were fixed on her. "I don't know."

"Are you angry?" She forced herself not to look away, to take the coward's way out.

"I don't know."

Alix couldn't read his expression, and it scared her. *He's more vulnerable than you might imagine.* Green's words came back to her in a rush of guilt. "I didn't plan this," she said. "This wasn't an ambush."

He snorted softly. "I know that. You're the most impulsive person I've ever met, Allie. Ardin is definitely your sign."

"So . . . you're not angry?" Gods, she was being pathetic, but she couldn't seem to help it.

"If I am, it's not with you." They were still tangled together, and Alix could feel his heartbeat, still fast. "I thought I was more disciplined than that. But you . . ." He played with a lock of her hair. "Well. As you see."

"I feel like I should apologise, but I'm not sorry. I hope you're not sorry."

In reply, he kissed her.

When she'd caught her breath, Alix said, "I have to tell you something. About Green."

Liam made a face. "Well that's a mood-kill, Allie."

"I'm serious. Green knows about us. Well . . . not this, obviously. But he knows there's something between us, and he doesn't approve."

"I'll make a note of it."

If only it were that simple. "Liam . . . is Green . . . is he your father?"

It was a mistake. Liam stiffened, and a shutter came down over his eyes.

"I'm sorry." Her hands flew instinctively to his face. "I'm

sorry, Liam, it doesn't matter. Please forget I said anything. It's just . . . Green worries me. He—"

"Stop." Liam's arms tightened around her. "Allie, I'm leaving in a few hours, and I'm going to be gone for a long time. I don't know when I'll see you again. I don't know *if* I'll see you again. I don't want to talk about Arran Green."

She nodded, biting her lip to prevent any further stupidity from tumbling out.

Liam reached behind his neck and drew forth a chain with a ring around it. Wordlessly, he slid the ring off the chain and dropped it into her palm. Alix peered at it through the darkness. It was an elegant wisp of gold wrought in the shape of ivy leaves. She had never seen anything so delicate; it was obviously the work of a master goldsmith. She looked up at Liam, speechless for a dozen reasons at once.

He gave her a wry look. "Don't panic, it's not like that. I just . . . I want you to think of me when I'm gone."

Still not trusting herself to speak, Alix tried it on. It fit around her baby finger—barely. She felt like an ox.

Liam grinned, reading her thoughts. "Mighty warrior woman." He twisted the ring on her finger. "It belonged to my mother. I'm not sure, but I think my father must have given it to her—my real father, I mean. My stepfather hated the thing. He made some nasty comment every time she wore it, and when she died, he wanted to sell it. Naturally, that meant I had to keep it, and wear it around my neck so that he could see it every single day."

Alix curled into him, lacing her fingers through his. She liked the way the ring felt, even if it was a little small. It seemed only fitting that it should hurt a little. "I will think of you," she vowed. It was the easiest promise she'd ever made.

She left him just before dawn, hurrying as fast as her weak knees would carry her. The world grew heavy as she walked. Her throat seemed to tighten a little more with every step. She fought with herself the whole way home, trying to gather some scrap of dignity about her as she shouldered past the guards at the gatehouse, and the guards at the door of the keep, and the guards at the entrance to the guest chambers.

There would be gossip, certainly. Alix didn't care, so long as it never reached the ears of Arran Green or the king.

When at last she reached her room, she leaned against the inside of her door and blinked furiously, forbidding tears, now or ever. Liam was gone. From this day forward, all that mattered was her duty.

NINE

"Again," Erik said, wiping sweat from his brow with his free arm. He rotated his wrist, sending his wooden sword twirling in a humming arc. He crouched, waiting, his breath blooming in the cold.

Alix feinted left, then lunged right. Erik deflected, but he grimaced in pain.

"Your Majesty—"

"Don't say it. I've got to push through. Again."

Sighing, Alix tightened her grip on her weapon. Wood it might be, but it was weighted with lead, and perfectly capable of breaking bone. More to the point, Erik's leg wasn't ready for the strain. He was going to hurt himself, but he would brook no argument. So Alix came at him again, and this time she didn't hold back. If the king insisted upon sparring, she was going to give him what he asked for.

The yard rang out with the dry cracking of staves coming together. Guards clustered on the ramparts and along the walls, watching. Though his leg was not fully healed, Erik was a capable swordsman, and Alix had had the best training gold could buy. They might not be as graceful as they would have been wielding bloodweapons, but they were putting on a good show, at least for those few privileged enough to keep the king's secret. The training yard was tucked behind the barracks, allowing the royal guardsmen to seal it off from prying eyes. Or it would do, if they were the least bit focused on their duties.

"You're guards, not spectators!" Alix called, pivoting to avoid a slash. It was all the distraction she could afford; Erik was coiling for another strike. She didn't wait for it to fall. She threw all her weight behind a single blow, bringing her sword down vertically at Erik's chest. The king crossed, shoved her back so hard she nearly lost her balance. He charged, trying to take advantage of her loss of footing, but she recovered quickly and twisted out of the way, swiping at him as he passed. His own momentum betrayed him, and Erik crashed to the ground, crying out as he landed on his bad leg.

Alix swore and fell to her knees beside him. "I'm sorry!"

"Gods' blood, woman!" He curled over his thigh, his teeth gritted in pain.

Her temper flared. "Well this wouldn't have happened if you weren't so *damned stubborn*!"

The king stared at her. Alix stared back, horrified.

Erik burst out laughing.

Alix dropped her gaze as the familiar blush spread over her cheeks. "I . . . don't know what to say."

"I think that will do nicely." He rolled into a sitting position. "I can't tell you how pleased I am that we've reached this stage in our relationship."

"I believe I detect some sarcasm."

"Sarcasm, dear lady? Whyever would you think that?" He accepted her help to stand. "What king wouldn't enjoy being knocked on his backside and scolded in front of his men?"

"It builds character."

"Excellent. At this rate, I will be the very paragon of character in no time."

Alix chewed her lip to get her smile under control. "In earnest, I am sorry."

Erik shrugged. "I thoroughly deserved it. I should be more patient. I'm just so blasted tired of this leg."

Alix couldn't blame him. It had been almost two months since the Battle of Boswyck, and still his leg gave him trouble.

He walked with only a slight limp, but anything more demanding left him stiff and sore for days. Not that he let that rule him. He insisted on sparring every day, both to push his recovery and to ensure his skills didn't fall into disuse. Alix appreciated their sessions as well, for like the king, she wanted her blade to remain keen. But she wished he wouldn't let his frustration get the better of him.

"One upside of all this is that I might just emerge a better swordsman," Erik said. "It's been so long since I had a blood-blade in my hand, I hardly remember what it feels like. By the time I get a new one, I'll be so accustomed to an ordinary weapon, I'll feel like Rahl himself when I take it up."

Alix failed to see the upside in her king being without his best protection. Only one known bloodbinder remained in the whole kingdom, and he was back at the capital. If there were others, they hadn't come forward, either because they didn't realise how truly rare their talents were, or because they wanted to avoid being pressed into military service. The gods only knew how long it would be until Erik could replace the bloodblade he'd lost at Boswyck, and until then, he would have to content himself with an ordinary sword. No matter how finely crafted, how well balanced, it would feel heavy and ungainly in comparison, and on the battlefield, that could make the difference between life and death.

You're worrying too much, she scolded herself. *Owning a bloodblade is a privilege, not a necessity. The vast majority of the Kingswords get on just fine without them, including Liam.*

The thought brought fresh worries of its own. "Any word from the front?"

Erik accepted a towel from one of his knights. "Not for a few days. The enemy is probably still licking his wounds after last week's skirmish."

Not a day went by that Alix didn't find herself thinking of Liam and the others, out there clashing with the enemy week after week. She imagined them sore and ragged, hungry and drained, their nights long and cold and full of dread. And then there was Rig . . . She hadn't had word of the missing Blackswords for over a month. The waiting, the not knowing, the hiding behind these walls, keeping secrets, while the war unfolded beyond the hills—it was killing her. Her guts felt like they were eating themselves from the inside out.

Her thoughts must have played clearly across her face, because Erik said, "I hate it too. That's why we need to keep at this. The sooner I'm well, the sooner we can be out there where we belong."

She nodded. "As long as we're pinning the enemy down, that's the main thing."

"For now. But if that host at the border moves . . ." He didn't finish the thought. He didn't have to.

"I hear Lord Brown is mustering again."

Erik winced. "Farmers and millers and merchants."

"They've had their two years of training, at least. That's the whole idea behind the King's Service, isn't it?"

"According to my great-grandfather's thinking, but those were different days. We don't—"

A pigeon leapt suddenly off the ramparts, wings whirring. Alix glanced up and saw a flash of metal in the sunlight. Her body was moving before her mind had even processed what she'd seen. She dove, tackling Erik to the ground just as a quarrel hissed though the air where he'd been standing.

"West wall!" she cried, covering the king with her body.

Guards burst into action. A silhouetted figure uncoiled from his crouch in the lee of the tower, dropping his crossbow as he made for the stairs. Alix craned her head to track his movements. Her men surged up the stairs and along the wall walk from both sides, cutting off the would-be assassin's escape. Alix watched as he contemplated a suicidal jump, ultimately hesitating too long and allowing himself to be overtaken. Swords flashed.

"Wait," she cried, "don't—" But it was too late. Half a dozen swords plunged into the assassin's body. He crumpled.

Alix cursed under her breath. There would be no questioning him now. "All clear?" she called.

"All clear, Captain!"

Only then did Alix recall that she was lying on top of the king.

"This seems oddly familiar," came a muffled voice from beneath her.

Alix looked down at him, incredulous. He was as bad as Liam. "It's not funny," she growled, rolling off him.

He sighed. "No, it's not." For the second time in the space of a few moments, he accepted Alix's help to stand. He dusted himself off and glanced up at the west wall, where the guards were already dragging the body away. "I will let you tend to this, Captain, and we can talk later." So saying, he headed for the keep, donning the detested helm as he walked. Alix snapped her fingers and pointed at him, and a pair of guards hurried after.

She drew a long, steadying breath, willing her pulse to slow. She had always known that it was only a matter of time until the secret of the king's survival was discovered. They'd all known it, but they hadn't been sure how the Raven would react, how far he would really go. It seemed they had their answer.

Commander Ormond Wildwood stuck his boot under the corpse and rolled it over. Bloodstained straw clung to the front of the dead man's tabard, obscuring his wounds, but there was no mistaking the livery: he wore the emerald-dyed linen of the Greenswords. The old knight frowned thoughtfully. "Don't recognise him," he said, though that didn't prove much; the garrison commander could hardly be expected to know every man in his charge. Ormond glanced at his second, a stout man-at-arms called Jarvis. "What about you? Seen him before?"

Jarvis shook his head and spat in the dust. "No Greensword, that one."

"One of yours, Captain?"

Alix suppressed an instinctive flash of outrage. The question wasn't entirely unfair. She'd had some of her guards put on Green livery, to make them less conspicuous on the walls. Kingswords milling around the bailey would not raise any eyebrows, but they had no business patrolling the ramparts. Disguising them avoided inconvenient questions from the rank and file.

She studied the dead man's face. It was narrow and ratlike, with prominent ears and a thicket of broken veins around the nose—distinctive enough for her to be sure she hadn't seen it before. "Not one of mine, either."

Ormond unsheathed his dagger and slashed the dead man's

tabard up the side, exposing boiled leather beneath. "No mail."

"Chain mail makes noise," Alix said. "He probably sneaked in overnight and stole the tabard from the barracks."

"A professional, most like," Jarvis said.

"Search him thoroughly, Commander," Alix said. "And when you've done that, I want to know how in the Nine Domains he got past your guards."

Ormond eyed her sourly. "You won't be staying?"

She could guess his thoughts. He was a knight and garrison commander, thirty years her senior and unaccustomed to taking orders from anyone but Lord Green. Well, that was just too bad. Alix didn't care one whit for his infringed ego. Half of her royal guardsmen were knights, and they had fallen in line when she'd made it clear she wouldn't tolerate anything less. Commander Ormond could bloody well do the same. "My place is with the king," she said coolly, and she left him.

Her hands balled into fists as she walked, and her strides grew longer with each step. She managed to hold on until she was inside the keep, but as soon as she reached the seclusion of the study, her temper broke free.

"Damnation!" She punctuated the oath by kicking Lord Green's chair over. Finding that surprisingly satisfying, she looked for something to throw, but a tiny, timid voice in her head reminded her that she was a guest here. So instead she paced the room like a caged animal, tugging at her braid and swearing under her breath.

Questions roiled in her mind, and though she had no answers, all the possibilities pointed to negligence on her part. Who had discovered the king's secret and betrayed it to the Raven? It could have been anyone—the spy they'd caught, a castle servant, one of the Kingswords. Even her own guards could have let the information slip in a moment of indiscretion. And then there was the question of how the assassin had managed to get past the royal guardsmen—in broad daylight, for gods' sake!—and get a shot off before he was discovered. Only his own clumsiness had exposed him. If he hadn't startled that pigeon . . . Alix shuddered. Then her guardsmen had killed him outright, leaving no possibility of interrogating him. She'd let it happen. Her incompetence was all too obvious.

She growled out loud, grinding the heels of her hands into her eyes. Where there was one assassin, there would be others. That was a certainty, a law of the world as firm and immutable as death itself. From this day forward, everything would be different.

"You're too hard on yourself."

Alix turned to find Raibert Green leaning on the door frame.

"You saved the king's life. You did your duty."

"Barely. It was luck as much as anything."

He shrugged, his thin face wise and weary. "We all rely on luck, every day of our lives."

Alix took little comfort in that. "How is he?"

"He waits for you. He'll put on a brave face, but he's shaken. Be gentle with him."

She frowned. "What do you mean?"

"Tether your temper, Captain. It will do the king no good to see you like this. Take a cue from him and project confidence, even if you don't feel it. Keep your doubts about your performance to yourself."

Alix paused. He had a point. What the king needed from his bodyguard was reassurance, not a reminder of how close he'd come to being murdered. She blew out a long breath. "Thank you, Lord Green. Your counsel is steady, as always. The king is fortunate to have you."

"He is fortunate to have you too," Raibert said meaningfully before leaving her.

She found Erik in the solar, sipping wine. He looked small and vulnerable in that grand room, its high ceilings stretching into shadow, its long table crowding him against the hearth. Firelight illuminated the reddish gold of his hair, cast the velvet of his doublet in a soft ruby glow. He was perfectly situated amid the sumptuous accents of the room, as fragile and beautiful as any of them, but so much more valuable. Alix felt the weight of her duty more heavily in that moment than ever before.

Erik poured a second cup of wine and pushed it wordlessly across the table. Alix pulled out a chair and sat. She took the cup, sipped from it.

"I might wish for something stronger," Erik remarked.

"I'll drink to that," Alix said, and she did.

The king leaned back in his chair and looked up at the ceiling. He seemed to be avoiding her gaze, as though he were having trouble keeping himself in check. "Who was he?"

"We don't know. I doubt we ever will."

"But we know who sent him."

Alix hesitated. "Perhaps."

"Say it," he commanded softly, still staring at the ceiling. "I want to hear you say it."

She sighed. "Most likely he was sent by Tomald."

"My brother." Erik's features were set in stone. "Commander of the White Wolves, and prince of the realm. My own blood." The bitterness grew with each word.

Raibert Green had been wrong. Erik was not putting on a brave face. Not this time. He was freely showing Alix the depth of his pain, and it was beyond fathoming. Tomald had been his only remaining family. Alix couldn't imagine how it felt to have someone so close turn on him so completely. Even his childhood memories must feel corrupted.

"Did you know I had a twin once?"

Alix started. "No, I didn't. What happened to him?"

"Her," Erik corrected. "Stillborn. I'm not surprised you didn't know—Father forbade anyone to speak of it. It wouldn't do for people to get the idea that the royal seed was somehow defective." He took a long sip of his wine, upending his cup before refilling it. "Tom and I were never close, and by the time I was ten or so, I realised we never would be. That was a lonely discovery. Even at that age, I wondered how many of my friends loved me for Erik, and how many just wanted the favour of the crown prince. It made it very hard for me to let my guard down around anyone. I started to wonder what things would have been like had my sister lived. I was sure we would have been the best of friends." A brief, haunted smile flickered across his face. "I mourned her for years, for all that I never knew her. And now, suddenly, I find myself mourning her again."

"I'm sorry." She couldn't think of anything else to say.

"It's all right. I may have been deceived in my brother, but there are others I know I can rely on. That is some comfort, at least." He looked over at her at last. "Thank you, Alix."

"It was my duty."

"No, not for that alone." He reached across the table and took her hand. "Thank you for being such a steadying presence through all this. You are a true friend."

"You're easy to be a friend to."

He sighed ruefully. "Perhaps that was true once, but now . . . These are complicated times, aren't they? What a shame we weren't friends before all this. Before I was such a gloomy creature, and you a Kingsword. It's terribly delinquent of your brother never to have brought you to court. I would have liked to meet you there. At a ball, perhaps." He paused, a crooked smile hitching his mouth. "Actually, that is something I would pay to see."

"What?"

"You, in a ball gown. I'm having a little trouble picturing it, Captain." His gaze roamed significantly over her armour.

"Well, you can stop trying to picture it right now, Your Majesty," she said, smiling archly. At that moment, in that grand room, a goblet of wine in her hand and the handsome young king before her, Alix could almost imagine herself back in her old life.

His smile turned wicked. "I'm not sure I can, actually."

She laughed, feeling some of the tension ease from her shoulders. She'd meant what she said about Erik being easy to get on with. His good nature was infectious, and he never allowed himself to brood for long. Yet there was something tragic in that. Only a few moments ago, he'd been hurting terribly, rolling the taste of his brother's betrayal on his tongue. Suddenly he was joking, flirting, radiating a warmth as golden as his hair. The royal mask was back, slipping over him so smoothly it was as if it had been there all along. *It must have taken him a lifetime to learn this skill*, Alix thought sadly. She wanted to tell him that it was unnecessary, that he could lean on her if he wanted to, that she wasn't afraid of his pain. But she couldn't. It wasn't her place. Not yet.

For now, all she could do was bask in Erik's sunshine, and hope that he found at least a measure of the solace that she did.

TEN

Alix rubbed the sleep out of her eyes, willing her head to stop throbbing. It felt like someone was mining for ore in her skull—someone tiny and vindictive and armed with a very sharp pickaxe. She would have traded her bloodblade for a single glass of cold water. She'd stayed up late drinking with Erik, which was unwise on many levels. The level that concerned her most at the moment was that of the floor, which seemed suspiciously uneven. The king, for his part, looked bright and shiny as always. Alix found that considerably less charming this morning than she had last night.

Focus, foolish girl. This is a very serious matter.

She realised that Erik and Raibert were staring at her expectantly. She sat up straighter. "Sorry. Pardon?"

Erik's mouth twitched. "Are you quite well, Captain? You seem a little out of sorts."

"I am quite well, Your Majesty, thank you for asking." She locked eyes with him, daring him to keep it up. She didn't care if he *was* king, he could bloody well wipe that glint out of his eye.

If Raibert noticed this silent exchange, he was too well

bred to let on. "I asked if you agree that we should increase the size of the king's detail."

"I do."

He nodded. "I thought so, but it will come at a cost in terms of secrecy. It is hard to be discreet with an armed escort."

"I don't see that as a problem," Alix said. "Not anymore."

Lord Green frowned. "Oh?"

"There's no point in continuing the deception, assuming we were deceiving anyone in the first place. Tomald obviously knows, and he's the one we were trying to keep it from. Now we're only keeping it from the people, and they're our greatest ally. Cloaking ourselves in shadow lets Tomald act against us with impunity. But if the people know their king lives, further treachery won't go unnoticed."

Raibert leaned back in his chair thoughtfully. "I see your logic. But if we go public with news of His Majesty's survival, it will force Tomald into a corner, and that will make him even more unpredictable. He might do worse than send assassins."

"Maybe," Alix said, "but I doubt even Tomald would risk a full-fledged attack on the rightful King of Alden. No one would dare to back such an audacious play. It would be the quickest way to scare off potential allies." Raibert eyed her appraisingly, and Alix couldn't help smiling. "We Blacks may be uncouth, my lord, but we're not completely ignorant of politics, gossip notwithstanding."

Raibert laughed. "Such gossip never came from a Green, I assure you." Alix doubted that. The Greens were the oldest and most venerable of the Banner Houses, and the Blacks were second only to the Golds for scorn. Alix would have given her right arm to restore her family's name to anything like the Greens' standing. But she appreciated the thought all the same.

Erik dismissed the idle chatter with a wave. "This is all well and fine, but it hardly qualifies as a plan. So we announce my survival. What then?"

"I don't think we should announce anything, sire," Alix said. "We should simply drop the secrecy. Let the news spread of its own accord."

"And then?"

"And then nothing. The next move is his."

"Why would we willingly give him the initiative?"

Alix suppressed a sigh. He was like a hound with a scent in his nose: fearless, brazen—and likely to send his prey bolting to safety. Fortunately, Raibert Green was older and subtler than his king. "I think I see. By not making a formal announcement, we do not officially challenge Tomald's version of events. That gives us room for compromise, if necessary."

"Exactly," Alix said. "We have to leave him room to save face, a way to back down peacefully, or we reduce our options later on. And by letting the news spread without bringing Tomald into it, we also draw attention away from him and put it back on the king, where it belongs. The moment word gets out that the king is at Greenhold, all eyes will shift here. Erroman will cease to be the centre of power, for now at least. Then we don't need to challenge Tomald; *he* must challenge *us*. And he'll have to do it openly, before the eyes of all the realm. He won't be ready to do that right away. He'll need to build up his alliances first. That's one of the reasons we wanted him to think the king was dead—so he wouldn't bother trying to bolster his position. Hopefully, we've bought ourselves some time."

"It's risky," Raibert said. "We are counting on Tomald to act rationally. There was a time when I would have expected that of him, but now, I'm not so sure."

Alix shared that worry. After what happened at Boswyck, she wouldn't have been at all surprised to learn that the Raven was barking mad. But what choice did they have? "It's the best option left to us."

"Very well," Erik said, "if this is the best we can do. Fly the royal colours over the gates, and let us see what happens."

Raibert inclined his head. "As you say, sire."

"Thank you, Lord Green. That will be all for now."

Raibert rose and took his leave. Alix stood too, intending to take her place outside the door of the king's sitting room, but Erik held up a hand. "Stay, Alix, please. There's something I would discuss with you." She sat, feeling uneasy. She had no idea what he was going to say, but somehow she dreaded it anyway. Maybe he saw it on her face, because he smiled. "You are gifted with surpassing good sense. I'm not sure you realise how valuable that is."

She dropped her gaze demurely. "Thank you."

"Truly, Alix. You have a keen mind, and you aren't afraid to speak it. Sometimes I wonder if you aren't wasted as my bodyguard."

"I don't believe that. Besides, if you find value in my advice, what better place for me than by your side?"

"But you must promise me that you won't hesitate to give it, even when things return to normal and we're surrounded by people who don't believe it's your place."

Alix laughed. "I can promise that easily. Holding my tongue is where I have trouble."

"Good. Then perhaps I might call upon your wisdom now. What I wish to discuss is a matter of some delicacy."

"At your pleasure."

His smile turned wry, as if to say, *You're going to regret saying that.* "You are aware, no doubt, of my prolonged betrothal to Sirin Grey."

Alix couldn't imagine what Sirin Grey had to do with anything, but presumably she was about to find out. She waited for him to continue.

"I have made something of an art of procrastination where my marriage is concerned, to the delight of gossips everywhere. Some interesting theories have developed to explain my delay. I imagine you've heard a few of them yourself." He gazed at her steadily as he spoke, as though daring her to look away. Alix forced herself not to react. She would rather leap from the ramparts than have this conversation, but she would do her best not to show it.

"I don't love her," Erik said flatly. "I never have. And I have no intention of marrying her, not if I can avoid it."

Unease gave way to mild panic. *Farika's mercy, why is he telling me this?* The king continued to stare at her, giving her no option but to stare back. He seemed almost to relish the impropriety of discussing these private details with her. He could not be oblivious to her discomfort, but for some reason, he was forcing the issue. Alix felt like a trapped animal.

He seemed to be waiting for a reaction. When none was forthcoming, he said, "You wonder why I'm burdening you with this."

"It's not a burden, Your Majesty, it's just—"

He flinched. "Don't do that. Don't put that distance between us, Alix, not now."

"I'm sorry," she said, and she was. Only last night she'd been wishing Erik felt more comfortable letting his guard down with her. Now he was doing just that, and she was squirming like a spoiled courtier. Impulsively, she took his hand. "Truly, I am. Please continue."

His fingers tightened around hers. "I'm telling you this because . . ." He hesitated.

Alix waited, frozen in the ice blue of his eyes. She saw uncertainty there. He seemed to be searching for words.

Abruptly, he released her hand and sat back. "I think that might be why my brother betrayed me."

Alix blinked. Whatever she had expected him to say, it wasn't that. "I don't understand. You think Tomald betrayed you because you wouldn't marry Sirin Grey?"

"Because he was afraid that I *would*." Erik's mouth twisted into a sour smile. "My brother and my betrothed are lovers, you see."

Alix clamped a hand over her mouth. For a long moment, all she could do was stare, wide-eyed.

That amused him. "I see you are sensitive to the awkward position that puts me in."

"Lovers? As in . . ."

"As in deeply in love. For years now. Since before our betrothal, in fact. My father was ever a *thoughtful* soul."

Alix had never heard him sound so caustic. Not that she blamed him. The very thought of it . . . The pain, the tension it must have created between the brothers . . . It was too awful to contemplate. "Did King Osrik know?"

"Oh, no. He was perfectly oblivious. He needed a match for his heir, and Sirin Grey was constantly in his view, since she spent rather a lot of time at the palace. Instead of reflecting on why that might be, he merely congratulated himself on a convenient solution."

"Merciful Nine . . ."

"Not in this case, I fear."

"Did you explain it to your father?"

"Of course, as soon as he told me of his decision. But by

then it was too late. He'd already spoken to Lord Grey, who was only too happy to have his own issue share the crown. If Father had backed out, he would have made an enemy of the most powerful of the Banner Houses—a dilemma that lingers to this day, else I would have called it off long ago. Lady Grey is as ambitious and powerful as her late husband, and she is determined to see Sirin share the crown, no matter that her daughter doesn't want it. Roswald is just as bad. I have him in my study at least once a month demanding to know why I haven't set a date for my marriage to his sister. With each passing day, it grows more difficult to deny him."

For a brief moment, Alix almost felt a pang of pity for Tomald White. Almost. *I should have seen that he was getting desperate.* Erik's words that day on the gatehouse tower, as they watched the battle from afar. Now she understood. But still, to go to such extremes . . . "Do you really think that would be enough for your brother to betray you?"

Erik's expression was unreadable. "Have you ever been in love, Alix?"

Her thoughts flashed instinctively to Liam. He was the closest she'd come, but love? *If not love, then what? Why else would you be clawing at the walls of Greenhold, yearning to rush to war?*

She didn't have an answer, but Erik didn't wait for one anyway. "They say a man will do anything for love."

Alix scowled. "Murder his brother? Betray his country?"

"I doubt he sees it that way. Most likely he's concocted some sort of narrative that justifies his behaviour. Tom was always good at that. Whatever road he takes, he convinces himself it's the high road. He always believes he's the hero of the story."

"I don't give a fraction of a damn what he believes," Alix hissed, dropping any remaining pretence of propriety. "He left his king and thousands of his own men to be butchered! There's no excusing what he's done."

Erik smiled faintly. "I won't argue."

"What about Sirin Grey? Do you think she knows what happened at Boswyck?"

He sighed and looked away. "I've been wondering that myself. I can't believe she would have anything to do with it.

Through all of this mess, she more than any of us has put her duty first. She would marry me without hesitation. However much it broke her heart, she would do it. She's told me so a hundred times, and Tom too. It's hard to imagine she would suddenly commit treason. But then, I never would have believed Tom capable of it, either."

Alix wasn't so sure. The Raven's extreme mood swings were the stuff of legend. She wondered if he'd always been like that, or if it was his troubled heart that made him wild. "For what it's worth, I'm sorry. For all of it."

He nodded absently. His gaze had grown distant and haunted. *He should be alone*, she thought. *This grief is not for my eyes.* "With your leave, sire," she said, rising.

"One more thing. I don't wish to cause you pain by bringing this up, but I wanted you to know that I haven't given up on finding Rig. Nor will I leave your family home to be picked over by scavengers. I've dispatched a small guard to Blackhold, to protect whatever might be left. I'm sorry I didn't think of it sooner. As to your brother—we'll find him, Alix, I swear it."

Tears stung her eyes. "I am grateful, my king."

Erik nodded, and for a moment it looked like he might say more, but instead he sighed and sagged back into his chair.

Alix bowed and left him to his thoughts.

A pair of Greenswords eyed the western tower of the gatehouse with matching frowns. There, on the ramparts, a knight in White livery was untying the emerald green banner of their lord from the long iron spike overlooking the bridge.

"What in the bloody Nine does he think he's doing?" one of the guards growled. His companion only shook his head.

Alix kept quiet, watching from her perch on the steps of the motte. The knight was slowly folding Lord Green's banner into smaller and smaller squares. Alix wondered if his deliberate pace was a mark of respect, or if he was simply relishing the drama of what he was about to do. A bit of both, perhaps. She continued with the pretence of honing her blade, but in truth, every sense stretched outward—over the bailey, along the ramparts, through the stables and the barracks and the armoury—as she braced for the reaction. Somewhere behind her, she knew, King Erik and Lord Green watched from the warmth of the keep.

The knight handed the folded colour of Greenhold over to his squire, exchanging it for a bundle of white. At first glance, it seemed only to be the banner of the Kingswords: a simple square of pure white. But as the flag unfurled from the spike, the golden sunburst flared as brash as dawn, and all around her, Alix heard sharply drawn breaths.

"Oy!" One of the guards stepped forward angrily—the same who had spoken before. He was a bull of a fellow, short and broad. An easterner, by the look of him, with more than a drop of Onnani blood. "If you're going to fly that, at least have the decency to add a mourning band!"

The knight looked down from the ramparts with a smug little grin. "The king is in residence."

"I never saw no one ride in," the second guard said in an undertone. "Must've come overnight."

"The Craven ain't been crowned yet. They got no right to fly that flag."

Alix smiled darkly. *The Craven.* Now there was a sweet bit of wordplay. Few would dare to openly name Tomald's retreat at Boswyck treachery, but fighting men would call it cowardice, at least among their own kind. Whatever happened, the Raven would have trouble regaining the loyalty of a large segment of the king's army.

The guard's voice must have carried on the wind, for the knight on the battlements only smiled wider and said, "I do not speak of Prince Tomald. I speak of His Majesty King Erik, who reclines in your lord's solar even now."

The guard flushed an ugly red. "You trying to be funny?"

He had a bold tongue on him, to address a knight so. *Must be his Onnani side*, Alix thought wryly. *Rebellion is in the blood.* But before the Kingsword could reply, a voice over Alix's shoulder said, "Alas, Commander Marvyn is not known for his sense of humour."

The guards turned, blanched, and fell to their knees.

"Your Majesty!" The easterner glanced up furtively, as if fearing that if he looked too squarely, the mirage might vanish. "You . . . you're . . ."

"Alive?" Erik came to stand beside Alix on the lowest step. "Most assuredly."

"The gods are good," the second guard said, his hand going to his heart.

"I will join you in that sentiment when the war is done, and the Oridians driven back to their own lands with their tails between their legs."

"Aye, sire," the guards said together.

"Please rise." They did so, Erik eyeing the bolder of the two appraisingly. "What is your name, soldier?"

"Smith, Your Majesty. Birk Smith."

Gods, he *was* bold. Not only had he taken a second name, he'd used it in front of the king. It was a brazen political statement. *I'm Onnani first and Aldenian second, and I believe every man has a right to a second name.* He must have been a blacksmith before joining the Greenswords. Fresh from the docks, this one.

Erik smiled benignly, as though the significance of *Smith* had passed him by entirely. "You strike me as a man of initiative, Birk. Is that so?"

The easterner drew himself up. "I like to think so, Your Majesty."

"Then I can entrust to you an important task?"

The man looked fit to burst with pride. "Aye, sire."

Alix felt a surge of admiration for her king. In the space of a few heartbeats, Erik had the rebellious self-named Smith eating right out of his hand. Charisma like that couldn't be learned. Erik had a gift.

"Go now," the king told Birk Smith, "and tell your comrades what you've seen here. Speak to as many of them as you can. I would correct this unfortunate gossip about my demise." The easterner bowed deeply, and he and his companion headed off for the barracks.

Erik lowered himself down beside Alix, watching the guards cross the bailey. She took in his sable-lined cloak and rich brocade doublet with a smirk. Throughout his stay at Greenhold, the king had kept himself well trimmed, but this was something of a different order. He positively *reeked* of royalty. "You enjoyed that," she said.

"Maybe a little." Rubbing his hands together, he said, "It's blasted cold out here. What are you doing?"

Alix glanced down at the sword dangling in her hand. She'd forgotten it entirely.

Erik followed her gaze. "Ah, yes. I've been meaning to ask you about that." He gestured at the egg-sized garnet embedded in the pommel. "Bloodforged, obviously. Is that the sword Rig had made for you?"

"For my sixteenth birthday," she said, surprised. "How did you know?"

"Who do you think gave Nevyn permission to travel all the way to Blackhold?"

Of course. She should have realised. Even in peacetime, the bloodbinders were jealously guarded by the crown, so rare and valuable were their talents. Rig would have needed permission to tempt one away from the royal forges, even temporarily. He could have taken his sister to Erroman, but that would have ruined the surprise. He'd been incredibly proud of himself for pulling it off.

Alix turned the shortsword over in her hand, admiring the way the sunlight licked the blade. "I was completely ungrateful at the time. I wanted a diamond necklace."

"Understandable. It's tradition, after all."

"I thought he was trying to send a message about my lack of devotion to my training. And I wasn't very excited about the idea of having my blood drawn, either." She flicked her wrist, slicing the air in a perfectly precise arc. "Now I can't imagine being without it."

Erik grimaced. "I don't have to imagine it. I'm living it. Every time I lift one of those practice swords, I feel like I might as well be fighting left-handed."

"Me too." Alix supposed that was one disadvantage of owning a bloodforged weapon. One grew to rely on the enchantment. So long as she wielded her own sword, forged with her own blood, she might as well have wielded an extension of herself. The bloodblade obeyed her utterly. It never slipped, never jarred, never threw her off balance. Striking with it was as natural as throwing a punch. But if she should become separated from her sword, the way Erik had, she would find it awkward to fight with an inert chunk of metal.

How would she cope with that on the battlefield? She hoped she never had to find out.

"Have you ever tried to use someone else's bloodweapon?" Erik asked.

She laughed at the memory. "Once. I took Rig's bow, just to see what would happen. I thought that since I was his sister, since we shared the family blood, maybe I could use it."

"And?"

"I couldn't even hit the wall of the armoury. The arrows just twisted around like a sow's tail, or bounced off the wood. I told Rig I thought it was defective, and he took it out of my hands and shot a fly from a pile of horse dung at twenty paces. I couldn't believe it. Apparently being siblings doesn't make any difference at all."

Erik shook his head. "Not unless you're identical twins. The blood has to be exactly the same. Otherwise, the enchantment works in reverse, just like it would with anyone else. I learned that lesson the hard way too, with my father's greatsword. Tom and I sneaked into the royal armoury. He wanted to try on my father's ceremonial plate, but I only had eyes for that sword." His smile widened, lost in the memory. "I must have been about fifteen—almost a man—but I couldn't even heft the thing. I managed to get the hilt off the ground, but the tip of the blade felt like it weighed a thousand stone. It wouldn't yield to me, even when I threw all my weight against it. Tom watched me struggle, but he never tried to help. I think he enjoyed seeing me so humbled."

His smile faded as quickly as it had come. Alix wasn't surprised. "They say the Priest knows the bloodbond," she said. Not exactly a cheerful change of subject, but at least it would draw his mind away from his brother.

"I'm certain of it. If not him, someone else who travels with that army. It seemed like half the men at Boswyck had bloodswords."

"It won't help them." Her voice was armoured with confidence, but inside, her guts twisted over themselves, as they did at least once an hour, whenever she thought of Liam.

Gods keep him safe, she prayed silently.

If only she believed.

ELEVEN

A lix peered down from the ramparts overlooking the road to town. It was quieter today, thank the gods. Only a few villagers clustered near the gate, laying sprays of winter flowers. The bouquets lined the curtain wall, nearly two weeks' worth, stacked waist deep in some places. Crocuses and pansies, roses and witchhazel, snowdrops and coralberry and chrysanthemums, many of them tucked in woven wreaths of wheat or rye. Alix's favourite were the dried lavender; whenever she saw them, she stole outside the gate to bring them inside, letting their rich, sleepy fragrance fill her room in the keep. The perfume wafting up to the ramparts was not quite as pleasant, the sweet scent of the new flowers lending a sugary coating to the decay of the old.

"We'll have to remove those," Commander Ormond said, as though reading her thoughts.

"Leave them awhile yet," she said. "The people deserve to express their joy. Gods know there's little enough of it to be had."

The garrison commander grunted. "At least they've left off the swarming. It doesn't do to have hundreds of peasants pressing in on my walls, however joyful they may be."

On that score, Alix agreed. She understood why they came,

of course. Their king had been miraculously restored to them in the midst of war. Erik's triumphant return had the quality of myth, and he the mythical hero. Understandable as the enthusiasm might be, however, it still made Alix nervous. Last week, when Erik had ventured forth into the throng (over Alix's strong objections), she'd lost sight of him immediately, and she'd been on the brink of ordering the royal guardsmen to extract him. But it proved unnecessary. Erik's casual charisma blunted the edge of the crowd's frenzy, inspiring a relaxed, festive mood. He traded well-wishes and anecdotes, flattered the women and joked with the men. And then he took his leave, without so much as an unwanted grab of his hand.

"The people must see me, Alix," he'd told her as they headed back through the gate. "They are my shield, and I am their hope."

Since then, the crowds had thankfully dwindled. "It looks quiet enough out there," Alix said. "I'm going."

Commander Ormond did not trouble to conceal his disapproval. "How many times is that now?"

"Four."

"Four evenings spent in that stinking tavern. And for what? To listen to ale-sodden oafs telling tales?"

"Taverns are a good place to hear news," Alix said, as though she were an expert on the subject. She'd never set foot in a tavern before the Crooked Mast. Her mother would have died all over again if she knew.

"And what news have you heard, pray?"

She shrugged. "Nothing much, but I choose to regard that as a good sign. It means people don't care enough about the Raven to gossip about him."

"And yet you go anyway."

"Someone needs to. We're blind and deaf behind these walls, Commander."

Ormond snorted, but he'd said his piece. "Do as you will, Captain."

As though I need your permission. She descended the steps from the wall walk, leaving Ormond to his thoughts. Two of her guardsmen trailed behind her. "Remember," she said, "four on the king at all times, and don't take your eyes off him for a moment. If any man so much as relieves himself without finding a replacement first, I'll have his head. Understood?"

"Understood, Captain."

The guardsmen left her, probably muttering to themselves about being taken for fools. Alix had given that particular speech several times over the past few days, but she still felt nervous about leaving the king alone. If only she could trust one of her men to do the reconnaissance work, she could stay with Erik, where she belonged. She'd tried sending some of her guardsmen into town, but it had proved to be a waste of time. The knights couldn't blend in to save their lives, and the common-born men didn't seem to know what they were listening for. All Alix ever got from them was drivel.

She found the Crooked Mast packed to the crow's nest, as usual. It seemed like every man in the Greenlands had decided to make the place a second home. Gratified as she was to see the people toasting their king, Alix wondered how much longer they intended to use Erik's miraculous resurrection as a pretext for public drunkenness. She bumped and jostled her way between the tables, her eyes already watering from the stench of sweat, beer-soaked rushes, and smoke. Wedging herself at a discreet corner of the bar, she slapped down a few coins and said, "Ale." She'd already tried the wine, and the experience did not bear repeating.

"Your money's no good here, milady!" The innkeep, beaming, sloshed a draught of amber liquid into a mug.

Alix eyed him warily. "And what have I done to deserve such a boon?"

"You should've told me who you were." He treated her to a theatrical wink. "The Hero of Boswyck can drink free for life."

"The *what*?" Heat crept into her cheeks as she leaned across the bar. "Listen, don't call me that. And keep your voice down."

He touched his finger to the side of his long, crooked nose. "Understood, milady. Keeping a low profile. You can count on me." He shoved the mug at her, winked again, and went off whistling.

Alix swore into the froth of her ale and resisted the urge to glance around and see who might have overheard. *The Hero of bloody Boswyck. Isn't that just perfect.* So much for catching people with their tongues unguarded. After all the trouble she'd gone to making sure that her clothing wouldn't mark her out for notice, the innkeep had practically announced her to the room like a sodding herald.

Fortunately, most of the patrons were too far into their cups to notice. Alix listened as they traded jibes and tales of the road, as they toasted their king and mocked their wives, as they cursed Oridians and foreigners in general. Everyone seemed to know someone who'd fallen at Boswyck, and many a tribute was drunk. Through all of it, Alix heard nothing of use.

She soon grew bored. Absently, she picked up one of the coins she'd left on the bar, running her thumb and forefinger over its textured surfaces. One side was stamped with a sun-burst, the other with the king's profile. Alix had never really looked at it closely. It was an acceptable likeness, she decided, though it didn't do Erik justice. He looked regal, certainly, but not quite as handsome as he ought. Something about the mouth was off, and the cast of the brow looked cold and arrogant. The strong jaw was there, though, and they'd gotten the nose right. Or was it more like Liam's nose? And the cheekbones, too, were like Liam. The more Alix considered the coin, the more she fancied she saw Liam's features.

She sighed, putting the coins away. Liam had been gone so long that she was beginning to see his face everywhere. Her mind was in constant pursuit of an excuse to think of him. *As though I have nothing better to worry about.*

She lingered another hour or so before giving up. On her way to the door, she elbowed past a raucous group of fellows with long blades and well-worn bows. *Sellswords*, she thought contemptuously. *On their way to the front, no doubt.* She won-dered where they'd come from. Not that it mattered—the hard truth was that the Kingswords alone could not hope to defeat the Oridians, not with their numbers divided between the Blacklands and Erroman. They would need all the help they could get, even if it came from brigands and knaves like these.

She spilled out of the tavern into the crisp-smelling air of late winter. The road to the castle looked deserted, a welcome reprieve from the press of filthy bodies inside. A pale winter sun slumped over the horizon as its watch came to an end. Somewhere over the edge of the world, the moon prepared to take over. Alix shivered against a blade-sharp wind, wishing she had her armour. The plate itself would do little to warm her, but the padding beneath would have been a welcome extra layer.

She was halfway home when a figure materialised at the crest of the road. A peasant on his way back from the castle, she presumed, though he didn't seem to be in any particular rush. On the contrary, he dawdled along, and as she drew nearer, she saw the outline of a sword at his hip. She tensed, reaching under her cloak to feel the reassuring presence of her own steel.

"Good evening, milady," the man called to her.

"Good evening to you." Her tone was standoffish enough to deter further courtesies.

Or so she thought. "Pleasant weather," he said, slowing.

Alix flexed her cold-stiffened fingers under her cloak. Either he hailed from the extreme north, or he was trying to get her to stop. She thought she knew which. "I'm in a hurry, friend."

"All right, then." The man flashed an oily smile. "Let's get this over with."

He was on her so quickly that she scarcely had time to react. She spun out of his path, drawing her blade as she moved. The man turned deftly and faced her, a shortsword gleaming in his hand. Alix flung her cloak over her shoulder and crouched.

Her attacker was left-handed, she noted uneasily. Rig had been nagging her for years to practice more with left-handed foes. She couldn't remember the last time she'd faced one. She would have given anything for a shield at that moment, but she didn't even have her armour. *Fool*. What kind of bodyguard leaves herself so vulnerable?

Her attacker dove in, but Alix was ready. She mirrored his movements as though he led her in a dance, pivoting her body away from his before rocking forward and slamming her blade down, driving the tip of his sword into the dirt. If only she'd had a dagger in her off hand, she could have ended it then and there. But she didn't, and he recovered quickly, leaping back and coiling for another strike. He lunged at her shoulder. The unfamiliar angle threw her off; instinctively, her arm flew up as though to block with her hand. Metal rang as the tip of her blade met the edge of his, knocking it aside. Alix staggered back, swallowing a thick knot of panic. If her sword hadn't been bloodforged, she would surely have missed that parry. Only the enhanced dexterity bestowed by the enchantment had saved her life.

Her fear made her reckless. She dove in too soon, hoping to tie him up at close range, and he lashed out with the hilt of his sword and clubbed her in the mouth, sending her reeling. Alix tasted blood. Her vision swam, and for a terrifying moment she thought she might swoon. A blur of movement brought her back to her senses; she swung out blindly, letting the bloodbond guide her hand, tuning her sword to the pitch of her subconscious. Her blade met resistance. The man cried out. A lucky shot, but as her vision cleared, Alix saw that it wasn't much. She'd drawn blood on his forearm, but not deeply. She gave her head a firm shake, spat a mouthful of blood at the dirt, and planted her feet.

Settle, damn you. You're the king's bodyguard, trained by the best master-at-arms in the realm. Your blade is enchanted to obey your every instinct. And who is this cretin? Some whoreson from the back alleys of Erroman? Quit flailing like a wounded goose and fight.

When he came at her again, she held her ground. *He is not my equal. He is nothing.* Her sword rang out once, twice, a third time, and went silent, its metal throat buried to the hilt. Blood ran warm over the pommel, over the dark red jewel that marked it as bloodforged. The man slumped into her, wide-eyed and gasping, one hand planted against her shoulder, the other clutching at the sword in his breast. Slowly, Alix turned aside and let him fall off her blade.

She left him twitching in the dirt, knowing that if she looked back, if she even paused to think, she might come undone. *Too close. You let that get way, way too close.* The man had been a mediocre swordsman equipped with an ordinary weapon, yet he'd almost had her. She'd nearly panicked herself into an early grave. *Learn from it,* Master Alvan's voice rumbled in her head. That's what he'd always told her in the yard, back when she was still learning. He would pick her up from the dirt and say, *Don't cry about it, girl, learn from it.* And so she would.

The sun had nearly set by the time she reached Greenhold. The far side of the bridge was deserted but for a single peasant crouched by the wall, perusing the flowers. Instinctively,

Alix tensed, even though the wall walk teemed with guards. Her encounter on the road had left her shaken.

"Evening, Lady Black," the man said, rising. "Had a spot of trouble on the road, I see. I thought you might."

Alix's sword sang out of its scabbard.

The man smiled and raised his hands. "That seems a little hasty." He spoke with a dark, rasping voice that might have been soothing had it not been cold as stone. Alix was certain she would have recognised that voice if she'd heard it before.

"All right down there, Captain?" One of the guards leaned out over the ramparts of the gatehouse. He'd seen her draw her blade. Perhaps he could even see the bloodstains on her forearm, though the light was failing.

"We'll see," she called. "Have archers ready."

The man's smile didn't waver. "Hasty *and* overdone."

Alix looked him over. Clad in black from hood to heel, he was difficult to make out against the slab of grey stone behind him. Other than that, there was nothing remarkable about his person—medium height, medium build, simple clothing. His features were bland and forgettable, the sort of man you could meet half a dozen times and still take for a stranger. He didn't appear to be armed, but he could easily have a dagger concealed somewhere. Alix kept her distance. "Who are you?"

"Best not to think of me as some*one*, Lady Black. Rather some*thing*."

"Some*thing*?" she echoed incredulously.

"That's right. Something very useful."

She scowled. "I'll ask you again, and I warn you not to test my patience. *Who are you?*"

He wasn't impressed by her bluster. "I'm not fond of giving out my name. It takes most of my employers years to earn the privilege."

"How do you know me?"

"Hard to mistake hair like that, Lady Black. A word of advice: If you're in the business of spying, it's a good idea not to stand out." He gestured at himself, as though to illustrate the point. "Next time, consider tucking those red tresses of yours under a hood."

She did her best to look unruffled. "I'm not in the business of spying."

His smile turned wry. "My mistake. Perhaps you just relish a drop of sour ale in the company of sellswords and swineherds."

"You've been following me."

"You couldn't have been more obvious if you'd dangled your banner from your belt. At least it was a fruitful evening. Tell me, who was he?"

"Who?"

"The assassin who accosted you on the road. I passed him on the way here, loitering about, advertising his purpose almost as loudly as you. He was going to offer you either his services or his sword. Judging by the blood on your arm, it was the latter."

"And you made no move to stop him?"

The man's eyebrows flew up. "Me? Oh no, Lady Black. I'm not made for swordplay. Listening and learning, that's my trade."

"So *you're* a spy."

He bowed mockingly. "Who was he, then? The fool who tried to best the mighty Hero of Boswyck?" He smirked, in case Alix had missed the sarcasm.

"He neglected to introduce himself," she said dryly.

"But you questioned him?"

She frowned.

"You examined the body, at least?"

Bugger and damn.

The man laughed softly, a smug, languorous sound like the purring of an old tomcat. "By all the Virtues, woman. You need me even more than I thought."

In the space of a heartbeat, Alix had closed the distance between them and pressed her blade to his throat. The creak of bows sounded from the ramparts above as the Greenswords took her cue. "For the last time, *who are you?*"

The man peered down his nose at the hilt of Alix's sword. "Now that's a blunder on my part. Misread your temperament. It's a delicate business I'm in, Lady Black. Not much room for error."

"Very true. Your next error will be fatal."

"I've come all the way from Erroman to see you, so I'd be grateful if you at least heard me out before opening my throat."

Alix backed off, but not much. She kept her blade raised.

He massaged his neck gently. "Word among fighting men is that the Raven quit the field in the heat of battle. Some call him a coward, but the way I heard it told, he was cool as mint when he sounded the retreat. Some in my trade wonder if the Raven hasn't taken it into his head to replace his brother."

"Do they."

"They wonder a lot else besides. There are whispers of civil war. Erroman is an orchard of whispers, Lady Black, and you need only a hand to pluck them for you, to see what seeds of truth you may find."

"How very poetic."

"I can help you. Let me be your eyes and ears in the capital. Never mind this backwater and its provincial gossip. I have connections at the highest levels of court and the lowest back-alley brothels. If you would know the Raven's mind—his ploys, his allies, his assassins—you have only to engage my services."

Alix's lip curled. "You're a vulture, feeding on the misfortune of others."

He shrugged. "I'm a man of enterprise, who knows how to match his talents with opportunity. Scorn that if you like. My feelings aren't delicate. But don't be too quick to turn away what I offer. You need it, else you wouldn't be leaving your king's side to swat hands off your arse at the Crooked Mast."

She ground her teeth, but didn't rise to the bait. "How do I know you aren't working for someone else? The Raven, for example?"

"Good girl. Now you're thinking sensibly. The answer is, you don't. Treat everything you hear, including from me, with a healthy dose of scepticism. Tomald White is not known for his subtlety, but he has many admirers, some of whom may have a lighter touch. Always consider the possibility of deception."

Alix hesitated. It *would* make sense to have a spy in their employ. She'd been thinking about it ever since Gwylim suggested it. She couldn't possibly trust this man, but he had the truth of it when he said that she shouldn't trust anyone, especially not someone good enough for the job. Any spy worth the name was inherently deceitful.

The man watched her chew over the dilemma. "If it will

help you decide, let me offer you a sample of my wares. The assassin you killed tonight—the one you failed to interrogate—does it surprise you that he came after you on the road like that?"

She frowned, considering. "I suppose it does, now that you mention it. Even if he'd managed to kill me, it wouldn't have helped him get to the king."

"No, it wouldn't. So either he was uncommonly stupid, or it wasn't the king he was after. Or perhaps a little of both."

Something cold wrapped itself around Alix's gut, like a snake constricting around its prey. "Why would an assassin want to kill *me*?"

"I expect twenty crowns is enough to tempt many a man to make a trophy of your lovely locks."

The cold thing constricted, leaving her queasy. "What are you talking about?"

"Why, the price on your head, offered to a certain guild of some renown. A pittance in comparison to what's on offer for His Majesty, of course, but enough. Fortunately for you, the guild doesn't seem to have estimated your skills very highly, or they wouldn't have sent such incompetents to do the job. I wouldn't count on them to make that mistake a third time."

"A third time?" The answer came to her as soon as she spoke. *The assassin on the wall walk.* Her fingers tightened around the hilt of her sword. "Who hired them?"

"That I cannot tell you—at least not yet."

"The Raven?"

"We can speculate, you and I, but that can be more dangerous than ignorance. Give me time, and a few crowns, and I will get you the information you need. Until then, be on your guard, and this time be serious about it. No more wandering alone and unarmoured, and no more rubbing shoulders with drunkards and sellswords. Don't leave your king's side for a moment, Lady Black, because the next assassin they send will be their best, you can count on it."

He had her, and he knew it. There was no point in trying to pretend. She sheathed her sword, untied her coin purse, and tossed it at him. He caught it with a soft *chink*. "Go then," she said. "Ride hard for Erroman, and I want to hear from you as soon as you arrive. We receive pigeons daily from Lord Green's estate to the west of the city." Not that they ever brought anything useful, but maybe that was about to change.

The man bowed. "You won't be disappointed. I will write you within a fortnight. In the meantime, try not to get yourself killed."

Alix stood in the moonlight and watched as the nameless spy vanished over the bridge.

TWELVE

† "**A**nd you just sent him off into the night?"
      "Lord Green, please, lower your voice." It was
not as though Alix could keep the incident on the road a
secret, but she preferred to tell the king in her own time,
once she'd had a chance to think things through. Obviously,
she should have considered that before she'd told Raibert
Green. She had scarcely washed the blood from her face before she happened upon the lord of Greenhold, and like a fool,
she'd blurted it all out. Now he was making a scene, right
there in the corridor.

"He could have been anyone," Green said, wearing a scowl
that was half anger, half fear. "How do you know he wasn't in
league with the man who tried to kill you? Awfully convenient, don't you think, that he should be waiting for you at
the gates only moments later?"

"What's this commotion?" Erik appeared around the
corner, four royal guardsmen in tow.

Alix cursed inwardly. "It's nothing to worry about, Your
Majesty."

"Olan's battered shield it isn't!" Green shook his head in
exasperation. "Do you really think you can trust a word the

man says? Like as not he'll fill your head with lies and herd you straight into a trap!"

Alix had never seen him so angry. Neither had Erik, apparently; he looked taken aback, his gaze alternating between Alix and Lord Green. "Will someone kindly tell me what in the name of the Nine we're discussing? What happened to your lip, Alix?"

Instinctively, she ran her tongue over the wound. Before she could think of a way to deflect the question, Raibert said, "She was attacked, Your Majesty, by another assassin."

Erik's eyes flashed. "Where?"

"On the road to town. She was alone, without armour, and he set upon her. And after that, she saw fit to hire a spy who happened to be loitering outside the castle gates when she got back."

Alix glared at Green as if he were a tattling sibling. Bad enough that he should make her sound like a fool in front of the king, but four of her own men were standing right there at the end of the corridor, trying their best to pretend they weren't listening to their commander being dressed down. "It all came out fine," she said, glaring.

Green snorted. "Indeed."

Erik frowned, and Alix experienced a flare of annoyance that he would look at her like that before she'd even had a chance to explain. *So much for deferring to my judgement.* "It's more complicated than it sounds, sire, as I was just attempting to explain to Lord Green."

The king folded his arms expectantly.

"I went to the Crooked Mast, as we discussed this afternoon. I've made several such trips—"

"Against my advice," Raibert put in, helpfully.

"—*without incident.* But this time, there was a man waiting for me on the road. He attacked me, and I killed him." She breezed through this part of the story with a dismissive wave. "Then, as I was approaching the gate, there was another man waiting for me. A spy, as it turned out, come from Erroman to offer his services. We talked, and he convinced me that he could be of some use."

"He convinced you." Erik eyed her doubtfully.

"All it cost me was a few coins. And I'm not so stupid as to trust him blindly. I'll treat the intelligence he provides with caution—as he himself suggested I should."

"Then what's the point?" Erik asked.

"If he's genuine, he could be extremely useful. He's already provided me with valuable information."

Raibert rolled his eyes. "How can it be valuable, if you can't even trust it?"

Alix paused long enough to beg blessed Farika for patience. "Because, Lord Green, in this case there's nothing to be gained by a lie. On the contrary, it only puts us on our guard."

"Let's hear this valuable information, then," said Erik.

"An assassin's guild has been hired to kill you."

Erik shrugged, but Alix wasn't fooled by it; his nonchalance was every bit as feigned as her own. "We knew that already, more or less. Whether it's a guild or a lone wolf, it makes little difference."

"Maybe, but the spy claims you're not the only one they're after. They've put a price on me, too." She would have said more, but the look that came over Erik silenced her.

"Lord Green." He addressed Raibert, but his eyes were on Alix, ice-blue and furious. "Would you excuse us for a moment?"

"Certainly, sire." Green bowed and took his leave, and Erik put his hand on Alix's elbow and steered her into the study, closing the door behind them. Alix cringed inwardly.

He didn't speak right away. Instead he stood with his back to her, seemingly collecting himself. At length, he said, "I'm trying to understand, Alix, how you thought it wise to do what you did today."

"I told you where I was going."

He whirled around. "But you left out a few choice details, didn't you? Alone, Alix? Without armour?"

She winced; she'd hoped those particulars had passed him by. *Damn Raibert Green.* "I didn't want to stand out. I wouldn't have learned anything if people knew who I was."

"Reckless," he growled, as though he hadn't heard her.

That got her back up. "I thought I was supposed to execute my duties in a manner befitting my judgement? Or was that just talk?" Somewhere in the back of her mind, a voice mentioned something about Erik being *king*, but she brushed it aside.

He threw her a sharp look. "If this is your idea of good judgement, then perhaps it should have been just talk."

"With all due respect, Your Majesty, you weren't there."

"No, I wasn't. I would never have put myself in that position."

"Your Majesty. *Erik.*" She took a step closer to him, met and held his gaze. The part of her that had been bred for court shrank at this brazen display of impudence, but the captain of the royal guardsmen could not afford to blink. "If I am to protect you, I have to be allowed to follow my instincts. We've talked about this."

"We've talked about the need for you to be independent. I never said anything about allowing you to behave rashly. It is completely unacceptable for you to risk yourself in that manner."

"It's my duty to risk myself."

"Not carelessly, Alix!" he cried, seizing her by the shoulders. "Not needlessly! What could you possibly have learned out there that was worth your life? Do you not know how valued you are? Do you not realise . . ." He trailed off, staring at her. She could only stare back, utterly at a loss. He sighed and shook his head. "You really don't see, do you? How can that be? It's not as though I've made any secret of it." Even then, she might not have understood. But when he laid a hand against her cheek, there was no mistaking it. An unexpected flash of heat swept over her. It was more than shock. His touch ignited something in her blood, something she hadn't known was there. Her breath came faster.

He brushed his thumb over her lip, swollen from the assassin's blow. "You always were oblivious," he murmured. "Too locked up in your own head to see what's right in front of you. Then again, perhaps I haven't been as plain as I thought. I can be plainer, if you'll let me." He drew closer, his gaze lingering on her mouth. "May I kiss you, Alix?"

A delicious sort of panic bucked in her chest. She could feel herself shaking with it. She nodded numbly.

He was gentle at first, coaxing. Alix closed her eyes as a silvery shiver ran down her spine. There was something so familiar about his kiss, so *right*. She felt her arms going around him, felt herself sinking into his embrace. Encouraged, he gathered her closer and deepened the kiss. The soft glide of his tongue into her mouth brought a fresh wave of heat, like a shot of whiskey down her throat. Alix was overcome. She surged into him, breathless and heedless and soaring. He matched her fierceness with his own, pulling her flush against him, as if he could merge them right then and there. Her fingers tangled in his hair, rumpled the shirt at his waist. He lifted her suddenly and hoisted her onto the desk. She locked her legs around him as his mouth wandered under her jaw, over her throat, finding the tender place behind her ear. Through the roar of her blood, she heard him whisper, "*Allie.*"

She stiffened. Everything shattered. She pulled away, gasping.

For a moment she was too muddled to speak. She hopped down off the desk, hiding her face behind a curtain of hair. "I'm sorry." Her voice trembled. "I don't think I'm ready for this."

He was a credit to his breeding. "I understand," he said, the words belied by the confusion, the disappointment, in his voice. "I didn't mean to push you."

"I'm sorry," she said again, and fled the room.

Holy flame of Ardin. What have I done?

Alix stared up at the ceiling, watching the scene unfold again and again through the lens of her memory. It was as if she observed herself from afar, her actions framed by the dark wood panels as though she gazed upon a moving portrait. A portrait of Alix Black kissing the King of Alden.

The king.

Erik.

Oh gods . . .

Alix clapped her hands over her eyes, but it did nothing to stop to the imaginary play. It simply went on in her head: Erik reaching for her, his thumb ghosting over the wound on her lip. His voice, low and honeyed. His eyes, so impossibly blue, wandering over her face until they found her mouth. *May I kiss you, Alix?*

She experienced it all over again—the flash of panic, the sudden thrill of longing . . . Even now, as she lay there, she could still feel him, his mouth and his arms and his body. And she *craved* it.

How did this happen?

It had taken her completely by surprise. Not just his desire, but her own. Especially her own. It couldn't have come from nowhere; it was too strong for that. It must have been there all along, lurking just beneath the surface, waiting to ambush her. How could she not have realised?

She'd *noticed* him, of course. How handsome he was, how charming. What woman wouldn't be swayed by that breezy confidence, that dignity, that quintessentially masculine beauty? But he was her king, and later, the man whose life lay in her hands. She couldn't possibly allow herself to think of him as a romantic prospect. And then, of course, there was Liam . . .

Liam.

A low note of despair sounded from somewhere deep within. *I've betrayed him.* A small betrayal, maybe, but it could easily have been much more. Alix knew instinctively that things would have gone as far as she'd let them—and for a moment, she'd been inclined to let them get very far indeed. That was the *real* betrayal—not what she'd done, but what she'd wanted to do.

What I still want to do . . .

She put her hand over her chest, and her heart raced a little more, just to show its agreement.

And then, abruptly, her mind was back in the woods, with the cold night air and the warm weight on top of her, and a tiny ache throbbed inside. She'd transported herself to this place so many times, and it never lost its power over her. She missed Liam so badly. It was like having a piece of her carved away. She'd known it would be; she'd gone through it before, with Rig. Maybe that was why she'd pushed Liam so fast. She'd been afraid of losing him, as she'd lost so many of those close to her. And now he was gone, and Erik was here . . .

Is that all this is? Am I just replacing Liam with Erik?

Alix swore and rolled onto her side. Her country was at war, her king under threat of assassination, and she was lying here worrying about romance? "You're a disgrace, Alix Black," she growled into her pillow.

She squeezed her eyes shut, took a deep breath, and willed herself to sleep. It would be a long day tomorrow, and the day after that. She needed her rest.

When she finally drifted off, it was to the sound of leaves rustling in the forest.

Erik White stared, unseeing, at the letter under his nose. The words on the page were little more than shadowy, meaningless scratches of ink. It did not help that the taper on the desk had slumped into a misshapen heap, its glow dwindling to a thin halo on one side of the parchment. With his back to the hearth, he could scarcely make out half the script. But that wasn't the real problem. The real problem stood ten paces behind him, in a discreet corner of the study, her presence tugging incessantly at nerves already taut with a thousand more kingly concerns.

He resisted the urge to turn around. It would only reveal his mind, and he had done quite enough of that already. *You should never have kissed her*, he thought ruefully. There was still a chance he could have talked himself out of this. Now . . .

Now it was too late. In a single unguarded moment, he had tipped his hand and sealed his fate. And yet if he had it to do over, he had no doubt he would kiss her again. That was how he knew he had wandered in deep. Too deep to ignore it, and too deep to wriggle out. All that was left to him now was to do something about it.

But perhaps that can wait until after the war, Your Majesty. He rubbed his eyes and focused his attention back on the letter.

There is little doubt they are preparing to march, the parchment told him, *but it seems only half the host readies itself. We have tracked a number of scouting missions looking to the east. It is impossible to know what the enemy is thinking . . .*

Of course it was. One could never truly know another's mind, no matter how hard one tried. The gods knew Erik had spent enough time trying to guess what Alix Black was thinking. But all he had to go on was the kiss, and he hardly knew what to make of *that*. One moment, she'd been all passion and fire; the next, shaken and distraught. He had triggered something when he called her *Allie*, something that broke the spell. *Thoughts of her brother, perhaps, or someone else?* A riddle, to be sure, and until he solved it, he sensed it would be unwise to try again.

He could not recall ever being so muddled over a woman, not even as an adolescent. Romance had always come easy to him; too easy, if he was honest with himself. Even after his betrothal, he had never wanted for female attention. Sirin could not very well deny him what she did not deny herself, and so she turned a blind eye to the occasional dalliance, so long as he was discreet. As for the women, they did not seem to mind the secrecy. On the contrary, most of them found it exciting. And if his court was not exactly fooled by his pretensions of faithfulness, well . . . he was hardly the first king to indulge in such recreation. All in all, relationships had never troubled him overmuch. But this was different. *She* was different. Alix Black rattled his confidence in a way that was profoundly disturbing—and intoxicating.

The letter, Erik. Focus.

They number slightly more than we estimated, he read. *However, that in itself does not concern me. The Kingswords are better trained by far, and a man defending crown and hearth is ten times as fierce as a man whose only aim is conquest.*

That was surely Destan's own truth. Erik had seen it for himself at Boswyck, when Alix had charged to his defence. That memory haunted his dreams. Even now, wide awake, he had only to close his eyes to see it: Alix descending on his attackers in a storm of wrath. Frenzied, undisciplined, magnificent. He would remember that image for the rest of his days. Even so, he could have made it easier on himself. He could have left her to her King's Service. She would be gone now, off in the Blacklands with Arran Green and the others. Instead, fool that he was, he had appointed her to be his shadow. How was he to stop thinking about her when she was *right there*, all day, every day?

If only we had met years ago. Before the war, before his

betrothal. She was a Black, the daughter of a Banner House. They could have . . .

No. Don't do that. He was restive enough without tormenting himself with what could have been.

Erik growled under his breath. He'd read the same paragraph three times over. This self-indulgence was unacceptable, a distraction he could ill afford. *Frivolous*, Tom would have called it, and he would have been right. *But how am I to make a decision, when I can't even concentrate?* He needed a second opinion.

"Alix." He didn't have to turn around to know where she was.

"Sire?"

"Would you please send for Lord Green?"

"Certainly."

She returned a moment later, and Erik waved her over. The very least he owed her, and himself, was to keep things from becoming awkward between them. "Take a look at this," he said, angling the letter to the light, "and tell me what you think."

He watched her read, those warm hazel eyes scanning the parchment, shapely eyebrows drawn together in thought. When his gaze strayed to her lips, he looked away. *Frivolous*, Tom's voice grated in his head.

"Hmm," Alix said.

Erik forced a smile. "Care to elaborate?"

"I see your dilemma. General Green can't defend the Blacklands and the Brownlands at the same time. If the enemy splits his host, as Green fears, you'll have to choose."

"Unless we take our two thousand from here."

"Leaving the Greenlands defenceless with the bulk of the Oridian army to the south."

"But if I do nothing, and the Brownlands are ravaged . . ."

She nodded grimly. "You could lose the loyalty of the Browns, and others besides."

He stared at the letter, scratched out in Arran Green's blocky script. "Tom might bestir himself to defend the Brownlands."

Alix grimaced. "In which case the Browns would throw in with him for sure."

She's right. Each scenario was gloomier than the last. Erik pounded the table in frustration. "Damn! Why do our allies sit idle? Surely the Onnani know they're next, or if not Onnan, then Harram!"

"They're afraid," she said, and Erik knew she was right about that too.

"Never have I regretted being landlocked more than I do now. If we had access to the old imperial ports . . ."

"Even if the Onnani let us use them, we'd still need a fleet. Our river craft won't be much good at sea."

"No." Erik's eyes drifted to the map of Gedona spread out beside the letter. The Trionate of Oridia, painted in crimson, sprawled like a bloodstain over half the continent. Even tiny Andithyri was red; someone had updated the map, inking over the Trionate's latest conquest so that the crimson came right up to Alden's southern border.

How long until my kingdom is red too?

To the west, the Broken Mountains formed a hard, impenetrable line. To the east, Onnan stood between Alden and the sea.

We're trapped.

Erik turned the map upside down, so that north was south, but that only made it worse. Now, Oridia seemed to crush Alden beneath its massive weight. It was no use—any way he looked at it, his kingdom was small, weak, and besieged. "Have I made a terrible mistake, Alix?" he asked softly. "Should I have left Andithyri to its fate, as Tom counselled me? Perhaps we could have avoided this war, if only I had not been so stubborn."

She rested a hand on his shoulder. "Don't do that. You were honour-bound and treaty-bound."

"Honour-bound, yes. But what good are principles if they come at the expense of everything we hold dear?" The question seemed to come from someone else, someone with Tom's voice.

"It's not just about principles. It's as you said—after Andithyri, it would have been us, and then our neighbours, and so on and so on. The Oridian gods demand conquest. They'll never stop until someone stops them. If it helps, I would have made the same choice."

Erik started to put his hand over hers, but footsteps sounded in the corridor, and Alix pulled away, retreating to her corner.

Her words did help, a little. But Erik couldn't shake the feeling that one day soon, he would regret his choice, and by then, it would be too late. It was already too late.

"Your Majesty," Raibert Green said as he entered the study.

"Lord Green." Erik stood and gestured at the desk. Then, glancing over his shoulder at Alix, he made an abrupt decision. "Would you give us a moment, please, Captain?" She looked taken aback, but she obeyed, withdrawing and closing the door behind her. Raibert eyed his king curiously, waiting for Erik to speak.

"I had hoped for your counsel," Erik said.

"It is yours whenever you wish it, sire, for whatever it is worth."

"It is worth a great deal, especially now. I have always relied on the wisdom of my counsellors, but now they're gone—at the front, or in the capital, or dead, and I . . ." He paused, swallowing. "I fear I am lost." He could never have admitted that with Alix in the room. It was hard enough admitting it to a gentle soul like Raibert Green.

"You are not lost, sire," Green said.

"No? What else would you call it when a man does not know which course to choose?"

"Wisdom." Green's pale eyes, so like his cousin's, met Erik's steadily. "Only a fool is certain of every step he takes. A wise man questions his decisions—before he makes them, and after. So long as he does not allow himself to become paralysed by doubt, questioning is healthy and necessary."

"Yet I am no closer to making a decision." Erik sighed and rubbed his stinging eyes yet again. "I've worn the crown for almost seven years, yet I never truly felt the weight of it until now. It's as though I've been playacting all along."

"You're too hard on yourself, sire. Generations of kings come and go without having to face what you're facing now. Your father never had to deal with such a crisis."

"True enough, and nothing he ever taught me prepared me for something like this." *Especially since we barely spoke to each other.* In truth, most of what Erik knew of kingcraft he had learned from Albern Highmount. His former first counsel had never shied away from giving advice, solicited or otherwise. *What would Highmount say if he were here now? He would lecture me, as Tom did. That much is certain.* "Tell me the truth, Green—is Tom right about me? Am I frivolous?"

Green did not respond right away. When he did, he seemed to choose his words carefully. "You and your brother are very different people. That has been so since you were children. For you, everything has always come easily. People are drawn to you. They instinctively want to please you. That breeds a certain style of leader, one who inspires his men to greatness. Tomald is a different animal. He lacks your easy way with people, so he has to rely on himself. That has made him strong, and strong-willed. Men like that don't seek to inspire greatness in others, they seek to embody it in themselves."

"You didn't answer my question."

Green sighed. "You are not frivolous, Erik. But we are at war, both within and without, and the world is not as simple as it used to be. You will have to dig deeper. I know you want to be a good man, and you are. But your duty is to be a good king, and from time to time, it may not be possible for you to be both."

Erik nodded, stiff and silent.

"Forgive me, sire," Green said, lowering his gaze. "I speak out of turn."

"No. I asked for your views, and you gave them. I thank you for it."

A wry smile flitted across Green's face, as if to say, *I doubt that.* "Will that be all, Your Majesty?"

"Yes, Lord Green, thank you."

Erik's gaze dropped back to the letter as Raibert Green quit the study. *You may have to choose, Your Majesty,* the letter told him, *and soon.* Arran Green was referring to the deployment of the Kingswords, but the words applied equally to what his cousin had just said, about being a good man, or a good king.

You may have to choose, Your Majesty, and soon.

THIRTEEN

"Sire." Raibert Green appeared at the entrance to the solar. "My apologies for interrupting your meal, but a supply party has just arrived from the front."

Erik stood, his food instantly forgotten. "I trust they have a report for me?"

"Indeed. A scout called Liam awaits you in the oratorium."

Alix's breath caught in her throat. *Finally!* Three supply missions had come and gone from the front since the Kingswords left Greenhold, all of them accompanied by scouts Alix barely knew. She'd begun to suspect that Arran Green was deliberately keeping her friends away from her. But now a fourth had come, and Liam with it. *The gods are good*, she thought, twisting the golden ivy around her little finger.

"Liam, is it?" Surprisingly, Erik seemed to remember him. "Let's be off, then."

They followed Raibert Green to the oratorium. A fire was just beginning to flare in the hearth behind the lord's table. The second hearth at the foot of the room sat dark, leaving the gallery cloaked in shadow. Standing at the edge of the firelight, at a respectful distance from the lord's table, was Liam. Alix's step faltered a little at the sight of him, but luckily, both the king and Lord Green had their backs to her. As for Liam, his eyes flicked to her only momentarily; he didn't dare seem more interested in the king's bodyguard than in the king himself. Instead, he did the safe thing and bowed deeply.

"Your Majesty." Liam's voice echoed under the high ceiling.

"Hello, Liam. Are you well?"

Alix felt a shy sort of pride at the king's solicitude. Liam, though, seemed to find it uncomfortable. He wrung out a nervous smile and said, "Very well, sire, I thank you." He hesitated a moment before adding, "Your leg. It, er, seems better."

"Much better." Erik didn't sit; instead, he leaned casually against the lord's table, smiling. Alix and Raibert Green exchanged a bemused look.

"Um," said Liam. As ever, being in the presence of the king left him awkward and tongue-tied.

"You have news?" Erik prompted gently.

Liam nodded enthusiastically, as though grateful for the reminder. "The commander general sends his regards, sire, and bids me begin by saying that things are going as well as can be expected. We've managed to stop the enemy from further pillaging. They're too busy trying to keep ahead of us. Since we deployed, only a single village has fallen prey to their attacks."

Alix found it difficult to divide her attention between the sound of Liam's voice and the news of her homeland. She tried to focus, but his nearness stirred her insides like embers, kindling a warm glow—and an ashen wisp of dread.

"So we have them on the run, then," Erik said.

"We did, until they reached the Scions. Now they've hunkered down inside the fork of the river."

"The Scions . . ." Erik shook his head. "It's been years since I've been to the Blacklands. I don't remember . . ." He looked over at Alix, inviting comment.

The conversation had her full attention now. "The Scions is the place where the Tyrant splits." She spread three fingers, demonstrating. "It creates two wedges of land, both of them hemmed in by water. The only way to reach them is by fording the north fork a few miles downstream." She pointed at the middle knuckle of her index finger. "All the enemy has to do is hold the ford, and they're virtually unassailable."

"Unless we go around," said Liam, "but the nearest bridge is over two hundred miles downstream, and if we made a move toward it, the enemy would have plenty of time to bring it down."

Erik frowned. "Attacking the ford sounds risky."

"Like laying siege to a castle," Alix said. "They can hold the ford with a fraction of their number."

"And that's exactly what they're doing," Liam said. "Did Your Majesty receive General Green's last letter?"

"I did. I take it the enemy has split its host?"

"Yes, sire. They've left about a thousand to hold the ford. The rest are making their way east, to the Brownlands. If we try to intercept them, we'll be leaving the Blacklands defenceless."

"But if you don't, the Brownlands will be virtually defenceless," Raibert said, stating the obvious.

Liam nodded. "I'm afraid so, my lord. General Green requests His Majesty's instructions."

Erik swore quietly and pushed away from the table. He started to pace. "Lord Green, how many men do you need to hold the castle against a siege?"

Raibert sighed. He knew where this was going. "Five hundred, I suppose. It depends on what the enemy has for siege engines."

"Meaning we could ride out with fifteen hundred. Liam, how many of the enemy march on the Brownlands?"

"Four thousand, sire."

Alix already knew what Erik's decision would be. It was written in the set of his eyebrows, the tension of his jaw. She knew that look.

Raibert knew it too. "They would outnumber us almost three to one," he said, as though Erik couldn't count. "We could not hope to defeat them."

"But we can slow them down, and that is exactly what we'll do. Send word to Adelbard Brown immediately. He must gather his garrison and whatever ragtag band of peasants he has managed to muster and meet us on the field. Together, we will buy time for your cousin to dislodge the enemy from the Scions."

Raibert frowned. "A costly purchase."

"That depends on how you calculate the terms. I don't dare leave the Browns to their fate, Lord Green. I must consider the fights we face in the future, as well as those we face now. I need Lord Brown's allegiance. We've discussed this already, you and I."

"We have indeed," Raibert said coolly, "and you know my views, but it seems you are decided. Apparently, those whose loyalties are beyond question must sacrifice for those whose loyalties are in doubt."

Alix winced, and Liam studied his boots. As for the king, he only sighed. "I do not ask you to leave your lands defenceless, Lord Green. If the host at the border so much as glances north, we will return with all haste. But I must remind you, if that happens, every Kingsword at my command will not be enough to drive the enemy from our lands. That power will remain beyond us until I return to Erroman and the armies of Alden reunite under me. For that I must have the Browns."

The anger bled from Raibert's eyes, and he nodded resignedly. "You have the right of it, Your Majesty, but it is a bitter draught to swallow."

Erik put a hand on his shoulder. "I know. And I will make it up to you, I promise." He glanced back at Liam. "You understand what you're to tell General Green?"

"Yes, sire."

"Good. Thank you, Liam, and let Olan be your sign." To Alix, he said, "Feel free to accompany Liam back to the camp. I'm sure you're eager for news of your comrades."

The delight that washed over Alix carried a distinct aftertaste of anxiety. "Thank you, Your Majesty."

Liam bowed again and headed for the double doors behind the gallery. He paused until Alix caught up, holding the door for her. A subtle grin played at his mouth, but he wiped it off as they made their way out into the crowded bailey. They walked in impatient silence, not even daring to look at each other until they were well down the path to camp. Then Liam put his hand on the small of her back and steered her into the trees, just as he had done all those weeks ago.

He crushed her to him the moment they were alone. "Allie," he murmured into her neck, "it's so good to see you." He hoisted her off the ground, extracting a squeal of surprise. Then he bent his forehead to hers and let out a long sigh, as though relieved of an ache.

Taking his face in her hands, Alix said a silent prayer of

thanks. "You look well." She brushed the thick stubble lining his jaw. "If a little shaggy."

Liam had several days' growth of beard, and a harder look about him than Alix remembered, but his crooked grin was as mischievous as ever. "Do you like it? I think it makes a very manly impression."

"It certainly made a manly impression on my neck." She rubbed a tender spot where his beard had chafed her.

"Completely intentional. Gives me an excuse to do this." He leaned in and kissed her throat.

Brutally overruling her instincts, Alix forced herself to step back. "So, who else came with you?" She was postponing the inevitable, but they'd had only a few moments together. She wasn't ready. It was like lingering in bed after the morning wake-up call, wringing out just a few more moments of peace before facing the day.

"Just Ide," Liam said. "Green wouldn't spare any more. The scouts are stretched thinner than ever, with so many fronts to watch. I've been crisscrossing the Blacklands for weeks, but I guess Green finally took pity on me."

"I'm surprised he sent you at all, considering how he feels about me."

"I don't think he had much of a choice. Like I said, we're stretched pretty thin."

"How's it going out there?"

Liam's smile grew taut. "It's not easy. The scouts have it okay, but the rest . . . We're losing a lot of men."

"But Green knows the terrain, and the Kingswords are so much better trained . . ." It sounded like wilful denial, even to her own ears.

"They have more cavalry, and there's some kind of consumption running through our ranks. Gwylim had it, but only for a couple of weeks, thank the gods. I think we've lost more to that damn cough than to the enemy, actually. And it's cold as hell up there in the highlands. Hard to sleep."

"How often do you meet in battle?"

"Less and less. It's like . . . have you ever seen a fistfight? A professional one, I mean?"

"Oh, sure. Every time I go down to the local tavern for a quaff with the lads."

"Well, excuse me, Lady Highborn. Anyway, you can imagine what it's like if the fight goes on too long. If neither fighter lands a knockout punch, they just keep going at it, swinging and swinging, bleeding and sweating, until they're so tired they can't even really fight anymore, and all they're doing is grappling, sort of like a big messy hug. We've kind of reached that stage."

"You must be exhausted."

He shrugged. "Maybe. It doesn't matter anymore. I'm here. You're here." He wrapped his arms around her again, and she couldn't bear to pull away, not yet.

Just a little longer.

"I couldn't stop thinking about you. About that night." She could hear the smile in his voice. "It kept me warm on many a cold night, I can tell you."

Gods, it was agony. And when he leaned in to kiss her, it took every scrap of her strength to back away. This was the moment she'd been dreading. "Wait. I have to tell you something."

"Uh-oh. This doesn't sound promising." His tone was light, but Alix saw the apprehension in his eyes.

She struggled to find the words. A confusing tangle of emotions battled for dominance, dread and guilt and longing. They were familiar to her now, a constant companion ever since that night in the study. "Something happened that I think you should know about. With Erik."

He nodded. "An assassin on the walls, I know. Green told me. You weren't hurt, were you?"

His trust cut Alix to the quick. That trust had allowed him to surrender to her before he was ready. And now it lay broken in her hands, fragments of something precious she couldn't put back together.

"No, not that. He . . . Erik, he . . ." Dread was winning the emotional war. She just wanted to get it over with. "He kissed me, Liam. And . . . I kissed him back."

There was a long, torturous pause. Liam just looked at her, as though unsure whether he'd heard correctly. "I see," he said eventually.

"I didn't mean for it to happen," she heard herself saying, sickened by the triteness of her own words.

He swallowed, shifted from foot to foot. "Did you . . . Are

you . . . ?" He couldn't bring himself to finish. Pain was blooming in his eyes like a drop of ink in clear water.

"No! Nothing like that!" She thanked the gods it was the truth. "It was only a moment, but it just happened so fast . . . I don't know how to explain it. It was like . . ."

"You don't have to explain." Liam's voice was heartbreakingly flat. "I understand."

"No, you don't! You couldn't possibly, because I don't understand it myself! I've gone over it a thousand times in my head, and I know what I felt, but it doesn't make sense!"

"What did you feel?" He looked at the ground, unable to face her answer.

Damn. She shouldn't have said that. Now she was going to have to explain, and that could well make things worse. She bit her lip. "When he touched me . . . this is going to sound strange, but . . . well, he reminded me of you."

Liam stared.

"I know how crazy that is, and it's no excuse. But there was something about the way he looked at me, the way he . . ." She paused, grasping. "I don't know how to describe it, Liam, but in that moment, it was like I was kissing you."

He squeezed his eyes shut. "This isn't happening. This is a bad dream."

A stream of defensive drivel started falling from her lips. "You actually look a bit alike, you know, once you get past the hair colour. You have the same jaw, and practically the same nose, and you even have the same expressions sometimes, especially when . . ."

Alix paused. She looked carefully at Liam.

Liam looked back at her grimly. It was that expression, one she had seen so often on the face of her king, that drove it home.

"Liam . . ."

"Don't." A command, a warning, but most of all, a plea.

Her hand flew to her mouth. "You . . . you and Erik . . . you're—"

"I think it would be best if you didn't finish that thought," Liam said firmly.

"Oh no . . ." Suddenly, everything made sense. Her body had known it, though her mind had not. *Not Liam Green.*

Liam White. Her hand went from her mouth to her stomach. She nearly doubled over. "Oh, gods, I feel ill."

"*You* feel ill?" He gave a humourless laugh.

"Why didn't you tell me?" She wanted to hit him. She wanted to kiss away that look in his eyes. She wanted to crawl off into the woods and disappear.

He scowled. "Is that a serious question? You're the daughter of a Banner House, surely you don't need me to explain it to you. Besides, what difference would it have made?"

"I would have been prepared!"

"For what? Do you think he would have been any less charming? Any less . . . *royal*?"

"I don't care about that!"

"Well, then you're a fool, because, trust me, it changes everything." He turned away, rubbing his jaw roughly. He stayed like that, his back turned, for a long time.

"Liam, please." Alix could hardly speak through the ache in her throat. "Say something."

He turned around, and the pain in his eyes was more than she could bear. She was the cause of that pain. She was the one who had led him here, pushed him faster than he wanted to go, only to lose her way. *Just as Arran Green knew you would.*

"Tell me this," he said, "and be honest. You say he reminded you of me. Was that the only reason?"

She could have lied. She could have told him what he wanted to hear, and maybe they could have forgotten it ever happened. But she hadn't forced herself to come this far, to hurt him this much, only to lie in the end. "I don't know," she said. "I don't think so."

Liam nodded slowly. In that moment, he withdrew beyond her reach. The windows of his eyes went dark. Those beautiful grey eyes, so full of warmth and mischief only moments before, now a dull void. "You should go to him. He'll be waiting for you."

She stiffened. "What, I don't get a choice in this?"

"Neither of us gets a choice. Not anymore." He turned to go.

"So that's it?" It came out more sharply than she'd intended. "You're just going to walk away?"

He spun around and threw his arms wide. "What do you want from me, Alix?"

"Don't you even want to try to work this out?" She knew she was pushing him, but she couldn't help it. In her desperation, offence seemed better than surrender.

"What is there to work out?"

"It was just a kiss!"

"He's the *King of Alden*, Alix! There's no *just* anything. You know that as well as I do, so don't stand there shouting at me as if this is my fault!"

"So it's my fault? I didn't plan this, you know. It was just a moment—"

"It's always just a moment with you! You never stop to think. And I know that about you, so I should have seen this coming. I did, in a way, but I guess I thought after what happened that night in the woods . . . but that was stupid of me, wasn't it? So maybe it's my fault after all."

"Of course it's not your fault. But I can't believe you're not even willing to fight for this!"

"You don't get it, do you?" He was truly angry now. "I'm a *bastard*. You're a Black. We're in the middle of a war. This was always going to be a fight. A losing one, but idiot that I am, I was still willing to try, because . . ." He choked on the words, swallowed them down. "But this . . . you and the king . . . it's too much."

Each word was a tiny barb in her heart, cold and sharp and fletched with truth. *He's right. This was never going anywhere.* She knew that—she'd always known it—but she couldn't let go. She was a snared creature thrashing in its death throes, knowing the fight is finished, but struggling just the same. "He doesn't own me," she said helplessly.

"Of course he does," Liam said, turning to go. "He owns us all." In a few lunging strides, he was through the trees and out of view.

Alix did not even remember the walk back to the keep. She simply found herself in her room, alone. She bolted the door and collapsed on her bed. Then she did what she had sworn she would never do.

She wept.

FOURTEEN

The horses jingled and stamped restlessly, as though they could smell the coming battle. Maybe they could. Alix had heard it said that horses could smell weather approaching, so why not death? They were warhorses; they knew the sharp scent of metal, the cold press of armoured knees at their flanks. They knew what it meant to have thick white war paint smeared on their haunches. She wondered if the paint made them feel stronger, as it was supposed to. Few people really believed in the talismanic power of war paint anymore, but it was still tradition, like carrying a banner onto the field. Maybe the horses drew courage from it, the way a knight draws courage from seeing his command standard flying bravely overhead. Or maybe it just itched.

Adelbard Brown swivelled in his saddle to survey the ranks. He'd done that several times over the last quarter hour, as if to reassure himself that they were still there. His eyes stared out through the visor of his impressive gilt helm, hard and unreadable. He stayed like that for long moments before turning back around. Alix scowled at the back of his head.

"You're doing it again," Raibert Green admonished quietly.

His mount was close enough to Alix's that Lord Brown couldn't hear.

"He's making the men nervous," Alix whispered. "Why does he keep staring at them like that? Like he's trying to memorise their faces?"

"These are his lands, Alix. Surely we can excuse a bit of agitation?"

He was right, of course. Lord Brown had every reason to be worried. The Oridian host had made faster progress than they'd hoped, leaving little time to evacuate the area. Brownhold itself was safe enough for now, but the Brownlands were heavily populated, especially here in the fertile hills. Every league of territory lost to the enemy would mean one more village burned, its inhabitants driven off or slaughtered.

There will be no victory here, Alix thought. Even with the modest addition of Brownswords, the Oridians still outnumbered them a little less than three to one. The Brownlands would fall. It was not a question of if, but when. Erik knew that; they all did. The king's goal was not to defeat the enemy host, but to slow its progress, skirmishing along its edges like a small predator harassing much larger prey. He did this to give people a chance to flee, and to buy time for Arran Green and the rest of the Kingswords to dislodge the enemy from the Blacklands.

It was hardly the stuff of legend, but that didn't stop Erik from speaking of it like it was the most glorious battle of their times. He'd greeted the morning with breezy talk of their inevitable triumph, clapping Lord Brown and his daughter Rona on the shoulder as though they were about to embark on a leisurely hunt. He'd addressed the men as heroes whose songs had yet to be sung.

"A good day," he'd told Alix that morning. "A day to remember."

Alix had seen him do this before, at Three Skulls, and again at Boswyck. She'd thought him vain and naïve. But seeing him now, resplendent in his white tabard and gleaming white helm, guiding his warhorse regally down the line, Alix understood. It wasn't vanity that prompted Erik to carry himself as though he were posing for a portrait. He *was* posing for a portrait, if only in the minds of his men. He was the heroic king who would lead them to victory, for the glory of Alden. Erik understood the power of symbol.

Not that it was entirely for show. There was no mistaking the excited glint in his eyes as he drew his horse up alongside Alix's. "You look vexed, Captain," he said lightly, raising the visor of his helm. "Aren't you glad to be up and about, instead of cooped up in the castle?"

"Not quite as glad as you are, sire. I do wish you would reconsider."

A shadow flickered across Erik's features. He lowered his voice. "We've discussed this, Alix. I'll not hear it again."

She nodded resignedly. It was pointless to argue. But she couldn't pretend to like it, not when he was putting himself in danger like this.

He leaned over his horse's neck so Alix alone could hear. "I haven't tried to dissuade you from *your* duty, however much I might wish to. We both belong here, and it's no use pretending otherwise."

"I know."

His gaze softened, and he started to say something else, but Raibert Green interrupted. "Scouts, Your Majesty!"

A figure on horseback pounded down the eastern slope, and a second appeared moments later. Half a dozen other scouts prowled the hills nearby, though they were invisible to Alix's eyes. The Kingswords had nestled themselves in the winding trough of the valley, using the hills as cover. They hoped to take the Oridians from the flank, for if they confronted the host head-on, they would be slaughtered.

The lead scout arrived in a flurry of hooves and turf, his mount foaming. "They're a half mile out, Your Majesty!"

"Did they see you?"

"No, sire, I'm certain of it. They're still pursuing our decoy upcountry, and we took out the only enemy scout that could have given us away."

"Good." Erik raised his arm, signalling the archers in the hills above. Alix watched them creep closer to the summits, readying themselves for the second signal that would order the volley.

The king turned his horse and walked it to the back of the

cavalry lines. Alix, the banner lords, Rona Brown, and the rest of Erik's guard followed. This minor concession was all Erik had allowed. He wouldn't ride at the vanguard, but he would ride all the same.

Tense moments crawled by. Alix licked her lips with a dry tongue. *You can do this*, she told herself, but the thought lacked conviction. She'd never been on the front lines before. She wasn't trained for it. She had barely been tested in battle at all. Her job was to guard her king against assassins, lone men armed with bows and daggers and poison. Now Erik was about to ride straight into an army. She couldn't protect him from that. She would be lucky to protect herself. She stared down the throat of the valley, at the place where it veered sharply to the west. Just beyond that blind corner, the valley spilled out into the plains, into the enemy. She couldn't see them, and they couldn't see her, but they were there. Any moment now, Erik would order the charge, and there would be no more time to fear.

A glint of metal flashed from the summit of the eastern hill. The signal came from the scouts; the enemy was in position. The king slammed down his visor. Then he nodded, and his standard-bearer raised the White banner high.

The northern sky darkened as a thick volley of arrows arced out from the hilltops. It was an awesome sight. Like a flock of slender birds moving as one, the arrows reached the apex of their flight, seeming to hang, suspended, before plunging down and out of view. Screams drifted on the wind. A second volley leapt after the first, sizzling through the air. More shouts, followed by the panicked call of a horn. A third and final time the sky bristled with death, and then Erik drew his sword. He glanced at Alix, winked, and let out a cry.

The Kingswords surged.

Alix rode as close to Erik as she dared. Raibert and Lord Brown flanked him on the opposite side, young Rona hard upon their heels. The rest of the cavalry, two hundred horses, thundered before them; the valley shuddered beneath the avalanche of their hooves. They burst onto the plain to find the Oridians in disarray, their ranks swarming as they tried to reposition their defences. Before the men even had time to set their pikes, the Kingswords were upon them.

Alix had never been trained to fight on horseback. All she could do was look to Erik for guidance. The king crouched in his stirrups, his body coiled to absorb the force of the blows he would deliver. Alix leaned forward a little in the saddle, doing her best to imitate Erik's posture. Then they crashed into the enemy lines, and there was no more time to think. She bore down on the nearest target and swung.

The impact nearly threw her down. Her sword bit deep into the man's breastplate, arresting her forward momentum so suddenly that she fell back in the saddle, her shoulder wrenching painfully. She barely managed to pull her blade free before she lost it.

First lesson: Don't follow through.

Bodies swam all around her. She lashed out blindly, using short, clipped blows. She aimed for necks and limbs instead of the sturdier core. That worked much better, and soon she had a steady rhythm. She hacked her way through the enemy ranks, blood spattering her greaves and sparkling off her blade. The carnage should have appalled her, but instead, she felt strangely removed from it all, looking down from above like some passing god. The men she cut down were faceless, fleeting, no more real to her than a straw man set up in the yard.

Suddenly, her horse screamed and heaved to the side. Alix managed to swing her leg over just in time to avoid being pinned as the courser went down. She leapt away from the beast and rolled to her feet, sword at the ready. She caught a glimpse of white: Erik, still heading west. She charged after him, engaging the first Oridian that got in her way.

She was lucky in her foe. The man was wide-eyed with fear, and he clutched his spear as though she meant to steal it from him. When he dove at her, she struck his weapon in half, then lashed out with her shield, catching him under the chin. His head snapped back, and Alix lunged, thrusting the end of her blade into his throat. The encounter lasted less than five breaths. It was a welcome reminder that unlike Alden, the Trionate of Oridia swelled its ranks by pressing untrained peasants into military service. Most of these men weren't professional soldiers. They were farmers and bakers and fishmongers. Blood-weapons or no, they were at a serious disadvantage.

Alix brought down a second foe almost as quickly as the first, and with each kill, her confidence grew. She let the bloodbond guide her hand. Her blade was a part of her, weightless and sure, an extension of her own reflexes and intuition. She slashed and parried and lunged and blocked without conscious thought. Even so, her progress was frustratingly slow. No sooner had she felled one opponent than another would appear to take his place. She could hear the cries of horses as cavalry went down all around her. She needed to find Erik.

She shoved a dying man off her blade and paused to reorient herself. The press of bodies grew denser by the moment as the Kingswords continued to pour out of the hills. Spears stabbed the air, and naked blades flashed in every direction. Even if Alix managed to avoid engaging anyone directly, she was liable to be skewered by friend or foe.

Between the heaving bodies, she spied the distinctive gilt helm of Adelbard Brown. She made for him, doing her best to see in three directions at once. An Oridian charged toward her, but she knocked him aside with her shield and kept running. She was close to Brown now, and she could see he was in trouble. He staggered backward as he fended off an ogre of a man armed with a two-handed greatsword. The Oridian looked to be an officer; he was covered in heavy plate from the waist up. His legs, though, were only protected by tassets, presenting a soft target from the rear. Alix took him unawares, slashing the backs of his knees. He buckled, and Brown's blade crashed into his head.

Lord Brown gave a brief nod of thanks before engaging a new foe, leaving Alix free to move on. Erik should be nearby; Brown wouldn't have strayed far from the king if he could help it. She spotted his daughter Rona nearby, hacking away from atop her destrier. Alix started toward her, and soon the king himself came into view. He was on foot, his tabard sprayed with blood, but it didn't seem to be his. His horse lay dead at his side, and he kept close to the animal's corpse, using its bulk to shield his flank as he fought.

Alix closed with his other flank, feeling more comfortable than she had since the battle began. It was relatively calm here inside the ring of Erik's knights; the king and his bodyguard had the luxury of facing their foes one at a time. Even so, Alix found little honour in her kills. The first Oridian to break through the knights was a mere boy, fourteen at most, and Alix cut him down in a heartbeat. The second was just as green, judging by his white-knuckled grip and white-rimmed eyes. He died with a sob on his lips. Meanwhile, Erik tangled with a real soldier, a man in full plate armed with a fearsome-looking mace. The king hunkered cautiously behind his shield, and it was only then Alix remembered that he was bereft of his bloodblade. The sword in his hand was ordinary steel, slow and heavy and awkward.

Just as she pivoted to help, a pair of Oridians rushed at Rona Brown. The young knight opened up the shoulder of the first and crossed swords with the second. The wounded Oridian barrelled on as though he hadn't even noticed. He came at Alix, swinging with a strength he was no longer entitled to. She was so surprised that she almost didn't put enough into her parry; his blade jarred to a halt barely a handspan above her collarbone. She shoved him back, but no sooner had he regained his footing than he swung again, totally undaunted by the bloody trench pumping its contents over his sword arm. Alix deflected the blow and followed it with a lunge that bit just below the ribs. He was too far out of reach for the blade to sink very deep, but it should have been enough to double him over. It didn't even slow him down. He slashed at Alix again and again, his exertion all but invisible on his face. Dead eyes stared out at her, glassy and dark like the surface of a well. Those eyes turned her guts to water.

She had all she could do to keep him at arm's length. He just kept closing in, as though he were trying to tackle her bodily to the ground. She got through his defences more than once, but no matter how much blood she drew, he didn't even flinch.

Panic welled up inside her. What was *wrong* with this man?

Eventually he found an opening, and he crashed into her, toppling her easily under his weight. A gauntleted fist clamped around her throat. Pain arced from her chest to her skull. Alix gasped and flailed. She tried to club at him with the hilt of her sword, but she couldn't get the leverage. Her chest bucked in a futile effort to draw air.

"Green!" Erik's voice, tinged with desperation.

"I'm coming!"

She could hear Erik struggling with his foe, cursing and grappling, his fury a surreal counterpoint to the dispassionate face looming above her. The Oridian's lifeless eyes seemed to grow, swallowing up her entire view until all she could see was a reflection of her own death. And then something crashed into them, knocking the weight off her. She gasped. A blade sang, heavy and wet. Alix rolled onto her side and found herself staring at a severed head, as expressionless in death as it had been in life. Some part of her registered Erik moving away from the corpse, but then blackness stole the edges of her sight. She lay still, trembling, coughing, while the fight went on around her.

For a moment, she lost track of everything but the burning in her lungs. And then, quite suddenly, the sounds of battle receded. Alix struggled to her feet, one hand wrapped gingerly around her throat. Erik and his knights were a good thirty feet away, and the Oridians seemed to be falling back.

Strange.

The Kingswords were supposed to herd the enemy northward, away from the hills, giving themselves space to retreat back into the valley. But the Oridians were moving west, meaning they'd been pressed from a second front—to the north, maybe, or the south. But how was that possible?

A few stray cheers went up from the surrounding Kingswords. Erik stood triumphant, his helm tucked under his arm, flush with victory and unexpected providence. Alix approached him on shaky legs. "Thank you, Your Majesty. I guess we're even now."

"Not yet," Erik said brightly. "I seem to recall something about you lying on top of me and stripping off my armour." Beside him, poor young Rona blushed to the tops of her ears and beat a hasty retreat.

Alix snorted. "I should slap you."

"Technically, that would be treason."

Raibert Green appeared a moment later. He had a long gash on his jaw, just beneath the edge of his half helm, but it didn't look deep. "I'm glad to see you're both all right." He took in Alix's face with an amused expression. "Why, Lady Alix, you look radiant. Blood is your colour."

Alix swiped a hand across her cheek; it came away smeared with gore. She shook her head. "What is it about battle that turns sensible men into buffoons?"

"It rather depends on the outcome, I think," Erik said, sobering. "I'm relieved you're all right, Alix. I don't know what the Trionate feeds its soldiers, but that *thing* that got hold of you was monstrous strong."

"And determined," she said, fingering her neck. "He was bleeding to death the entire time we were fighting, but he just kept coming. It was like he thought killing me would end the whole war . . ." She trailed off, shuddering.

Erik frowned into the distance. "And what happened to the Oridians? Not to sound ungrateful, but I don't understand why they turned tail and fled like that. Green, did you see what happened?"

"Another force took the field," Raibert said, pointing north. "I saw some of them, and they didn't look like ours."

"Then whose were they?"

Just then, Alix spotted one of them, a knight giving orders to his men. Dark, unruly hair spilled out beneath a helm she would have known anywhere, for she had seen it hanging above the mantel at Blackhold since birth.

"Rig!"

With a joyful cry, Alix flew into the arms of her brother.

FIFTEEN

† "Gods be praised." Rig clutched her so tightly it hurt. "I didn't know if you were alive or dead."

"Nor I you." Alix shook violently, joy and relief crashing into blood already spiked with the rush of battle. She clung to Rig as if he were a stone in the tides, heedless of who might see her so undone.

"Hush," he murmured, stroking her hair. His touch was her father's, and her mother's too. His voice was the sound of memory, and his skin the smell of home. Alix gave herself a moment to soak it in, feeling truly safe for the first time in months. Then she drew a deep, shuddering breath and released him.

Rig laughed, though his own eyes were shining. "Gods, you look a fright. Here." He handed her a square of cloth to wipe away the blood and tears.

"You keep a handkerchief under your armour?"

"A true knight always keeps a handkerchief on hand." When Alix gave him a sceptical look, he added, "Actually, it's a bandage, but let's keep that between us."

She choked out something between a laugh and a sob. "Same old Rig."

But that wasn't quite true. Rig looked different. Even through plate and mail, Alix could see that her brother was stronger, more rugged. His beard was long and scruffy, and his coal-black hair was almost to his shoulders. His eyes were coal too, hard and black, with a fierce gleam that hadn't been there before. She'd seen a similar change in Liam. She wondered if Rig could see it in her too.

"Riggard Black, you unconscionable laggard! Where have you been?"

Rig grinned as he turned to clasp arms with the king. "A fine greeting for the man who just saved your hide."

"Rubbish! We were only toying with them. Isn't that right, Green?"

Raibert smiled indulgently. "As you say, Your Majesty."

Erik clapped Rig's shoulder. "Bloody good to see you all the same. I was beginning to think you'd gotten lost."

"Alas, you're not rid of me yet."

Alix watched the exchange with a mixture of pride and bemusement. She'd always known that her brother and the king were friends; they were nearly the same age, and Father had made a point of taking Rig to Erroman often, to rub shoulders with his fellow heirs. But like all of Rig's dealings at court, his relationship with the king was something that took place a world away, beyond her ken or caring. She hadn't seen the two of them together since she was a child. It felt strange to listen to them talking to each other like brothers. Strange, and strangely satisfying.

Rig sobered quickly. "I can't tell you how relieved I am to see you well, Your Majesty."

"I have your sister to thank for that," Erik said. At Rig's puzzled look, he added, "We have much to discuss, but we can't do it here. We may have caught the Oridians unawares, but it won't take them long to realise they outnumber us. They'll be back, and we had best not be here when that happens. How many are you?"

"A little over six hundred."

"Cavalry?"

"About half."

"Good. We've a dire need for horses. Speaking of which . . ." Erik called for a squire.

Rig, meanwhile, turned to one of his knights, a man Alix didn't know. "Morris, tell the men to form up. We're getting out of here."

Commander Morris nodded smartly. As he walked away, his squire raised the Black banner, crying, "Blackswords!"

"Not anymore," Rig said. "We're Kingswords now."

They left the serious business until after the meal, as was proper. It was a tight fit in the king's pavilion. Erik sat at the centre of his table, flanked on either side by Lords Green and Brown. Across from him sat Alix, Rig, and Rona Brown. The servants had all they could do to squeeze between the table and the canvas walls, but somehow they managed. They kept the food hot and the wine flowing as Rig demonstrated his famous appetite for one and all. Alix shook her head as her brother helped himself to yet another plate of fruit. He'd been on the run for months, but still—manners were manners. Mother would have been appalled.

"We played cat and mouse for weeks," Rig was saying, his dagger flashing as he carved the pit from his peach. "Every time we tried to come out of the marsh, the enemy was waiting for us. And then, all of a sudden, they weren't. We had no idea where they'd gone, but we didn't care—we jumped at the chance to get to high ground."

"That must have been when Arran Green arrived with the Kingswords," Erik said.

Rig bit a slice of peach off the tip of his knife. "I'd assumed it was you."

"Alas, I wasn't able to ride at the time."

"Oh?"

"Your sister broke my leg," Erik said severely.

Alix *tsk*ed. "I was indirectly responsible for your leg being broken. Hardly the same thing."

"Quibbling," Erik said with a dismissive wave.

Rig gave them both a funny look, but did not otherwise comment. "Anyway, I thought about sending scouts to locate whoever was giving the enemy trouble, but I couldn't spare the men. I barely had enough to watch our flanks. I figured our armies would meet up sooner or later anyway. We laid low for a while, healing up and resupplying where we could. I even managed to recruit a few able bodies. And then the gods saw fit to strike the enemy stupid, and we pounced."

Erik arched a red-gold eyebrow. "Meaning?"

"The Oridians have overstretched themselves. Their supply lines are exposed. We've been hitting at them relentlessly ever since they left the Scions. By the time they reach Brownhold, they'll be hungry and spent—if they get there at all."

Erik leaned back in his chair, a wondering expression on his face. "Do you mean to tell me you've been pitting your six hundred against a host of four thousand? And succeeding? Remarkable!"

Rig sipped his wine. "It's a question of tactics. We're not strong enough to confront the enemy directly, but we've become quite adept at hit-and-run strikes—taking out their scouting parties, raiding their camps, targeting their supply lines, that sort of thing. Some of the men disapprove of such devices—they've got fool-headed ideas about glory and honour—but I'm no martyr. I do what I can with the resources at my disposal, and no more."

"You're a hero, Lord Black," Erik said. "Few men would show the courage and resourcefulness that you have. It seems to be in the blood."

Alix smiled down at her plate. She could feel the king's eyes on her. And her brother's eyes on both of them.

"You certainly did us a great turn today," said Green. "You've proved that even a small force can take the enemy by surprise and prompt him to do something rash. That is comforting, given how much our own strategy rests on that very assumption."

"In theory, that's true," Rig said, "though we got lucky today. We didn't come across many thralls. Most of them were probably in the vanguard."

The others exchanged confused glances. "What's a thrall?" Erik asked.

"That's what we've been calling the bewitched fighters." More puzzled looks. Taking in their expressions, Rig's mouth tightened grimly. "So you haven't faced one yet. In that case, I'm afraid I have some grave news, Your Majesty." He put down his wine cup and pushed it away. "It seems the rumours about the Priest are true. He does wield some kind of dark power over his men, or some of them, at any rate. It lets him control them like puppets. Eeriest thing I've ever seen."

Alix's supper churned in her belly. She thought she knew where this was going. So did Erik, judging by his sudden pallor.

"We can't prove it's the Priest," Rig went on, "but I don't see any other explanation. These men are definitely under some kind of spell. They feel no pain, and no fear. You can wound them as many times as you like and it barely slows them down. Imagine fighting someone who puts no value on his own life. The conventional rules of swordplay just don't apply. All your training, your experience—useless. Worse than useless. If you try to anticipate them, you're dead. They strike when they ought to fall back, use the sword when they should use the shield. And it's all but impossible to incapacitate them. You can cut off an arm—it doesn't matter. You have to kill, and kill instantly, or they'll keep coming until one of you is dead."

"The man who tried to choke me today," Alix said quietly.

"Yes." The king's eyes were chips of ice.

Rig sighed. "So you have seen one, then. I killed a thrall myself today. So far, they're not that common, but the men say they're turning up more and more."

"But how is that possible?" Raibert Green looked half fearful, half disbelieving. "We've been hearing rumours about the Priest for years, but I've never put any stock in them. After all . . . *magic*? Who can credit that?"

"What about the bloodbond?" Rona Brown gestured to where her sword lay propped in a corner of the tent. "It turns an inert object into a part of your body, maybe even your soul. What is that if not magic?"

"Alchemy is not magic, my dear," her father said. "It's mysterious, to be sure, but not supernatural."

The young heiress frowned. "With respect, Father, alchemy is just another word for something we don't understand."

"Magic or no," said Green, "these thralls are real. I saw one with my own eyes. The man who attacked Alix had been hacked half to pieces, yet he did not even flinch. His Majesty had to lop off the thing's head before it was over."

"What else can you tell us about them, Lord Black?" Erik asked.

"Nothing for the moment, except that we presume the Priest rides with that host. I've promised a thousand gold crowns and a title to any man who brings me his head."

"A bargain at ten times the price, if all that you say is true." Erik shook his head. "Soldiers who feel no fear or pain . . ."

"Gods preserve us," Adelbard Brown muttered.

"They'd better," Rig said. "One of those abominations is worth three ordinary soldiers on the field. If you thought we were outnumbered before . . ."

"And they still have their fifty thousand at the border, just waiting to swoop down on our carcasses," Brown said. Alix's supper moved again, this time perilously close to her throat. The thought of their *carcasses* almost pushed her over the edge. "We're outnumbered and outflanked," Brown continued, in case there was anyone at the table not yet contemplating his doom.

"Meaning Lord Black's raiding tactics are more important than ever," Erik said. He paused, steepling his fingers. He was brewing an idea, Alix could tell. If he held to form, it would be more vision than detail, but that was well and proper for a king, as far as she was concerned. Let his lords and knights fill in the particulars. "If I were to allocate more men to your command, would it hamper your effectiveness?"

Rig considered. "I don't think we could conduct our style of operation with more than, say, eight hundred men. Half to strike, half in reserve in case things get ugly."

"Eight hundred it is, then. You shall have two hundred of mine, along with my blessing and thanks for your continued efforts. We can discuss division of labour tomorrow."

"Thank you, Your Majesty. And what are your plans?"

"We'll have to deal with my brother eventually, but for now, we will continue as you see us, buying time for the Greys to muster, and for General Green to clear out the Blacklands. When that is done, we'll be ready to march for Erroman."

"And when you do, the Black banner shall be yours," Rig said gravely.

Erik nodded. "I count on it." He rose, and the lords did the same, bowing their heads before taking their leave. Alix hovered near the tent flap, intending to take her place outside, but Erik said, "Go, be with your brother. Commander Elan can watch my tent."

Murmuring a heartfelt thanks, she slipped out into the night.

Rig was waiting for her. "Let's find someplace private to talk. I want to hear everything that's happened since you left Blackhold, and I doubt we'll have much chance later."

"Down by the river," she suggested.

The riverbank smelled of mud and moss and new spring leaves. Rig plonked himself down with his usual abandon, small stones scraping noisily beneath him. Alix sat beside him and drew her knees up under her chin. For a fleeting moment, it felt like they were children again, sitting on the banks of the Black River—before the fall of Blackhold, and the massacre at Boswyck. Before the war, and the Great Fever . . . before, before, before, when things were simple.

"So," Rig said.

"So."

"Things aren't going exactly the way we imagined, are they?"

"Not exactly."

"I'm going to have a hell of a time marrying you off now."

She smiled. "Because I'm the king's bodyguard, or because we're utterly ruined?"

"Either. Both. Gods only know when Erik is going to let you go. Not anytime soon, by the looks of it."

"I'll bet I can still hook an Elderfir. Or a Stonegate, maybe."

Rig sighed theatrically. "If only I had your lovely face. I think the best I could do at this point would be a Middlemarch."

Alix laughed heartily at that, and it felt good. Prospective marriage matches had been a running joke with them since they were children. At first it was a means of deflecting their mother's constant machinations; later, a lighthearted way of coping with their declining prospects. It was comforting to slip back into the old routine, if only for a moment.

Then silence fell, and the shadows crept back in.

"Have you had any word of Blackhold?" she asked.

"No." He stared out at the river, his strong features sketched in moonlight. His jaw formed a square line, and his heavy eyebrows sat dark and brooding. "It's killing me, Allie. To not even know if our home still stands . . . I failed our people, and I don't know how I can ever redeem myself as their lord."

She grabbed his hand. It was hard and rough beneath her fingers. "You didn't fail. Everyone escaped with their lives, thanks to you."

"Everyone at Blackhold, maybe. But after that, I didn't do a thing to stop those bastards from burning their way through our lands. How many people did they slaughter? And how many more will die of deprivation?"

"You couldn't have stopped them."

"Maybe not, but it's no comfort."

She squeezed his hand, her chest aching.

"So much for restoring the Black name."

"Don't say that," Alix said fiercely. "We will. We are." She needed to believe that, now more than ever. Maybe the war should have driven that desire from her, rendered it small and insignificant, but it hadn't. Instead, she felt it more keenly than ever, as if some part of her feared that it was the only mark she could hope to leave on the world, and she was running out of time. "Erik said it himself. You're a hero."

He didn't even hear her. "I keep telling myself that I'll have my revenge. First on the Oridians, and then on Tomald *fucking* White."

Alix winced at the coarse language. In spite of their reputation among the other Banner Houses, the Blacks had never been given to tavern talk. Then again, perhaps she shouldn't be surprised. She'd already noticed subtle changes in her brother. His eyes glinted with steel, and his deep voice was edged with something dark. At supper, she'd noticed the calluses on his hands, and the way his forearms moved with muscle as he broke bread. And when Erik had spoken of Tom, of his spies and assassins, the expression that came over Rig . . . He'd looked half feral.

"Part of me can't believe it," he went on, "and part of me feels like we all saw it coming. Tom was always erratic. And deep down, he thought he'd be the better king. You could see it in his eyes. Hells, you could hear it in his voice. *Frivolous,* he always used to say. Anything Erik did or said—*frivolous*. The snivelling little bootlick."

"Bootlick? Prince Tomald?" The Raven had always struck her as haughty.

"Bootlick," Rig repeated with a scowl, "at least where his father was concerned. After Erik and King Osrik fell out, Tom saw his chance to be the favourite son at last. He did everything he could to earn his father's favour. I swear, sometimes he went out of his way to make Erik look bad. Not that it ever worked. All Erik had to do was flash that smile of his, and he was forgiven anything. The Raven would always end up looking the fool, and Erik none the wiser."

A hate that strong can't be invisible. Maybe Erik had been right after all. Maybe he really had been the only one not to see it. "I don't understand how anyone could hate Erik," she said.

"Oh, I don't think Tom hates him. I think he idolises him. Most of the time, anyway."

"That doesn't make sense. Why would he want to destroy someone he idolises?"

Rig smiled ruefully. "Ah, Allie, love, sometimes I forget how young you are."

"You're six years older than me, Rig."

"It's an important six years."

"If you say so." She hugged her knees. "All I know is that it's never stopped us from understanding each other. Erik and Tom aren't even two years apart, but it might as well be twenty."

"Some siblings are closer than others, I guess."

"I guess," she agreed dryly. Her brother had always had a talent for understatement.

Rig paused, glancing at her out of the corner of his eye. "Seeing how we're so close, dear sister, why don't you tell me what's going on between you and the king?"

That caught her off balance. She shrugged, trying for nonchalance. "I'm his bodyguard."

He snorted. "That's not what I'm talking about and you know it. Come on, Allie. I have years of experience watching Erik flirt, but the way he looks at you—that's something else entirely."

Alix chewed her lip. She could tell him about the kiss, but that wouldn't explain much. The only way he could truly understand was if she told him everything. And so she did. It felt good to confide in someone.

"You shameless little vixen!" Rig's laughter ricocheted off the trees. "In the *woods*, in the middle of an army camp! Ardin's flame, Allie, that's bold, even for you."

"Keep your bloody voice down, will you?"

Rig swiped at his eyes, still laughing. "So you dallied a little with this Liam chap. What does that have to do with Erik?"

She groaned. "Everything. He's . . ." She hesitated. "Rig, you have to promise never to repeat this."

He raised his eyebrows. "This should be good."

"Promise me."

"All right, I promise."

Alix said the words aloud for the first time, if only in a whisper. "Liam is Erik's brother."

Rig looked at her blankly. "What do you mean?"

"Just what I said."

"That can't be."

"No? Think, Rig."

He paused. "A bastard? Are you sure?"

"I didn't figure it out until later, but I'm positive." She spoke so quietly that she could barely hear her own voice. No doubt many powerful people had gone to great trouble to preserve that secret, and the gods only knew what would happen to Liam if it got out.

Rig's eyes widened as he processed the full implications of this revelation. "And you and he . . . and then Erik . . . Oh, *Allie.*"

She sighed. "Indeed."

"So what now?"

She picked up a stone and tossed it into the brooding water. She had no answer to that. Erik hadn't tried to kiss her again, and she hadn't encouraged him. What happened with Liam still haunted her, and until she was able to put it behind her, she didn't dare embark on something new with Erik, however tempting the prospect. And it *was* tempting—achingly so. Her insides fluttered every time he looked at her *that way*, the way Rig had noticed at dinner. But she didn't want to rush into anything, not this time. She had promised herself not to make the same mistake with Erik that she had made with Liam.

"Do you love him?" Rig asked.

"Which one?"

He winced. "*Shit*, Allie. Either of them, I suppose."

"I don't know what I feel. I care for both of them, deeply. Erik is everything I could ask for, and then some. When I'm with him, it feels so natural, like we belong together. The idea of taking that further . . . I can't tell you how tempting it is. But Liam . . . He's rooted so deep, it's like he's a part of me now. I can feel him inside, somewhere down here." She gestured at herself.

Rig eyed the position of her hand, hovering over her lap. "Please tell me we're talking about your guts."

"Rig."

"Sorry."

"I feel like I'm being pulled in two directions at once, and it's tearing me apart. It's like this damn war. I know my duty is here, by the king's side, and yet I can't help feeling like I should be at the front, fighting with my comrades. I want both. I *need* both." She threw another rock, listened as it clattered coldly off the shore. "That sounds childish, I suppose."

Rig was quiet for a long moment before answering. "You've never really taken much time to think about what you want, Allie. You've always just gone where the wind takes you, and that's been okay, up until now. You're young, and I've always trusted that you'll find your path eventually, even if you take a few wrong turns along the way. But this is different. You need to be careful. Erik is the *king*. And Liam . . ."

"Liam is no less complicated. He's Erik's brother."

"No, he isn't." Rig paused to let that sink in. "Look, I haven't pressed marriage on you, even though I probably should have, because I want you to be happy, and besides— I'm hardly setting an example myself. But I'm a banner lord, and I have responsibilities. So do you, and it's past time we faced up to them. Even if Liam is a son of Osrik, he's still a bastard. It can't happen, Allie."

"I know." Sighing, she added, "Anyway, I don't think you have to worry about that. I'm fairly certain Liam will never speak to me again."

Rig flicked his eyes skyward. "You and your drama."

She scowled, but when he put his arm around her, she let him gather her close, just like he used to do when she was a child. "You just tell me if you need any brotherly assistance," Rig said. "I don't know about this Liam, but I outweigh Erik by at least two stone."

"Erik says hitting the king counts as treason."

"It's that or marry a Middlemarch. I think I'll take the treason, frankly."

Alix laughed, letting her head fall back against Rig's shoulder so that she gazed up at the glittering sky. The stars burned brightly tonight, without a single wisp of cloud to soften their splendour. Their inscrutable patterns revealed the future, it was said, though it was written in a language long forgotten. Alix didn't need to read the stars to know that there would be dark days ahead, darker even than those that had gone before. But for the first time since she left Blackhold, she felt she had everything she needed to get her through.

She had family.

SIXTEEN

"Give me a week, Your Majesty, and I'll see it
done. The enemy will ride straight into your arms."
Rig started to bow, but Erik was having none of it; they
clasped arms instead.

"Let Olan be your sign, Lord Black."

Rig grinned. "Courage has never lacked in my family.
Wisdom . . . there's another matter."

"In that case," Erik said, "let Eldora be your sign."

"I'll try, but she doesn't seem to fancy me." So saying, Rig
slung himself into his saddle. Alix reached up and took his
hand, and he gave her fingers a reassuring squeeze. Then he
wheeled his horse around and joined his knights.

He'll be fine, she told herself. *He's been doing this for
months.* Still, she couldn't help picturing the dead eyes of the
Oridian soldier who had tried to choke her two days before.
How many more had the Priest bewitched? And what if he
could turn his sorcery on his enemies? It didn't bear thinking
about.

Erik headed back to his pavilion while the Blackswords
formed up. About two days northeast of here, they would
come across the enemy encampment. Rig's job was to herd

the Oridians, slowly and subtly, toward the Kingswords. They had chosen their battlefield carefully, and once again, the Kingswords would rely on the element of surprise to keep them alive. To preserve that advantage, Rig and Erik had each assigned a small army of scouts to track and kill their enemy counterparts. It was exactly the sort of mission Alix would have excelled at—except that she had other, more pressing duties now.

She watched until Rig and his men were little more than a dark smudge on the horizon before following Erik's path to his pavilion. Stepping through the flap, she paused to let her eyes adjust to the relative gloom, and gradually, she took in a scene of regal disarray. Erik's cot was a jumble, the furs cast carelessly into a pile in a corner. A half-empty bottle of wine stood open on his writing table, the surface of which had been disfigured by globs of beeswax from the dozens of tapers that had burned the night through. An untouched plate of fruit was beginning to attract tiny flies. At the centre of it all, a riot of maps lay scattered across the dining table, completely obscuring its surface. Erik had banished his servants from the tent the previous afternoon, adamant that nothing should disrupt the military planning. Their absence showed. Though the king himself was always immaculate—clothing crisp and fresh, red-gold hair pulled back in a short, tidy tail—his fastidiousness was confined to his person. Left to his own devices, Erik was as orderly as a tornado.

Oblivious to the chaos, the king leaned over his pile of maps, frowning. "I wish we had more cavalry."

"We don't need them." Alix joined him at the table. "If we do this right, we can pin them between the Kingfisher and the hills, just here. The riverbend is the perfect choke point. Having too many horses would compromise the archers."

"Perhaps, but I'd still rather have a reserve, especially if the vanguard folds more quickly than we anticipated."

He had a point. A second wave of horses would help hold the enemy down. Alix chewed her lip in thought. "We have a week. Maybe we should try commandeering horses from some of these farms?" She spread her fingers over the map, gesturing at a clutch of farmsteads just to the south of their position. "The enemy may have gotten to them already, but it's worth trying."

"That's very beautiful," Erik said, randomly. Puzzled, Alix followed his gaze.

He was looking at the ring on her little finger, the one Liam had given her—how long ago? *A lifetime.*

"It's nothing," she said, straightening.

"Wait." Erik reached out and took her hand in both of his. Was it fear that spiked her pulse, or his touch? Maybe both. "It looks familiar." He turned her hand gently, letting the light glide over the finely wrought ivy leaves. His eyes narrowed.

Now it was definitely fear that seized her. Was it possible he'd seen it before? Surely fate couldn't be so cruel?

"It reminds me of a ring my mother used to have. It's not exactly the same, but I'd be willing to bet it came from the same craftsman. Where did you get it?"

"It belongs to a friend," she said as casually as she could manage. "I'm . . . sort of borrowing it."

"She has excellent taste." Erik let her fingers slip through his before turning back to his map.

Silently, Alix let out the breath she'd been holding. Satisfied that Erik's attention was elsewhere, she brought her hand up close, studying the ring. She'd grown so used to wearing it that she almost never looked at it anymore. Instead, she played with it compulsively, especially when she thought of Liam. She wondered if Erik was right, if it was indeed of the same make as some of Queen Hestia's jewellery. If so, it could hardly be coincidence. Alix didn't know much about Liam's mother, but judging from his accent, she had been of common stock. It was highly unlikely that she would possess anything of such fine craftsmanship as befitted a queen—unless it had been a gift from a king.

"Erik?" Alix heard herself speaking before she'd made a conscious decision to do so. He looked up at her expectantly; she had no choice but to forge ahead. "May I ask you a personal question?"

Amusement tugged at the corner of his mouth. "Of course you may, Alix." *We've shared more than that*, his eyes reminded her.

"Why didn't you tell me Liam was your brother?" Her cheeks stung even as she spoke. It was impertinent. Outrageous, even. She had no right to ask, no right to know. And if he should wonder why she'd suddenly brought it up . . .

Erik stared. Had she known him less well, she might not have noticed his shock, for he reined it in so masterfully that it was gone almost before it appeared. "Did Liam tell you that?"

"No. I figured it out on my own. Eventually." Even now, her throat ached at the memory.

Erik regarded her for a long moment, a hint of anger in his eyes. Then he surprised her by saying, "Perhaps I should have. The two of you are friends, and I suppose it was inevitable that you would find out. But I've grown accustomed to secrecy where Liam is concerned, for his safety and mine."

"He wouldn't say it, even after I challenged him." Erik needed to know that. If the secret was out, it was none of Liam's doing.

Erik nodded. "He has always been discreet. One day I'll tell him how much I appreciate that." The anger faded from his eyes, replaced by a contemplative look. "You know, seeing you and Rig together, I can't help but wonder if Liam and I might have had something like that, given the chance." He sighed. "I may never know, and I have only myself to blame."

"What do you mean?"

"Let's just say I didn't react especially well to the news that I had an illegitimate brother." He flashed a tight smile. "I was young. Hotheaded."

"How young?" Alix knew she should drop it before she gave herself away, but she couldn't resist.

"Seventeen. Liam would have been . . . what, eleven? I overheard Father talking to his first counsel about a boy whose mother had just died. Father wanted Highmount's advice as to whether he should take the boy in."

"What did Highmount say?"

"He was against it. He brought up that old yarn about Ysur the Bastard almost taking the crown. 'A hundred years is not so long in the public memory, Your Majesty.' " Erik's impersonation of Highmount was stiff and pompous, leaving little doubt as to what he thought of the first counsel's advice.

But Alix couldn't help feeling that Highmount had a point. It might seem like ancient history, but the White War was still a scar on the nation's body politic. Ysur's rebellion had been brief, bloody, and very nearly successful. Men like Albern Highmount could hardly be blamed for concluding that royal bastards were not a matter to be taken lightly. Doubtless several had been sired since the White War, but they were kept secret—or not kept at all.

"That's how I figured it out," Erik continued. "There was only one reason Highmount would bring up Ysur the Bastard. This *boy* was my father's son. I was outraged. I barged into the room and demanded answers. The conversation did not go well." Even now, Erik's voice grew taut with anger.

So that was it! Alix fought to keep her surprise from showing. The infamous rift between the king and the crown prince, a rupture so public, so toxic, that the entire realm knew of it. Court gossip had never settled on an explanation, but all agreed that the relationship had never recovered. To think it was over *Liam* . . .

"I was furious that he would betray my mother, sickly as she was. To leave his ailing wife and children back at home while he sought his pleasure in the arms of another woman—it was unforgivable." Erik paused, sighing. "At least I thought so at the time."

"You obviously won the argument. He didn't take Liam in."

Erik closed his eyes briefly, as though the memory pained him. "He never spoke of Liam again. He abandoned one son to appease another, but by then it was too late. I never forgave him."

Alix wondered if Erik knew what had become of his brother after that. And then he ran a hand over his face and shook his head, and she had her answer. "It wasn't your fault," she blurted.

Erik tensed, his eyes guarded. "What do you mean?"

"What happened with Liam's stepfather. You couldn't have known."

"Liam discussed his stepfather with you?"

"You get to know your comrades pretty well out there on the road. People will tell you just about anything to pass the time." It was only half a lie.

Erik nodded absently. "I didn't realise what I had done until a couple of years later, when my father started going into decline, and I began handling his affairs." His gaze dropped to the table, anger mingled with shame. "To this day, I wonder if I was the first to hear of the beatings, or if my father knew and just did nothing."

"And when you found out?"

"I was wracked with guilt, of course. How not? I'd condemned my own brother to . . ." He trailed off.

"It wasn't your fault," she said again.

He didn't seem to hear. "I knew I needed to do something, but I didn't dare bring him to the palace. Perhaps if I'd had the courage to confront my father again, tell him I'd changed my mind . . . But by then we were barely speaking. So I called upon the only man I thought I could trust."

"Arran Green," she said, the last piece falling into place.

He smiled wryly. "Out of the forge and onto the anvil, perhaps."

Alix's memory returned to Greenhold, to Erik peppering her with questions about her stern commander. She'd wondered why he was so curious. Now she understood. "Liam was happy with Green. He told me so himself."

"He would be happier if he were a knight, I'll warrant. Green should have consulted me before he dismissed Liam. I would not have allowed such a blow to his honour, even if it does keep him out of harm's way. I'll see to that too, when I can."

"He'll be grateful. The Kingswords are his family. You made the right choice."

"Bit of a bother about the war, though," Erik said dryly.

"There is that."

He sighed and stretched expansively. The all-night planning session was catching up with him. Alix must have been tired too, because she found herself fixated by the way his broad shoulders moved as he stretched. Thankfully, he didn't notice. Instead, he seemed to be taking in his surroundings for the first time. "Merciful Nine, it's a disgraceful mess in here!"

She hid a smile. "Shall I send for the servants?"

"I think you'd better." They rose together, and he took her

hand. "I find myself thanking you again, Alix. You should be careful—I could get used to burdening you with my sighs and woes."

"It's no burden. It's a privilege to have your confidence."

"You've earned it," he said, his eyes filling with warmth. He hadn't let go of her hand.

She could have pulled away, made her excuses, and fled, but she didn't. Maybe she was testing herself—the race of her pulse, the shallow draw of her breath, the sudden tilt of her insides. *Does it compare? Do I want him less, or more?* He seemed to sense the question, or at least the opportunity, and he didn't hesitate. He pulled her in, one arm wrapping possessively around her as he bent his head to kiss her. Alix couldn't help it—she met him halfway, her lips parting for him, her tongue searching for his and finding it just where she wanted it. And then the wanting was all she could think of, all she could feel. She pressed into him. His hand slid down to the small of her back, pulling her hips against his. Some unseen cliff loomed closer, only a few steps away, the distance between a table and a cot . . .

She broke away before she fell over the edge.

"I'm sorry," he said immediately, but he didn't look sorry. He looked like a starved wolf with raw meat in his sights.

"It's not . . . don't be sorry." Alix swallowed hard, fumbling for something reasonable to say, trying to pretend that look in his eye didn't pluck something taut in her nethers. "It's my fault. But it's still not . . . It's not a good idea right now." *Right now.* She could almost see the words reflected in his eyes. So much for not encouraging him. "You should rest," she said, stupidly.

His mouth twitched, as if he were biting down on some wicked reply. "As should you."

"I'll try," she said with a fleeting smile, and she left him.

SEVENTEEN

Stupid. So stupid. So gods-damned stupid. Alix stomped through the undergrowth toward the river, willing the flash of heat in her skin to subside. Why had she done that? Why? What could possibly be gained by it? Testing herself, indeed. As if there could be any true test. Liam wasn't here; she hadn't seen him in weeks. All that remained was the piece of him wedged deep inside her, and when she reached down into that place, all she felt was hurt, like a shard of glass buried in her belly. How could she weigh her desire for Erik against the pain of Liam's loss? She might as well weigh water against wind.

Discussing Liam with Erik had been delicious, in a frightening and forbidden sort of way. If she could have drawn it out even further without arousing Erik's suspicion, she would have. It was the closest she could come to Liam right now, and she was greedy for any excuse to think of him. And yet she had kissed Erik, passionately, and very nearly done more than that. *Again.* How could she reconcile those two things?

A tremendous weariness came over her. She would drive herself crazy with this. And yet her mind was already whirring with ideas, treacherously plotting new ways to broach the subject of Liam again. It didn't help that Erik had been so forthcoming, as though part of him had needed it too. It had almost felt like a confession. Probably he had no one else to confide in, at least not on a matter so delicate as this. No one except . . .

Alix paused. Tom must know about his half brother. If he wanted Erik dead, might he want Liam dead too? *I wonder if Erik's thought of that?* She would have to mention it to him when he woke up. She could not have invented a better reason to bring it up again . . .

She sighed. Thinking about Liam was like worrying a loose tooth, an irresistible compulsion that was somehow satisfying even as it made her bleed. Unlike a loose tooth, however, Liam refused to be dislodged.

She resumed her stride, uncorking her empty water skin as she neared the riverbank. She had almost reached the water's edge when an uneasy feeling prickled under her skin. She sensed something, a cue too subtle for her conscious mind to identify. She was being watched. Slowly, deliberately, she scanned the trees. Sunshine lanced through the branches, piercing the undergrowth with shafts of light and shadow that played tricks on the eye. Leaves shuddered and stirred all around her. The birds continued to trill, oblivious to anything amiss.

Alix felt the air move on her skin, as gentle as the breath of a lover. She spun, leading with her elbow, and was rewarded with a sharp impact and a grunt. Before she had even completed her turn, she threw herself into the hooded figure, tackling him to the ground. Her dagger flashed, pressed against warm flesh. She looked into dark eyes wide with shock, even as they glinted with amusement.

"I believe this is about where we left off, Lady Black, albeit with a slightly smaller blade."

"You." She started to pull back, but thought better of it and stayed where she was. "State your purpose!"

The spy raised an eyebrow. "I've returned with information, as we agreed. Please don't say you've forgotten me already. My pride might never recover."

She relaxed a little, but she didn't put her blade away. "You're an idiot. I almost killed you."

"So it would seem."

"Why are you sneaking around in the woods? You should have announced yourself to one of the knights."

"What an excellent idea. 'Good morning, Commander Valiant, what a cosy little war camp you have here. Could you kindly inform the king's bodyguard that I would like to see her? No, she doesn't know my name. No, I'm afraid I can't tell you why I'm here. Now be a good knight and fetch her, will you?' "

"Point taken," she said wryly. "What are you doing here?"

"I believe we just went over that."

"We agreed that you would send a message. By *pigeon*." She pointed her dagger at the sky.

"Indeed, yet my missives to Greenhold went unanswered. A problem with the quality of my birds, perhaps. They seem to have difficulty finding an army in the field."

Alix paused. "I hadn't thought of that."

"So I surmised."

She clambered off him and extended a hand. "How did you find us?"

Only after he'd brushed the leaves from his cloak and drawn the hood back up over his face did he answer. "How did I find two thousand metal-clad men in an open field?"

"Are you always this sarcastic?"

"Alas, I lack the wit for subtler humour."

Alix doubted that, but she wouldn't flatter him by saying so. "Our enemies don't seem to find it so easy to locate us."

"Your enemies might have a harder time than I do plying the locals for information. People are surprisingly uncooperative with foreigners who just left off burning their fields. Besides"—he cocked his head back over his shoulder—"you can't be that difficult to find. Unless my eyes deceive me, that is a band of sellswords encamped at your flank."

Alix made a sour face. "Yes, well . . . desperate times, and all that."

"Who are they?"

She shrugged. "They call themselves the Fist. They showed up last week, claiming a burning desire to defend the realm. This in spite of the fact that at least half of them are foreigners, as far as I can tell."

"Alden inspires love far and wide."

"Especially its gold."

"I'm sure I don't need to tell you that mercenaries cannot be trusted."

"You're right," Alix said, "you don't. So why don't you tell me something else, starting with what I'm paying you for?"

Though his features were largely obscured in the depths of his cowl, Alix could hear the smile in his rasping voice. "I really must thank you, Lady Black. I always enjoy my work, but this contract is something special. His Highness makes for gripping drama. The peaks and valleys of his humours, especially. Maybe I should be taking notes. Then one day, when I'm old and tired, I can write an epic play about it. A tragedy, naturally, in which the hero has only himself to blame for his downfall."

She clucked her tongue impatiently. "Get on with it."

"Very well. First, I can confirm that the Raven does not act alone."

"How do you know?"

"I came upon a letter, written in his own hand, addressed to our Oridian friends."

So there it is. Alix felt ill. "What did it say?"

"His Highness pronounced himself exceedingly vexed by the continued presence of foreign forces on his soil. He demanded to know why the Oridian army was not turning back as agreed, and reiterated his commitment to declare neutrality in the wider war as soon as the last Oridian soldier quits Aldenian territory."

Every muscle in Alix's body went taut; for a moment, she couldn't speak through the knot of rage in her throat. "Tom offered Erik's head in exchange for peace."

"Peace, and a crown."

"But the enemy reneged." It was all she could do to hold herself together against the fury rattling inside her.

The spy merely shrugged. "Perhaps the Oridians believe it was the Raven who reneged. After all, King Erik lives. Or perhaps the Raven was simply treating with the wrong Trion."

"What do you mean?"

"The letter was addressed to Varad, the King. By all accounts, he is the least powerful of the Trions. It's the Priest whose gods demand conquest, and the Warlord is said to lust for battle above all things. Even if Varad wanted to withdraw, it's possible the other two overruled him."

"You seem to know a lot about Oridian politics."

If the spy noticed the suspicion in her voice, it didn't trouble him. "More than the Raven, apparently."

"How did you come by this letter? It seems awfully convenient that you should find it."

"It was far from convenient, Lady Black, and that's all I'll say. Men who reveal their sources don't last very long in my trade."

Alix paused. Something uncomfortable had just occurred to her. "Did you kill anyone? For the letter, or anything else?"

He cocked his head, considering her. Though she could see little of his features, Alix felt the weight of his gaze upon her. "Perhaps it is better to avoid seeking details that might offend your delicate sensibilities," he said.

It wasn't often that someone accused a Black of having delicate sensibilities, but then again, the spy presumably moved in different social circles. Clearing her throat, Alix said, "All right, so his plans aren't unfolding exactly the way he'd hoped. What's his next move?"

"Since his allies abroad seem to have abandoned him, he looks closer to home. He would turn the nobility against King Erik."

"That's absurd," Alix scoffed.

"Is it?"

"Yes, it is. All the Banner Houses support Erik. Only the Golds are uncertain, and the Goldswords are too few to make any difference to either side."

"All the Banner Houses, you say." There was something unmistakably smug in the spy's tone. "Are you sure?"

She narrowed her eyes. "The Blacks, Greens, and Browns are all here with the Kingswords, and the Greys are tied by marriage."

"Ah, but that's not quite so, is it? The Greys are not tied by marriage. They are tied by a *promise* of marriage, a promise that seems certain to be broken."

Alix feigned indifference. "I don't know what you mean."

"Come, Lady Black, you cannot think so little of my skill, or you would not have hired me. However discreet the Raven and his lover may be, there are no secrets at court, at least not among my kind. And King Erik has made it clear that he would like nothing more than to wriggle out of his betrothal. Lady Grey may have concluded that her daughter's only chance at the crown lies with Prince Tomald. If that's so . . . well, you certainly don't need me to tell you how powerful the Greys are, especially with the other Banner Houses brought low by the war."

By the Virtues, he's right. The Greys have every incentive to back Tom. And if they do . . . "It's not even their swords that matter," she said grimly. "The Raven has more than enough of those already. It's their influence."

"Many a lesser lord is beholden to the Greys," the spy agreed. "And an ambitious nobleman might smell an opportunity in all this. The venerable old Banner Houses are humbled, too weak to defend their positions, but many of the lesser houses are as yet untouched by the war. Perhaps a new king might bestow new banners."

Alix shivered. "Would people truly be so disloyal?"

"Someone thinks so. A group calling itself the White Ravens has started posting notices all over the city, denouncing King Erik and his vainglorious war and praising Prince Tomald's steadfast leadership."

"A propaganda campaign? Surely people will see through that?"

"Some no doubt will, but the White Ravens have marshalled more than a few sheets of parchment to their cause. Rumour has it they are disposed of a handsome coin purse, and they will loosen its strings for any noble family willing to declare for them when the time comes. I think we can guess who is master of those purse strings."

"The Greys."

"Or perhaps the Raven himself, if he has wrested control of the royal treasury. It doesn't really matter in the end."

Alix found herself pacing, the undergrowth crackling beneath her boots as she traced a short, restless path in front of the spy. "If these White Ravens can paper Erroman with their cant, so can we. Recruit as many helpers as you need. I want every tavern and market stall covered in notices. The people will know of the Raven's treachery."

"That may persuade the common man, but what of the nobility? The more ambitious of your peers won't give a boar's backside about what really happened at Boswyck, if you will pardon me for saying so. They will smell the winds changing, and ready their sails for whatever tack will carry them to wealth and power."

"In that case, we'd better convince them that tacking toward Erik will be to their profit, and Tomald their ruin."

"What do you propose?"

"Put it about that King Erik has a spy among the White Ravens, someone keeping track of every lord who promises himself to Prince Tomald. The king knows who they are, and what they've been offered, and when he returns to Erroman, there will be a reckoning."

"Interesting." The spy sounded amused. "I've never been asked to disseminate misinformation before."

"But you can do it?"

He shrugged. "Easily, but to what end? Will it be enough to deter these opportunists?"

"Maybe not, but it should give a few of them pause, at least. And it will sow mistrust among them. All we really need is to keep them guessing until Erik is ready to return to the capital."

"Well, well, Lady Black." Once again, she could hear the smile in the spy's dark voice. "Perhaps I misjudged your affinity for espionage. You seem to have rather a knack for it."

"I'm flattered."

"I'll set to work immediately."

"Good." Alix reached for her belt and unhooked her coin purse. "Another instalment," she said, tossing it at him.

He caught it with a deft swipe of his hand. "Thank you. And now let me offer you one last thing in return, as a token of our continued partnership."

Alix raised her eyebrows expectantly.

"Saxon," the spy said.

"I beg your pardon?"

"My name, though I'd thank you not to spread it about."

"Saxon." It was probably a false name, but even so, she found herself oddly pleased at the gesture.

Saxon bowed, his movements as graceful as the shadows of the leaves. Then he turned and melted into the forest, leaving Alix blinking after him.

EIGHTEEN

"**E**rik."

He looked up to find Alix peering through the tent flap with a worried expression. He stood. "What's the matter?"

"Sorry, I didn't mean to alarm you. It's just . . ." She blinked and shook her head, as if she couldn't quite believe what she was about to say. "Albern Highmount is here."

Erik stared at her in astonishment. *"What?"*

"He just arrived, and he wants to see you. I wasn't sure . . . Shall I admit him?" She sounded as perplexed as Erik felt. *We were only just discussing him . . . what, a week ago? No*, Erik realised, *longer.* Three weeks. Three weeks and three battles. An age in wartime.

"Did he come alone?"

"Not quite. He brought a handful of guards and retainers."

Erik shook his head in disbelief. What in the Nine Domains was Highmount doing here, of all places? The man was too old to be riding halfway across the country, especially a country at war. *He must be here for Tom,* Erik thought. *My brother has sent him to treat with me.* He felt his gaze harden. "You may admit him, Alix, but keep a close eye on his men."

She nodded and disappeared through the tent flap. Moments later, Highmount himself pushed through, bowing as low as his rickety frame would allow. "Your Majesty."

"Lord Highmount," Erik said. "You look well."

It was an empty courtesy. Highmount looked pale and drawn. His beard was a dull grey, not the glossy silver Erik remembered, and the dimples that had once been the only sign of humour on the first counsel's face had slumped into long, deep crags in his flesh. Only his piercing eyes and hawkish nose remained undaunted; if anything, they were more prominent than ever against that wasted face, lending him the look of a bird of prey. *And so he is*, Erik thought, perhaps uncharitably.

"Your Majesty is more kind than truthful," Highmount said with a wisp of a smile. "In truth, I am weary from my journey."

"I don't doubt it." Erik gestured at a chair. "It is a long way for you to have come. You serve a hard master, it seems."

"What an odd thing to say, Your Majesty. I serve you."

Erik frowned. "I dismissed you. Over a year ago."

"I recall," Highmount said as he sank into his chair. "War has made you blunt, sire. Or perhaps it is merely efficient." His eyes did a slow tour of the tent. It must have seemed terribly austere to him, accustomed as he was to the finery of King Osrik's hunting pavilion. Even Erik scarcely recognised it as his refuge from a few weeks before. Everything that did not serve a purpose had been removed. There were no rugs, no silk hangings, not even a bottle of wine. Erik's writing desk was meticulously tidy, his maps scrupulously rolled. Coloured inks were arranged in neat ranks, from archer red to infantry black. Aside from the desk, the cot, the dining table, and a few functional chairs, the tent was barren. It had been transformed from royal sanctuary to war room.

"War makes a man efficient, it's true," Erik said. "I've found it necessary to curtail my indulgences, idle chatter among them. So forgive me if I ask you to come directly to the point. Why are you here?"

Highmount folded his hands in his lap. "But I have already told you, Your Majesty, I am here to serve. I may not be first counsel any longer, but I still serve the realm, and therefore, its king."

"Tom sent you."

"He did not."

Irritably, Erik grabbed a chair and sat. "I'll not play volley with you, Highmount. Speak plainly. How exactly do you mean to serve me?"

The old man regarded him steadily. "Though you may not realise it, you are still in need of my counsel, now more than ever before. I swore an oath to your father, may he find peace in his Domain, and I mean to keep my word. Your brother is a traitor, though all of court feigns ignorance of that fact, and he will have your crown unless you stop him."

"I'm well aware of that."

"And yet I find you here." Highmount spread his hands, condemning his surroundings. "Instead of in the capital where you belong."

"I'm fighting a war," Erik said between clenched teeth. It was all he could do to keep his temper in check. No one in the realm got under his skin like this man. Surround him with fools and liars and worse, and Erik would never let his smile slip, but Highmount found every gap in his armour, whether he meant to or not.

"Fighting a war, yes," the old man said, "and weakening yourself with every passing day. The Brownlands are a lost cause, as you must know, and the Brownswords too few to make much difference. Meanwhile, your brother's army stays healthy and rested, and he spends his time recruiting allies whose strength may actually matter when the time comes. The longer you leave him unchallenged, the stronger he becomes. If you are to have any hope of dislodging him, you must return home immediately."

"You would have me leave my kingdom undefended against the invaders? Are you so eager to join the Trionate?"

"You cannot defeat the Oridians with your paltry force. The best you can hope for is to stay alive a little longer—that is, unless the main host at the border should stir. If that happens—*when* that happens—you will be caught in the field without shelter or hope of reinforcement. Your swords are in Erroman, and it is to Erroman you must go. You are fighting this war in reverse, Erik, and it will be your undoing."

"I had no idea you were a military strategist."

Highmount made a dismissive gesture. "One hardly needs to be a military strategist to see the truth of this. A basic command of mathematics should suffice. If you cannot see your doom galloping toward you, then it falls to me to describe it to you."

Erik bit back a scathing reply. He would be damned if he let Highmount bully him into behaving like a petulant child. Calmly, he said, "If you think I am under any illusions about my situation, you are mistaken. I understand perfectly well the need to deal with the enemy within before I face the enemy without. But in order to do *that*, I need the loyalty of the Banner Houses, which my presence here has secured."

Highmount nodded gravely. "A wise precaution. But the task is complete, and now it is time to move on. There is no further loyalty to be gained from Brown or Black or Green by staying here and allowing your meagre forces to be ground down by attrition."

"We are buying time for Arran Green to uproot the enemy from the Blacklands. I'll not give Oridia a foothold this deep inside our territory."

The old man ran a thumb and forefinger over his thick moustache, his expression thoughtful. "How much more time does Green require?"

"I wish I knew. We haven't heard from him in over a week. At last word, they were headed over the Catsback bridge to take the Scions from the east."

"A risky operation. Is Liam still his squire?"

"No, but he is among Green's men. It does worry me." Highmount was the only person in the world he could admit that to. Highmount, and perhaps Alix.

The old man grunted. "Do you still harbour the same intentions toward him?"

"I do, and that's all the discussion I care to have on that subject." If the old man was as wise as he claimed, he would recall what happened the last time he had aired his views on the matter, and he would hold his Hew-cursed tongue.

"It sounds as though the battle for the Scions will decide matters in the Blacklands," Highmount said.

"It should."

"And when that is through, you will ride for Erroman?"

"Provided we can find enough horses," Erik said wryly.

"Good. And now that you have ensured the loyalty of the Banner Houses, you must make a show of rewarding them for it. You are already well on your way, whether you realise it or not."

Erik narrowed his eyes, suddenly wary. "What do you mean?"

"Your brother—or rather his pet, Roswald Grey—has made it clear that wealth and power await any lord who throws in his lot with the White Ravens. However shabby the tactic, I fear it will be effective. The Whites have gone too long without bestowing a new banner, as I warned your royal father many times, and the lesser nobles grow weary of playing squire to the musty old Banner Houses. Their loyalties are ripe for the purchase."

"And so you counsel me to make a counteroffer?"

"Someone already has. I received an interesting message while on the road. It seems that a group styling itself the White Crowns has begun papering the city with pamphlets, promising a clever mix of carrot and stick to give the ambitious pause."

Erik smiled. *Alix's work.*

"That is well done," Highmount went on, "but now you must lend credence to the rumours by making a show of rewarding loyalty."

"How?"

"Appointing Arran Green commander general of your armies was a good start."

"I appointed Green because he was the best man for the job."

Highmount shrugged. "No matter. You threw the Greens a juicy bone, and now you must throw more."

"Such as?"

"Formalise Riggard Black's command. Give him the White Wolves."

"The White Wolves are disbanded."

"The White Wolves *were* disbanded," Highmount corrected patiently. "Reconstituting them is your prerogative."

He had a point. The White Wolves were merely a name—and a storied one at that. Their legacy would strengthen him, if only symbolically. In time, perhaps they could even be restored to their former glory. "Go on," Erik said.

"You must also deliver a blow to the Greys. Punish them for their disloyalty."

Erik frowned. "Will that not make them my enemies?"

"They are already your enemies, Your Majesty, or at least, Roswald is. His mother is a more calculating woman. Deal her a blow, yes, but one that leaves room for reconciliation later on. She will bring her son to heel."

"You obviously have something in mind." Why did he feel a tingle of dread working its way down his spine?

"A stick for the Greys, and a carrot for the Blacks, all rolled into one." The old man smiled, visibly pleased with himself.

Erik squirmed. "I don't follow," he said, but that was a lie, and Highmount knew it.

The old man indulged him anyway. "Announce your intention to marry Alix Black."

Erik couldn't help it; he burst out laughing. The irony was just too much for him. "After years of badgering me to marry Sirin Grey, you counsel me to put her aside? And for a Black, no less! *Those wayward children,* isn't that what you called them? Forgive me, Highmount, but I can't quite believe it. This must surely be a sign that the dragon is nigh and the world will soon end."

"It is a sign that the situation has changed," Highmount said. "An engagement is a promise, one that can be broken—or remade. You will send a powerful signal, not only to the Greys, but to all those who are considering throwing in with Tom."

"And Alix and Sirin—they will do as they're bid, no doubt." That amused him too. The old man obviously didn't know either of them.

"I am surprised at you, Your Majesty. I would have thought you would welcome the chance to be open about your lover."

Erik laughed again, but this time there was an edge to it. "Someone's been having you on, I'm afraid. Alix Black and I are not lovers." *Not quite*, he allowed himself silently.

"The servants at Greenhold tell a different story."

Erik suppressed a growl. Did the man have spies *everywhere*? Aloud, he said, "If you pay for gossip, you can hardly be surprised if it is always in good supply."

"You would do well to be mindful of gossip, Your Majesty. It can be enormously valuable. And if I have heard the rumour of your involvement with Lady Alix, you can be sure the Greys have too."

Erik winced. He had not thought of that. "I hope you're wrong."

"Unlikely. In which case, the best thing you can do is turn the rumour to your advantage. Announce your betrothal, and back it up with action. Make sure you display your affection for all to see. You may even consider inviting her to spend the night in your tent. Indiscreet, to be sure, but under the circumstances—"

"Did you not just hear me say that we are not lovers?"

"That can be remedied, surely."

"I'm flattered by your confidence," Erik said wryly, "but I assure you it isn't as easy as that."

"So you have tried, then?"

"*Olan's battered shield, man!* My bed is not your business!"

"Your bed is the kingdom's business, Your Majesty," Highmount returned implacably.

Erik sprang from his chair and began to pace. He did not dare to speak, lest he say something he regretted later. Was it so unreasonable to want something for himself, something untouched by grubby politicking and the vagaries of court?

"You may even decide to go through with the marriage," Highmount continued. "The Blacks are not what they once were, certainly, but—"

"Enough." Erik silenced the old man with a sharp gesture. "I will not have you speaking of Alix like she is a brick to be added to my fortress. Nor do I intend simply to cast aside my vow to Sirin Grey."

Highmount's lips pursed in displeasure. "Your vows cannot rule you, Your Majesty. Honour is a fine virtue, but a luxury in times like these. You have a higher duty to your kingdom."

"So I am constantly being told," Erik snapped. *So I am beginning to tell myself*, he might have added. "I will consider it, Highmount, and that is all. Leave it now. I have a battle to prepare for."

For a moment, Highmount looked like he would argue. At length, however, he sighed and leaned back in his chair. "Very well. I will let this subject alone for now. Do not think it gives me any pleasure to broach these matters with you. I only want what is best for you, and what is best for Alden. I owe your father's memory no less."

Clever touch, old man, bringing my father into this. He did not doubt Highmount's sincerity, but that did not make him any less manipulative. He was a good man, but a classic creature of court. He saw all the angles, spied every risk and every opportunity. Erik admired the man's savvy, even as he despised it. Part of him wanted to learn those skills, and part of him was afraid he already had.

But I need him, now more than ever. He's right about that, and a lot else besides. In truth, Erik had known all along that he had been wrong to dismiss his first counsel. It was done out of anger, left unresolved out of pride. Erik did not have the luxury of such rashness now. "Let us speak no further of this," he said in a conciliatory tone. "You are weary from your journey. Take some rest. Tomorrow, we can discuss next steps."

"Then you will permit me to remain?"

Swallow your pride, Your Majesty. "If you would do me the honour of being my first counsel again, I should be very pleased." The words did not taste quite as bitter as he had feared.

Highmount rose and bowed. "The honour is mine, Your Majesty," he said without a hint of smugness. "And you are right—I am exhausted. I daresay I shall sleep very well to-night." He turned to go. Then he paused at the tent flap, casting a final glance around him. "You have changed, I think."

"Betrayal and disappointment will do that to a man."

"So it is that we grow wise," Highmount said, and for the briefest moment, Erik glimpsed a lifetime of hard lessons in his eyes. Then he turned away and was gone.

A **chill mist** clung to the camp, draping over the shoulders of the tents like a rain-sodden cloak. It was strangely cool for the season. It was as though nature itself were nervous before the battle, dew collecting like beads of sweat on the pale brow of dawn. Men stumbled over tent posts hidden in the fog, slipped on grass slick with damp. If Erik had been a superstitious man, he might have considered it an ill omen.

Alix stood at his side, as always, copper hair curling gently in the humidity. Erik longed to reach out and touch those shining waves, beautiful and slightly wild. His thoughts returned, as they had so often, to that night at Greenhold. The softness of her hair, the sweet sigh of her voice in his ear . . . He could almost bring to mind the faint scent of lavender as his lips brushed the perfect white skin of her neck.

She gazed out over the camp, unaware of Erik's eyes on her. Would she think him weak, if she could hear his thoughts? Would she question the worth of a king who allowed himself to be so distracted on the morning of battle?

She looked over at him and smiled. Erik smiled back, but a part of him felt uneasy. There was something surreal about this moment, something portentous. It felt a little like a dream, as though his mind wanted him to remember. Erik shivered. He was not normally given to anxiety before a battle. Perhaps he had not slept properly.

Highmount was up and about, though he did not bother with the pretence of armour. He was too old to fight, and had probably never been much of a knight to begin with. He would remain at the camp, along with the healers, smiths and sundry others whose efforts were the backbone of the army. Surprisingly, he had not attempted to persuade Erik not to fight. Perhaps Highmount was beginning to take his young king seriously at last.

Erik struck out into the fog, Highmount at his side, Alix trailing just behind. He always walked among the men before battle. He had read somewhere that a good general avoids fraternising with his troops, so as not to compromise his ability to take difficult life-and-death decisions. It was important to see one's men as weapons, rather than people, or so the theory went, lest one hesitate to sacrifice them to military necessity.

Erik had a different theory. It was good for his soldiers to see their king up close. Let them put a face to the man who would lead them into battle, and draw strength from his confidence. It was important to show them that he cared to know their names, what village they came from. A king who cares for his people is one who will do what is necessary to protect them.

"Victory, Your Majesty!" one of the men called.

"Let Rahl be your sign today, sire," said another.

Erik approached a young soldier polishing his weapon. It was a massive two-handed greatsword with an elaborately carved hilt, most likely a family heirloom. The man froze when Erik drew near, then leapt to his feet and bowed, the tip of his blade sinking into the dirt. Even with a few inches of it buried, the sword was nearly as tall as the young man himself.

"That's quite a weapon," Erik said. "Was it your father's?"

The young man flushed at being thus singled out. "Aye, sire, and his father's before."

"Was your father a giant, by any chance? Or perhaps a little Harrami blood?" A ripple of laughter went through the gathering crowd of soldiers. "Honestly, man, how do you even lift that thing?"

The young soldier tilted his chin proudly. "I'm stronger than I look, Your Majesty."

"You must be." Gesturing at the surrounding crowd, Erik added, "But if I were you lot, I'd give this man plenty of space when he winds up." More laughter. Erik continued on.

He stopped to speak to several others before heading back, and gradually, his mood began to clear. He had long since realised that these walks were as good for him as they were for his men. Just as the soldiers drew strength from his confidence, he drew resolve from their trust. These ordinary men and women reminded Erik why he was here, and what they were defending.

A soldier walked toward him, smiling broadly. "Good hunting today, Your Majesty," the man said as he approached, reaching out to clasp Erik's arm. He was a stocky fellow, with thick arms and beefy hands. The one that reached for Erik bore a tattoo of a snake. And something else . . .

A blade flashed. Someone cried out. Erik was seized from behind and spun around, his body wrapped in another as he turned. He felt an impact against his back, heard a grunt. The arms around him went slack. Erik whirled to find Alix staring at him. There was a great commotion behind her, men surging and grabbing and shouting. Alix stood perfectly still, her face strangely expressionless.

She buckled. Erik lunged and caught her under the arms. Over her shoulder, he saw the hilt of a dagger. She had shielded him with her own body, and the blow aimed for Erik's heart had instead found her back. It was an armour-piercing blade. An assassin's blade. Alix opened her mouth to say something, but she only managed a cough, wet and wheezing.

Erik eased her down onto her side. Highmount was shouting for a healer. Erik sank to his knees in the grass, momentarily paralysed with fear. Alix's breath rattled in her throat, and a pink froth appeared on her lips. Her eyes glazed over. He grabbed her shoulder and leaned in close. Her eyelids started to flutter. "Don't you dare," he hissed. "I forbid it, Alix."

She focused on him for a moment, nearly managed a smile. Then her eyes closed, and she went limp.

NINETEEN

†A lix woke to darkness. She lay on her stomach, her back exposed to the open air. A knife was embedded in her flesh, just to the right of her spine. At least that was what it felt like. Alix had never been stabbed before, not even in battle, but if she'd had to guess what lacerated muscle felt like, it would have been this. The sensation of being *torn* was unmistakable. And excruciating.

She tilted her head, scanning the shadows. She recognised the vague outline of her own tent. She shifted, her elbow bumping the small bedside table and nearly knocking over a cup of water that had been placed there. The sight of it awakened a powerful thirst. Gingerly, Alix propped herself on her elbows. A jolt of pain lanced through her back, but her thirst would not be denied. She grabbed the cup.

"Hey," a voice said irritably, "I could have got that for you."

Alix craned her neck to locate the source, and found Erik sitting vigil near her bedside. She was too busy gulping water to respond right away. "I didn't know you were there," she said between swallows. She could barely see him, it was so dark. It must have been late.

"I shouldn't be, but I just had to see for myself that you

were all right. I'll go . . . in a moment." He spoke in a low voice, not wanting to draw attention to his presence.

Alix peered at him through the shadows. She could only see the outline of his face against the pale backdrop of the canvas. "Are you all right?"

He shrugged. "A few scrapes and bruises, but nothing to worry about."

Scrapes and bruises? He must have fought the assassin after she passed out. She would have assumed the soldiers had killed him by then. "That was close," she said. "I hope Saxon was right, and the guild sent their best this time. Any better, and he'd have had us."

She sensed his frown. "Saxon?"

"The spy. That's his name." She wondered if she was wrong to repeat it.

"You should rest," Erik said, rising. "If they find me here, I'm liable to be flogged." He sounded sullen, and his voice was deeper than usual. Alix wondered if he was unwell. He paused at the tent flap. "Good night, Allie."

She gasped, twisting all the way around before she realised what she was doing. Her gasp turned into a cry as pain flared through her body.

"Are you insane, woman?" Strong hands eased her back onto her stomach. "You do remember about the knife and the almost dying, don't you?"

"Liam," she whispered through a haze of pain.

He lowered himself to a crouch by her bedside. Even in the darkness, she could see the concern in his eyes. "What do you need? How can I help?"

Alix reached out and ran her fingers through his short-cropped hair. "It's really you." The familiar contours of his face were brushed in moonlight. Gods, he was beautiful.

"You thought maybe it was a bad dream?" A ghost of his roguish grin appeared, only to dissolve into a pained look. Alix realised that she was stroking his hair with the tips of her fingers. Liam closed his eyes and turned his face into her hand. His breath flitted along her wrist like a shiver. She started to pull him near, but he rose swiftly out of reach. When he spoke again, his voice sounded rusty. "If you want, I'll have Gwylim come by tomorrow. He's got this wonder poultice, better than any of the stuff the healers use. It smells like something died in that jar, but it's worth it."

"Please stay."

"I'd better not. Angry healers are up there with skunks, bears, and Oridian thralls on my list of dangerous fauna. Besides, it's late, and you should rest."

"Liam, wait. How long will you be in camp?" If he said he was leaving at dawn, Alix was getting up out of this cot, knife wound be damned.

"We're back for good," he said, "all of us. We defeated the enemy at the Scions. They've scattered, probably heading south to regroup with the main force. Green says we've done all we can. We meet up with your brother tomorrow, and I guess I don't really know what happens after that." A slice of moonlight appeared as he pulled back the tent flap. "I'll see you around," he said, and was gone.

Alix nearly gagged when he opened the jar.

"Sweet Farika, goddess of grace!" She twisted to look back over her shoulder, just far enough to see Gwylim smirk.

"You were warned."

It was true, she *had* been warned, but she had never imagined a stench like this. "What is *in* that stuff?"

"You don't want to know. Hold still, please, your bandage is stuck." Alix hissed in pain as Gwylim tugged at the dried blood caking her stitches. "You bled through last night. Here, let me soak it off." He dipped a rag in water and gently dabbed at the wound.

"Thanks."

"Don't thank me yet. If you think this stuff smells bad now, wait until you've sweated in it awhile." He patted her dry and took up the clay jar. Alix buried her face in her pillow and breathed deeply of goose down. "This is going to sting a little," Gwylim said.

It stung a *lot*, as if he had squeezed a lemon over the wound. Alix screwed up her face and gritted her teeth. "This had better be worth it," she growled, a little ungratefully.

"It will be." His hands were gentle and steady, and after a

moment, the burning wore off, replaced by an almost icy feeling. "They think the dagger nicked your lung."

"I guess that explains why I couldn't breathe." Alix shuddered at the memory.

Gwylim's hands left her; Alix could hear him putting the stopper back in the jar. "I passed His Majesty on the way in," he said as he pressed a fresh bandage to her back.

"He was here when I woke up."

"Mmm," said Gwylim.

Alix frowned at her pillow. "What?"

"He almost didn't let me in. Blocked me bodily at the tent flap until I explained myself. Almost as if he were your bodyguard, and not the other way around."

Alix was glad her face was half hidden by the pillow. *I wonder if my neck blushes*, she thought sourly. Aloud, she said, "He doesn't know you, that's all."

"Mmm," said Gwylim.

Alix hastened to change the subject. "Where did you learn how to make this stuff, anyway?" She raised herself up on her arms as he wound the dressing around her ribs, just under her breast band. If it had been anyone else, she would have worried about her modesty, but for some reason, it never occurred to her to fret about Gwylim.

"You learn lots of things when you're studying to become a priest," he said. "Herbology especially. Herbs and potions let you commune with the Virtues."

"Oh?"

She could hear the smile in his voice. "That's what they say."

"Doesn't sound like you believe it."

He tied off the dressing with a clever knot. "I've had a vision or two thanks to a leaf or a mushroom, but I can't say I've ever felt holier for it."

Alix snorted into her pillow. "You don't paint a very flattering portrait of religious life."

"I give credit where it's due. The priestly orders have contributed their share to society. Longlenses and fireworks, literature and poetry, and of course medicines like this one."

"Hopefully they don't all smell like death washed through a sewer."

Gwylim laughed. "You won't mind so much by tomorrow," he promised.

Alix fell asleep after that, and by the time she woke up, it was late afternoon, and her brother was at her bedside. He stayed all through the night, was still there the following morning when Erik appeared with breakfast. Later, Gwylim arrived to change her bandages, and Kerta and Ide came too. Albern Highmount sent his regards through the king, and even Arran Green dropped by to wish her well.

Liam, though, did not return.

He didn't come the next day, or the day after that. He didn't even send word. That hurt more than any knife wound, for it confirmed Alix's fears. Not only was he no longer her lover, he was no longer even her friend. She'd lost him completely.

After four days, Alix could finally stand without assistance, and Erik ordered the camp struck. The march to Erroman had begun at last. They'd waited so long for this moment, it seemed to Alix that it ought to feel somehow momentous, but it didn't. It felt like any other march on any other day, with weary soldiers and bad weather and many miles ahead. Alix bounced along in the back of a supply wagon, wincing at every bump in the road and wishing fervently that she could walk. *So this is how Erik felt after the Battle of Boswyck.* She'd known he was uncomfortable, but the humiliation of it, the sense of being utterly powerless, was something she hadn't fully understood. He'd borne it with more dignity than she could ever hope to.

The sky opened up that afternoon. Rain cleaved through the fog in frigid sheets, clattering against armour and beating the road into muck. The men swore and grumbled. Alix managed to hunker down under some canvas, but even so, she was soaked to her smalls. From under her makeshift tent, she glimpsed Liam and Kerta following along behind the wagon. Kerta had her arms looped through Liam's, and they were laughing. Kerta wore a helm that kept the rain off her perfect blond curls, but Liam's hair was plastered to his forehead, streaming with wet. Kerta reached up and slicked it back for him. Liam grinned down at her, making some remark that had Kerta giggling and simpering like a little girl. Then Ide trotted up and handed them each a corner of a blanket, and they opened it out above their heads and huddled under it together. Alix thought about calling to them, but they would never hear her above the rush of the rain, and anyway, she didn't want to intrude. They'd been on the road together for months, had tasted battle and blood together. Alix wasn't a part of that, not anymore.

The rain finally let up when evening came, and the sky filled with stars. The air smelled fresh and new, perfumed with wet clay and tree bark. Alix breathed deeply of the scent as she walked through the camp. She'd grown fond of living outdoors, despite the inconveniences. There was something so alive about it, so primal and true. Out here on the road, one didn't need to be refined—not that she'd ever been very refined to begin with. How often had her mother despaired of ever making her a proper lady? And that was before Rig's dubious tutelage. Alix smiled ruefully at the thought. *Oh, Mother—what would you think of me now?*

She spied Erik standing near his tent, on a bluff overlooking the river, and she made her way over. At Alix's suggestion, the men had erected Erik's pavilion on elevated ground in order to afford the royal guardsmen a better view of the surrounding camp. Everyone was on edge following the assassination attempt, Alix most of all. She was herself useless until she recovered from her wound, so she compensated by doubling the king's detail. Erik now had eight men with him at all times, a situation he plainly disliked. Even so, he didn't try to talk her out of it.

The king gazed out over the water, hands folded at his back. He seemed deep in thought. Alix hesitated, but he'd heard her approach, and he turned. "Ah, Captain." He addressed her formally for the benefit of the guards. "I'm pleased to see you up and about. Join me, won't you?"

She stepped to his side, following his gaze out to the river. The waters coiled silver and silent in the moonlight.

"How do you feel?" Erik asked, keeping his voice low. He was more discreet in public lately. Alix suspected it had something to do with Lord Highmount's presence.

"It's improving. Hurts like a bitch, though, begging His Majesty's pardon."

He smiled. "It doesn't seem to have dampened your spirits any." He paused for a long moment. When he spoke again, his smile was gone. "I don't think I can do this anymore, Alix."

"Do what?"

"Let you put yourself in harm's way on my account."

She gave an incredulous laugh. "Erik—"

"I know what you're going to say," he interrupted with a scowl, "and of course you're right. Which is why I've decided that I no longer want you to be my bodyguard. We need a new arrangement."

Alix stared. "You can't be serious."

"I'm perfectly serious." He dropped his voice still lower. "You know how I feel, Alix. Last week I held you in my arms and watched the light go out of your eyes, and I didn't know if it would ever return. Can you imagine what that was like?"

Silence descended between them. Alix was grateful for the dark, for the guards couldn't see the flush of her skin. Neither could they see the look in Erik's eyes, a fiery mixture of fear and want.

"I don't know what to say to that."

His gaze drifted to her mouth, where it lingered. "How I resent these guards. I would give anything to be alone with you right now. Then again, perhaps it doesn't matter anymore."

Alix's breath quickened. Erik stirred.

"Your Majesty!"

Alix nearly jumped out of her skin. Turning, she saw her brother standing at the base of the hill.

"The war council is ready," Rig called.

"Good." Erik started for the tent.

Alix grabbed his hand, heedless of the eyes upon them. "Please, Erik, don't do anything rash. We'll deal with your brother soon, and then things will be different. Until then, you need me. Let me do my duty."

He regarded her silently for a moment. Then he sighed. "We'll discuss it later. That is all I can agree to for now." He turned away.

Alix hung back, struggling to compose herself. She watched Erik disappear into the tent. Taking a deep breath, she followed. Rig waited for her outside. She could feel his gaze, in spite of the dark. "Don't say a *word*," she growled as she passed.

Rig only shook his head and lifted the tent flap.

TWENTY

"First, the grim news," Highmount said, eyeing each of them in turn. He sat on the king's right, opposite Arran Green and Adelbard Brown. Raibert Green, Alix, and Rig rounded out the assembly. Taken together, they were something of a crowd, in Alix's estimation, and she found herself pining for the tidy trio of their Greenhold days, when she and Erik and Raibert Green had formed the sum total of the decision-making apparatus. Spacious as the king's pavilion was, Alix feared it was too small to accommodate the egos around the table.

"General Green, if you please," said Highmount.

Green inclined his head gravely. "Our scouts report that the enemy host at the border stirs. They are building siege engines, taking advantage of the abundant forest of Boswyck Valley. There can be little doubt that they mean to march in the coming days."

A spasm of fear wrenched Alix's insides. They'd known it was only a matter of time, but it still came as a nasty shock to learn that the moment was here. *Siege engines. They make for Erroman.*

"They are fifty thousand strong," Green went on, as though

any of them could have forgotten. "The coming battle will be like nothing this country has faced since the days of the old empire."

"You mean when the Harrami sacked Erroman?" Rig asked. "Or were you referring to the Onnani rebellion? Hard to say which was the more glorious moment in our history, but it's good to hear that this might top them both."

Highmount fixed him with a look of elegant distaste. "Lord Black, please. This is hardly the time for levity."

Arran Green ignored them both. "We have a substantial head start on the enemy, and the siege engines will slow his progress. Even so, we must increase our pace. I recommend adding two hours per day to the march, plus a night march every three days. It will be difficult, but we have little choice. We must allow ourselves enough time to deal with matters in Erroman before the Oridians descend upon us in earnest."

"Very well," said Erik. "There is little else we can do for now. We will begin tomorrow. Now—what else? Have we any news from the capital?"

"Thankfully, of a more positive nature," Highmount said. "As of last intelligence, Tomald remained lodged in his own apartments."

Erik was unimpressed. "I'm afraid I don't understand your point. Where else would he be lodged?"

"Why, in your royal suite, Your Majesty. Moving into the king's lodgings would have sent a powerful signal."

"My brother has sent plenty of signals," Erik said dryly, "but I'm gratified to hear that he has drawn the line at occupying my bed."

"It has always been difficult to know your brother's mind," Highmount said, ignoring the king's sarcasm. "Any small insight into his thinking is valuable. From that perspective, his decision to remain in his own quarters is instructive."

"And what does it teach us?"

"That for all his manoeuvrings, Tomald is not yet ready to proclaim himself king."

Erik didn't look convinced, but he held his peace. It was Raibert Green who asked the obvious question. "But what will he do when we approach the city? What if he bars the gates?"

"Then we attack," said Rig.

"Impossible," said Arran Green. "They outnumber us nearly fourfold."

"Do they?" Rig arched an eyebrow. "How many King-swords will take up arms against their rightful king? Seems to me that we have allies within the walls, and plenty of them."

"Perhaps, but it would be foolish to rely on that."

"It does not matter," Highmount interrupted with an impatient gesture. "The king cannot attack his own city. It would make him appear weak, as though *he* were the challenger for the crown. And besides, it would do significant damage to the city, which in addition to weakening our defences against the Oridians, would cost him dearly in terms of popular support."

"What do you suggest, Highmount?" asked Lord Brown. "Should we stand outside the gates and ask nicely?" He and Rig exchanged a *look*; plainly, they did not think Highmount had any business in the war council. *As though this is a military question*, Alix thought irritably. By all accounts, Highmount was a shrewd politician, and he came with fresh intelligence from the capital. If anyone had a right to speak on the matter, it was he. *Too many egos, not enough information.* She didn't envy Erik the task of sorting wisdom from bluster.

"I do not believe Tomald means to bar King Erik from the city," Highmount said. "He can no more afford a direct confrontation than we can. He recognises that, else he would not have troubled with assassins and spies. He needs at least a veneer of legitimacy for his actions."

"You can't be sure of that," Erik said.

"Letting us into the city would squander a major military advantage," Arran Green said. "The Raven is too smart for that."

Alix could hold her tongue no longer. "I agree with Lord Highmount." Unsurprisingly, this announcement earned her a glare from Arran Green. *He can scowl all he likes*, she thought, meeting Green's eyes with a level stare. She was not his to command anymore, or to reproach. Erik had always encouraged her to speak her mind, and so she would. "If Tom meant to challenge His Majesty through force of arms, he wouldn't bother investing so much in his propaganda campaign. The White Ravens are proof that he craves popular backing."

"Crave it he might," Arran Green said, "but that does not mean he will renounce a military option."

Erik surveyed his counsellors with narrowed eyes, his chin propped on his hand. "Suppose you're right, Highmount. What would you do in Tom's place?"

"I would meet you in parley. I would attempt to convince you that the crown is already lost, and demand that you stand aside."

Erik laughed bitterly. "He knows me better than that."

"He knows you will do what you believe best for the kingdom. Therefore, he will seek to convince you that opposing him will only bring blood and ruin to all of Alden."

"You're wrong, Highmount," Erik said. "Tom thinks me *frivolous*."

"He thinks you a fool," Highmount said blandly. Alix's jaw dropped, and she wasn't alone; every pair of eyes around the table glared at the first counsel. If Highmount noticed, he didn't care. "He also thinks you are principled to a fault. Recall the arguments you employed in favour of going to war with Oridia."

"I said we were honour-bound to stand by our allies."

"You also said that however painful for Alden, it was for the greater good. If I were your brother, I would appeal to that very sentiment, and argue that yielding to me would be for the greater good."

Erik grunted thoughtfully. "You may be right."

Alix wasn't sure. If Tom believed his brother was principled to a fault, he might just as easily conclude that Erik would dig in his heels no matter what.

"Your brother has gathered many allies," Highmount said. "How many, I cannot say. He obviously hopes that the balance of support weighs in his favour, and he may not be wrong."

Rig scowled at that. "Nearly all the Banner Houses are represented at this table."

"With due respect, Lord Black, the Banner Houses are not what they used to be." Highmount raised his eyebrows at Rig, as if to say, *Especially yours.* "The lesser houses outnumber you tenfold. Many of them are far wealthier and spend more time in the capital, meticulously tending to their alliances. Their influence cannot be underestimated. Moreover, they breed prodigiously, no matter if some consider it vulgar, and that makes them hungry." He pulled his collar down to reveal his marriage chain, two large gold loops and four smaller, proclaiming him the father of four children. "I myself have three daughters and a son, gods help me, and nearly a dozen grandchildren. We must find a marriage and lands for each of them. Unlike the Banner Houses, the lesser lords take marriage very seriously." In case anyone had missed his meaning, he fixed Lords Black and Green with a reproachful look. Rig should have been married years ago, it was true, and it had been nearly a decade since Raibert Green's wife died in childbirth. Neither had heirs, and Raibert lacked even a single sibling. If he fell tomorrow, the Green banner would pass to his cousin Arran.

"On this, at least, we agree," Lord Brown said. "The Swiftcurrents have more gold than the royal treasury, and the Middlemarches are shameless climbers, and breed like rabbits besides. Who can say what families like that will do?"

Highmount levelled his hawklike gaze at Erik. "Your brother hopes you will see the allies arrayed at his back and conclude that opposing him would tear the country apart."

"And if I fail to reach that conclusion?"

"Then he will attack," Arran Green said, "and he will win."

Silence settled like ash over the table. The assembled lords looked at each other grimly. Erik sat straight and proud, jaw taut, blue eyes chiselled from ice. "It's hopeless, then?"

"Not hopeless, Your Majesty," Highmount said. "I cannot agree with General Green. I do not think it inevitable that your brother will attack, at least not straightaway. Tomald is not entirely without honour."

Arran Green snorted, but did not otherwise deign to reply. Part of Alix was in sympathy with the commander general, but another part recalled a conversation at Greenhold, half a lifetime ago. "Your Majesty," she said, "you once told me that Tom always believes he's the hero of the story," she said. "If that's true, then maybe Lord Highmount is right, and there's a chance he can be convinced to back down."

Erik cocked his head. "Go on."

Alix felt the weight of the gazes upon her. They were expectant, even hopeful. For once, none of the great lords looked at her as if she were an impudent girl, not even Arran Green. She should have felt vindicated; instead she felt more nervous than ever. She cleared her throat. "If Tom fancies himself the hero, then let him be. Hand him a narrative that makes him the saviour. What happened at Boswyck changed you forever. It hardened you, forced you to grow wiser. You understand now what Tom was trying to tell you all along, that war with Oridia was folly. It's too late to stop it now, but you're twice the king you once were, and together, you and Tom can defeat the enemy." It rolled off her tongue so easily that Alix wondered if some of it might even be true.

Highmount stroked his beard. Alix could see the thoughts churning behind his sharp eyes. Aloud, he merely said, "Interesting."

Erik did not share that assessment. "You want me to say that I was wrong to honour our oath? That I should never have declared war? I don't believe that, Alix."

"You are not the one who needs to believe it, Your Majesty," Highmount said. "You need only play the part long enough for your brother to concede. Then you may do with him what you will."

Erik turned a cold gaze on his first counsel. "You propose that I deceive him into surrendering and then take his head?"

"If that is what you must—"

"No." Erik didn't raise his voice, but he didn't have to. The word carried absolute finality. "He is my *brother*. If I accept his surrender, then I accept it. I will not betray him, no matter that he has betrayed me."

Alix suppressed a sigh. Destan himself couldn't have been more stubborn where honour was concerned. Admirable though Erik's principles might be, they were not always practical. Then again, honour was a Holy Virtue; pragmatism was not.

"The good news is, you probably won't need to make that choice," Rig said wryly. "Tom will never stand aside, not when he's this close to getting what he wants."

"Then I will give him what he wants."

Highmount was aghast. "Your Majesty, you cannot turn over the crown!"

"It's not the crown he wants, not really." Erik smiled sadly. "The crown is only a symbol. Alix has the right of it—what he wants is to be the hero. He wants to prove that he is better than me, once and for all. I can give him that. And I can give him Sirin Grey."

"A risky ploy," said Raibert Green. "He will have to believe you are absolutely sincere."

"Yes."

Rig shook his head. "In that case, may Hew be your sign, Erik."

Alix would have thought to go to her grave without ever hearing her brother invoke the god of wit. Courage and strength had always been his watchwords. *The world must be coming to an end after all.*

"His Majesty must be armed with more than a clever tongue," Highmount said. "We must do everything we can to strengthen his position before the parley."

"You obviously have ideas," Lord Brown said.

"Indeed. First, there is the matter of the White Wolves. Have you considered my proposal, Your Majesty?"

Erik gave a thin smile. Turning to Rig, he said, "Congratulations, Lord Black. You are now commander of the White Wolves."

"His Majesty is too generous." They shared a hollow laugh, oblivious to the look of outrage that came over Arran Green. The commander general didn't appear to see the humour in mocking the legendary Wolves, a unit he himself had commanded before the Raven came of age.

"And my other proposal?" Lord Highmount said.

Erik stiffened, but made no reply. His reaction piqued Rig's curiosity. "What proposal is that?"

Highmount glanced at Alix, and suddenly she knew what he was going to say. "I have suggested that His Majesty betroth himself to your sister."

Alix's gaze snapped to Erik, but he looked away before she could catch his eye. "I told you I'd heard enough of this," he growled, sounding more embarrassed than angry.

"And I agreed to leave it be for a time, but it is my duty as first counsel to give you the benefit of my wisdom, and I firmly believe that an alliance with the Blacks is the most prudent step you could take right now."

"He *has* an alliance with the Blacks," Rig said, frowning.

"That may be, but it is not enough. It is the symbol we require, and a symbol must be visible in order to be effective."

"My sister is not a game piece for you to move about," Rig said, his voice cooling with every word.

"No indeed, Lord Black, and this is not a game."

"She's an adult. She makes her own decisions."

"She is the daughter of a Banner House. That comes with obligations, especially to her king."

"I have not even discussed this with her," Erik put in. "A decision is certainly premature."

"She isn't—"

"Could everyone kindly stop talking about me as though I weren't here?" Alix glared at the men around the table.

Rig surged to his feet, his face flushed with fury. Luckily for Highmount, he was well out of reach. "Alix is right—she can speak for herself. On my own behalf, I'll say this: If you ever presume to lecture me or mine about duty again, you *will* regret it. My sister has gone through more in her short life than a pompous prat like you ever will. She deserves to make her own choices." With a final, furious look at Erik, Rig punched through the tent flap and disappeared.

"How invigorating," Highmount said.

That was too much for Erik. "This council is adjourned."

"Your Majesty—"

"Get out."

Alix started to rise, but Erik stayed her with a subtle gesture, so she sank back into her chair and squirmed while the lords filed out of the pavilion. When they had gone, Erik passed a weary hand over his eyes. "Gods, Alix, I am so sorry. I never—"

"It's all right. Highmount is an ass, but he's right—I'm the daughter of a Banner House. I have no delusions about deciding my own destiny." Even now that they were alone, Erik wouldn't look at her. It was more than embarrassment. *Is he afraid of what I'll see in his eyes?* She was half afraid of what he might see in hers. The thought of marrying the king was terrifying. The thought of marrying *Erik* . . . that was terrifying too, but in a very different way.

"I want you to know that I haven't been plotting with him," Erik said. "He brought it up, it's true, but I made it clear that I did not want to hear it."

"I believe you."

He sighed and would have said more, but Rig poked his head back in the tent. "Sorry," he said gruffly, "a word?"

Erik waved him in.

Rig only entered far enough for the tent flap to close behind him. "I apologise, Your Majesty. My behaviour was inappropriate." His gaze shifted to Alix. "I'm afraid that when it comes to my sister . . ."

"I understand," Erik said. "But I cannot have threats and insults in my war council. Our situation is precarious enough as it is. We cannot afford to be divided now."

"It won't happen again." Rig bowed stiffly and went out.

Erik stared after him, thoughtful. "He loves you very much, Alix."

She felt a little pang, part affection, part sadness. "He's always been protective. He's . . ." Words failed her.

"He's your brother."

"He's more than that. He's my best friend."

"That is as it should be." Erik's gaze had taken on a faraway look. Abruptly, he stood. "Excuse me, Alix, there's something I must do. Good night." Without so much as a backward glance, he slipped through the tent flap.

When Alix stepped outside, she found Albern Highmount waiting for her. "I beg your pardon, my lady, but I wonder if I might prevail upon you for a brief word?"

"All right," she said coolly.

"I apologise if the conversation a moment ago was awkward. However, I am sure you appreciate that for a woman of your station, marriage is an obligation, not a privilege."

She ground her teeth together, but managed a polite, "Of course."

In the deepening darkness, Highmount's face was little more than a shadowy sketch, but Alix could feel his eyes appraising her. "In truth, I think a betrothal between your ladyship and His Majesty would be more than a prudent political match. You complement each other well. His Majesty looks to you for counsel, and from what I have seen, your advice thus far has been admirably pragmatic. That is a crucial trait for a king, one His Majesty has only recently begun to embrace. You would do your country a great service if you helped him to nurture it."

"Erik doesn't need my help. He's already a great king."

Highmount cleared his throat delicately. "Even a great king can be greater."

"Is that all?" If she didn't get out of here soon, she was going to lose her temper, and Erik would not thank her for that.

"No. I'm afraid I must beg your indulgence with a favour."

"Go on."

"So long as a marriage alliance between yourself and His Majesty is under discussion, your conduct must be beyond reproach. There can be no more gossip about you, Lady Alix, nothing that might jeopardise your suitability as queen."

"What do you mean, gossip?"

"Forgive me if I am indelicate, but tales of a certain late-night visit to the Kingsword camp some months ago have circulated rather widely."

Alix cursed inwardly, her face burning. She'd known the guards would whisper about her stealing away from Greenhold that night, but it had never occurred to her that it would reach the ears of someone like Albern Highmount.

"I do not know who he was," Highmount said, "and it does not matter. But if he is still among the Kingswords, you must not be seen with him again. It would not do to have it about that you were . . . *familiar* . . . with other men."

"You have nothing to fear on that score, my lord. That is long over."

"I am gratified to hear it. Good evening, my lady." He retreated into the shadows, leaving Alix to glare at his back.

Erik strode briskly between the tents, doing his best to ignore the eight armed men jostling noisily to keep up with him. His purposeful gait masked his uncertainty. He was nervous, more so than he had any reason to be. Perhaps that was because he was unprepared. The impulse had come upon him suddenly, and part of him wondered if he was making a mistake. *Perhaps Alix is right. Perhaps I am behaving rashly.* The evidence was not promising. He had almost kissed her in front of the entire camp, for Ardin's sake. As uncertain as he was, however, he was determined to act on the impulse before he lost his nerve. *This is long overdue*, he told himself firmly.

He found the scouts without much difficulty. A cheerful fire danced and crackled on the fringes of the main camp; by its glow, Erik counted four silhouettes. The curious faces that turned to greet him made him feel uncharacteristically awkward, a sensation that only grew as they exclaimed in surprise and scrambled to their feet. "Please," he said, raising his hands, "don't trouble yourselves. I have no wish to disturb you. Gods know you have earned your rest." His gaze sought out a particular face among them. "Liam, may I have a word?"

Liam froze halfway to his feet, momentarily stunned. Then he straightened like a soldier under inspection, doing his best to avoid the questioning looks of his companions. His own expression was one of mild panic, as though Erik had just ordered him to the gallows. *At least I'm not the only one who's nervous*, he thought wryly.

He gestured for Liam to join him, heading for the relative seclusion of the river. They walked in silence. He could sense Liam's unease, but it could not be helped. He did not want to be overheard. He waited until they had passed beyond the soft globe of firelight surrounding the camp. Darkness enfolded them, and a chorus of frogs drowned out the muted sound of nearby voices.

Erik turned to his guards. "We will speak alone. You may remain here." So saying, he led Liam up the bluff overlooking the river.

His brother waited for him to speak.

Brother.

Erik turned the word over in his mind. It was strange to think of this young man as such, after so many years of rejecting the very idea of him. Yet even through the shadows, he could recognise his father in Liam's features, and Tom too. He could even see himself. *Yes, this man is my brother.* Only half, perhaps, but what did it matter? They were bound to each other by blood, and blood could no more be parsed than water. The bond between them could not be undone by word or deed, nor diluted by a lifetime of vastly different experience. That was something to be respected. Cherished, even. Erik had ignored it for far too long.

"I'm sorry to have come upon you so suddenly," he said. Liam did not reply. He was submissive, his gaze downcast, waiting for Erik to continue. When he did glance up, his eyes were full of dread. It was as though he expected Erik to deliver some piece of bad news, or issue some terrible edict. Erik tried not to be annoyed. Given their past history, could he really blame Liam for assuming the worst? "We will reach Erroman soon," he said, choosing his words carefully. He had not had time to prepare, and he did not know Liam well enough to anticipate how he might react. "The enemy will be hard upon our heels. The time has come to deal with my brother. It is likely that Tom and I will meet in parley, and try to resolve this without bloodshed."

Liam remained mute. His silence was presumably meant to be deferential, but it only made Erik more uncomfortable.

"I would like you to be there, Liam."

There was a stretch of silence. When it became clear that a reply was expected of him, Liam said, "As you wish, Your Majesty."

"You understand that I'm asking for more than just your presence. I would like your support."

"My support? You have it, of course, but . . . Well, if you don't mind me asking, what good is that? I'm nobody."

"*Nobody?* Liam . . ." Erik felt sick. This was his doing. His father's doing, and Arran Green's too. *It must have been pounded into him from birth.* Erik was not his family. Erik was his *king.*

It was even worse than he had imagined. *What shall I do now? Do I dare to unmake this?* To acknowledge Liam as family would be to admit he had been wronged as a child, to confess to years of neglect and mistreatment, all of it Erik's fault. That might unlock a torrent of resentment. Perhaps the only thing preventing Liam from hating Erik was that he didn't think he had the right.

"You are my brother, Liam." *There. Too late to back out now.*

Liam opened his mouth. Closed it with a snap. He frowned.

"I have been remiss not to address this sooner." Erik felt himself flush for the first time in years. "I should have . . . found a way. I'm sorry." It felt foolish and inadequate, but he could not think of anything else to say.

Liam did not answer right away. He met Erik's eye at last, revealing a mix of emotions. There was confusion, unease, and, yes, anger. Of course it was there. How could it not be? For the first time, Erik realised that Liam was several inches taller than him.

"You want me to be with you when you meet the Rave . . . Prince Tomald . . . in parley." Liam spoke slowly, as though to make sure he had understood correctly.

"I don't command it of you, Liam, but I ask it. Stand beside me, and let us face our brother together."

Liam regarded him warily, as though half expecting some trick. "There will be other people there . . . besides His Highness, I mean."

"Yes."

"And you want them to know about me? Isn't that . . . a bad idea?"

"No one should have to hide who he is, Liam. You've been forced to do that for too long, and I can never make up for that. But it ends here, if you want it to."

Liam chewed on that for a moment. "I appreciate the sentiment, but I have to ask, why now?"

It was a fair question. Erik sighed. "There is no simple answer to that. I've meant to do this for so long, but it never seemed like the right time. So much has happened over the past months, and . . ." He stopped himself. He was being needlessly obscure. Perhaps it was simple after all. "What it comes down to is this: We are at war, and my kingdom threatens to rip itself apart. In times like these, a man turns to family above all else. You are my family, Liam." *The only family I have left.*

Liam's eyes were guarded, even suspicious. Yet Erik fancied he could also see hope, however timid, peeking through. Liam *wanted* to believe him.

Erik put a hand on his arm. "Think about it, brother. When you're ready, you know where to find me."

He withdrew, heading down the bluff to rejoin his guards. When he glanced back, he saw Liam staring out over the water, arms folded, head bowed. *He'll come around*, Erik told himself. The past was the past. They had both been young. Things were different now.

He would never give his brother cause to resent him again.

TWENTY-ONE

"It's looking a lot better," Gwylim said, peeling the bandage away from Alix's ribs. "I think the poultice has done all it can."

"Thank the Nine Virtues," Alix said. "As much as I appreciate the healing power of that stuff, I've had about all I can take of people covering their noses and fleeing upwind."

"You sure that's the poultice? You haven't bathed in a while."

"Funny."

Alix felt cool water against her skin as Gwylim dabbed at the wound. "You can probably go back to your regular routine now. As long as you make sure the stitches dry out before you cover them, you can soak them if you like."

"In that case, leave the bandage off. I'll head down to the river and have a good wash, and you can put it on later."

Gwylim helped her wriggle into her tunic. As she was pulling it over her head, he said, "I hear congratulations are in order."

She froze, peering at him through the neck hole. "What?"

"Your betrothal." Gwylim's expression was unreadable.

Alix yanked the tunic down a little too forcefully and was

rewarded with a sharp pang in her back. "Word certainly travels fast."

"It does."

"Nothing has been decided. It's politics."

Gwylim nodded inscrutably. *He sees right through you, Alix.*

"Has . . ." She paused, feeling her skin warm. "Has everyone heard?"

"Has Liam heard, you mean?"

There was no point in pretending. She gave a miserable little nod, absently twisting the golden ring on her baby finger.

"I'm sure he has, but I haven't spoken to him about it. I doubt he would welcome any of us broaching the subject."

Alix swore under her breath. *Poor Liam.* As though what had happened weren't bad enough, he had to face the awkwardness of all his friends knowing about it.

Gwylim seemed to read her thoughts. "At least Green promised to make him a knight. That should be some consolation."

Alix brightened. "He did? That's great!" She thought immediately of Erik, how he had promised to speak to Green about Liam's situation. *I wonder if he had anything to do with it . . .*

"After the Battle of the Scions, even Green couldn't deny that Liam was wasted in the scouts. He's with the infantry now."

Her smile withered. The infantry meant the front lines. It meant marching straight into the teeth of the enemy. Four fifths of the men they'd lost were infantry. "Is he . . ." Alix swallowed. "Is he happy about that?"

Gwylim appraised her with kind green eyes. "Why don't you ask him?"

Because he doesn't even speak to me. Aloud, she said, "Maybe I will."

Gwylim rose. "Don't wait too long. There's a war going on, you know."

Alix vacated the tent as soon as Gwylim had left, making way for a pair of soldiers to pack it up for her. The coddling made her feel like a fool, but Erik would brook no argument, so she simply nodded to the men and left them to their business. She made for the river, heading downstream of the camp to find someplace private to wash. She chose a spot where the foot of the bluff was screened by shoulder-high grass. The water sparkled brightly under the morning sun, looking cold and fresh and wonderful. Alix couldn't wait to wade in. She dropped her swordbelt onto the rocks and pulled off her boots. Then she stripped to her smalls and stepped to the river's edge, pausing to enjoy the soft, sucking mud between her toes. She waded in tentatively. By the time the water had reached her navel, she was gasping with cold, and her fingers were rigid around the cake of soap in her hand. She wouldn't last long, but at least she could give herself a good once-over.

She was sitting on the rocks, freshly washed, pulling her boots back on, when a rustle in the grass drew her gaze over her shoulder.

"Oh," said Liam, drawing up short. "Hello."

She straightened. Liam did not look happy to see her.

"Sorry," he said, "I didn't know you were down here. I'll just . . . leave you to it."

Alix's cheeks stung as though she'd been slapped. *So he has been avoiding me after all.* She'd tried to convince herself she was imagining it. It would be awkward to talk in front of the others as they marched. He didn't want Arran Green to see them together. Erik might grow suspicious if Liam tried to seek her out. All this had been rationalisation, lies she told herself to ward off the hurt. The truth could not be more plain: Liam wanted nothing to do with her.

He turned to go.

"Liam, wait."

He pursed his lips with obvious reluctance, but he waited. Alix hesitated a moment, Highmount's warning fresh in her mind, but this was something she had to do. She picked her way over the rocks, her heart in her throat. She couldn't meet his gaze. "I just wanted to say that I'm sorry, for everything. If I could undo it . . . but I can't. I know that I wronged you, in more ways than one." She forced herself to look up.

Liam was fidgeting. He looked like he would rather be facing down a horde of thralls than having this conversation.

She cursed herself silently. All she was doing was making him uncomfortable. Overcome with self-loathing, she said, "You have every right to hate me."

Liam scowled. "Don't be ridiculous, of course I don't hate you. How could you—?" He broke off, shaking his head irritably. "I don't *hate* you, Alix. I could never hate you. I'm not even angry, really—not anymore. I know you didn't do it deliberately. You just go with your instincts, which is one of the things I . . ." He paused, swallowed. "Anyway, I don't hate you. I just . . . can't be around you."

Alix looked away. She didn't want him to see how deeply his words cut. "I understand. I just want you to be happy."

"Don't worry about me. I'm fine, really." He shrugged.

I'm not fine, she wanted to say. And if Liam was recovering nicely, she had a pretty good idea why. The words were out of her mouth before she could stop herself. "How's Kerta?"

His eyes narrowed; for a moment, Alix thought he wouldn't reply. "She's great," he said coolly. "Look, I'd better go. If we don't talk again for a while . . . Well, good-bye, I guess." Hesitantly, he put his arms around her. He was stiff and awkward, and his armour dug into her rib cage, but Alix melted into him anyway. It was all she could do to keep her tears in check. After a moment, he relaxed, holding her more closely. She was acutely aware of his breath on her hair, his hand on the curve of her back. His scent filled her nose, familiar and comforting, leather and metal and something that made her think of home. She moved her head a fraction to drink it in deeper, bringing her lips against the bare flesh of his neck. The urge to kiss him, even just the faintest pressure, was almost overwhelming. A moment more and she might have succumbed, but he pulled away, and she felt the loss of him like a physical chill. He started back toward the bluff.

A light winked somewhere downriver. "What was that?"

Liam paused. "What?"

"I thought I saw . . . There it is again." Just a momentary glint, as of sunlight on metal. "Someone's down there."

"Well, there are about eight thousand of us, so . . ." He shrugged and turned away.

"But there shouldn't be anyone downstream." Something began to gnaw at her gut, subtle but persistent, like a meal that didn't quite agree with her. "I came down here specifically to avoid the others."

"Probably someone else had the same idea."

"I'm going to check it out."

He frowned. "You shouldn't go wandering off by yourself."

"So come with me."

"Alix . . ."

"It'll only take a moment." She picked up her swordbelt and started off. Grumbling under his breath, Liam followed.

The riverbank narrowed as they went, the steep bluff crowding them against the water's edge. They weaved their way through towering temples of grass. Trees played peek-and-hide through the swaying screen, but there was no sign of man or beast.

"You must have imagined it," Liam said. "We should turn back."

"Hush. Did you hear that?" Quietly, Alix drew her sword.

"I didn't hear anything." All the same, he pulled his own blade and swung his shield down from his back.

A twig snapped somewhere nearby. They froze.

Alix licked her lips, her eyes raking the greenery for signs of movement. Her blood rushed in her ears. *It could be anything*, the sensible part of her argued. *A rabbit. A bird. And even if you did see metal, it was probably just a Kingsword, like Liam said . . .* Sensible, all of it, but she knew it wasn't true.

They waited a few more moments in silence. Slowly, the tip of Liam's sword began to droop. "Alix—"

Something erupted from the grass and charged at them. Alix saw a flash of crimson and a glint of metal. Liam grunted in surprise, but he got his shield up in time to block the sword humming toward his neck. Alix lunged, thrusting her blade and withdrawing it in a single motion. A man's body slumped to the ground. Alix tensed, ready for the next attack, but the grass was still.

Long moments passed. The only sound was the soft gasping of the Oridian scout dying at their feet.

"Do you think he was alone?" Alix whispered.

"No way to tell." Liam glanced back over his shoulder. "You should go warn the others. I'll stand guard."

"Not bloody likely."

Liam's jaw twitched. "We don't know what's out there. And you're wounded, remember?"

"I'm fine. I'm not leaving you alone. Anyway, we're within shouting distance of the camp. If we get into trouble, we can call for help."

"Oh, right, well, that makes *perfect* sense. I'm sure the enemy won't mind waiting around for our friends to join us before they kill us."

"Are you coming or not?"

He blew out an exasperated breath. "Gods' blood, woman, you're going to be the death of us both." A graceless surrender, but a surrender nonetheless. Alix parted the grass with the tip of her sword and peered beyond. Nothing. Steeling herself, she plunged through.

The scene before her looked just like the one behind: grass, trees, rocks. No movement. She forged ahead, rolling along the arches of her feet to muffle her footfalls. Liam followed almost as soundlessly, in spite of his plate and mail. The Kingswords trained their scouts well.

About fifty paces on, the ground fell away to the east, offering a good view of the terrain beyond. A thousand shades of green shivered against a canvas of stark blue sky, and the river scattered over the rocks in glistening threads of spun glass. But it was not the beauty of the vista that drew Alix up short. "Oh no," she whispered, her sword nearly slipping from numb fingers.

There were thirty of them, maybe more, their crimson tabards flowing over the rocks like a spreading pool of blood. They moved furtively, their blades already drawn in anticipation of battle.

"Would this be a good time to say I told you so?" Liam asked dryly.

"I wouldn't recommend it."

The raiding party was closing fast. It wouldn't be long before they fell upon the Kingsword camp. *They'll catch the men unawares, but still . . . they'll never get out alive.* Thirty against eight thousand. What were they thinking?

There was no time to worry about it now. "Options?" she asked.

Just then, an Oridian looked their way and pointed. As one, the men turned their heads.

Liam sighed. "I'd say it boils down to running or dying."

The Oridians charged.

Alix and Liam sprinted back upstream, but they didn't get far. A pair of enemies rushed at them from the grass—more scouts, moving out ahead of the pack. Alix crouched, keeping tight to Liam's shield side for added protection. It proved a wise move, for the first Oridian that lunged at her was nearly decapitated by Liam's shield. He used it like a weapon, slicing out with a snap of his elbow at the man's unprotected throat and sending a sheet of blood arcing through the air. It cut through far too cleanly for an ordinary shield. Liam must have filed the steel banding down to a razor edge. A clever trick; Alix hoped he had more of them.

The second Oridian came at them more cautiously, harrying them just enough to pin them down while his comrades caught up. Within moments, it was three on two. They doubled up on Liam, while the third went for Alix. Her attacker was quick, but not quick enough; she turned aside his downstroke and cleaved off his hand. He kept attacking, barrelling into her with his shield, but Alix spun aside, ramming her blade into his exposed flank. *Thrall*, she thought grimly as he fell. He hadn't even flinched when she cut off his hand. "Fall back! Where the bank narrows!"

Liam obeyed, and they let themselves be driven back until they reached a thin strip of rocks hemmed in by bluff and deep water. The defile was only wide enough for two or three to fight abreast—a perfect choke point.

"Better, but we're still in trouble." Liam drove the point of his sword into a man's chest, then planted a boot in his gut and sent him sprawling backward into the gathering crowd. Two more Oridians surged forward to take his place, stepping over their fallen comrade without so much as a glance. *More thralls. How many of them can there be?* Alix looked into their flat, soulless eyes, and saw the truth. *All of them. Gods have mercy.*

She fought shoulder-to-shoulder with Liam, beating them back as best she could, but she knew they couldn't hold out for long. Thralls were piling up at the choke point, jostling to get by one another in their frenzy. It was like holding back a riot. A thicket of blades flashed in every direction. Blood spattered across Alix's chest as the Oridian she was fighting lost an arm to the man behind him. Men in full plate armour waded out into the river, only to be dragged under by the current. Others tried to scrabble up the embankment. Alix and Liam fell back again, but they were running out of room, and still the crowd pressed in. *They're going to trample us*, she thought dully.

Suddenly, thralls began to stagger and fall. It took Alix a moment to understand what was happening; then she spied the arrows raining down from above, and she looked up to find the top of the bluff studded with archers. A war cry sounded, then another, and Kingswords poured down the embankment with sword and axe and mace.

"Thank the gods," Alix breathed.

Erik's men slammed into the enemy like an avalanche, driving them back into the water and down the riverbank. But it wasn't over yet. Liam was still locked with a huge thrall, his face contorted with exertion as he tried unsuccessfully to push the Oridian back. Their swords were crossed; the Oridian leaned into Liam with all his considerable weight. Over his shoulder, an even bigger thrall loomed, a fearsome war axe clutched in both hands. Alix watched in horror as he twisted his body, ready to deliver a swipe that would fell both combatants in a single blow.

Crying out, she threw herself at Liam's knees, toppling him and his foe both as the axe groaned uselessly overhead. The two men crashed down on top of her in a heap of armour and agony. Luckily, she didn't have to endure it for long. Somehow, through a struggle she couldn't see, Liam slew both of his enemies without even getting up.

Alix groaned as Liam rolled off her. Pain throbbed in her back, and she felt a warm, sticky wetness. Gwylim would not be pleased.

They lay still in the mud, regaining their breath as the Kingswords finished off the enemy. "Thanks for that," Liam said. "You're getting pretty good at the saving thing."

"Lots of practice."

He heaved himself up, then helped Alix to sit. "Right, let's have a look." He lifted the back of her shirt and peered underneath. "Not good, Allie."

She winced. "I figured."

"Wonderful." A shadow spilled over them, and Alix looked up into the angry face of her brother. "Missing the leisurely rides in the supply wagon, were you?"

"Hello to you too, Rig. Glad to see you're all right."

Liam drew back, smiling awkwardly at being caught looking under Alix's shirt. "Er, hi."

Rig flicked him a glance, but his attention was all on Alix. "Did it occur to you at any point while you were wading through a sea of Oridians that there was an entire army right on the other side of this bluff?" He pointed with a blood-stained blade.

Alix opened her mouth to reply, but at that moment, Arran Green appeared, looking no more pleased than Rig. Liam swore softly.

"You disappoint me again, Liam. It is precisely this kind of recklessness that has delayed your knighthood for so long."

Rig looked sharply at Alix's companion. *"You're* Liam?"

Liam raised his eyebrows. "Pleased to meet you?"

"And you just let her march straight into an entire raiding party?" Rig gestured impatiently at Alix. He hadn't even considered the possibility that Liam had gone first. He knew his sister too well.

"Wait, how did this become my fault?" Now Liam was the one waving irritably at Alix. "She wouldn't listen to me. She never does!"

Alix threw her hands over her ears. "Argh! Enough! I'm sorry, Rig. I'm sorry, Liam. I'm sorry, General. Are we through here?"

Rig sighed and shook his head. "You are *impossible,* Allie." He adopted a thoughtful look. "I blame Father."

Alix grinned. Rig never could stay angry with her for long. Arran Green, though, was not so easily appeased. "Your carelessness could have cost many lives, including your own. The fact that you both sit here alive and well is down to luck and no more. If you cannot exercise better judgement than that, you do not belong in the Kingswords, still less at the side of the king. Am I understood?"

"Yes, General," Alix and Liam said in unison.

Liam leaned over to help her stand. His eyes sparkled with mischief, and the corner of his mouth curled in a hint of that grin that had snared her so long ago. "Some things never change," he whispered in her ear.

Alix shivered warmly. He was right about that.

TWENTY-TWO

✝ "I don't understand it," Erik said, surveying the carnage. He looked ill, and Alix couldn't blame him. Bodies littered the riverbank. Blood swirled in nooks and eddies, and limbs could be seen poking out of the water like driftwood. Only a handful of the dead were Kingswords, but it was a sickening sight all the same. "What did they hope to accomplish?"

"An excellent question, Your Majesty," said Arran Green. "They could not have thought to deal much damage with so few men. Even if they were thralls."

Impossibly, Erik paled even more. "What—all of them?"

"All of them. According to Liam and the captain, at any rate."

Erik's gaze snapped to Alix and Liam, and she caught the briefest flicker of fear before he mastered himself. "You're certain?" he asked her.

"Positive. They came at us like a starving mob after the last loaf of bread. I've never seen anything like it."

"Keep your voice down, Captain," Arran Green said with a frown. "You will sow panic among the men."

Rig, who had observed the exchange in silence until now,

said, "There's your answer, Erik. What they hoped to accomplish was fear. They're flaunting the Priest's power. They want us to lie awake at night terrified that we'll be set upon at any moment by a horde of thralls."

Green gave a thoughtful grunt. "If that is their goal, they may well have succeeded. Some of the men may have recognised the signs, just as the captain did. If so, word will spread through the ranks, and if the Kingswords are infected with fear, they will bring that disease into the city as well. All of Erroman will succumb."

"We must not let that happen," Erik said. "A frightened people is a broken people."

Rig leaned on the crossguard of his greatsword, head bowed in thought. The garnets embedded in the hilt threw bloody droplets of light over his breastplate. "If we strike back, it might placate the men somewhat."

"But it will take time," Erik said, "and we need to get to Erroman. The fifty thousand at the border must have begun their march by now."

Liam stirred. He was standing right next to Alix, but he'd been so quiet that she had almost forgotten he was there. He shifted restlessly from foot to foot; he obviously had something to say, but he hadn't been given leave to speak. Fortunately, Alix no longer suffered from such reservations. "What is it, Liam?"

He blinked at her, half amused, half mortified. "Well . . . er . . ." He glanced at the king, but Erik only returned his gaze expectantly. "It's just . . . Based on the enemy's last known location, they're too far away to have staged that raid. A smaller group must have broken off and followed us. A very small group, or our scouts would have spotted them."

"True enough," said Arran Green, "but even so, His Majesty is right—we cannot spare the time to deal with them. The whole of the Oridian strength might even now be making its way to our doorstep."

"What if it's worth our while?" Liam said, uncharacteristically bold. "They can't be far, and if those raiders were thralls—"

"Then the Priest is probably with them." Rig's eyes lit up with a predatory gleam. "By the gods, he's right. If Madan has left himself so exposed . . . We'd be fools to pass up this chance, Erik."

"We cannot be certain the Priest is nearby," Green said, but the protest lacked conviction. Even the commander general was tempted.

Erik eyed both knights appraisingly. He glanced again at the wreckage of corpses at their feet. His jaw set grimly. Alix knew what his answer would be. "You're right, we cannot afford to ignore this opportunity. Destroying the Priest would deal the enemy a massive blow. But I'll not throw my men against an unknown foe. Green, you will take a scouting party and track them down. If you see a chance to kill Madan, take it. Otherwise, report back to me, and we will decide what to do from there."

"As you wish, Your Majesty, but this mission will not be easy. We must do more than determine the enemy's location. We must confirm that the Trion is among them. For that, we will need to get close—very close. Stealth is of the utmost importance. I will need our best."

"Of course, I assumed . . ." Erik paused, eyes narrowing. "Wait. Are you saying that you wish to take Alix with you?"

"She is the stealthiest of all the scouts—or at least, she was. Assuming her skills have not grown dull, she is the best we have."

Alix struggled to keep her surprise from showing. She had thought her scouting days done forever.

"I don't think so," said Erik.

"Out of the question," said Rig.

"She'll do great," said Liam.

Erik regarded his brother in mild disbelief. "Pardon?"

Liam fidgeted, but he stood his ground. "I've been on loads of scouting missions with Alix, and there's no question she's the best. She can get within slapping distance of the enemy without being seen. Plus, she's a great fighter. It would be crazy not to take her." Alix couldn't decide what amazed her more—Liam's confidence in her, or his confidence in himself. *What's gotten into him?* He had always been so awkward in front of Erik.

"I appreciate your faith in my sister's talents," Rig said coolly, "but she's wounded."

Alix shrugged. "I'm not worried about myself—"

"What else is new?" Rig snapped.

She ignored him. "—but I *am* concerned about the king. I don't like the idea of leaving His Majesty alone, even for a short while."

Erik locked eyes with her, his gaze full of the unspoken. She could read his frustration. There was no argument he could make that would not mark him a coward or a lover, and he wouldn't risk appearing to be either. He gave a tiny shake of his head, his lips pursed in displeasure. "Go, then, but we will need to discuss arrangements for your absence. Come by my tent when you're through here." Alix watched him go with a heavy feeling. She was not looking forward to that conversation.

Green gave the scouts two hours to prepare themselves. Though Erik had instructed her to go directly to his pavilion, Alix sought out a healer instead. She had no desire to face the king until she was whole. She sat in sullen silence while the healer stitched her back up, only half listening to his lecturing. She would have to find Gwylim too, and get more of that gods-forsaken poultice, but even that would be pleasant in comparison to the conversation that awaited her in the king's tent.

All too soon, Alix found herself standing outside the royal pavilion. She hovered there a moment, gazing unenthusiastically at the tent flap, but she'd put it off as long as she dared. Steeling herself, she called, "Your Majesty?"

"Come in."

He sat at his desk, a book laid out before him. Alix knew him to be an avid reader, but it didn't look like he'd been deeply engrossed. The book was pushed away from him, as though he'd given up on it, and when he looked up at her, his expression made it clear he was in no mood for reading.

Alix sighed. "You're angry."

"What did you expect?"

"I'm sorry, Erik, but I can't just sit back and stay out of trouble. Anyway, I'll be fine. I was a scout before I was your bodyguard."

He was unmoved. "I wonder, do scouts generally consider thirty-to-one odds favourable?"

"Ah. That." Alix looked away. "There may have been a lapse in judgement there, I admit."

"*May* have been? One of these days, your recklessness is going to cost you dearly. Cost all of us, perhaps. Do you not realise what's at stake here? We could be conquered. Gods, we're half conquered already! By a man who knows how to *enslave men's minds*, no less. This is not a game!"

"I know that."

He sighed. "I know you do. But you cannot afford to slip into old habits anymore. Neither of us can." He got up and started to pace, his gaze trained on the ground. The gravity of his countenance sat oddly on a man of his youth, and Alix was struck yet again by how much Erik had changed these past months. Much of it was undeniably for the better. He was a subtler creature, more inclined to take counsel, more critical of himself and those around him. He no longer trusted so easily, or made decisions so quickly. But it had been a long time since Alix had seen a glimpse of Erik's sunshine. He smiled, he laughed, but it wasn't the same. His youthful optimism was spent; in its place was worry and doubt. Alix knew it was for the best, but part of her was sorry for it.

Erik stopped before her, his expression resigned. "It's futile, isn't it? No matter what I do, you will be in danger."

"And so will you."

"It seems we're doomed to worry about one another."

Alix looked down at her boots. "I suppose we are."

He lifted her chin gently, and Alix found herself swimming in the blue sea of his eyes. He brushed his thumb over her cheek, setting her blood thrumming. He was so near, but he didn't close the space between them. Instead, he held her gaze intently, as though searching for something. They stayed like that for long moments, neither of them moving. Then Erik's eyes clouded over, and he dropped his hand, turning away.

"I can't wait for you forever, Alix," he said quietly. After a pause, he added, "I will have to move out in three days. I've told Green that if you're not back by then, we start for Erroman without you."

"All right."

"I don't want to do that."

"Understood." She started to reach for him, thought better of it. Her hand dropped to her side. "Farewell, my king."

He turned around and took her shoulder. His lips brushed her forehead. "May the gods watch over you," he said, and he let her go.

Alix struggled through the undergrowth, doing her best not to sound winded. She hadn't been on a trek this long in months, and it showed. Or rather, it felt. Even in leather armour, her limbs were starting to feel heavy and awkward, and her lungs protested noisily, though she tried to hide it. Meanwhile, just ahead, Kerta sprang lightly through the brush, as graceful and silent as a deer. Sullenly, Alix mimed drawing a bow at her back.

"Not nice," said a low voice from just behind her.

Alix flushed. She'd thought she was bringing up the rear, but obviously not; Gwylim appeared beside her, a wry grin on his lips. "Not her fault you're out of shape," he said with his usual tact.

"Have I told you how much I missed having you around? No? Must have been an oversight."

"Must have."

"Quiet," Arran Green snapped over his shoulder.

Just behind him, Liam turned around and feigned a scowl, pointing severely at Alix and Gwylim. He'd been in a playful mood all afternoon, delighted at having been asked to join the mission. Like Alix, he was technically no longer a scout, but he had more experience than any of them, and Green wanted him along. Erik hadn't been happy about that either, but he couldn't very well intervene, not without raising eyebrows. Besides, he probably knew his brother wouldn't welcome his interference. For all his jests, Liam valued Arran Green's good opinion above all else.

"We can't be far now," Gwylim whispered. "There isn't much forest left before we reach the fields again."

Alix nodded in agreement. If the Oridians had been camped on open ground, they would have been spotted by one of the routine scouting missions. The terrain was too flat to hide them. Only the narrow strip of trees around the river offered any cover, and it ran out a few miles ahead, where the river bisected Anderly town. Unless the Oridians had turned back, they were almost certainly nearby. Arran Green must have had the same thought, because he came to an abrupt halt.

"We will fan out," he said, "in the usual pairs." That meant Alix and Liam, Gwylim and Ide. Nik had been slain at Boswyck, leaving Kerta to pair off with Green. *One light, one heavy*, the commander general called it, reflecting his old-fashioned views. Women were stealthy but weak; they needed strong men to protect them. Alix wondered how he accounted for a small man like Gwylim, or an ox like Ide, or if he even bothered to think about it.

Alix took the point position, as always. Liam fell in behind wordlessly, both of them settling back into the old routine as easily as if no time had passed. That was why Green had put them together, in spite of everything; a military man knew better than to disrupt a good team. And they were a good team. The best. It felt so natural that for a moment Alix forgot to be afraid. She listened to the soft crackling of Liam's footfalls, felt his reassuring presence at her back. It was like scratching an itch she hadn't known was there, and something inside her relaxed. She wondered if he felt it too. Her thumb drifted instinctively to the ring on her little finger. *Should I say something?* But it was hardly the time. The enemy might be . . .

"Wait." Liam's whisper cut through the trees.

Alix froze, silently rebuking herself for letting her attention wander.

"Do you smell that?"

She drew a deep draught of air. *Smoke.* If Liam hadn't said something, she would have missed it altogether. Licking her finger, she held it up to the wind. *Northeast*, she decided, pointing. Quietly, she unsheathed her dirk and scanned the gloom between the trees. This too felt familiar, bringing to mind the raid they'd stumbled on only hours before. Liam's thoughts must have taken a similar turn, because his lips pursed grimly. He cocked his head upwind, and they started out.

Alix picked her way carefully through the brush. She had donned her old scouting gear, trading her heavy boots for doeskin, her plate and mail for dark leather that blended into the shadows. Liam wore similar garb. Only the blades of their dirks, barely longer than daggers, risked catching the light, and Alix kept hers tucked close to her body as she had been taught. Every few paces, she stopped and listened, straining to hear through the subtle din of wind, leaves, and birdsong. She closed her eyes, the better to shut out distractions.

Her nose caught smoke again, stronger this time. She pressed herself up against a tree, motioning for Liam to do the same. She listened. When she was satisfied all was still, she darted ahead a few paces and ducked behind another tree. She waited. Behind her, Liam traced her steps. Bit by bit they moved forward, until Alix spotted a flash of colour. She dropped low and peered around the tree trunk.

A sentry leaned against a white-skinned poplar, looking bored. His crimson tabard did him no favours; he stood out like a wildflower after a fire. Alix chewed her lip uncertainly. If Ide were with them, she might have dropped the sentry with an arrow. As it was, Alix could think of only one way to deal with him, but it was risky. She looked back over her shoulder, her eyes scanning the undergrowth. At first she saw only empty forest, but after a moment, Liam peered around a tree and met her eye. She mimed tossing something, and he nodded. Moments later, a branch spun through the air to land with a leafy rustle behind her. Alix flattened herself against her tree and waited.

A crackle of brush signalled that the sentry had taken the bait. Alix clutched her dirk to her chest and held her breath. The footsteps drew close. Stopped. Alix's heart hammered in her ears. Another snap and rustle, and he was on the move again. A flash of crimson appeared in her peripheral vision. Alix waited until the sentry had passed, then slipped up behind him and slashed her blade across his throat. He folded over himself with a gurgle and slumped to the ground. Alix briefly considered dragging him off someplace out of sight, but dismissed the idea. It would take too long and make too much noise. She settled for arranging the brush around him as best she could.

A little farther on, she spotted the first sign of the Oridian camp: a heavy wagon hunkered in the shade of an immense oak tree. She frowned. *Why would they struggle through the woods with* that? She shifted position to get a better look, and she had her answer. *Prisoners.* A dozen or more, packed so tightly into the wagon that elbows and knees and hands protruded between the wooden bars. *What in the gods are they taking prisoners for?* There was no call for rounding up civilians like cattle. *Savages*, she thought bitterly.

The prisoners complicated matters. Alix wasn't under any illusions about rescuing them—Arran Green would never permit a risk like that—but a dozen prisoners had a dozen pairs of eyes, and she couldn't be sure what they would do if one of them spotted her. She crouched, debating her next move.

Voices sounded nearby. Alix tensed and ducked lower. A pair of Oridian soldiers made their way toward the wagon, and when the prisoners caught sight of them, they began to whimper and plead.

"Please don't take me," a man's voice said. "I'm too old."

"Not my son!" a woman wailed. "Not my son!"

The Oridians ignored them. One soldier unlocked the rear door of the wagon, while the other stood with a crossbow trained on the prisoners. They dragged a young man out by the hair and tossed him off the back before locking up the wagon once more.

The young man lay still, trembling. It was not until the soldiers hauled him to his feet that he spoke. "Please," he said. "Please don't take my blood. I don't want to be one of them. I'll fight anyway. I'll do whatever you want." One of the soldiers cuffed him into silence, and together, the Oridians lugged him away.

Alix's blood had gone cold. *I must have misheard. I must have misunderstood.* Instinctively, she turned around to look at Liam. He stared back at her, his eyes round with horror, and she knew she hadn't misunderstood.

They're bleeding the prisoners. Merciful Nine, they're turning them into thralls. Our own people . . .

Rage pooled in her guts, searing hot and sickening. Her fingers tightened around the hilt of her dirk. *Arran Green be damned. I'm getting these people out.* Liam would help her. She knew he would.

Alix rose from her crouch. No sooner had she done so than a terrible sound ripped through the silence and froze her veins all over again.

Kerta was screaming.

TWENTY-THREE

A lix whipped around to look at Liam, but he had already bolted from his hiding place and taken off in the direction of the sound. She charged after him, her mind a tumult. Kerta's screams shredded her concentration, leaving her with only ragged scraps of thought. *Pain, or fear? Liam too fast. Going to get caught. Take our blood.*

Liam coursed through the trees like a hound with a scent; Alix caught only glimpses of him amid a flurry of green and amber and brown. It was all she could do to follow. Branches caught at her armour and stung her cheeks, and she nearly turned an ankle stumbling over a root. With each step, she fell farther behind. She had the vague sense they were headed back the way they had come, but the screaming disoriented her. It bounced off trees and filtered through brush, seeming to come from several directions at once.

"Liam!" Her voice was lost in the crashing of her own footfalls. She tried again, louder this time. "Liam!"

He heard me. I know he heard me. Still he ran on.

"Damn it, Liam, *stop!*"

He held up, whipped around. "What?"

"We have to slow down." She trotted up to him, panting. "We're making too much noise—"

"Noise?" He gestured furiously at the trees. "Are you *listening* to that? You know what they're doing to her! You heard what they said!"

"We can't help her if we're dead. You keep moving like that, you're going to bring the whole camp down on our heads."

"She's one of *us*," he snapped. "You used to know what that meant."

Alix flinched, stunned into silence.

"Shut it, both of you!" Ide's scowling face popped out from behind a screen of leaves. "Gonna get us all killed!"

Gwylim materialised at Alix's side. "She's stopped," he said. It took Alix a moment to realise what he meant. The woods were silent. Kerta was silent.

Oh, gods. Alix felt a stab of guilt for every unkind thought she'd ever had about Kerta Middlemarch. *Please let her be all right.*

Liam was beside himself. "We have to find her! And Green—where in the hells is he?"

"We'll find them," Gwylim said. "*Quietly.* This way."

They threaded through the trees, moving cautiously once more. The sudden calm chewed at Alix's nerves. Where was the wind? The birdsong? It seemed to her that the forest held its breath, disturbed by the unnatural forces at work in its midst. The only sound was their footfalls rustling and snapping, a veritable clamour against the eerie hush.

A slash of crimson appeared in the undergrowth. Alix tensed, but Ide raised a hand and mouthed, "*Dead.*" She patted her bow by way of explanation. Alix wondered how many more sentries might be about. If Kerta and Arran Green had been taken, the Oridians would probably assume there were more enemy scouts nearby. *Four against gods know how many, and miles from any help.*

A voice sounded from just ahead. Alix and the others dropped to the undergrowth. Another voice, closer at hand, gave answer. Alix caught the Oridian word for "carry," but the rest was gibberish. Not for the first time, she cursed herself for not paying closer attention to her lessons. *A woman of your station must know her languages,* her mother used to say, though Alix doubted these were quite the circumstances she'd had in mind.

She could see them now: a pair of soldiers crouched over something in the bushes. They straightened, hauling a limp form between them. Green. The commander general was motionless, his head drooping to his chest. Unconscious or dead? At this distance, it was impossible to tell. *They're moving him. They wouldn't bother if he were dead.* So she told herself, but who knew what grisly uses the Priest might have for a corpse? She pushed the thought away.

Gwylim's ash-blond hair poked up from the leaves. He met Alix's eye and jerked his head in the direction of the departing Oridians. *We follow.* Alix nodded her understanding.

The Oridians dragged Arran Green all the way back to their camp, but they didn't take him to the prisoner wagon. Instead, they deposited him outside a large pavilion ostentatiously stitched with the golden trident of Oridia. The guards flanking the entrance barely spared a glance for the body at their feet; apparently, they had seen it all before. One of the two soldiers who had brought Green ducked inside the tent. The other waited with the guards, arms folded, a bored expression on his face. Alix imagined an arrow sprouting from his eye, as though wishing it could make it so.

Moments later, the first soldier reappeared, accompanied by a thin man in blood-red robes. Alix recognised the raiment of an Oridian priest, and her breath caught in her throat. But when she looked at Gwylim, he shook his head. *Not him.* He gestured at his chest, tracing a pattern with his fingers. Something about the robes was wrong, apparently. A design was missing, something that would identify him as the Trion. *But still, I'd bet all the gold in the Black River that Madan is in that tent.*

The robed man squatted over Arran Green's inert form. He nodded and said something to the soldiers, and they hauled Green up again. As they talked, a second priest appeared from inside the pavilion carrying a shallow silver bowl. He took a few steps away from the tent and lunged, sending a sheet of dark liquid crashing into the bushes. The move dislodged a cloud of flies, and above, a trio of crows cackled approvingly. *Blood*, Alix thought, bile rising in the back of her throat.

The priests both disappeared back inside the tent, leaving the soldiers to drag Arran Green away. They didn't go far, circling the pavilion and dumping Green in a small clearing behind the tent. There, another priest hunched over a body like an ungainly red vulture. Alix couldn't see what he was doing, but when he moved, she spied a flash of spun gold against a pale brow. Kerta. The priest stood. In his arms he carried a silver bowl identical to the one his comrade had carried. Alix had no doubt what was in it. The priest started to make his way toward the pavilion. Now she was certain Madan was in there. The blood was being brought to him so he could perform whatever gods-cursed ritual he used to turn human beings into his personal puppets. He was about to perform that ritual on Kerta, to bind her with her own blood. *Farika's mercy, we can't let them make her a thrall. Better she dies . . .*

The soldiers standing over Green suddenly drew their blades. The commander general was stirring. One of the soldiers raised his sword over his head, ready to club his prisoner back into unconsciousness. Alix nearly choked aloud. Without Green, they had no chance.

There was no time for planning. No time even for decisions. Alix let out a cry and charged.

The soldiers whirled at the sound. One of them took a step toward Alix, but he staggered suddenly, one of Ide's arrows lodged in his throat. Alix closed in on the second soldier, her dirk at the ready. From behind came the sound of her companions crashing through the brush.

The priest with Kerta's blood hesitated, looking down into the bowl uncertainly. Self-preservation won out; he dropped the bowl and fled. Gwylim gave chase, kicking the bowl over as he passed. Alix had never seen him look more determined.

The guard circled her, demanding her full attention. She coiled for a strike, but Liam never gave her the chance. He flew past her in a blur, launching himself into the air and slamming the point of his dirk into the narrow gap between spaulders and breastplate, dropping the soldier with chilling precision. He was on the move as soon as his boots hit ground, squaring off to face a guard who'd come running to help. Alix grabbed the fallen soldier's sword and tossed it to Liam. He'd do better with a longer blade.

She glanced over at Green. Ide knelt at his side, helping him to sit. Satisfied that her commander was seen to, Alix moved to flank Liam's foe. But by now the second guard had arrived, and Alix had problems of her own. The guard was armed with a two-handed greatsword, too much weapon to counter with her slim dirk. If only she'd had her bloodblade, they might have been more evenly matched, but like Liam, she had traded protection for stealth. To make matters worse, the garnets studding the crossguard marked the weapon as bloodforged. It would be lighter and nimbler than a conventional greatsword, making it harder for Alix to compensate with speed. But there was nothing to be done about it now. Swallowing down a thick knot of fear, she braced for attack.

He came at her with a thrust. Alix leapt aside, instinctively bringing her blade down to cross, but the dirk only glanced off the sturdy edge of the greatsword. The move cost her balance, and a second lunge nearly took her in the midsection. She spun, trying to get behind her attacker, but he pivoted with her, keeping the point of his sword trained on her. He was too smart to try a slash; she would just get under his backswing, or dart into his follow-through. Instead he lined her up for another thrust, feinting left before diving right. Alix read his footwork in time, but just barely, and she was too unsteady to mount a counterstrike. At this rate, she would be exhausted before she landed a single hit.

The guard dove again, and this time, when Alix stepped aside, he tried to smash her in the face with the butt of his sword. She ducked the blow and managed to get her dirk up under his arm, burying it to the hilt. The guard grunted and staggered back. The dirk was wrenched free from Alix's grasp; it dangled for a moment before dropping to the ground, a streamer of blood trailing after it. *Let's see how well you handle that steel now.* Bloodblade or no, the greatsword weighed too much to use one-handed.

But he wasn't dead yet, and Alix was without a weapon. The guard took his sword half-hand, grasping the blade to steady it. He charged. Alix twisted behind him. As he came around, she grabbed the hilt of his sword, grappling with him just long enough to slam a boot into the back of his knee. He buckled, and in one smooth motion, Alix scooped up her dirk and opened his throat.

More soldiers crashed into the clearing. Alix eyed the fallen greatsword regretfully. Even if she'd been strong enough to wield it, the blade had been forged of someone else's blood; it would never obey her. Her dirk would have to do.

Beside her, Liam finished off the guard he was fighting and engaged a new foe. Ide had jumped into the fray, and Arran Green too, though the commander general looked a little unsteady on his feet. Their numbers were almost evenly matched. *So few*, Alix thought, confused. *We should be over-whelmed by now. Where are the rest of them?*

"The Priest!" Arran Green called as he crossed swords with a guard. "Find him, Alix!"

She obeyed, heading straight for the pavilion. As she rounded the back corner, she came upon the priest who'd been collecting Kerta's blood. He lay on his back, eyes staring sightlessly at the sky. He'd been opened from navel to breastbone. Gwylim's work. But where had he gone? Her answer came as she spied a long slash in the canvas wall of the pavilion, as though someone had taken a sword to it. She hesitated only a moment before diving through.

She had barely stepped inside before her boot caught something, and she nearly went down. As her eyes adjusted to the gloom, the heap at her feet resolved itself into Gwylim. He lay prone near the opening, hair matted with blood. He gazed up at her groggily. He started to gesture at something, but then his eyes went wide. Alix spun in time to see the flash of a blade. She threw herself to the ground and rolled into a crouch. An Oridian guard loomed over her. He started to lunge, but Gwylim stuck his knee out, sending the guard sprawling into Alix's arms. She killed him cleanly.

A scramble of movement on the far side of the tent drew her eye. Another guard was rushing toward her. Beyond him, a pair of priests struggled to help a third man to his feet. Alix could see him only in profile, but he looked ancient: thin, hairless, bloodless. The priests were shouting at him as though he were half deaf. Alix recognised a handful of words. *Danger. Go.* Then the guard was upon her, and she was ducking out of the way of another blade. At her feet, Gwylim groaned; Alix glimpsed the look of pure desperation in his eyes as he struggled to sit. "Madan. Getting away. Don't let him, Alix . . ."

She deflected one blow and stepped inside another, landing an ineffectual cut against the guard's breastplate. He tried to pivot around her, but Alix grabbed his wrist and immobilised his sword hand. They struggled. Across the tent, the priests had finally managed to get the third man to his feet. He sagged between them, as though he lacked the strength to stand on his own. He turned his head toward the commotion at the back of the pavilion.

Deep shadows sketched the angles of a hollowed, ashen face. Sunken eyes met Alix's, took the measure of her from across the tent. There was no fear in those eyes. There was nothing at all. Madan gazed at her long enough for her heart to beat, to send her blood coursing through every inch of her body, to sound a single, dull thud in her ears. Then he looked away, and his priests dragged him through the tent flap and beyond.

Alix cried out in frustration, summoning all her strength, but the guard was too strong, her blade too short. Her knees were slowly giving out beneath his weight. Determination melted into despair. *He was right there. Right there, and I let him get away!* The guard hooked his boot behind her ankle, trying to drag her leg out from under her. Then Gwylim was there, lurching into the guard and tangling him up just enough for Alix to break free and jab her dirk up under his chin. He jerked and gasped and died on his feet.

Shouts sounded outside the tent. *Attack. Hurry.* Alix slipped her arm under Gwylim's. "Madan," he breathed.

"We have to go. More of them are coming." She started to steer him away.

"Escaping . . ."

"He's gone, Gwylim. We have to get out of here." He slumped against her resignedly, and they ducked outside. There, they came upon a bloodied Arran Green. "The Priest got away," Alix reported before he could ask. Green said nothing. He just nodded and took Gwylim's other arm.

They rounded the tent to find Liam and Ide flanking a single, grim-looking Oridian. He didn't put up much of a fight. He tried his luck with Ide, but she parried easily, and Liam took him in the back. With his death, the scouts suddenly found themselves alone in the clearing.

"There are more of them on the far side of the tent," Alix said. "They'll be here any moment."

"Doubtful," said Green. "They are focused on getting the Priest out of danger. But once that is done, they will come back. We must be gone by then."

Liam gathered a limp Kerta into his arms and looked her over, stricken. "Probably just blood loss," Gwylim said, still sounding woozy. "They wouldn't have hurt her too much if they wanted to make her a thrall."

Liam nodded, but he didn't look comforted. "Let's get out of here," he said, cradling Kerta protectively against him.

"Wait," said Alix, "the prisoners . . ."

"No time," said Green.

"But there's only a handful of enemy soldiers left. It looks like this was just a staging point—"

"*Enough.*" Green's eyes were as hard as his voice. "We do not know how many they are. Gwylim and Kerta cannot fight, and I am not at my best. Do you intend that three of us should face the enemy alone?"

Alix felt heat rise to her face. She opened her mouth to retort, but the words died on her lips. Green was right. There was no way of knowing how many Oridians were left, but it was almost certainly too many. And they would be back any moment now. As soon as their Trion was safely whisked away, they would return for their prisoners—and for revenge.

Green stared her down until the defiance drained from her eyes. "This way," he said, and he led his ragged, broken party back into the trees and out of sight.

Alix sat perched on the edge of her cot, staring into nothing. She'd been there for half an hour, maybe more, just sitting in her armour, the blood of the men she'd killed still caked on her skin. She'd managed to remove her swordbelt; the weapon stood clutched in her hand, tip resting on the ground. But that was as much as she'd been able to accomplish. For the rest, it was as if she had arrived only moments before. She felt hollow. Frozen. Blank but for a single thought that haunted the empty corridors inside her:

You let him get away.

He was *right there*. Madan. The Priest. The most powerful of the three Oridian lords, the zealot who drove his country to war again and again to please his gods. The bloodbinder who kept his army equipped with enchanted weapons. The dark witch who enslaved men's wills, turned them into mindless monsters. He'd been fifteen feet away at most, so feeble he could barely stand. And Alix had let him escape.

There would never be another chance. Not like that. Alix had failed her king and her country. How many more would die because of her? How many more turned into puppets? The terrorised faces of the Aldenian prisoners seemed to stare out at her from the shadows, accusing. *You left us behind. You left us to* him. Would she recognise one of them someday, on the wrong side of the battlefield, charging toward her with a blank face and a bloody blade?

She closed her eyes to ward off the tears. Then she heard a rustle near the door, and she opened them again. The king stood inside the tent flap.

He didn't speak. He just gazed down at her, taking in her filthy state with an unreadable expression. The light from a tallow candle flamed along the contours of his armour, giving him a strange glow, as if he were some heavenly being come to judge her. Perhaps that was not far off. Erik would certainly have been informed by now. He would know of her failure, how she had let their greatest enemy slip through her fingers. She tried to meet his eye. Couldn't. Couldn't even draw herself up straighter to receive his judgement. She hadn't the dignity. She stared at the ground and waited.

But Erik wouldn't let her off that easy. He dropped to his haunches before her, bringing him to eye level. Alix tried again to look at him, but she still couldn't bear it. She got as far as his breastplate before she froze, trembling, unable to continue. He took her chin and tilted her head until she had no choice but to meet his gaze. Then her eyes swam with tears, and she saw no more.

Erik rose and turned away. *He's leaving*, Alix thought dully. *He's too disgusted even to speak.* But instead he went to the basin and poured out a pitcher of water, returning a moment later with a bowl and a damp cloth. He sank to his knees. Gently, he pried the sword from her fingers and set it aside. Then he took her face in his hands and began to dab at it. Alix started to reach for the cloth, to take it from him, but her arms wouldn't move. It was as if she were numb from the neck down. Rivulets of water mixed with the tears sliding down her cheeks as he caressed her face with the cloth, lifting away the blood and dirt. He worked in silence, as methodical as any healer. When he'd finished, he went on to her hands, washing her fingers with his own. Alix watched him, mesmerised, shame and despair and warmth and want mingling like blood and water in a bowl. She was still trembling, but she was no longer sure why.

The water and the tears dried together. Alix tried to find her voice, but she was afraid of breaking whatever spell had brought the King of Alden to her tent, to his knees, to wash away her sins.

Erik took her hand in both of his and turned it over, exposing the buckles of her vambrace. He started at her wrist and worked his way up, first the right vambrace, then the left. When the armour came free, he set it aside and took up the cloth again, washing away the dirt that had been trapped underneath. The newly exposed skin thrilled to his touch. Next, he reached for her chest, tugging at the laces and loosening them around her breasts. Alix's breath came faster. Erik glanced up, but said nothing, moving on to the buckles. Moments later, he lifted the leather free. Sweat had plastered Alix's thin shirt to her body, leaving every contour exposed. She felt herself blushing, but Erik just moved on to her boots.

When he was through, Alix sat half naked on her cot, shivering. Erik reached past her to pull down the blanket, and when he leaned in, Alix turned her face into his, brushing his lips with her own. He hesitated. Alix felt his hand go to her thigh, felt the pressure of his fingers. He stood. He cleared away the bowl and placed her armour in a pile in the corner. Then he snuffed the candle with his fingers and was gone.

TWENTY-FOUR

†Mud sucked at the horses' hooves, lending a grim rhythm to their grim procession. The slurping reverberated off the underbelly of the stone arch and rolled the short length of the tunnel, making it sound as though they were a hundred horses instead of twenty. If only it were so—then maybe Alix wouldn't feel so exposed. Even the protective stone canopy of the Elders' Gate failed to ease her fears; instead, it felt like the jaws of a trap. Alix couldn't help glancing over her shoulder at the ranks of men marching behind, and as the column emerged from the far end of the gate, she twisted in her saddle to look up at the ruined ramparts of the old curtain wall. Her gaze scoured the crumbling stones like a hawk searching for a meal, but instead of lizards, she looked for bowmen; instead of food, she looked for death.

He wouldn't ambush us here, the reasonable part of her argued. If the Raven meant to attack them, he would hardly wait until they were on the very doorstep of Erroman before falling upon them. There were plenty of better places to spring a trap, places that weren't a horn's blow away from the new city walls and the thousands of eyes and ears they sheltered. Or if he didn't care who might see, if he judged that the whole of Alden already knew him for a traitor, he would simply sweep down on them with a thousand horses and break them as surely as the Harrami hordes had broken these old walls in the days of the empire. So Alix told herself, but it was little comfort.

The wet slurping of mud gave way to the dry clatter of cobbles as they passed down what had once been the temple road. It was cool here in the lee of the gate tower, the only part of the ancient Erromanian fortifications to remain intact. The afternoon's heat still radiated up from the paving stones, but it was nothing compared to what had beaten down on them for the past two hours. Though it was nearing dinnertime, the sun still wreaked havoc in the western sky. Rahl's watch grew long as the season progressed, and he surrendered his shift more reluctantly each night.

If Erik suffered under the heat, he gave no sign. The king rode straight and tall, splendid in his shining new armour and flowing white cape. Brownhold's master smith had done himself credit on such short notice, for though plain, the plate and mail gleamed as though wrought of purest silver. The king's horse, the proudest destrier left at Brownhold, was barded all in white silk, a fine, exotic weave worthy of a bridal gown. Young Aina Brown had surrendered the fabric gracefully. She'd only smiled and declared it an ill season for a wedding, and when it came time to stitch the golden sun on the king's cape, Aina had taken up the needlework herself. *Farika must be your sign, my lady*, Erik had told her as he kissed her hand, and Alix thought the girl might faint clean away.

At the king's left rode the Greens—Raibert, nearly as grand as his king in spotless armour and emerald cape, and Arran, dour and dark and dressed like a soldier. To Erik's right was Rig, whose black hair and black cape and black horse gave him the look of a living shadow. Adelbard Brown rode on Rig's other side, his daughter Rona, heir to the Brown banner, next to him. The White, Green, Black, and Brown banners marched all in a line, each one mounted on a gilded spear. Taken together, they were an impressive sight— or so the great lords hoped. So intent were they on the symbolism of it all that they hadn't allowed Alix to take her customary place at the king's flank. Instead, she rode directly behind him—as though she could do anything to protect him from there.

At last, the city gates loomed into view. They stood open, with only a few guards flanking them. Alix let out the breath she'd been holding, and Rig threw a relieved look over his shoulder. Then Alix felt another pair of eyes on her, and she turned to meet the icy gaze of Albern Highmount.

"Forgive me, my lady," the first counsel said, "perhaps you have forgotten, but the idea here is to look confident. *As bold as a Black*, is that not what they say? For once, it would be preferable for you to live up to your family's reputation."

Alix muttered a particularly bold suggestion under her breath, but otherwise focused her attention on the approaching walls. She could see archers prowling the ramparts, but that was nothing out of the ordinary. Even in peacetime, the city was well protected. She was more disturbed by the quiet on the road. It wasn't market day, but even so, the city gates should have seen a steady flow of traffic. Instead, the road was virtually deserted save for a single oxcart lumbering under the archway. Tensions were running high in the capital, it seemed. *Is it the Oridians the city fears most, or civil war?* It had been too long since she'd had news from Saxon.

The guards at the gate stood stiff as statues, their spears pointed at the sky. They would have been warned hours ago of the king's coming, but what were their orders? It was the first real test. Alix scanned the impassive faces for some sign of their intentions. Erik, though, did not so much as glance at them. Instead, he rode straight through as if nothing were amiss, as if it were perfectly normal for the king's long-awaited return from the front to be greeted with such edgy silence. *It feels more like a funeral march than a homecoming,* Alix thought grimly as the banner lords folded in behind the king.

She followed Erik's lead and made herself stare straight ahead as she guided her horse through the gate. The temple road unfurled before them, its black paving stones glittering with flecks of mica. *The Street of Stars.* Alix couldn't help smiling a little. The last time she'd seen the famed causeway of the capital, she'd been nine years old and half dazed with awe. *Look, Papa, there it is! It sparkles just like you said!* Her father had smiled and tweaked her braid. *You should see it after dark, my love, when the lamps are lit. Too bad it'll be past your bedtime . . .*

The memory evaporated like heat from the paving stones, and Alix's smile with it. The Street of Stars held no enchantment for her now. It did not lead anywhere she wanted to go.

Lower Town was quieter than she remembered, but it still swarmed with activity—at least until the king's party started up the Street of Stars. Then people began to stop and stare at the riders, and when they saw who led the column, they fell as still as the guards at the gate. The murmur of voices died down. Merchants ceased to cry their wares. Mules and oxen were drawn up. Soon, the only sound was the clatter of hooves and the steady, cheerful gurgle of the Fountain of Virtues. Erik gazed ruthlessly ahead, but Alix could see his shoulders stiffen beneath the cape. *They just stand there, stunned, as if he were a ghost.* The White Ravens had obviously done their work. The people had no idea how to react to the unexpected appearance of their half-deposed monarch. It was almost too much for Alix to bear. *Here is your king!* she wanted to shout at them. *Don't you know your true king when you see him? Don't you know how he fights for you?*

A young girl stepped away from her flower cart, pushing to the front of the crowd to get a better look. She was a scruffy thing, no more than twelve, with a faded ribbon in her hair and dust clinging to the hem of her frock. In her hand, forgotten, dangled a rose she'd been trimming when the world around her had gone still. She gazed up at the king, eyes wide, mouth half open. Something about her drew Erik's attention, and he slowed his horse. The girl glanced down at the flower in her hand, then stood on her toes to offer it to the king. Erik reached down and took the rose. He smiled.

It was like sunlight melting the ice. The street came suddenly alive. People began to call out. Only a few voices at first—a prayer, a hail, a timid cheer—but it soon built into a chorus. The crowd pressed in, hands reaching out to brush Erik's fingers, to touch his gleaming greaves, to stroke the silk barding of his horse. They fell in beside the column, following alongside and clasping the arms of any rider they could reach. Alix flinched at the first touch on her leg, and her horse muttered suspiciously, but there was nothing threatening in any of it, and for once Alix didn't fear the press of people around her king. *Erik needs this. And Tom will hear of it too.* She wondered if anyone had given the Raven a rose when he returned from Boswyck. She doubted it. *For all his strength, Tom can never compete with Erik for the people's love.*

The crowd grew as they rode on. Scores joined them in the Temple Square, and even more in Upper Town. By the time they reached the Gallery of Heroes, Erik's informal retinue stretched back as far as Alix could see. *That's better than a hundred banners*, she thought smugly, and she even shared a grin with Albern Highmount.

The palace gates swung open as the riders drew near. Alix wasn't sure what to make of that, and from the look of Highmount, neither was he. The crowd peeled away as the column rode between the great iron-banded doors, and Alix felt exposed all over again. Erik must have felt it too, for no one was more conscious than he of the protection the common people afforded him. As before, however, he gave no sign of anxiety; he just nodded coolly at the palace guards as he rode past. They wore the same raiment as Alix's own royal guardsmen, as did the men on the ramparts. *That might get confusing later on*, she thought darkly.

The bailey, like Lower Town and the Imperial Road before it, was quieter than it should have been. Guards stood at attention, their faces seemingly carved from marble, but no one else was about. Where there should have been grooms and footmen and various other servants, there was only an empty yard. The Three Keeps loomed over it all. Somewhere inside one of them—the North Keep, Alix presumed—Prince Tomald White waited for his brother.

Erik's squire played the part of groom while the king dismounted, and Alix wasted no time getting to his side where she belonged. Her fingers curled around the hilt of her bloodblade, but she did her best to keep her face as inscrutable as those of the guards.

"Your Majesty!" A thin, piping voice cut across the courtyard. A portly man in a white doublet rushed Erik so enthusiastically that he was fortunate not to have died upon Alix's sword; only the king's hand at her elbow stayed her.

"I should be obliged if you didn't kill my steward, Captain," Erik said with a wink. As for the portly man, he just blinked stupidly.

Alix scowled, unsure which of them she was more annoyed with. She threw her blade back into its scabbard with a deliberate *snap*.

"Your Majesty." The man bowed as deeply as his gut could accommodate. "I cannot express my joy at seeing you safely returned to us. The gods are good."

"Thank you, Arnot. It's good to be home."

Arnot the steward licked his lips. "His Highness Prince Tomald bids me . . . ah . . . that is, he regrets the breach of protocol, but . . . ah . . . ." He patted a handkerchief to his balding brow. The poor man was sweating like an overheated cheese.

Erik put a hand on his shoulder. "It's all right, Arnot. What message did my brother give you?"

"His Highness has decided to spend a few days on the Grey estate, Your Majesty, at the invitation of Lord Roswald. For, ah, a spot of hunting, I believe. But once Your Majesty has settled in, His Highness would be pleased to call upon you."

No trace of emotion touched Erik's face. "Very good. Tell my brother I shall receive him in one hour."

Erik and his lords were ushered into the North Keep. Arnot explained the accommodation arrangements as they walked, but Alix wasn't listening. Instead she scanned her surroundings, doing her best to memorise everything they passed. *By dawn tomorrow*, she vowed, *I'll know every inch of this keep.* Every door, every twist and turn. All the ways in, and all the ways out. Every stairwell and where it went, every secret place a man could hide himself. *Every inch, even if it means I go without sleep.*

"That will all be fine, Arnot," Erik was saying, "except that I shall require another set of rooms to be prepared in the royal suite. The Crimson Rooms, I think."

The steward was too well trained to show his puzzlement; only the barest blink gave him away. "Very good, sire."

Erik turned to his lords. "We will greet my brother in the oratorium in one hour. I trust that will give us all enough time to refresh ourselves."

"Your Majesty," Alix said as the others were led away by

the servants, "with your leave, I would like to examine the oratorium."

He gave her a knowing look. "Reconnoitre it, you mean. Alix, we've been on the road since dawn. You must be as exhausted as the rest of us. Besides, if my brother meant me harm, he would hardly stash assassins in the oratorium. The palace has been his for months. He has no need of such devices."

Alix couldn't deny his logic, but she didn't care—she didn't want Erik meeting the Raven in a room she hadn't inspected first. He obviously read as much from her face, because he sighed and said, "Very well, but you are still a Black, and your brother will want you to look the part."

"My brother, or my king?"

"Both."

She smiled. "Don't worry, I'll wash up."

She did as promised before setting off to find the oratorium. It wasn't difficult—the room was large enough to hold at least five thousand people. The gallery alone required four separate hearths to keep it warm, and the benches could seat at least five hundred, Alix judged. She wondered what sort of audience would require the room to be filled to capacity. Royal weddings, certainly, and funerals. And coronations. The oratorium would have been full to bursting when King Erik White was crowned at the age of twenty-one. *I wonder who will bear witness to his overthrow, if it comes to that?* Alix pushed the thought away.

Sunlight slanted down through arched windows of coloured glass. Nine windows lined the west wall and nine the east, each one bearing the symbol of a Virtue. Olan's shield cast an orb of silver-grey over the gallery rail, and Ardin's flame bathed the benches in orange and yellow and red. Garvin's tears were picked out in cut crystal, scattering tiny rainbows across the polished stone floor. Alix passed beneath each of them slowly, craning her neck to see. She started to say a prayer beneath Eldora's all-seeing eye, but changed her mind and appealed to Hew's crow instead, for it seemed to her that Erik would need wit more than wisdom.

Albern Highmount was the first of the lords to arrive. He'd changed into a conservative doublet of brown velvet trimmed with gold, and his high leather boots were so shiny that the firelight seemed to lick at his toes. He paid Alix little heed, treating her to a curt nod before surveying the room as though expecting to read the future in the elaborate loops and whorls of the gallery rail. Erik himself appeared soon after, his steward in tow. "Did you find him?" the king was asking.

"Yes, Your Majesty. We had just enough time to polish his armour while he washed. He awaits your summons."

"No, that won't do. I'm not summoning him. Take me to him."

This time, the steward could not conceal his surprise. Erik was king; it was for men to come to him, not the other way around. "As you say, Your Majesty," Arnot replied bemusedly.

A second surprise was in store when Alix started to follow. Erik drew up short, looking uncertain. "Captain . . ."

He can't be serious. Not now. "Your Majesty," she said, "this is not a good time for you to move about unprotected."

He hesitated a moment longer, then sighed. "Yes, very well. Come along."

Arnot led them into an anteroom, where the biggest surprise of all was waiting.

"Hello, Liam."

"Your Majesty." Liam was clean-shaven, hair washed and combed, armour burnished to a high shine. All this must have been accomplished quickly—and, judging from his expression, somewhat traumatically.

"I expect Tom any minute now," Erik said. "What is your decision?"

Liam shifted uncomfortably. "You think now would be a good time to . . . ?"

"It's now or never. I'm sorry to press you, but we cannot defer any longer."

Alix burned with curiosity, but Erik obviously wanted this conversation to be private, so she withdrew to a discreet remove and pretended to admire a tapestry on the wall. Even so, she couldn't help overhearing.

"What would I have to do?" Liam asked.

"You have only to be there. Speak if you wish, hold your tongue if you don't. I ask only that you support me."

A pause. "Are you sure about this?"

"I am."

"All right, then." Liam sounded reluctant.

Erik called Alix over. "From now on, Liam will require his own retinue of guards." Seeing her confusion, he added, "I don't believe Tom will try anything drastic, but if he does, he may not stop at one brother."

One brother? Alix's eyes widened as she realised what he intended. *He's going to acknowledge Liam. Now, of all times.* With his position already under threat, he was going to introduce another possible heir into the mix. *Oh, Erik, have you thought this through?* But she could see from his expression that he'd made up his mind, so she held her peace.

As for Liam, he looked miserable, but determined. "We're going public, Allie," he said quietly.

Erik glanced sharply at his brother. His eyes registered something fleeting, but it was gone before Alix could make it out. "Tom knows about you, of course, but I never discussed my plans to bring you into the family, so this will come as a surprise. Speaking of which, we had best head back and inform the others. It wouldn't do to have them caught unawares in front of Tom."

They returned to the oratorium to find the banner lords and a few chosen knights fully assembled. The lords were dressed in their finest silks and velvets, while the knights, including Arran Green, had their armour gleaming. Most registered little interest in the newcomer, but few things escaped the notice of Albern Highmount. His eyes narrowed. "I see an important decision has been reached," the first counsel said coolly.

"A long time ago," Erik returned even more coolly. "All that remained was to carry it out."

The other lords were curious now, and they scrutinised the mysterious Kingsword more carefully. All except Arran Green, who regarded Erik with a puzzled expression, no doubt wondering what the king was about.

Erik wasted no time. "My lords, may I present my brother, His Royal Highness Prince Liam White."

Liam said, "Hi."

Erik's smile was laced with triumph. But it was Liam's smile—embarrassed, apprehensive, but unmistakably hopeful—that brought a sting of tears to Alix's eyes.

The room was momentarily struck dumb. Even Highmount

said nothing; he just shook his head. It was enough. With eyes as cold as hailstones and hair the colour of a thundercloud, Highmount could storm without a sound. He had too much sense to vent his displeasure aloud, however, and when he turned his gaze on Liam, he was the very picture of courtesy. "Your Highness," he said, bowing, "it is good to meet you at last."

The other lords were quick to join in. Poor Liam would have been smothered in courtly syrup had not Arnot's thin voice cut through the well-wishes like a hot knife through treacle.

"His Highness Prince Tomald approaches."

TWENTY-FIVE

Boot heels rang out from the corridor, a chill counterpoint to the deathly hush that had fallen over the oratorium. Erik tensed, and his lords and knights tightened around him. Out of habit, Liam started to fall in behind Arran Green, until Alix met his eye and cocked her head in Erik's direction. Grimacing, Liam stepped to his new brother's side.

This would be the ultimate test of Erik's self-control. Alix could feel the rage rolling off him like heat from a bed of coals, but his posture appeared relaxed, his expression revealing nothing. Alix hoped he could draw strength from the banner lords and Highmount, all of whom looked masterfully blank. Even Rig had spent enough time at court to learn the value of a wooden mask.

Tomald White swept into the room without preamble, trailed by a clutch of knights, a few lesser lords and ladies, and a tall man with an ash-coloured cape who could only be Roswald Grey. The Raven's stride was as purposeful as ever, but nothing else about him was the way Alix remembered. Maybe it was the white velvet doublet in place of a breastplate, or the smooth cheeks in place of a neatly trimmed beard. Maybe she had just reimagined him as a monster, something cold and ugly and larger than life. Whatever the reason, the first thing that occurred to her as the Raven walked through the door was how very much he looked like Erik.

Tom's raven-black hair set him apart, and he was smaller and lither than his brother, but he had the same piercing blue eyes and proud features. He moved with a grace matched only by its authority, more panther than raven, and his gaze glittered with a fierce intelligence. Alix watched him with something close to awe. *He's beautiful. How could I have forgotten?*

But she hadn't forgotten how dangerous he was, and as he came closer, she stepped between him and Erik, her hand going to the hilt of her sword. Those piercing blue eyes met hers, but only for a moment; the Raven glanced at her and dismissed her in the same breath. The banner lords got much the same treatment, but there was one face among the group that he couldn't dismiss so easily. Tom's gaze lingered on Liam for just a fraction too long before returning to the king. "Erik."

"Tom."

"Welcome back."

Welcome *back*, not welcome *home*. Alix wondered if the choice of words was deliberate. Knowing the Raven, it was. And knowing Erik, he'd noticed.

A brief silence descended. The brothers eyed each other as though they were the only two people in the room. "I've taken up residence at the Grey estate," Tom said at length, inclining his head at the tall young man in the ash-coloured cape. "I thought it best to give you some time in the palace." *Before I take it from you.* The unspoken words hung in the air, heavy, malignant.

"That's good of you," Erik said, "though you really shouldn't feel underfoot. We are enough of a crowd that I'm sure one more would make little difference."

The Raven had no trouble grasping the subtext. He smiled. "Yes, you are an impressive lot, to be sure. The Greens, the Browns, the Blacks . . . And I see you have even mustered the bastard."

Erik went rigid. "You *will* mind your tongue, Tom. He is our brother, and a prince of the realm."

"Is he now?" The Raven looked amused. "Let me

guess—you plan to name him your heir. Do you really think that will change anything, or is this just another sop to your precious honour?"

"Some of us take honour very seriously."

"At least you're taking *something* seriously. If only it were the well-being of your kingdom."

Erik drew a long breath, and when he spoke again, the edge was gone from his voice. "You never knew me very well, Tom, and I fear you know me even less now. Much has changed since we took the field together at Boswyck."

That piqued the Raven's interest. His eyes narrowed. *Good recovery,* Alix thought. He'd begun spinning the tale. If he spun it well, Tom would see him as a changed man, a stronger, wiser king who had found his path to redemption—thanks to his little brother.

"I have no wish to stand here squabbling before the high lords of the realm," Erik continued. "The matter before us is too grave, and I'm too weary. Give me two days to settle in from my journey, and then let us meet again to discuss the future."

"The future is upon us, Erik. Discussing it does no good." Tom sounded almost regretful.

"I have never known you to ride into battle without learning all you could about your enemy and the field you will meet him on. You know far less of either than you think. In two days, you will know more. Two days is not so much to ask, Tom. Let us meet in parley, and I swear that no weapon shall be raised against you."

The Raven's blue eyes studied his brother's. Alix would have given all the gold in the Black River to hear his thoughts, but they were hidden behind a shield of ice. "I have no more desire to see bloodshed than you do. You have your two days, Erik, but do not deceive yourself with false hopes."

Erik gave a thin smile, as though swallowing a caustic reply. "Until then."

Tom and his retinue withdrew, their footfalls tolling a cold, haughty exit. When the sound had receded, Erik turned to Alix. "What do you think? That went as well as could be expected, I suppose."

She had never seen him look so uncertain. *And it's my*

reassurance he craves. It's as though we're married already. The thought thrilled her and scared her in equal measure. "You did wonderfully," she said with an encouraging smile. He smiled back, and for a moment Alix forgot they had an audience. Then she felt Liam's eyes on her, and she dropped her gaze.

"Now, if you will all forgive me—" Erik began.

"Your Majesty!" A page rushed toward the king. Thankfully, he had the good sense to stop far enough away to avoid a glimpse of Alix's blade.

"What is it?" Erik sounded incalculably weary.

"Lady Sirin approaches, sire."

Erik suppressed a groan. Sirin Grey was the last person in the world he wanted to see. The lords and knights beat a hasty retreat, all except Liam, who hovered awkwardly. "Might I have a word, Your Majesty?" His eyes were cold and hard.

As though I haven't enough to deal with, Erik thought, perhaps ungraciously. "We don't have much time. What's on your mind?" Liam hesitated, still unaccustomed to speaking his mind in front of his king. "I can see you're angry about something," Erik prodded impatiently. "Out with it."

"All right. Tell me the truth—was I just a prop in your little play back there?"

Erik stared, stunned. "Of course not. Why would you think that?"

"It seems awfully convenient. After ten years of ignoring my existence, you suddenly decide to acknowledge me at the precise moment you're confronting your brother over the crown."

Erik's heart sank. *He thinks this has been politics all along.* In hindsight, perhaps the timing did look suspicious. Liam had no way of knowing how long Erik had been planning this; bereft of that context, it was easy to see how his actions might appear more self-serving than generous. Still, he had been clear that he wanted Liam's support for the parley. Why Liam should choose this precise moment to be angry about it, he could not guess. "I'm sorry you feel that way," Erik said. "I wish I had time to discuss it, but I'm afraid

I must ask you to excuse me, for I'm obliged to have an equally pleasant conversation with my betrothed."

Sirin was approaching them, clad in a silk dress of ivory and silver that reminded Erik of a pearl-handled dagger. Liam glanced at her, and when he looked back, his gaze softened a little. "Good luck," he said in an undertone before stepping aside.

"My king." Sirin started to reach for him, but Alix swept between them, one hand raised in a warding gesture. Sirin paled in anger. "How dare you?"

"Stand down, Captain," Erik said, putting a hand on Alix's shoulder. She turned, hazel eyes filled with worry, and for a moment he feared she would argue. But she relented and stepped aside.

"Come, my lady," Erik said, unable to keep the weariness from his voice. "Let us speak in the Banner Room." He gestured toward the western antechamber, and Sirin complied, crossing the hall in crisp strides, leaving Erik to follow. He could hear Alix trailing behind, but he knew she had understood him and would keep her distance.

Sirin paused in the centre of the antechamber, beneath her own banner, as though to remind Erik of who she was. The dangling silk panels fluttered gently overhead as he closed the door. As soon as it came to, Sirin spun to face him. "So you think me an assassin now?"

"If I did, I would hardly follow you into a room without my bodyguard."

Sirin's lip curled. "Your bodyguard, is she? That is not how she is described at court."

Erik did not even bother to point out her hypocrisy; he just folded his arms and leaned against the wall. "We have more important things to discuss than Alix Black, surely."

The fierceness drained from Sirin's eyes. Suddenly, she looked as weary as he felt. *She's thinner*, he realised, taking in her jutting cheekbones, her narrow hips, the way her dress hung loosely on her frame. Her dark braids were untidy, like frayed ropes, and her silk gloves slouched around her wrists. Erik had never seen her looking anything but immaculate. He was more disturbed by the sight than he cared to admit.

She laced her fingers in her lap. "I'm sorry, Your Majesty,

I did not mean to speak sharply. The last thing I wish to do is to aggravate you."

"Why are you here, Sirin?"

"First, to tell you that whatever wrongs Tom has done you, I had no part in them."

He considered her carefully. He knew Sirin well enough to know she could lie to him, and smoothly. But she was a proud creature, and there was defiance in her eyes, as though she were daring him to call her false. He decided he believed her—at least in part. "Are you telling me you know nothing of what he's done?"

"That's not what I said. I have heard the whispers, and I have seen the White Raven pamphlets for myself. I know some and suspect more. But Tom would not speak to me of any of it, not even . . ." She looked away, but not before Erik saw the glimmer of tears in her eyes. In all the years he had known her, he had never seen her cry. "He withdraws more every day," she continued, a slight tremor in her voice. "Now he barely speaks to me at all. He says it's for my own good, but I think he . . . I think he's afraid that I . . ."

"That if you knew the truth, you would forsake him?" It came out more harshly than he had intended.

Sirin turned her back on him and hugged herself. "He believes he's doing the right thing. He's not power-hungry. You know that. He—"

"He thinks I'm leading my kingdom to ruin."

"He believes the Oridian threat is greater than you know."

"What a coincidence—I think the same of him. Only I didn't try to *murder* him."

The air seemed to go out of her at that. She sagged, her hand going to her stomach. "Oh gods . . . Erik . . ." He waited for her to continue, but in vain; it seemed she had no more words.

"Tell me, has he despised me all along?"

She sighed. "Is that what you think?"

"He does give that impression."

"He doesn't despise you. He just can't see the world the way you do, no matter how much he might wish it. And he does wish it, Erik, so much . . . You can't know . . ."

"We see the world the way we choose. Tom chooses to be bitter."

She shook her head miserably. "You have never understood him."

"There we agree." Erik lurched away from the wall and began to pace. "What would you have of me, Sirin? Tom has committed treason many times over. You say you know little of his crimes. Would you like me to list them for you?"

"No." She shuddered. "Please don't."

"I thought not."

"His moods. You know how he suffers . . ."

"Should that excuse treason?"

"It's been so hard for him."

"For all of us."

"He is your *brother*, Erik. Your own blood."

She had found her mark. He stiffened. "I'm not the one who forgot." The words chafed his throat.

There was a stretch of silence. Then she asked, "What will you do?"

Good question. None of the options were appealing. "I don't know, but whatever happens, I must put my kingdom first. I am king; that is my duty. You of all people should understand that."

"He's your brother," she said again, pleadingly.

Erik sighed. "Go now. I cannot give you what you want. I can't even be sure I'll still be alive in a few days' time."

She turned. "Erik, you can't really think he would—"

"*Go.* If you would keep Tom safe, convince him that his plans are folly. If he will listen to anyone, it's you."

She started to say something, then bit her lip and brushed past him.

"Sirin."

She paused, her hand on the door.

"You have always known where your duty lies, and you have always been prepared to do it. Don't waver now."

Her head drooped, but she did not turn around. She left the room in silence.

TWENTY-SIX

Alix knocked on the heavy wooden door, her gaze drifting absently over its elegant carved panels. It felt strange to be in a castle again, after so many weeks on the road. It felt stranger still to be in the royal palace, and strangest of all to be knocking on the door of a prince who had once been her lover.

A prince. The irony of it was almost too bitter to bear. Liam, a nameless bastard all his life, finally had a name, and it was *White*. He could choose any bride he wanted, any position at court, any grand estate. Everything that had once made Liam an impossible prospect for her had changed. His birth, her duty, the long miles between the Blacklands and the Greenlands . . . None of it stood between them anymore. And it was too late.

The door swung open to reveal Liam, looking surprised—and surprisingly frilly.

"What are you wearing?" The words tumbled out before she could stop herself.

He scowled. "Yes, thanks for noticing. Because what I really needed was someone pointing out how ridiculous I look." He was dressed in a silk shirt and soft leather breeches, with a red velvet vest elaborately embroidered in blue and gold thread. Alix wouldn't have batted an eye to see Rig or Erik in such garb, but Liam looked so miserable that she had to bite her lip to keep from laughing.

"Very princely," she said.

"That's just great, Allie." He stood aside for her to enter. "You really know how to make a fellow feel comfortable."

"It's fetching."

"No, no. Too late for that. It's already settled—I look like a cockerel."

She laughed. "You do not."

"A velvet pincushion, then. Or a particularly handsome bit of upholstery."

"You can't be in armour all the time."

"Why not? Women love armour. It's dashing and dangerous. The only thing dangerous about this outfit is that I might be mistaken for a traveling acrobat, and that can only end badly."

"Women love princes too."

"Do they? I'll have to remember that."

"Anyway, it can't be that bad. You're smiling."

"Only because your laugh is contagious. Stop it at once."

"As you command, Your Highness."

He made a face. "I should have seen that coming. Did you come here to torment me, or is there something I can do for you?"

Alix's smile faded. She did indeed have a purpose, and not one she relished. But there was no help for it; she'd put it off long enough. "I thought I should give this back to you," she said.

Liam gave her a quizzical look. "Oh," he said when she dropped the ring in his hand. "Right."

"I should have given it back a long time ago. I'm sorry."

He nodded, his gaze on the golden twist of ivy in his hand. Silence settled between them.

Alix cleared her throat. "Do you still have the chain?" *Gods, what a stupid question.*

He didn't seem to hear. He toyed with the ring, lost in his own thoughts. "So," he said eventually, "when will you be married?"

She winced. "I'm not sure. I mean, it's not even decided. It was Highmount's idea, and I don't really know what Erik wants to do." *I guess I'll find out tonight*, she realised with a flutter of nervousness. Erik had been avoiding the issue, but putting it off any longer would squander the political advantage. He needed to decide before the parley.

Liam started to say something, thought better of it. He slipped the ring into his pocket.

"Liam . . ."

"It's all right, Allie," he said quietly. "It's not your fault."

To her horror, her eyes started to fill. She turned away, feigning interest in the sumptuous interior of his apartments. The sitting room alone was three times the size of her own bedchamber, every inch of it trimmed in velvets and satins and rich, dark wood. The accent pieces were all in crimson— Harrami tribal masks studded with beads, coral figurines carved in the shapes of fantastic beasts, even a collection of lacquered ceramics from ancient Alawar. "They certainly didn't waste any time turning you into a prince, did they?"

"No."

"You don't sound very excited about it."

"I don't know. There was a time when I thought I wanted all this, but now . . ."

"What's changed?"

She turned to find him looking at her with a resigned expression. It was the only answer she got.

"I'd better go," she said. "I need to work out the security arrangements for the oratorium. That room is a nightmare. Too many ways in and out."

"You'll manage. You always do."

"If I don't see you before the parley . . . Good luck." She hesitated, wondering if she should hug him. He made the choice for her, pulling her close and putting his arms around her. The relief that washed through her was chased with heat, like a sip of warm wine. He was so close, and she fit so neatly against him . . . She thought of the last time they'd embraced without armour between them, and a flush crept over her.

She pulled away before she forgot herself. "See you later," she said, her voice thick in her throat.

As she closed the door behind her, Alix let out a long breath, her thumb brushing the empty space where Liam's ring had been. She'd almost come undone with him—again.

She understood why he avoided her. Things between them were still too raw. It wasn't fair to keep coming back to him like this. He was trying to move on, and she needed to let him.

She made a vow then. If she and Erik didn't marry, she would find somewhere else to be, someplace far enough away that Liam could heal in peace, and Erik could find someone worthy of his affections. It would tear her heart out, but she owed them that much at least. *When all this is done, I'll disappear, and Erik and Liam can learn to be brothers.*

Assuming any of them lived that long.

Erik paused outside Liam's door. He hadn't spoken to his brother since yesterday, a conversation that had not gone well. He had no desire to repeat the tone of that exchange, and if he could have, he would have given Liam more time before broaching the subject again. But time was a luxury they did not have, so Erik knocked.

"Come in."

Gesturing for his guards to remain outside, Erik entered. Liam was seated at a small writing desk near the window, his head bowed in thought. When he saw who entered, he started to rise, but Erik waved a hand and dropped into a chair. "You don't have to do that. In fact, you should probably get out of the habit. It will look a little strange if the prince leaps to his feet every time a lord enters the room."

Liam nodded, slumping back into his seat. "It'll take some getting used to." As he spoke, he flicked a small gold coin between his thumb and forefinger, sending it spinning across the surface of the desk.

"I wanted to discuss our plans for the parley. There are some things you should know."

"All right." Liam didn't look up.

He's angry with me again. Or was it still? Perhaps he had been angry all along. Erik sighed and pressed on. "I presume you have questions as well."

Liam didn't reply; he was too busy watching the bit of spinning gold. As it slowed, Erik realised that it was not a coin after all, but before he could make out what it was, Liam slapped it down under his palm.

"The laws of parley forbid me from arresting Tom, or raising weapons against him. In theory, he is bound by the same laws, but I have seen too much of my brother's treachery to doubt that he will do as he pleases. I suppose what I'm saying is that it could be dangerous, especially for you."

Liam picked up the bit of gold and sent it spinning again. *Is he even listening to me?* "What is that, anyway?" Erik asked irritably.

"What, this?" Liam arrested its momentum long enough for Erik to get a good look. *Alix's ring. What's he doing with that?* "It's nothing," Liam said, turning the ring over in his fingers. "Just something of my mother's from a long time ago."

Erik closed his eyes. He had convinced himself that his suspicions were unfounded, that a nickname meant nothing. But deep down, he had known better.

He swept to his feet. "Perhaps we had better do this another time." Liam looked up, confused. He started to reply, but Erik was already at the door. "I'm sorry, I just remembered there's something urgent I must do." That was a lie, but he had to get out of there. He strode down the corridor as briskly as dignity would allow, though he had no clear idea where he was going. Behind him, his ridiculous retinue of guards clattered to keep up.

He felt numb. He had thought himself prepared, but he had never imagined that fate's designs could be so sublimely cruel. He had long suspected that Alix's heart was spoken for. That day in his tent, when he had agreed to let her go with Arran Green, he had tested her one last time. He hadn't kissed her, instead waiting for her to take the final step, to come to him on her own. But she had not, and he knew then that she never would, not truly, not until the hold on her heart was released. She might kiss him, even take him to her bed, but she would not *give* herself to him. However much they shared, some part of her would remain locked away, beyond his reach. It would never be enough. So he had resolved to put it out of his mind, to focus on Tom and the war. He might even have managed it, had he not heard Liam in the anteroom the day before.

Allie, he called her. The nickname no one but Rig used. The word Erik had whispered in her ear all those months ago, that had caused her to go rigid in his arms. He should have recognised the ring. He should have put it together. It explained so much. *No wonder he resents me.* How could he not? There was such a twisted poetry to it that Erik almost laughed. The two things he wanted most in this world could never co-exist. To have one was to renounce the other forever. Worse still, he had blundered on in ignorance for so long, it seemed all but certain he would have neither.

Erik paused. His path had brought him to the oratorium. He was not surprised; this place had been the site of many of the most important days of his life. Tomorrow, it would play that role again. Tomorrow, he would stand here with his brothers and his lords and fight the final battle for his crown, though whether with words or swords, he could not say.

He was not afraid. He would be surrounded by friends and allies. He had always been surrounded by people who loved him, ever since he was a child. Strange, then, that he should feel so utterly alone.

"I'll want crossbows on the balcony," Alix said, pointing, "and I've asked that all the anterooms be sealed off."

Rig grunted approval. "Don't overdo it, though. Erik won't violate the laws of parley, and besides, too much security will make him look weak."

"You're starting to sound like Highmount."

Her brother gave her a sour look. "Don't ever say that again."

Alix scanned the room. "He would be crazy to try anything. Wouldn't he?"

"The Raven?" Rig shrugged. "I think so, but I'm not the tactician he is. Then again, planning battles isn't the same as setting a trap."

"He doesn't even need to set a trap. If it comes to steel, he'll just call his most trusted Kingswords and round us up. We'll all die by the gallows."

"Treason traditionally calls for beheading," Rig pointed out, helpfully.

"Captain. My lord." An unfamiliar knight approached them. "Pardon me for disturbing, but there is a man outside the gates requesting to speak with the captain."

"Who is he?" Alix asked.

"He wouldn't give his name."

She frowned. "What does he look like?"

"A commoner, by his dress. His face . . . it was . . . Well, he had . . ." The knight paused, his brow furrowing. "I'm sorry, Captain, I couldn't describe him to you. I guess I didn't look very closely. I'll go back . . ."

Alix smiled. "No need, Commander, that's description enough. Take me to him." Ignoring her brother's puzzled look, she followed the knight.

They found him on the far side of the gate, leaning casually against a wall. He straightened when he saw Alix. "A very pleasant morning to you, Lady Black," he said in his voice like dark slate. The spy had traded his customary black garb for a dun-coloured tunic and breeches, but otherwise looked the same as the last time Alix had seen him—which was to say, completely unremarkable. Only the hood he wore seemed out of place on a warm spring day such as this. Even so, it was not enough to draw attention, for it had a stiff brim, as though he merely meant to shade his face from the sun.

It was good to see him, Alix had to admit—though she didn't have to admit it aloud. "You know, technically it's *Lady Alix*, not *Lady Black*. My brother holds the banner, not me."

"An exception can be made for a hero such as yourself, surely." Somehow, everything Saxon said sounded vaguely mocking. "Besides, I hear it will be *Your Majesty* soon enough."

Alix made a face. "Half the realm has heard that. Anyway, I don't pay you to dredge up gossip on me."

"No indeed, but you do pay me handsomely, and my clients always get what they pay for." Alix could just glimpse his smile under the hood as he held out a sheet of parchment.

She took the page. As she scanned it, her eyes widened. "Is this what I think it is?"

"I have turned a lie into truth. A cunning bit of alchemy, if I do say so myself."

Alix couldn't disagree. She had charged Saxon with disseminating false information—namely, that the king had a list naming every family that had gone over to the White Ravens. The spy had done his work; Highmount himself had confirmed it. But it seemed Saxon had done even better than that. "Is this confirmed? All these families are for Tom?"

"Considering it, at least. Much will depend on the outcome of your parley, I think."

"What about the Kingswords, the ones who stayed behind when the rest of us marched to the border? What will they do?"

"Some of the officers belong to the Raven. Others remain loyal to the king. They vie for influence over the rank and file. How the balance of power will play out, no one can say."

Alix read the list over again. *Woodridge. Greenbarrow. Alansport.* Names she knew. People she'd grown up with. Did they know the truth about Tom, or did they believe whatever lies he'd concocted? It was impossible to know, and it didn't really matter anyway. "We can't have these families attending the Raven at the parley. If he feels too secure, he won't listen to anything Erik has to say. It will end up being a formality, just going through the motions so he can say he did his best to avoid bloodshed."

"Perhaps if some of them were to meet with unfortunate accidents . . ." Saxon's eyes glittered from the depths of his hood.

Alix considered it long enough for her stomach to turn over. "No. Erik wouldn't want that on his hands, and neither would I."

"In that case, perhaps these families need only *believe* such misfortune might befall them."

"Go on," she said warily.

"They are brave because they are hidden. If their identities were known, their boldness might desert them. You are not a known commodity at court. You have not spent enough time in the capital. No one here can say what you're capable of. Let these families fear you."

Yes, she thought, *let them fear me. And let them fear Erik as well.* "Pay a visit to every one of these estates, and paint a raven on the door. Let them know they aren't hidden anymore."

He bowed. "It will be done tonight."

An idea occurred to her. "What if we were to use blood instead of paint? Or is that going too far?"

The spy smiled. "This is war, Lady Black. There's no such thing as going too far."

TWENTY-SEVEN

A lix found the king in his study, as expected. He was exactly where she'd left him last night: at his desk, writing. She'd stayed with him well into the dark hours, but he'd virtually ignored her, and eventually he had sent her off to bed. She'd fallen asleep just before dawn, to fitful dreams of princes and ravens and marriage. She wondered if Erik had slept at all.

He didn't look up as she entered the study, but gestured at a chair across from him. *This is it*, she thought. *We're going to discuss the betrothal.* As much as it terrified her, she would be glad to settle it once and for all.

"I'm sorry it took me so long to come," she said as she drew up the chair. "There always seems to be one more thing that needs doing."

He nodded vaguely, his quill scratching.

"I hear the priests have refused to align themselves with either side."

"Yes."

"Gwylim says that the gods take no part in the quarrels of men. Maybe that extends to the priests too." *Or maybe they're just waiting to see who comes out on top.*

Erik said nothing.

"Are you sure I can't persuade you to wear armour?" His doublet was exquisite. Ordinarily, she would have admired the artistry of the stitching, the way the dye brought out the blue of his eyes. Instead, she found herself wondering how heavy brocade would stand up to a dagger.

"It sends the wrong message," he said.

Alix studied him worriedly. The strokes of his quill were as clipped as his words, and his shoulders sat rigidly square. Everything about him screamed of tension. Understandable, certainly—so much would be decided this day. But she'd seen Erik ride down the throat of an army with a wink. If ever there was a time for his breezy confidence, it was now.

He scattered a handful of sand across the parchment and put it aside. Only then did he look up, leaning back in his chair with an unreadable expression. "May I ask you a personal question, Alix?" She scarcely had time to register the ominous familiarity of the words before he added, "Why didn't you tell me Liam was your lover?"

A sharp breath jolted out of her, as if she'd been punched in the stomach. She would have looked away, but Erik's eyes pinned her as surely as if she'd been forced against a wall. She could only stare at him helplessly, her mind swimming, her thumb moving instinctively to the empty place where her ring had been.

"You're surprised, I see. Collect your thoughts. I can wait." His tone was smooth and cold and fragile, like a dangerously thin layer of ice.

Damn you, Alix.

She forced her voice past a raw throat. "I didn't know he was your brother, not at first. By the time I realised it, everything was already falling apart. And then we weren't lovers anymore."

Erik was unimpressed. "So you thought it didn't matter?"

"I . . . I should have told you. I know that. But I just couldn't."

"I don't even have to ask if he knows about me. That much is obvious." His tone grew more brittle with each word. The ice was starting to crack.

"I had to tell him. It wouldn't have been fair to continue on as if nothing had happened."

Erik closed his eyes and shook his head, as if she'd confirmed a fear. "Let me guess: It was at that point that you ceased to be lovers."

"I should have told you, but I didn't want to hurt you. After what happened with Liam . . . I just wasn't ready to cause that kind of pain again."

"*You* weren't ready?" He leapt to his feet and went to the window, his left hand balled into a fist at his side. He was struggling to keep himself in check, but Alix wished he wouldn't. She deserved the full force of his anger. "This isn't about *you*, Alix. It's not even about me. Don't you see? You know what Liam has gone through, how hard it's been for the two of us to get to this point. I've been so careful—perhaps too careful—but he's finally here, and I dared to hope that we could be brothers at last. And now his trust may be destroyed forever, all because of an injury that I dealt in ignorance." When he turned away from the window, his eyes were accusing. "Everything Liam has suffered has been my fault. My father wanted to bring him home, but I stood in the way. I took *everything* from him—his family, his future, even his safety. For seven years, I have been trying to give something back, only to discover that instead *I have taken from him again*! If you cared for him, Alix, if you cared for either of us, how could you just stand there and watch it happen?"

Alix's heart broke a little more with each word. The guilt she had carried for months, that had weighed her down in heart and mind—it was a pittance. A fraction of what she owed. In the hundreds of hours she'd spent obsessing about her relationship with Liam, and with Erik, she had never once considered their relationship with each other. How could she not have seen? It was *she* who stood in the way of *their* future. After seven years of trying to clear away the rubble of the past, Erik had finally found a path to his brother—only to have Alix throw an even bigger obstacle between them, one they might never overcome.

"I'm so sorry." Her voice shook. "You're right. I've been a fool." *A wretched, reckless, self-absorbed fool . . .*

Erik sighed, long and deep and weary. The flame faded from his eyes. He took a step toward her, but she sprang out of her chair before he could speak. She deserved every arrow he'd spent, and she would not let him take a single one back.

"I'll see you in a few hours," she said, her voice sounding distant to her own ears. "You should try to relax, if you can. I'll have the servants bring tea." She bowed, spun on her heel, and left the room. As she closed the door, she heard the sound of papers being swept violently to the floor. She prayed to the Virtues that it was the last gasp of Erik's temper, for he needed to be ready for what lay ahead.

The oratorium thrummed with tension. Though empty but for the guards and a handful of chosen lords, the vast chamber felt confined and oppressive. The ceiling clamped down on them like the lid of a boiling pot; at any moment, it seemed likely to fly off from the pressure. The hairs on Alix's arms stood on end, though that might just have been the chill. Arnot had ordered only two of the hearths lit. "Better too cool than too hot," the steward had told her, "for the room, and the tempers."

Alix scanned the row of doors along either side of the hall. Each was flanked by a pair of guards, even though most had already been barred with thick beams of oak. Only the door at the back of the gallery had been left unsealed, and it was through this that the Raven and his entourage would enter. It was an insult to force a prince of the realm to come in through the commoners' door, but Alix didn't care—it would keep Tom and his men out of the main part of the keep, obliging them to use a corridor that ran directly from the courtyard to the gallery. The more she could control the Raven's movements, the better.

She looked up at the balcony again, reassuring herself that the crossbowmen were still there. *As though they might suddenly have vanished.* She blew out a frustrated breath. *You're obsessing. You've done all you can.* She met Rig's eye and gave him a curt nod. Satisfied that the room was in good hands, she left to take up her place at the king's side.

When she reached the door to the study, she hesitated. She

hadn't seen Erik since that morning, and the wound was still raw. But she couldn't afford to think about that now, and neither could he. *He's got more important things on his mind than you.* Thus fortified, she went in. Erik stood at the window, hands clasped behind his back. His posture seemed relaxed, but when he turned, his eyes burned like the blue flame of coal. That was no bad thing, Alix decided; he would need that intensity to match the Raven's.

"What is it like in the room?" he asked her.

"Edgy."

"I'm sure. You've half an army in there."

"I wanted the other half too." She glanced around. "Where's Liam?"

"He'll be along."

Probably throwing up, she thought. The only person who made Liam more nervous than the king was the Raven. "He'd better hurry. Tom will be here any moment."

"Tom can wait. It won't hurt to remind him who is king." Muscle stood out in Erik's jaw, and his fingers twitched restlessly at his side.

"Are you ready?" She regretted the question as soon as she'd asked it. How could he possibly be ready for something like this? "Sorry, that was stupid of me. Again."

His eyes filled with remorse. "Alix . . ."

She swept forward and threw her arms around him, and he clasped her tightly, burying his face in her hair. "It's all right," she murmured. "Everything's going to be fine." It sounded so trite, as if she were comforting a child, but it seemed to help. He relaxed in her arms with a sigh. "I'll be right behind you," she said, "and Liam too."

"Thank you." He drew back, a shadow of a smile on his lips. "That's just what I needed to hear."

A knock sounded at the door, and Liam appeared. Alix couldn't help gaping a little. He looked like a *prince*. His clothing was as grand as Erik's, his unruly hair tamed by a trim and a sound combing. But the expression on his face—as determined as if he were going into battle—was pure Liam. "I heard voices as I passed the oratorium," he said. "I think they're here."

"Then we begin," said Erik, heading for the door.

Liam stopped him as he passed. "I stand with you, brother." He held out his hand.

Alix directed her smile at the floor as they clasped arms. She could practically sense the strength flowing into Erik through Liam.

They arrived at the oratorium to find Tom, Roswald Grey, and a handful of others Alix didn't know standing in close formation near the king's table. Albern Highmount, Arran Green, and Lords Black, Brown, and Green were on the opposite side. The table formed a no-man's-land between them. All eyes turned to watch the king as he approached, his brother and his bodyguard trailing behind. Alix had begged Erik to let her go first, but he wouldn't hear of it, just as he wouldn't hear of wearing a sword or armour. He didn't want to look fearful.

The Raven hadn't troubled himself with such considerations. He wore no body armour, but a sword and dagger hung from his belt, and his leather-bound kite shield was strapped to his back. Alix did a quick scan of his men and found that they were all similarly armed. Roswald Grey even wore a breastplate. She glanced up at the balcony yet again. The crossbowmen were there, weapons cocked and ready. Rig was armed too, as was Arran Green, both of them too much soldier to do otherwise. That was something, at least.

"Good afternoon, brother," Erik said. "You are punctual as always."

"And you are late as always."

Erik ignored that. He scanned the half-dozen men Tom had with him. "You are fewer than I expected."

The remark was guileless—Alix hadn't had a chance to tell him about Saxon and his bloody ravens—but Tom couldn't know that. His lip curled. "Yes, a number of my friends appear to have gone hunting, or taken suddenly ill. Well played, brother."

"This isn't a game, Tom."

"No, it isn't."

"Let's get to it, shall we?" Erik gestured at the chairs that had been placed around the king's table, but Tom refused with a sharp shake of his head. Erik sighed. "Relax, brother. I am bound by the laws of parley. I cannot arrest you, and if I wanted to murder you, all I would have to do is give the signal to those bowmen. You know me better than that, or you would not have come."

"It's true, I do know you better than that." His gaze shifted to Alix. "But I don't know *her*, and rumour has it she is rather fond of you." He smiled in a perfect mockery of charm.

"She's not the Black you need to worry about," Rig growled, before Erik silenced him with a hard look.

"Very well," Erik said, "let me ease your mind. Bowmen, leave us!"

No!

Alix didn't dare gainsay the king in front of everyone, but she glared at him for all she was worth. He ignored her, and the crossbowmen filed out of the oratorium, taking Alix's only shred of comfort with them.

The Raven, for his part, studied his brother with narrowed eyes. Doubtless he wondered what game Erik was playing. Alix wondered the same. In the end, he took the proffered seat, his men following suit. They were a little over a dozen in all, eight on Erik's side, nine on Tom's, facing each other across the polished oak table. *We look like we're negotiating a treaty*, Alix thought. And in a sense, they were.

"You say you have intelligence about the enemy that I lack," the Raven said. "I doubt that, but I would hear what you think you know."

Erik leaned on the table, lacing his fingers together before him. "I presume you know that the Oridians have divided their forces. The main host makes its way up the old imperial road from Boswyck. A second force plagued the Blacklands until recently, but General Green smashed them at the Scions. A third force, which we judge to be approximately three thousand, remains in the Brownlands."

Tom made an impatient gesture. "We know all this."

"The Priest rides with them," Erik said.

"I have heard that rumour."

"It is no rumour," Arran Green put in. "Alix Black and one of my scouts saw him with their own eyes."

The Raven regarded him coolly. "In that case, it is a pity you did not make him pay for his recklessness. His presence no doubt inspires his men."

"It is far worse than that," Erik said. "Madan does more than nurture their faith. His dark powers have given them a strength we could never have imagined."

Tom snorted. "You read too many tales, Erik. The Priest is no dark wizard, and this war is not some epic struggle against evil. It's just an ordinary, shabby squabble that need never have involved us at all."

Erik regarded his brother almost pityingly. "You could not be more wrong. Tell him, Lord Black."

Rig's gaze was considerably less sympathetic. "If you had bothered to lift a finger in defence of the kingdom, you would know that the Priest's powers are no tavern tale. He's found a way to pervert the bloodbond, to use it to make soldiers. Men under his power are no more than husks, and he throws their lives away just so. His thralls know no fear and no pain. They're hard to fight and harder to kill. And he has hundreds of them, if not thousands."

Harsh laughter rang off the polished stone walls. All eyes fell upon Roswald Grey. Until now he'd been content to sneer in silence, but it seemed he could no longer restrain himself. "Is this some kind of jest, Lord Black?" He took full advantage of his imposing height to look down his nose at Rig.

"You cannot seriously expect us to believe such superstitious nonsense," said another of the Raven's flock, some lesser lady with more gold than breeding, judging from her tastelessly flashy garb.

Before Rig could answer, Arran Green said, "It is of no consequence what you believe, my lady. It is the truth. I have fought more thralls than I care to count. Some are nothing more than bewitched peasants. Their primary purpose is to get in the way. Others are trained soldiers, and they do not fall without a bitter contest. Every man and woman on this side of the table has seen one. All but one of us has faced one in battle. Thralls are very real, and very dangerous, and we have no idea how many of them the enemy has made."

The Raven listened attentively, his eyebrows knit in a thin black line. Tomald White and Arran Green had known each other a long time. They had trained together, commanded armies together, shed blood together. Tom knew what kind of man the commander general was, and he knew that Arran

Green did not lie. "How is such a thing possible?" he asked, ignoring an incredulous look from Roswald Grey.

"We don't know," Erik said. "Nevyn tells me he has never heard its like. But he is confident that the bond can be broken if the bloodbinder is slain."

"Then Madan must die," Tom said.

"We reached a similar conclusion," Rig said dryly.

"We almost had him," Erik said, passing a weary hand over his eyes. "We were so close . . ."

"A disappointing failure," Arran Green said, "for which I take full responsibility. The mission was not a total loss, however. We discovered something important. The Priest is using our own people against us. He has been taking Aldenian prisoners and turning them into thralls. We have no way of knowing how long he has been doing this, or how many he has taken, but he could potentially have swelled his numbers enormously."

Tom's face darkened at that. *So he does care what happens to his people*, Alix thought. *Too bad he hasn't done a damn thing about it.* The rest of the Raven's flock had changed colour as well, pale or green or red-faced—a veritable rainbow of fear. All except Roswald Grey, who was too busy watching Tom's reaction, presumably in order to decide his own.

"This explains the Andithyrians, perhaps," the Raven said meditatively.

"You can't be certain of that," Grey said.

"No, but it is a better theory than yours. It is simply beyond credit that so many Andithyrians would be eager to fight for their conquerors."

Erik looked from one to the other. "What are you talking about?"

"Your information is incomplete, brother," Tom said. "The main host is over fifty thousand strong, yet my scouts report that fully half have the white hair of Andithyri."

Erik's mouth pressed into a thin line. "The Priest. He must have bound them before he left for the Blacklands."

"He's probably been binding them for months," Rig said. Alix thought back to Madan's wasted frame, and she knew her brother was right. *He's probably been at it night and day since they invaded Andithyri. No wonder he's so weak . . .*

"We have known about the Andithyrians for some time," Tom said, "but we assumed they were prisoners. And then suddenly they began to march. It puzzled us greatly, but now it seems to make sense."

"The Priest probably went straight back to Boswyck Valley after we flushed him out of the Brownlands," Rig said. "His puppets were just sitting idle, waiting for him to come and pull their strings."

"And now he has," said Tom, "and they will be here in a fortnight."

"No matter," said Roswald Grey. "We have twenty thousand Kingswords. More than enough to hold the city."

Rig snorted. "Are you such a bloody fool?"

Roswald Grey flushed an ugly pink. "You're the fool. Everyone knows you need ten times the number of defenders to take a city."

Tom gave his ally an impatient look. "Have you understood nothing? This is no ordinary army. The Oridians march on us with tens of thousands of thralls, bloodforged of their enemies. What do they care how many white-hairs fall? They will show no caution, no scruple. They'll throw everything they have at the gates, and even if half their host is cut down before they break through, they will still outnumber us. They'll put the city to the torch, and it will be over."

His last words echoed ominously under the high ceiling. Alix shuddered.

For a moment, no one spoke. Then Erik said, "Under the circumstances, I trust you will agree that we cannot afford to be divided now."

"I do agree," said Tom. For half a heartbeat, Alix thought they'd won. Then he added, "Which is why you must step aside. Your ruinous leadership brought us to this place. We should never have started this war, and our best chance now is to find a diplomatic solution."

Erik's eyes iced over. "Your efforts to find a diplomatic solution have not borne fruit so far. Why should you imagine that will change, especially now that the enemy has us by the throat?"

Tom blinked. It wasn't much, but it was enough.

"Yes," Erik said coldly, "I know about your secret dealings with the enemy."

Tom gave a well-studied shrug. "Of course I attempted to treat with the enemy. It was only prudent."

"It was prudent to offer them your king's head?"

Shocked breaths came from both sides of the table. Erik had not shared that secret with all of his people, and apparently neither had the Raven.

"You are beneath contempt, Tomald White," Arran Green said in a tone capable of freezing solid rock.

"I made no such offer. The offer was made to me."

"And you accepted it," Erik said, very quietly. "You abandoned us on the field of battle, hoping the Oridians would do your work for you. And when that failed, you set assassins upon me, and upon those sworn to protect me."

Tom frowned at that. Alix thought he might have glanced at Roswald Grey, but it was too quick to be sure. "I did not come here to face accusations," he said. "I came here to give you a chance to surrender peacefully. This kingdom cannot survive another day of your reign. You may already have destroyed us, and all the realm knows it."

"I admit that I underestimated the threat we faced," Erik said.

Good. Now he would say what they'd planned—that Boswyck had opened his eyes, made him a wiser man and a better king.

"There are so many things I would have done differently . . ." He hesitated.

Come on, Erik, Alix urged him silently. She knew it would sit badly with him to forswear his decision to go to war, like confessing to a crime he hadn't committed. But he had to do it.

Tom interrupted him. "You are a good man, brother, but you are a fool." He said the words gently, even regretfully. "You have coasted through your reign as you have your life, getting by on a wink, counting on your charm to carry you while you left the difficult work to others." He swallowed, his face tightening with barely suppressed emotion. "Father never saw it, not even after you forsook him. But the rest of us see. *I* see. I told you that we could not win this war, Erik. I told you that our allies would not stir. But still you insisted on your damned treaty. You would not soil your precious honour, so I soiled mine. I did what I had to do, for the realm. Just as I am doing now."

Erik was very still. "So you will not stand down?"

"Not for you. Not for a king who lets his pride get in the way of sensible compromise. A king does not have the luxury of cleaving to his principles when every shred of evidence points to its folly. Alden needs someone who is prepared to do whatever it takes to defend the realm."

"You're right," Erik said with that same frightening calm. "I have taken that lesson to heart, though I cannot bring myself to thank you for it."

Alix bit her lip. It wasn't the most gracious admission, but at least Erik was saying the words. *Now he needs to convince Tom that he's changed enough to keep the crown . . .* It wasn't too late. Erik could turn this around . . .

But instead, the king said, "Guards."

They poured in from two doors flanking the king's table, doors that Alix had ordered sealed. Two dozen royal guardsmen, weapons in hand. For a moment, the hall was shocked into silence. Then Roswald Grey leapt to his feet, crying, "What treachery is this?" The rest of the Raven's flock took up the call, springing from their chairs and flapping and squawking their outrage. "Parley!" they cried, as though the word itself were a shield. As for Tom, he just sat there, stunned, like a bird that has just slammed into an invisible pane of glass.

"Your word," he said. "You swore."

"Yes," Erik said sadly, "I did." He pushed his chair back and stood. Tom stared for a moment at the empty seat. Then he looked up at his brother. He smiled.

The guards closed in. Roswald Grey broke into a run, heading for the door at the foot of the gallery. Alix didn't bother to give chase. There were guards at the door, and more in the courtyard; he wouldn't get far. But the guards only nodded to Grey as he went by, and suddenly men in strange livery were streaming in through the gallery door.

Alix's heart froze in her chest.

The attack came from above.

TWENTY-EIGHT

An arrow slammed into the table and stood between the brothers, quivering. Quicker than Alix would have thought possible, the Raven was diving over the table, swinging his kite shield down from his back. Alix grabbed her blade, but she was too late. Tom reached for his brother . . .

. . . and pulled him behind the shield just as another arrow buried itself in the wood with a meaty *thunk*.

Arran Green shouted at the guards. Rig was already halfway across the room, blade in hand, rushing to intercept the men pouring in through the gallery door. Liam grabbed the table and upended it, and the rest of them hunkered down behind the makeshift cover.

"Grey!" Tom snarled, daring a glance over the top of the table. "I should have known!"

Adelbard Brown threw the Raven an incredulous look. "You expect us to believe you had nothing to do with this?"

At that moment, Alix didn't give a flaming fig who was behind it. Erik was in danger, and she needed to get him out. But that would be no easy feat. The clash of metal told her the battle had been joined, but from what she'd seen, Grey's men outnumbered the royal guardsmen. Most of the doors were still sealed. Instead of trapping their enemies in, Alix had trapped the palace guards out. And there was still the matter of that archer.

"There's only one of them on the balcony," Liam said, as though reading her thoughts. "Does anyone have a dagger?"

Tom unsheathed his and handed it over, hilt first. "A tricky throw. Are you sure you can make it?"

"Nope." Liam peered over the top of the table.

"Then let me," Tom said.

Liam hesitated, but at a nod from Erik, he passed the dagger back. "Get ready," he said. He lifted his head above the table again, just long enough to goad the archer into a shot. Another shaft slammed into the wood. Quick as a snake, Tom uncoiled from his crouch and whipped the blade. There was no scream, but Alix heard the sickening sound of a body hitting the stone floor, and she knew the Raven had made his throw.

Liam vaulted over the table, grabbed the sword of a slain guardsman, and joined the fight. Raibert Green found a blade for himself, and after a moment's hesitation, Adelbard Brown followed. Rig and Arran Green fought at the centre of the melee, surrounded by the king's men, but they were still outnumbered by at least half, and there was no telling how many more Greyswords might be in the corridor.

The Raven whirled on Alix. "Get the king away from here."

She didn't need to be told twice. She put a hand on Erik's arm. "Come on!"

He pulled away. "I need a sword. There are enough of us. We can—"

Tom shoved him so hard that Erik nearly lost his footing. *"Go, fool!"*

Erik's jaw tightened, and for a moment Alix feared he would argue. Then he cursed and spun on his heel, letting Alix herd him toward the door.

They spilled out into a deserted corridor. "This way," Erik said, taking off at a trot. Alix followed, her gaze scouring their surroundings for any sign of threat. They passed a branching hallway where a pair of royal guardsmen was scrambling to unbar the door. The alarm had obviously been sounded, but where were the rest of the guards? And how in the bloody hells had the Greyswords gotten in?

Her questions would have to wait. She recognised Erik's path; they were headed for the main doors, and the courtyard beyond. "Wait, we can't go that way!"

"Why not?"

"They came in through the gallery door. That gives straight onto the courtyard. There might be more of them out there. For all we know, Grey has every sword in his service attacking the palace right now."

"You're right." Erik glanced indecisively at the branching corridors on either side of them. His eyes widened. "The tunnel!"

Alix shook her head, lost.

"There's a secret tunnel under the palace," Erik explained. "It was built after the White War, so the royal family could escape in case of attack. It runs from the wine cellar all the way to the Crying Keep. But we needn't go that far—there's another way out through the base of the gate tower."

That was good enough for Alix. "Let's go." Erik looked surprised when she darted past him, but she didn't need to be shown the way. She'd kept her promise to learn every square inch of the keep, and that included what lay below. She hadn't turned up any secret tunnels, but she could lead them to the wine cellar easily enough. She went left, then right, then right again, shoving past startled servants carrying pails and brooms and bundles of linen. They were almost at the entrance to the wine cellar when they came upon a clutch of guards racing in the opposite direction. "Here," Alix called to them, "the king needs a sword!" A young guard unsheathed his blade and offered it up two-handed. Erik looked relieved to be holding steel again.

They hurried on. Soon, they came upon the heavy oak door leading down to the cellars. It stood slightly ajar, but Alix wasn't surprised; servants beat a steady path up and down these stairs all day long. Torches lit the way down wide stone steps worn to a shine with use. Alix led, the shadow of her blade stretching and writhing along the wall like some great dark serpent. The air grew cool as they descended, and it wasn't long before she could smell damp wood and wine. When they reached the bottom of the stair, Erik said, "This way."

Row upon row of casks marched in neat ranks before them. Erik weaved his way between them for what seemed like forever, turning this way and that until he came to a door almost hidden behind the barrels. They passed through it into a smaller room with even more wine casks stacked in clusters beneath peaked stone vaults. "The finer vintages," Erik said, as if he were giving her a leisurely tour of the palace. He pointed with his sword. "The tunnel is just through there, in that alcove."

"Let me go first." Alix ducked to pass beneath the low stone archway.

Just as she crossed the threshold, something darted out from the shadows and caught her boot. She went down hard. There was a rustle of movement, and cool steel pressed against her throat.

"Well, now, Lady Black," said a familiar, rasping voice. "Here is a reversal. Usually it's *your* blade at *my* throat."

Alix opened her mouth to reply, but Saxon yanked her to her feet, his dagger still pressed against her. Erik crouched in the archway, ready to spring. Only the blade at Alix's throat held him back.

"Stay where you are, Your Majesty," the spy said as he dragged Alix backward.

"What are you doing?" she hissed. Her guts twisted in fear. Had she misjudged the spy after all?

Her answer came as Saxon lowered his knife. "Avoiding death. My apologies, but His Majesty looks to be in a *kill first, ask questions later* sort of mood. It seemed wise to put a little distance between us before I let you go."

Erik stepped carefully through the archway, the tip of his sword levelled at the spy's chest. "Do you know this man?"

"I do. He's with me."

Erik's expression did not soften. "Then why did he attack you?"

"I beg your pardon," Saxon said. "I was concealed in the shadows, with only my ears to guide me. I was not sure who you were."

"Who are *you*, and how did you get in here?"

"A humble spy in the service of my lady of Blackhold," Saxon said with a little bow. "As to how I come to be here, I followed one Roswald Grey."

Alix spun instinctively, her fingers tightening on the hilt of her sword. "He's here?"

"I believe so, though I am not entirely sure where *here* is."

"He must know about the tunnel," Erik said. "Someone in my service has loose lips."

"Someone in your service is no longer in your service at all, Your Majesty," Saxon said. "Many *someones*, in fact."

Alix had no time for the spy's dramatics. "Speak plainly!"

"I fear I have let you down, Lady Black, a fact that I am only now coming to realise, and rather by accident. You see, I found myself curious as to the outcome of today's events, so I came to the palace. I was content to loiter outside the gates, waiting to see who emerged, but then I saw something strange. One of the guards at the gate managed to slip away when his comrades weren't looking. I followed him, and whom should I find him speaking with but Lord Roswald Grey? I knew then that I had gravely miscalculated. I have been so busy seeking out White Ravens among the nobility that I did not think to seek them among the palace guards. An unforgivable oversight, I humbly admit. When the Greyswords arrived at the gates, a moment's bloodshed was all it took to eliminate those guards who were not already in Grey's pocket. When they raised the portcullis, I stole inside. I thought to find you, but I couldn't make my way into the oratorium without being seen. And then I heard shouting, and swordplay, and then Grey reappeared. I followed him down here, only to lose him in this maze of barrels. And here we are."

"How many Greyswords got into the palace compound?" Alix asked.

"A hundred, perhaps more. They control the gate. They lowered the portcullis as soon as they were inside."

"Meaning the Kingswords cannot get in," Erik said.

Saxon nodded. "I heard them blow the horn at the barracks, but the portcullis was already down by then."

"There aren't enough palace guards to hold them off," Alix said. She was stating the obvious, yet something didn't make sense. "Even if they take the keep, what then? With the Kingswords outside the walls, they'll never be able to fight their way back out again."

"It's not the keep they're after," Erik said, sounding incredibly weary. "If they had managed to take me, they would not need to fight their way out. Kill me or hold me—either way, they win."

Of course. That's why Grey came down here. He knew Erik would come this way . . . "We have to go. Right now."

Erik led them deeper into the shadows of the alcove. There were no torches here; the walls were more felt than seen, close and dark and radiating cold. Erik knelt. "Help me, Alix." She crouched, and Erik took her hand and guided it to a leather loop. A trapdoor. "On three." He counted, and together they pulled. Wood groaned against wood, and the trapdoor came free.

Alix went first. The drop wasn't long; her boots immediately hit stone, sounding dull and flat in the confined space. She reached up and brushed the ceiling of the tunnel with her fingertips. Erik would probably have to duck to keep from hitting his head. "I need a torch," she called up.

They brought two. Alix led the way with one, and Saxon brought up the rear with the other. Torchlight gleamed off wet stone walls as they hurried along. The tunnel curved gradually to the left, taking them under the keep and toward the palace walls, and before long, they came to a flight of steps branching off into darkness. The gate tower exit, Alix supposed, but given what Saxon had told them, she meant to take the tunnel all the way to the Crying Keep.

Erik had other ideas. "Wait," he said in a tone Alix had learned to dread. "If we took those stairs . . ."

"If we took those stairs, you would head straight back into danger. The Greyswords hold the gate, remember?"

Erik continued as if he hadn't heard. "We could raise the portcullis and let the Kingswords in. They would smash the Greyswords in moments!"

"Our men are probably already finding a way to climb the walls," Alix said, but it sounded unlikely even to her. They would need time to find ladders or grappling hooks or some such.

"Come on." Before Alix could stop him, Erik had shouldered past her and started up the stairs. All she could do was curse and follow.

Another trapdoor brought them into the cellar of the gate tower. Torches illuminated rows of blades and bows, ready to be taken up in defence of the gates. On the far side of the room, another stairway led to the main floor, and the portcullis. Dimly, Alix could hear the sound of blades clashing in the courtyard.

Erik heard it too. His eyes gleamed. "Let's go."

"Erik, wait!"

He ignored her, bounding up the steps two at a time.

A knife flashed through the air, tumbling end over end. It was aimed at the king's back, but the throw was ill-timed, and the weapon bounced uselessly off one of the steps. Erik continued on, oblivious, vanishing into shadow as he climbed. Alix whirled to find a blurred form charging toward her. She barely had time to recognise Roswald Grey before his sword greeted her at a run. She turned the slash aside, but he didn't slow, crashing into her and driving her to the hard stone floor. The air left her lungs in a *whoosh*.

Grey pinned her beneath his body and wrapped a hand around her throat. Alix tried to drive a knee into his groin, but he got his own knee inside hers and wrenched her leg aside. She bucked and twisted, panic threatening to overtake her. The memory of her encounter with the thrall was still fresh; it seemed to her that Grey's eyes were lifeless and flat, filling her vision . . .

A boot connected with his face, snapping his head back, and a second blow knocked him aside. Saxon hauled Alix to her feet. She clutched at him, half leaning, half shoving. "Go," she gasped, "find the king! Help him!"

"I am no warrior . . ."

"You're all he has. *Please.*"

Saxon hesitated a moment longer, but he did as she asked, bolting up the stairs after Erik.

Grey had regained his feet by then, but he didn't attack right away. He faced Alix warily, reluctant to make the first move now that he had lost the element of surprise. Instead, he tried to intimidate her. "He's a fool to go up there." Grey jerked his head toward the stairs. "My men will open his guts for him."

"You've obviously never seen Erik fight." Alix hoped she sounded more confident than she felt.

Grey dove in, but his attempt at distraction hadn't worked; Alix batted him aside easily. He had a bloodblade, as befit his station, but even the enchantment wasn't enough to make a swordsman out of him. His feet were too close together, his hand too tight to the crossguard. His weapon might be lighter, his reflexes better, but he was still visibly unpractised. Alix tried a lunge of her own, testing him. He parried, but it was a sloppy, graceless thing.

"I've seen more of Erik White than I care to," Grey said, "but that will be over soon enough. If my men don't kill him, I'll do it myself."

"Is that what you think?" She laughed, sharp and mocking. "You should have run when you had the chance. You're as much of a fool as my brother says."

His face darkened. He tried another swipe, this one even uglier than before. *It's working.* She'd seen how Grey reacted when her brother ridiculed him at the parley. That kind of pride could be turned against a man easily enough. She kept at him. "*This* is the best you can do, and you thought to beat Erik? He's been fighting a war while you hid behind your mother's skirts. Look at you—you can't even best a *girl*."

That earned her a flurry of blows, each one better placed than the last. Alix wondered fleetingly if she'd miscalculated, but it was too late to back out now. Grey looked half a gargoyle, lips curled over his teeth like a wild beast, eyes glazed with rage.

Alix summoned her nastiest smile. "I've saved Erik from the Greys once already. Thanks to me, he won't have to marry your sister. I can't tell you how relieved he is. He'd rather face an army of thralls than become part of your family. Now that I've met you, I can understand why."

Grey lunged at her with a wordless cry, bringing his weapon down in a savage cut. She twisted aside and slammed her blade into his side. The blow rang harmlessly off his armour, but it enraged him even further. He swung his sword two-handed, putting all his weight behind the slice. It was a mistake. He left himself completely open, unable to arrest his momentum. Alix stepped in, close enough to embrace him, and smashed the hilt of her sword into his face. His nose opened in a spray of blood. He staggered backward, and before he could regain his balance, Alix thrust her blade through his unprotected throat. Then she hooked her boot behind his heel and drove a shoulder into him, riding him to the floor. Roswald Grey died with blood on his lips and disbelief in his eyes.

Alix charged up the stone steps and shouldered her way through the door. Bodies littered the floor of the gatehouse, Kingswords and Greyswords both, but there was no sign of anyone living. She raced outside. For a moment, the sun was so bright that she had to shield her eyes. She scanned the bailey through a sheen of tears. Her heart leapt a little when she saw the portcullis was open, leapt a lot when she saw Erik standing behind a wall of Kingswords, his sword dangling idly at his side. There was no sign of Saxon. Shouts still sounded here and there, but the clamour of battle had largely died. *Is it over?*

Her answer came a moment later as Arran Green burst through the doors of the keep, Rig and Liam in tow. They were tattered and bloody, but none of them looked hurt. Only then did Alix allow herself to feel relief.

She stayed where she was, vaguely aware that her knees were shaking, though whether from fear or the aftershock of battle, she wasn't sure. They'd nearly lost Erik in the oratorium. If it hadn't been for the Raven . . .

"Correct me if I'm wrong," said a familiar voice, "but isn't a bodyguard supposed to keep the body she's guarding *away* from danger?"

She scowled. "Do you honestly think I'm in the mood for that?"

Liam lacked the good sense to cower before her fury. He just shrugged. "I have trouble gauging a woman's mood when she's covered in blood."

Alix looked down at herself. The top of her breastplate was lacquered in a sticky layer of crimson. "Grey's," she said, half to herself.

Liam's grin vanished. "*Roswald* Grey?"

"He tried to ambush Erik, but he botched that as badly as everything else. He's dead."

Liam blew out a breath. "What a mess. The Raven insists he had nothing to do with it. Part of me believes him."

"Me too. Tom is a master tactician. It's hard to imagine him planning something this half-hatched. Grey didn't even have the sense to know when he was beaten. He sacrificed a hundred of his men for nothing. He could have at least used the battle as cover to escape."

"I guess the king will have to sort it out. For now, we've got the Raven under guard, and he'll be in irons within the hour."

Alix knew she should be happy, but instead she felt strangely hollow. She could not even imagine how Erik must feel. "I should go to him," she said, and she was almost too numb to feel guilty when the shutters closed over Liam's eyes. Almost.

She made her way across the bailey toward her king. Erik stood with his head bowed, oblivious to everyone around him. Already, she knew, he was thinking about what came next—for his brothers, for the war, for himself. He had terrible choices ahead of him, and very little time to make them. Alix wished she could do something to ease his burden, but she knew better. All she could do was stand beside him and try to lend him strength. That, and perhaps pray.

TWENTY-NINE

Alix brushed her hair for the third time that morning. She twisted it around her fingers, smoothing it into loose ringlets. Then she swept it up at the sides and affixed it with pins. She considered her reflection in the mirror. It was a flattering hairstyle, framing her face in soft waves of copper. Such things had mattered to her once, though she couldn't recall when, or why. She wondered if they would ever matter to her again.

Yanking the pins free, she let her tresses tumble down onto her shoulders. She gathered her hair into a fist at the nape of her neck and began tugging it into an austere braid. Gradually, mercifully, the noblewoman in the mirror vanished, replaced by the practical image of the king's bodyguard. The captain of the royal guardsmen didn't need to worry about betrothals or Banner Houses or failed loves. All she needed to worry about was her duty.

Which would be much easier if Erik would actually let her do it. Instead, he'd sent her away, banished her from his side to occupy herself with gods-knew-what while he brooded alone in his study. She understood why he didn't want to see her, but that didn't make it any easier. He might not want her, but he *needed* her. Only he was too angry to see it, and she had herself to blame.

A knock at the door startled her. She wasn't eager for company, so she took her time opening it. By the time she did, her visitor was halfway down the corridor.

"Oh." Liam sounded almost as surprised to see Alix as she was to see him. "I wasn't sure whether I should expect to find you here."

"The king . . . er . . ." *Can't stand the sight of me right now.* ". . . gave me some time off from my duties. To rest up and everything."

"Right. Good of him." If Liam's breeches had had pockets, his hands would have been jammed in them. Instead, he raked his fingers through his dark hair, leaving it dishevelled.

Alix was immediately wary. Liam had been avoiding her for so long that she couldn't imagine he brought good news. "What's up?"

"Well, listen—maybe this isn't the best timing, but I was hoping I could ask a favour."

"All right."

"I need some advice. I've spent the last two days being poked and prodded at by the king's people, trying to make something vaguely royal out of me, and it's driving me mad. They're obsessed with status symbols, especially clothes." A pensive look came over him. "I think I made the tailor cry this morning."

"Nice."

"Anyway, they've finally suggested something I actually sort of like, and I thought you could help me pick it out, since you've got experience with this sort of thing. It wouldn't take long—I've asked a merchant to come here to the palace." Liam jerked a thumb over his shoulder. "He's waiting in the courtyard. What do you think?"

She frowned. "Why are you being so coy?"

"Why are *you* being so suspicious? I'm just asking for a little friendly advice. I promise it won't kill you."

Alix didn't hesitate for long. It wasn't as though she had anything better to do, and besides, it would be good to get her mind off Erik. "I suppose I have time. Lead on."

The bailey was a bustle of activity, with a steady stream of servants, pages, and guards flowing in and out of the Three Keeps. Normalcy had returned swiftly to the palace following the dramatic end to the parley. Now that it was clear who was in charge, there was plenty of work to be done, and Liam and Alix had to weave their way through a small crowd as they headed toward the stables. Amidst the din of voices, Alix gradually became aware of a sound that didn't belong, a strange chorus of yips and growls coming from the paddock just ahead.

"What kind of merchant is this, anyway?" she asked, her mind forming the answer even as she spoke.

The paddock teemed with small, bristling balls of fur with sagging ears and furiously wagging tails. They tumbled and tussled, chased and chewed, all tangled together in a writhing mass of play. There were almost a dozen of them in as many shades of brown and grey, each no bigger than a small cat.

Liam leaned over the rail. "Wolfhounds. Hard to believe these little bits of fluff will grow into fifteen-stone killers, isn't it?"

"You're getting a puppy?" Alix knew she was grinning like a fool, but she didn't care.

"It won't stay a puppy for long. It'll turn into one of those great grey monsters King Rendell was famous for. You've seen his portraits all over the keep, haven't you? Apparently, His Majesty was never seen without his dogs."

"So they figure if you have one, people will immediately think of your grandfather." The idea had Albern Highmount written all over it.

"Exactly. That way, no one will notice I'm a bastard."

They shared a wry look.

"I need you to help me pick the foulest little beast we can find. We're going for maximum manliness, you understand. Something that won't hesitate to savage smaller, cuter creatures and drag their entrails over the expensive carpets."

"Your Highness!" An eager-looking fellow was hurrying over. Liam didn't react at first, only belatedly realising he was the one being addressed.

"Oh, right, that's me. You must be the breeder."

The man sketched a hasty bow. "This is the finest stock of wolfhounds in all of Alden, Your Highness . . ."

Alix wasn't the least bit interested in the man's sales pitch, so she left Liam to it. She propelled herself over the rail and waded into the throng. Immediately, the pups mobbed her, gazing up at her with wet, eager eyes, their tails thrashing. She squatted and ran her hands over coarse fur warmed by the sun. The pups heaved and flowed under her touch, unable to sit still even for the attention they so desperately craved. One of them set to gnawing at her boot, his needle-sharp teeth dragging ragged lines through the leather.

"There's a candidate." Liam came up behind her, having somehow managed to extricate himself from the breeder. "Let's put him in the maybe pile."

Alix spotted the runt of the group and dragged him out from under his brothers and sisters. He lapped at her fingers with the unbridled affection only puppies can manage, covering her hand in slobber.

"Nope," said Liam, "that one won't do. He's soft."

"He's adorable." Alix tousled the puppy's ears.

"I thought I was clear. We don't want adorable, we want ruthless killer. I'm supposed to be acquiring a symbol of princely virility, remember?" So saying, he plopped himself down in the dirt. "All right, fleabags, do your worst!"

A man sitting prone on the ground was too tempting a target for a wolfhound pup to ignore. The pack broke away from Alix, rushing Liam in a tide of fur and tiny teeth. They clambered over his knees and chest until he was overwhelmed. He rolled onto his back, laughing, letting the pups swarm all over him.

Alix was laughing too. "You're going to get yourself killed."

"Nonsense." Liam's voice was muffled beneath the seething mass of fur. "I'm perfectly—Ow! You little blighter!"

Later, Alix and Liam sat with their backs against the rail, exhausted, filthy, and happy. Alix tugged at the ears of the pup in her lap. It dozed in the sunshine, its legs occasionally twitching as it chased some imaginary prey in its head.

"I thought we agreed that one was no good," said Liam.

"What can I say? I've always had a soft spot for the defective ones. You should know."

"Oh, very nice."

"Sorry, couldn't resist." She paused, smiling up at him. "Are you really getting a puppy, or did you just arrange this to cheer me up?"

"Saw through my elaborate ruse, eh? Well done, you." He reached down to scratch the pup in Alix's lap. "I might do. I've never had a dog before. What about you—do you want to keep him?"

She considered, but only for a moment. "I couldn't possibly take care of one, not now. Everything's so uncertain . . ."

His smile faded. "I know what you mean." Patting the pup one last time, he got to his feet and stretched. "I'd better go. I've got to track down the king."

"You might consider bathing first."

He pretended to sniff himself. "You think so? Nothing says *I'm sorry* like a heady perfume of dog."

Alix dusted herself off, avoiding the unhappy stare of the breeder, who had apparently concluded that he wasn't going to make a sale today. "What do you have to apologise to Erik for?" It wasn't really any of her business, but that had never stopped her before.

Liam sighed. "I haven't exactly been overflowing with gratitude since he . . . er . . . acknowledged me." He was still uncomfortable talking about it, and Alix had yet to hear him refer to Erik by his given name. "I know he's trying to do something nice for me, and I should just focus on that."

"But?"

"I . . . don't know how to explain it." Judging by the guarded look in his eyes, Alix thought it more likely that he didn't *want* to explain it.

"Anyway," she said, smiling, "thank you for bringing me. I really needed that." She stood on her toes and gave him a peck on the cheek.

He shifted awkwardly. "Yes, well . . . Your brother mentioned you were feeling down, so when Highmount started in about the dogs . . ."

Liam had always known just what she needed, but this time he was wrong. She wanted to tell him the truth—that it wasn't the puppies that had brought a smile back to her face. But no good could come of saying such a thing, so she touched her thumb to the empty space on her little finger and kept the thought to herself.

A ragged breeze shivered through the rosebushes, dislodging delicate petals onto the sparkling white gravel of the pathway. The duck pond shied away from its touch, rippling frantically, and the loose rose petals collected in the shadowed corners of the hedgerows, as though hiding. The wind came from the south. From the thralls. It had grown stronger over the course of the day, and cooler too, carrying ominous tidings of an impending storm.

Ten days, the scouts reported. Ten days, and the Oridian army would reach Erroman. *Ten days*, Erik thought, *and the fate of my kingdom will be decided, one way or another.*

The Kingswords could not prevail, not with twenty-five thousand thralls at their gates. The enchantment had to be broken if they had any hope of holding the city. Erik knew what he had to do, but how? The Priest was surrounded by an army of thousands, half of them his own creatures. Killing him would not be the work of a general, not even one as talented as Arran Green. They needed a hunter. An assassin. Erik did not know any assassins. *Perhaps I should ask my brother*, he thought bitterly.

He sighed and rubbed his eyes. Moping about the rose garden was surely not helping matters. He had just made up his mind to seek out Arran Green when a figure appeared around the corner of the hedge maze.

"Thank the gods!" Liam put a hand to his stomach in a parody of relief. "I've spent the last half hour blundering around those sinister roses of yours. I was beginning to think the war would be over by the time I found my way out."

Erik mustered a smile. "That would be quite something to explain to General Green."

"Wouldn't it, though. 'Sorry about sticking you with the thralls, General, but I hope you'll accept this lovely bouquet of roses as a sign I was thinking of you.'"

Erik had heard much of Liam's wit, but had never actually seen any evidence of it until now. Not for the first time, he wondered how his brother managed with Arran Green. Aloud, he said, "I see my tailor has found you."

Liam plopped down on the bench beside him. "What gave it away?"

"Your shirt. The man is unreasonably fond of purple. And did he try to fit you for a cape?"

"He did. Horribly distressing. I almost slammed the door in his face."

Erik laughed. "It wouldn't be the first time. But he won't let it go, I promise you. I've learned that it's better to surrender peacefully."

The subject of the tailor spent, an awkward stretch of silence ensued. They both gazed out over the duck pond. Liam shifted restlessly on the bench. He had something to say, but Erik was in no mood to pry it from him, so he waited.

"Listen," Liam said eventually, "I wanted to apologise for the other day. What I said . . . It was unfair. I guess this whole . . . prince . . . thing will take some getting used to."

Erik smiled inwardly. His brother said the word *prince* the way a finely dressed lady steps in a mud puddle.

"When I was younger, I thought I wanted to be a prince, but it was made clear to me that was never going to happen. I came to accept that, eventually. Maybe I was even grateful for it. But now . . . everything's been turned on its head. I guess I'll have to learn to cope."

Erik did not reply straightaway. Part of him wanted to end the conversation here, at an awkward apology they could both pretend had cleared the air. But that would only defer the problem. Even now, there was a sullen tint to Liam's voice. The underlying implication of his words was obvious: He had been manoeuvred into this, even though he didn't really want it. Once again, Liam had done what he felt was obliged of him.

"What is it you *do* want, Liam?"

He shrugged. "You mean besides an inexhaustible supply of beautiful women and fine wine?"

Erik, of all people, knew a mask when he saw one. "Do you always deflect difficult questions with humour?"

Liam scowled and looked away. "What do you want me to say?"

"I want you to answer the question, if you can."

"What's that supposed to mean? Since when has it mattered what I want, anyway?"

Erik felt his own temper stir. "Has it occurred to you, Liam, that your life might not actually be so terrible if you just learned to take some initiative? The gods know you had a difficult childhood, but that's behind you now. You don't have to be a victim of circumstance anymore."

"Is that so?" Liam's scowl darkened. "Well I must be a bloody idiot, because here I thought my life was still being dictated by my blood." He looked uncomfortable as soon as he'd said it, no doubt realising how ridiculous it was to complain of his royal blood to the King of Alden.

"I'm not forcing anything on you," Erik said. "I'm giving you the option to *choose*. Gods' blood, man, you're like a prisoner who doesn't know what to do with an open cell door! Decide what you want, and *take it*!"

Liam sprang to his feet so suddenly that Erik reeled back, momentarily convinced that his brother meant to strike him. But the anger in Liam's eyes was eclipsed by something else, something nearer to grief. "You think I don't know what I want? Well, you're wrong. But it isn't that simple, is it? You're the king—I shouldn't have to explain to you about duty and sacrifice and all the rest."

Erik broke away from his brother's gaze. Words tumbled uselessly in his head, his mind refusing to grab hold of any of them. His tongue sat rebelliously idle. He had goaded Liam this far, but now that they were on the brink of it, he had seemingly lost his nerve. *One thing. I asked for one thing for myself.*

But that was not true. He had asked for two things. The gods had given him a choice, and he had already made it. He would not look back now. "You don't have to step aside for me, Liam," he said quietly. "Not anymore."

He was met with silence. When he looked up, Liam was watching him with a wary expression. Erik could not bring himself to say it any more clearly, so he waited for Liam to draw his own conclusions.

"I'm not sure I know what you're talking about," Liam said.

"I'm quite sure you do," Erik returned, his voice strangely expressionless. He felt numb, his nerves buzzing like the white noise of the sea.

Panic flickered across Liam's face. "Wait . . . did she tell you? I mean, are we really talking about . . . ?"

"She didn't tell me, and more's the pity." The words could have sounded bitter, but Erik had already spent his anger on that point. All that remained was emptiness.

Liam sat down heavily, looking a little ill. "I'm . . . not sure what to say."

That makes two of us. They sat in silence, listening to the wind rustling through the rosebushes. Liam furrowed his brow, as though he were choosing his next words carefully. "Are you . . . Are you saying it's over between you?"

Erik's reply stuck briefly in his throat before forcing its way out. "I'm saying it never began."

Liam's frown deepened. "I don't understand. What about the engagement? You and Alix were supposed to . . ."

Supposed to. Erik had believed that once, believed it with the force of fate. That belief was gone now. In its place, there was only a hollow space. "It was discussed," he said. "High-mount wanted to send a signal to the Greys, and to others considering throwing their lot in with Tom. But the Greys are disgraced, and Tom is no longer a factor. For the moment at least, my enemies have no one to rally behind. I still need a bride, it's true, but it does not have to be today, and it does not have to be Alix."

"So you're going to give her up? Just like that?"

Just like that? I should hit you, you ass. "I'm not giving her up, Liam, because I never had her. Believe it or not, I do not consider the royal prerogative to extend to Alix's heart. She makes her own choices."

"Of course she does!" He flushed all the same. "I just thought . . . this whole time . . ."

Erik dropped his head between his knees, laughing humourlessly. "You know something? You *are* a bloody idiot. You've been in such a quality sulk that you haven't even seen what's right in front of you." He looked up, and he could feel his eyes burning. Liam shrank a little beneath his stare, but he didn't care. "That ring of yours? Alix has been wearing it for months. She never took it off, at least not that I saw. She chose you a long time ago, or at least she would have, if you'd let her. But instead you've been too busy revelling in your martyrdom. Forgive me, Liam, but I'm well and truly tired of being your excuse to hide behind your own self-doubt. I've offered you what I can. Take it or leave it, but I have nothing left." *Nothing at all.*

He stood abruptly, wanting nothing more than to be away from this place.

Liam, for his part, stared down at his boots. His cheeks were flushed, though whether from anger or embarrassment, Erik could not tell. "You could give Arran Green a go when it comes to lecturing," he said. "I don't think I've been told off that thoroughly since I was a squire."

Erik blew out a long, weary sigh. "That's what older brothers are for, Liam."

He retreated to the head of the path, where his guards waited. Instinctively, he reached inside for the discipline to wipe his face clear of emotion, but he found he did not need it. His step was surprisingly light, considering what had just happened. It was as though some hitherto unknown burden had been lifted. It left a hole behind, and there was pain, certainly. But it was not etched in hard lines, as he might have expected. Instead, it was painted in the soft hues of a watercolour.

The first hint of rain spattered the pathway. The rosebushes ducked and shuddered under its touch. Wind gathered and gusted, and a moment later, the sky opened up in earnest.

Absurdly, Erik found himself smiling.

THIRTY

Four shadows prowled the inner walls of the Red Tower, circling Erik like a pack of wolves as he climbed. The rest of the pack waited for him at the top of the narrow stone steps, swirling around each other hungrily, their forms growing darker as the men casting the shadows drew near. Torchlight bathed the windowless walls in a bloody hue, but it was not the glow of the torches that gave the Red Tower its name. Erik stood aside as one of his guards pushed open a thick door banded in iron, and his gaze fell upon the machine. He hated the sight of it—always had—and he tried to avert his eyes as they walked past. But inevitably, he found himself staring at its sinister iron skeleton, its spikes and cranks and rollers, and picturing some poor, wretched creature pinned to it by his own flesh.

I should have had that thing removed years ago. It must weigh an unholy ton, but there had to be a way to move it. It did not belong within the palace walls, not even in the Red Tower. This place was a prison now, not some barbaric Erromanian hell where Onnani rebels and enemies of the emperor met their slow and agonising end. Erik swore he could still smell the blood, but perhaps that was just the sharp scent of iron from the dozens of rusted manacles dangling from the ceiling. They grasped at his shoulders as he weaved his way through, their touch cold as death. *I'll have this floor torn out*, he vowed, *as soon as the war is over.* Perhaps he should have the whole tower pulled down. There were better prisons in Erroman now, civilised places built to incarcerate men, not break them. Only the worst criminals in the land were still kept in the Red Tower—murderers, rapists, and, of course, traitors.

Traitors like Prince Tomald White.

Erik paused at the foot of the last flight of stairs. The air seemed colder above, though that was probably his imagination. *What good can come of this?* a voice inside him whispered. But he had no choice. Whatever else Tom might be, he was Erik's brother.

He made his way to the fourth floor. Alix and his other guards tightened around him. She had been prepared to give him space until now, but by the time they reached Tom's door, she stood right at his elbow, her hand resting on the hilt of her sword. As the jailer fumbled with his keys, Erik said, "I will go in alone." Alix started to object, but he raised a hand and said, "There's nothing to fear. He is unarmed, and you will be right on the other side of this door."

"What good is that?" The words were scarcely out of her mouth before she coloured. Alix's occasional flashes of insolence were rarely so ill-timed as this, and she knew it. She gave a stiff little bow. "I apologise, Your Majesty. It's just . . . this makes me extremely uncomfortable."

"We are all of us uncomfortable, Alix."

She flushed deeper and nodded, and when the jailer pushed the door inward, she stood aside without even baring her blade.

Tom sat beneath the window with his back to the wall, one arm draped across his knee. He made no move to stand as Erik entered. He did not even raise his head.

"Hello, Tom."

"I expected you yesterday."

"I wasn't ready for you yesterday." He was not ready now.

"Too busy laying battle plans?" Tom asked, looking up at last. A little smirk of contempt hitched one corner of his mouth. *For me*, Erik wondered, *or himself?* "I hear the enemy is moving faster than we thought. Less than a week away, they tell me. Will you evacuate the city?" Seeing Erik hesitate, his smile widened. "How much you have changed, brother. Not so long ago, you thought your charm enough to keep every man in the kingdom pecking out of your hand like a sweet songbird. Now you think your hold so weak that I might betray your plans to the enemy, even locked up in here."

"I didn't come here to discuss the Oridians."

Tom's gaze took in the bandage on Erik's forearm. "New sword?"

"I didn't come here to discuss bloodblades, either."

"Why did you come?"

"To decide," Erik said wearily.

Tom snorted and shook his head. "When you broke your word at the parley, I dared to hope you had grown up at last, but perhaps that was wishful thinking. What is there to decide, Erik? You know what must be done. Why come here and make it harder on yourself?"

"Because you're my brother. That may not mean anything to you, but—"

"Fool!" Tom shot to his feet so suddenly that Erik took an involuntary step back. "It doesn't matter! You are *king*, and I am a traitor! We are not just men, you and I. We don't have that luxury. You've never understood that! You should have married Sirin and made an heir. You should have had the bastard's head off the moment Father died. You should have thrown me in here months ago, when I made it clear I would never support your war. Time and again, you avoid the difficult decisions. Enough, Erik! It's time to be a king!"

"Is that what you were doing on that bluff at Boswyck? Being a king?"

The fury fled Tom's eyes as quickly as it had come. He turned and went to the window. It was little more than a square cut from the stone, not even wide enough for a child to crawl through, but it let in the air. Tom drew deeply of it before answering. "Varad wrote to me before we left Erroman. His spies must have heard us arguing, knew I opposed the war. Still, the sheer audacity of it . . ." He shook his head. "I burned the letter and didn't think of it again, until . . ."

A long pause. When Tom spoke again, he sounded hollow. Scraped out. "I sat atop that bluff and looked down over the enemy, and I knew we could not win. Even the Pack wouldn't have been enough to tip the balance in our favour. The battle was lost before it began."

"You could have signalled to me. I would have sounded the retreat."

"Yes." Tom turned back around and met his eye. "But you would have regrouped and insisted we fight another battle. And another battle after that, again and again, until the last Kingsword fell."

Erik could not deny it.

"I didn't even *decide*, not truly." Tom's gaze took on a far-away look. "I just turned my horse and signalled the men. Some followed, some didn't. I barely remember the ride. But I remember the sounds." He squeezed his eyes shut. "I will never forget the sounds."

"Nor I," Erik said, his voice thick in his throat. "Any more than I will forget the eyes of the man who tried to plunge a knife into my heart as I walked among my own men. Alix saved my life, and nearly paid for it with her own. The woman I . . ." He swallowed. "The woman sworn to protect me. How do you justify *that* to yourself, brother?"

"This again. You spoke of it at the parley." Tom shook his head in disgust. "I should have known Grey would not stop at mere bribery. He has been busy, it seems."

"You blame Grey?"

"I've just admitted leaving you to die on the battlefield, Erik. Why would I lie about this?"

It was true, Erik supposed; he had no reason to lie. And the gods knew Roswald Grey was capable of it. "You had no idea what he plotted?"

"It seems you are not the only one blindly confident in the faith of his followers." Tom flashed a bitter smile. "I knew what he was, and I knew how badly he wanted Sirin to share the crown. I should have known he would stoop to anything. His little White Raven scheme . . . I went along with it willingly enough. I thought that if I had enough allies, I could persuade you to step aside without a fight."

"You would still have had me executed."

"Yes." He looked Erik right in the eye as he said it. "I would have. But not because I wanted you to die. Whatever you might think of me . . . You are my brother, Erik. I never wanted . . ." He faltered, his whole body seeming to wilt like a sail with no wind to fill it, and for a long moment he stared at the floor, empty. Then his hands curled into fists at his side, and he drew himself up again, taut and strong. "I did what I had to do, but I would never have agreed to send some back-alley brigand to do my work for me. There is no honour in that."

Honour. After all this, he still believes he has acted honourably. A ghost materialised before Erik, a small, black-haired boy with fierce blue eyes. "I'm Eldrik the Lion," the boy said as he duelled his brother with a wooden sword. He was always Eldrik the Lion. Erik had played them all—kings and conquerors and great champions, every paragon worthy of a place on the Gallery of Heroes. But Tom had only ever had one hero, a king renowned for his prudence—and his brutal justice. *I wonder how Eldrik would have dealt with Prince Tom the traitor?* Erik thought he knew the answer.

Tom was facing ghosts of his own. The faraway look had returned. "Sirin. What will become of her?"

"I don't know."

"She is blameless in this. I swear it."

"I believe you."

Tom turned back to the window. "You should go," he said, his voice as cold and spent as a heap of ash. "The longer you stay here, the more your resolve will weaken. You know what you must do."

I can't. He dared not say it aloud. Tom would only despise him for it.

"All I ask is that you do it by your own hand, and quietly. Don't make a spectacle of me."

Erik sighed, a long, tortured thing that felt ragged in his throat.

"Your regret is misplaced," Tom growled, a cinder coming to life amid the ashes. "If the situation were reversed, I would not hesitate. I have committed high treason, and if you don't put me to death, all the realm will know you for a weak king. The nobility is divided. You dare not misstep now. You must—"

"*Enough*, Tom. I don't need your lectures anymore." *I*

never did, he wanted to say, but it was too late for that. *Let him die with his delusions. They are all he has.*

"Good." Tom leaned against the window, nodding to himself. "You have changed, it's true. War has made you stronger. What's the saying—*It takes hammer and flame to forge a sword*. I thought I was the sword, but perhaps I mistook myself. Perhaps I mistook us both. No matter. If I have not played the part I thought I would, at least I played a part. I am at peace."

Erik turned on his heel and left. He did not say farewell. He wanted those words to be the last he ever heard from his brother. If he tried hard enough, he might even believe them.

Evening found Erik at his desk, rubbing his eyes for the umpteenth time. The correspondence he was supposed to be reading blurred beneath his bleary gaze, refusing to resolve itself into comprehensible lines. Ordinarily, he would have allowed himself a pause, but there was no point. Should he break off from his work, he would find only dark thoughts waiting for him.

"Is there anything I can get you?" Alix asked from somewhere over his shoulder.

Half a dozen sarcastic replies floated through his mind before he settled for, "No, thank you."

"You'll wear yourself out, Erik."

"I'm long past worn out, Alix." He felt her hand squeeze his shoulder, and he put his own over hers. "I'll be fine," he said more firmly. "Now is not the time for me to start feeling sorry for myself."

Her reply was cut off by a knock at the door. Alix strode across the study and opened it a crack, sticking her head out through the gap. Erik heard a murmured exchange.

"It's Liam." She cocked a questioning eyebrow. Erik nodded, and she stood aside, letting Liam pass.

"Your Majesty." Liam ducked his head awkwardly. He glanced at Alix, then back at Erik. "Er," he said.

Erik understood. "Alix, could you excuse us for a moment?"

"Certainly." She vanished from the study as though only too happy to oblige.

"Have a seat." Erik gestured at the chair across his desk. "What's on your mind?"

Liam lowered himself into the chair, avoiding Erik's eye. "I wanted to talk to you about the other day."

"That's not necessary . . ."

"Yes it is. Just hear me out, please." He blew out a breath, as though steeling himself, and met Erik's gaze.

"Very well." Erik sincerely hoped he was not in for another tantrum. He doubted his ability to cope gracefully just now.

"I've been thinking a lot about what you said, and you're right—I have been using you as a sort of excuse. About a lot of things, but especially about"—he dropped his voice until it was barely above a whisper—"about Alix."

"All right," Erik said, for lack of anything better.

"For the longest time after my mother died, all I wanted was to find my way back to a family. A *real* family. Not that Arran Green wasn't . . . you know . . . Anyway, I used to lie awake at night and wonder what my father was like. I wondered if he loved my mother, whether he still thought about her sometimes. I thought about you too, and Tom. I used to imagine you being curious about me, asking all sorts of questions about who I was and what I was doing. I pretended that you wanted to come and find me, and that one day the three of us would escape together and have all sorts of adventures." Liam looked a little embarrassed, but he was smiling, and Erik found he was smiling too.

The moment was short-lived. Liam sighed and raked a hand through his hair. "So if all that's true, why am I being such an ungrateful *git*? Here you are, offering me a family after all this time, and all I do is throw it back in your face." Erik started to reply, but Liam cut him off again. "Don't, Erik. Don't make excuses for me. I've made enough of them for myself."

Erik could only stare in mild amazement, some part of him registering that Liam had just called him by his given name for the first time.

"When you asked me to stand with you at the parley," Liam continued, "you said that in times like these, a man needs his family more than anything else. You were right about that too. What I wanted to tell you the other day, what I was too clumsy and angry and *stupid* to say properly, is that you'll never know how much I appreciate being given the chance to be your brother. And I promise that from now on, you won't have cause to regret it. You had the strength to put your own feelings aside so that we could be brothers, and I can do no less."

Erik's brows gathered. "What exactly are you saying?"

"I'm saying that I would be an idiot to let anything come between my brother and me, and that includes Alix. I can't know for sure what kind of future I might have had with her. Lots of love stories end badly, right? What I do know is that you're my only family, the only person since my mother who's ever really wanted me around. I won't risk that. I can't. If you can leave Alix aside, so can I."

Erik studied his brother in silence. Liam's sincerity could not be doubted; he genuinely believed he could let Alix go. But the strain in his voice, the tightness in his shoulders, the quiet hurt in his eyes, gave the lie to his words. He could no more let her go than he could cut off his own arm. A week from now, a month, a year, he would realise his mistake, and he would hate Erik forever. *He doesn't understand. He actually thinks you're doing something selfless, and he feels guilty.* Erik smiled sadly. "Once again, brother, I'm forced to support your conclusion that you're an idiot."

Liam blinked. He opened his mouth. Closed it. He scowled. "You're pretty hard to please, you know that?"

Erik laughed. "Not as hard as you might think. I appreciate the gesture, Liam, more than you know. But it's not the same for you as it is for me, and I wouldn't be much of a brother if I let you go through with it."

"How is it not the same?"

Because if I choose her, I'll lose you forever, and I've lost far too much already. Because I need a brother more than I need a lover. Aloud, he said, "Because it's you she wants." It was the truth, if only part of it, and it hurt less to say it than he would have guessed. "This isn't me being noble, Liam. If I thought for a moment that she felt for me what she feels for you, I would never have the strength to stand aside. However, I'm not afflicted with any such conviction. I'd also like to point out that you've found a new excuse for not trying, and thus not risking rejection."

"That's not what this is about."

"Really?"

Liam glared at him. "You know what? I take it back. If this is what it's going to be like, I'll take my chances with Alix."

"You do that. Take your chances, Liam, and take them soon. Either you'll win her heart, or you won't, but I promise you this: If you don't even try, I *will* have you thrown in the Red Tower. Now if you'll excuse me, I have three inches of correspondence to get through by supper."

Liam rose, but he did not leave straightaway. Instead, he just stood there, hovering over the desk in silence. When Erik looked up, he was surprised to find Liam smirking at him. "You've got a head start on me with all this brother stuff. Seems like there's a lot of lecturing and name-calling involved. Anything else I should know about?"

"The occasional wrestling match, but I don't much fancy my chances, so I'm sticking with name-calling for the time being." They shared a laugh, and Erik felt as if someone had lifted heavy plate mail from his shoulders.

A moment after Liam quit the study, Alix reappeared. Erik watched her cross the room, returning her smile as she took up her place behind him. What he had told Liam was true; he doubted very much that Alix felt for him what she seemed to feel for Liam. That doubt was his salvation. If he was right, he would never have won her anyway. And if he was wrong, he didn't want to know about it.

He turned back to the hated pile of correspondence. To his relief, the words were sharp and clear, and his quill began to move of its own accord. Sometimes, he reflected, if one is patient, things simply fall into place.

Tom died at dawn, by the freshly forged edge of Erik's bloodblade. No announcement was made, no crowd gathered to see. Only a few guards bore witness, along with what remained of Tom's family. Liam was there to watch his new brother die, and Sirin Grey as well. She did not weep. She did not even speak. She just stood there, as silent and white as a statue, even as the blade fell. But when she turned to leave, her legs buckled beneath her; she would have fallen had Liam not been there to catch her. He helped her away, leaving Erik alone with what he had done.

The king knelt in a spreading pool of his brother's blood. It felt as if it were his own, seeping from him slowly, darkly, until all that was left was an empty husk. He curled his hands tightly around the hilt of his sword, so his guards would not see him shaking. Then he bowed his head and prayed. To whom, he could not have said.

THIRTY-ONE

† A thin stream of blood followed the sinuous path of the runes, tracing arcane patterns across the surface of the bowl as it trickled down to the bottom, where it gathered in a dark pool. Erik watched, fascinated, as Nevyn swirled the shallow silver dish in his hands, making sure the blood touched every corner of every symbol. The bloodbinder whispered to himself as he worked, though whether it was an incantation, or just distracted muttering, Erik could not tell. He had seen this process dozens of times before, but he had never had the stomach to ask how exactly it worked. He was not sure Nevyn would enlighten him anyway. Bloodbinders were notoriously jealous of their secrets.

Nevyn leaned over the mould, pouring the dish out into molten steel. The droplets of blood hissed as they met the glowing metal; an unpleasant smell filled the smithy.

"Well, that's foul," Liam said, wrinkling his nose. He looked a little pale, and the knuckles that held the bandage to his forearm were white.

"Don't distract him," Erik warned.

"It's fine, Your Majesty. The difficult part is over." Nevyn motioned for his assistant, and the young man poured out another layer of molten steel, filling the top half of the mould. The heat seared Erik's face, forcing him to close his eyes. When he opened them, Nevyn was gesturing at the door. "We're through here, Your Highness. Let us withdraw somewhere more comfortable while the blacksmith works."

"Wait, aren't you the blacksmith?"

"I am the bloodbinder, Your Highness. I prepare the raw materials, but I don't fashion the finished product. This way, please."

He led them to his study, a dark little room at the far end of an uncomfortably warm corridor. Erik had offered him chambers farther away from the forge, but Nevyn insisted that he did not mind. *It's not as though I live here*, he had said, *and anyway, I've spent most of my life at the forge*. Erik supposed that was true. Nevyn had been serving the Whites since before Erik was born. He was the youngest of them; in all that time, not a single new bloodbinder had emerged, and now Nevyn was the last. Alden was a small kingdom, and there had never been more than half a dozen known bloodbinders at any time. But to be down to one— during a time of war, no less—was nothing short of a national crisis. Erik would happily have offered Nevyn an estate if he thought it would help the man do his job. Fortunately for the royal treasury, Nevyn had simpler tastes. All he wanted was rest and a little privacy. Erik could grant him the latter, at least.

"Would you like to look at some designs for the hilt?" Nevyn drew a thick leather book down from a shelf. "I'm afraid we won't have time to etch the blade, if you need it as soon as you say . . ."

"I'm a little more worried about how I'm going to use the thing," Liam said. "I mean, is this really the right time for me to get a new sword? I won't be used to the enchantment."

"You can practice with it in the yard," Erik said. "See how you feel. If you prefer to fight with your old sword, no one will criticise you for it."

"Are you sure? Highmount seems to be able to criticise anything."

Erik smiled. "Speaking of which, I'd better go. I have appointments all day. But before I do . . . Nevyn, is there really nothing more you can tell me?"

The bloodbinder shook his head. "I'm sorry, Your Majesty.

I've looked through every book in my library, but there is no reference to anything like this power the Priest wields. If it's ever been done before, no one in Alden has written about it."

"So it is magic, then?" Liam asked. "The Priest, the bloodbond—all of it?"

Nevyn shrugged. "Everything is magic to those who can't master it."

"I guess so. But it didn't look to me like you did much of anything. No offence."

"None taken. In fact, I agree. It is simply a question of preparing the blood correctly. Once that is done, it can be added to any substance with which it can be properly blended or soaked in. Molten metal for a sword, wood or hemp for a bow . . . anything. The technique does not seem so very mysterious to me, but even I can't explain why one man can do it and another cannot. Is it innate, or just very difficult to learn? No one knows, Your Highness."

Erik had heard this explanation before, and it still sounded evasive to him. But he had bigger concerns at the moment. "You still believe that if we kill the Priest, the bond will be broken?"

"I do."

Liam regarded him curiously. "So if I were to kill you right now, all the bloodweapons you've made would stop working?"

"For gods' sake, Liam . . ." Erik shot the bloodbinder an apologetic look.

"It's all right, Your Majesty." Nevyn smiled. "No, Your Highness, slaying me would not undo the bloodbond. I am the one who forges the link, it's true, but once that is done, my role is ended. But if my theory is correct, the Priest has found a way to become part of the bond itself, and to reverse its power."

Erik frowned. "What do you mean, reverse it?"

"In conventional bloodbinding, the blood of the man is mixed with the weapon, thus giving the man command over the weapon. In this case, the power appears to work in reverse. The Priest is the weapon, and he controls the man."

"How would he achieve that?"

"I'm not sure. Perhaps he imbibes the blood himself."

Liam made a face. "Tasty."

"That is why I believe slaying the Priest will break the bond. At the very least, it should prevent him from giving instructions to his thralls. If I'm right, that is."

"And if you're wrong?" Liam asked.

"Then you needn't worry about learning to use a new sword," Erik said, "because magic or no, it won't make a damned bit of difference."

Alix shucked her armour off slowly, wincing at the stiffness in her muscles. It had been a long day spent on her feet while Erik received a steady stream of visitors. Alix wasn't sure which breed of courtier she found more distasteful—the sycophants and supposed well-wishers, or the swaggering, self-entitled oligarchs who scarcely made it through the obligatory niceties before launching into a list of complaints and demands. *As though half these cretins weren't licking Tom's boots a fortnight ago*, she'd thought at least a dozen times over the course of the day. If Erik felt the same, he gave no sign, treating each and every lord and lady like a proven stalwart.

Alix had scarcely dropped the last of her armour into a heap in the corner when a sound at the window made her spin. Even as she reached for her dagger, she recognised the form lounging on her windowsill, and she relaxed. "How long have you been here?"

"Longer than you have," came the rasping reply. "I thought it best to make my presence known before you disrobed any further. I wouldn't want you to mistake my intentions." Saxon was perched with his back against the window frame, one leg tucked up to his chest, the other dangling casually into the night. He twirled a rose between his fingers, presumably pilfered from the king's garden. "For you, Lady Black," he said, handing it over.

"How did you get in here, anyway?"

Saxon shrugged. "We all come from somewhere. Before I was a spy, I was a humble thief. I have a gift for sneaking."

Alix couldn't help smiling. *You and me both.* "I didn't get a chance to thank you for what you did the other day. For me, and for the king. It was . . ." She wanted to say *unexpected*, but that might sound insulting. So instead, she said, "exceptional."

"I could do no less. My oversight with the guards very nearly cost my client everything, and I have a reputation to maintain."

"Purely business, then?"

"Always."

Alix wasn't sure she believed that, but she didn't press the point. "What can I do for you?"

"It's a sad excuse for a spy who comes to his own client for information, but these are strange times."

"What information?"

"Is it true that the enemy is at our gates?"

She sighed. "Near enough. They're a few days away at most."

"Will it be a siege?"

"If we're lucky. More likely . . ." She didn't finish the thought.

Saxon's dark eyes studied her. "I've heard it said that the Madman has been butchering Aldenian children and using their blood for witchcraft. They say he cast a dark spell over his army to make them invincible."

Alix forced a brittle laugh. "And people believe that? I'm not aware of any children being butchered, and his army isn't invincible. Tales like that only serve our enemies."

The spy wasn't fooled. "Even the tallest tales often have roots in the truth."

Erik had forbidden them to speak of the Priest and his thralls, for it would only incite panic. But that didn't mean Alix had to lie. Saxon had served her loyally and well; he deserved as much of the truth as she could give him. "If you have the means to leave this city," she said, "I suggest you do so."

He nodded slowly. "I thank you."

"Where will you go?"

His only reply was to take her hand and kiss it. "Farewell, Lady Black. I hope we meet again." Without another word, he slipped out into the night and vanished.

The spy had barely been gone a quarter hour when there was a knock at Alix's door. Suppressing a groan, she opened it.

Her surprise at finding Liam was no less than it had been a few days ago, especially given the hour.

"Sorry to bother you so late," he said, before Alix could even greet him, "but if I don't get this off my chest now, I might explode."

Alix had no idea what to say to that, so she simply stood aside, sparing an anxious glance into the corridor lest anyone should see the prince enter her sleeping chamber at such an inappropriate hour. As difficult as it was for her to think of Liam as a White, her upbringing would never permit her to forget appearances.

He hovered awkwardly in the centre of the room, his gaze flitting around without really settling on anything.

"Is everything all right?"

"Fine, thank you." Belatedly registering the worry in her voice, he added, "Oh, right. No, everything's fine—don't worry. It's just . . . Well, I'm not very good at this sort of thing."

"What sort of thing, exactly?"

He pushed his dark hair back in the familiar nervous gesture. "Well, I could make you a list, but I doubt you have that kind of time." He gave her a thin smile, but before the joke had time to fall flat, he continued, "Anyway, the short answer is, I came to apologise."

Alix stared at him, bemused. "You seem to be doing a lot of that lately," she said, a little ungraciously.

"Don't I know it. You'd think with all the practice, I'd be better at it by now."

Silence collected in the space between them. "I'm sorry, but . . ." Alix shifted in mounting impatience. "You'll have to refresh my memory. What exactly is it that you're apologising for?"

"For everything, Allie." He said it with such quiet intensity that something flipped over in Alix's belly.

"I'm not sure I follow," she said.

"I'm sorry for pushing you away," he said in the same quiet, searing voice. "I acted like you were something Erik was entitled to, just one more thing that was meant for him and not for me. As if you didn't even have a say in the matter. I think maybe I wanted to believe you didn't have a choice, because I was sure you wouldn't choose me anyway. I guess part of me thought that I didn't deserve you. But it wasn't just my feelings I was putting aside—it was yours too. I didn't have the right, and I'm sorry."

Alix broke off from his gaze, afraid of the sting building behind her eyes. "You might have been able to put your own feelings aside, Liam, but you can't speak for mine."

His eyes widened a fraction. "No, wait. I didn't mean—" He made a frustrated sound and shook his head, momentarily at a loss. Then he reached into his pocket and withdrew something brightly coloured. "Do you know what this is?"

It looked like parchment in the shape of a five-pointed star. "It's a squashed flower."

He scowled. "It's not *squashed*, Alix, it's *pressed*. Haven't you ever kept dried flowers between the pages of a book? Or is it only sentimental idiots like me who do that? Anyway, it's a fire lily, or at least that's what Gwylim says. I picked it in the Blacklands. Not so far from Blackhold, actually, where the foothills start to rise. The others thought I was mad, I'm sure, since we were half surrounded by Oridians at the time. I was lying there on my belly, trying not to be seen . . ."

Now he was just babbling. Alix wondered if she should stop him.

". . . saw it there, and it was just the most amazing colour. Something between red and orange, like sunset over the Scions, or—"

"Liam . . ."

"—or the red clay of the foothills, or—"

"*Liam!*"

"—or the colour of your hair."

Silence.

"Which, as it turns out, is my favourite colour," he finished quietly. "I guess what I'm trying to say is that I never stopped thinking about you."

Alix stared at him mutely.

Her silence only agitated him more. "I'm making a complete hash of this, aren't I? Look, can we just skip all of it and pretend that I've just delivered the most romantic apology in history, and that I ended it all by saying what a beautiful and amazing creature you are?" He thrust the flower at her, like he couldn't wait to be rid of it.

Alix took it with numb fingers.

Liam's grey eyes were pleading. "Allie, for the love of Farika, say something or just kill me now."

Her lips parted long before she found words. "I'm having a little trouble understanding this. Until a few days ago, you barely spoke to me in complete sentences. What's changed?"

"Nothing." He grabbed her hand. "That's what I'm trying to tell you. Nothing has changed, not from the first day I met you. It just took my brother threatening to have me imprisoned to find the courage to say so."

There seemed to be a lot of significant information buried in that remark, but she couldn't sort through it now. All of her energy was devoted to suppressing the joy that surged against her willpower like a raging river trying to breach a dam. She could no longer afford to be impulsive, self-indulgent Alix. There was too much at stake; Erik had shown her that.

Seeing her waver, Liam pulled her closer, lacing his fingers through hers. "I want to try again."

His eyes held a warmth she hadn't seen there for a very long time, and she almost faltered. But she couldn't let herself give in, not until she'd had time to think. If Liam was just experiencing a moment of weakness, a spasm of regret that was destined to pass, accepting him now would only make things worse. "I need to think, Liam."

"I was afraid you'd say that." His fingers slipped away from hers. "I'll leave you alone, then. You know where to find me." He left without another word.

Moonlight bathed the corridor in a silvery glow, lending the polished stone floor the appearance of a frozen river. The marble was cold beneath Alix's bare feet, and she shivered, drawing her shirt more tightly around her. The thin fabric was designed to be worn under armour, not paraded about after dark. The heat of the day had long since leaked from the castle walls, leaving a chill borne on the breath of the river.

She stopped in front of a sumptuously panelled door, knocking softly. She was surprised when it opened; she'd expected him to be asleep. "Didn't I post guards outside this door?" she asked.

"Um." Liam glanced into the corridor, as though perhaps he'd misplaced them. "Yes, well . . . I may have reassigned them. Turns out I have that authority. Prince and all."

Alix only half heard the reply, fixated as she was on the sudden realisation that Liam was naked from the waist up. The ridiculousness of the situation hit her full force then, and she had to suppress a mad giggle. Here she was, standing outside the prince's sleeping chambers in the predawn hours, both of them scantily clad. So much for being conscious of appearances.

As though reading her mind, Liam said, "I think you'd better come in before a patrol comes past." He shut the door behind her. He waited.

"I've been thinking," she said, stupidly.

"Right."

"What you said before . . . that nothing has changed . . . that's not really true, is it? I mean, there's Erik. I don't think we're engaged, but I'm not sure. We haven't really talked about it."

"You're not," Liam said. "Engaged, I mean."

She frowned. "How do you know?"

"Because he told me. He told me a lot of things, Allie."

"You talked to him about me?"

"It's all right." He took her hand. "This isn't about Erik, not anymore. This is about you and me."

You and me. Something broke free then. Whether it was the last lingering bit of doubt, or merely her discipline, she would never know. The dam burst, and the torrent overwhelmed her. She had only one more question. "Are you sure?"

"Am *I* sure? Allie . . ." He pulled her into him.

She met his kiss with an urgency born of fear, some part of her convinced that this wasn't really happening, that she'd fallen asleep and would wake up to a rude dawn and the sinking realisation that Liam hadn't really come to see her. She pressed her fingers into the muscles of his back, drew in the scent of his skin and the heat of his mouth, rallying the support of every sense to confirm that he was real. She couldn't take in enough of him, and a small, desperate sound escaped her throat. Her fingers fumbled with the laces at his waist, but he caught her wrist in a firm grip. He broke off from the kiss, leaving them both panting.

"Slow down, love. We have plenty of time." His mouth drifted over her neck, barely glancing off her skin. "I want to learn everything about you, Alix Black," he murmured, the richness of his voice setting her nerves thrumming. When his lips caressed the tender spot behind her ear, her knees nearly gave way. "There, you see? I've learned something already."

He was lowering her onto the bed, though she had no memory of crossing the room. Her fingers traced the firm contours of his chest, swells and canyons brushed in the amber glow of lamplight. Her mouth followed, gently raking his skin with her teeth. He sucked in a breath and pulled her hips against him, and for a moment Alix thought his resolve would waver. But instead he pulled her shirt over her head, and she felt the warmth of his tongue dart over her skin. When he found her breast, her back arched in reply, and she gasped. She felt him sigh, his body moving against hers in a slow, steady rhythm filled with promise.

"Gods, Allie, you're so beautiful." He continued on his exploration. Her remaining clothing was removed with almost reverential care, each newly exposed bit of skin greeted with kisses and the caress of his tongue.

He was thorough. A sweet ache built all over her body, pulsing from her core. Her fingers twisted in the bedsheets as she sought an outlet for the tension. Finally, she could bear it no longer. *"Liam, please."*

He answered, and the relief was exquisite. She clung to his neck, moving against him, her mouth fixed beneath his ear so that he could hear every strained breath. When her body began to tense around him, she nipped his neck, and a moment later, he gave a low growl and shuddered against her.

His lips continued to roam against her throat as they recovered their breath. Alix raked her fingers through his hair, overwhelmed by the swell of feeling cresting inside her, the unlooked-for joy of reclaiming something precious she'd thought lost forever. "Liam," she said against his ear, "I love you."

He drew back, peering down at her with glazed eyes. "Did I really just hear that?" He paused. "Because if this is a dream, I'm going to be *very* cross."

Alix laughed as he left a trail of kisses along her jaw. "You really just heard that. And now you're going to leave me hanging?"

He stroked her hair back from her face. "Never. I love you, Allie."

She wasn't sure how long she lay there, smiling up at him, but eventually, the real world began to creep back in. She sighed. "It's going to be complicated, you know."

He rolled onto his side. "In spite of recent evidence to the contrary, I'm not *completely* stupid." He shrugged. "We'll manage. We belong together, Allie. Nothing's ever going to change that."

At that moment, in the soft cocoon of their happiness, Alix believed him. The dawn would almost certainly bring doubts, and worse besides. But in the dark hours before daylight, there was only Liam, and the sweet promise of peace.

THIRTY-TWO

"It has begun, Your Majesty," Arran Green said.

Erik's posture stiffened, but otherwise he remained admirably calm. "What is their exact position?"

"They have put up their tents on both sides of the old imperial walls. About five thousand within, the rest without. They have battering rams and siege towers and trebuchets."

"Not to mention about twenty-five thousand thralls," Rig added, in case anyone might have forgotten. Liam blew out a breath, and Raibert Green swore a quiet oath. Adelbard Brown tugged at his beard. As for Alix, she just swallowed hard and tried not to look afraid.

"The gates?"

Rig shrugged. "As fortified as they're ever going to be, and we've crammed as many men as we can along the ramparts. But if they storm the walls all at once . . ."

"They will." Arran Green's pale eyes scanned the drawing spread out before them, as though he might suddenly spot something he hadn't seen before, something that would deliver them.

"Sound the horns, then," Erik said resignedly. "The people must take cover."

Alix wondered how many places in the city afforded cover from a trebuchet flinging giant slabs of rock, but it wouldn't do to ask. Once again, her eyes strayed to Liam. He met her gaze, and for a moment she found the comfort she'd sought there. Then, slowly, the familiar burn began to spread through her body, and she forgot all about trebuchets.

It had been the same for days now. Every look that passed between them soon turned into a silent declaration of want. Alix was painfully aware of how ridiculous it was to be thinking carnal thoughts at a time like this, but she couldn't seem to help herself. She had never been so addicted to anything in her life, and apparently even a thrall army at their doorstep wasn't enough to curb her cravings.

War council, Alix, please?

She broke off from Liam's gaze and stared determinedly at the map.

"However," Arran Green was saying, "there is a small piece of good news. We know where Madan is."

Erik's eyes blazed. "Where?"

"At the Elders' Gate, ensconced in the tower."

Alix thought back to the ancient gate they had ridden through on their way into the city. It remained largely intact, in spite of the centuries, and would offer the Priest a good place to shelter while he plied his dark arts. *Smart*, she thought grimly. *It'll be almost impossible for us to reach him in there.*

Erik was aghast. "How can that be? I thought we posted men in the tower?"

"Archers and scouts, lightly defended. Their job was to watch for the enemy, not defend the gate. The structure itself is useless, except as a command post for an army in the field. Our army is not in the field."

"But the enemy's is. We should have destroyed the gate!"

"We had not the time, sire. In any event, what is done is done—the gate is in enemy hands."

"And you're certain it was the Priest?"

"Perhaps you would like to speak with the scouts yourself." Arran Green motioned to one of the guards, and the door of the study opened to admit Gwylim and Kerta. They were fresh from the field, their scouting leathers covered in dust. Kerta looked especially worn. The bruise under her eye had almost healed, but she was still pale. And afraid—that much was plain from the grim set of her mouth. Alix couldn't blame her. Kerta had barely recovered from her last encounter with the Priest. She couldn't have been eager for another.

"You saw the Priest yourselves?" Erik asked without preamble.

"We did, Your Majesty," Gwylim said. "I've seen him before, so I was certain of it. They were taking him into the tower with a heavy retinue of guards. He had his general with him too."

"We glimpsed him through a window on the fourth level, Your Majesty," Kerta added, her gaze lowered demurely. "They seem to have settled him up there."

"Makes sense," Rig said. "Harder for us to reach him."

"We won't be able to reach him at all, my lord," Gwylim said, "not without a miracle. They sent at least twenty guards up there with him, not to mention his general. The only chance of getting to the gate unseen would be to send one or two scouts, but even if they managed to get in, they'd be cut down before they made it anywhere near the Priest."

"Perhaps we could target the gate with catapults?" Raibert Green suggested.

His cousin shook his head. "The imperial walls are well out of range. If we are to have any chance of destroying the Priest, we must remove him from the gate tower."

"How?" Erik asked.

Arran Green shook his head. "I do not know, Your Majesty, but we must. Unless we break the bloodbond between the Priest and his thralls, the city is lost." *And so are we*, Alix added silently.

Gwylim stirred. "Your Majesty, General, if I may . . . I have an idea." All eyes turned to the small man with the ash-blond hair. Even Kerta looked surprised. Whatever Gwylim was brewing, he hadn't shared it with her. "Black powder," he said. Seeing only confused expressions, he explained, "They use it in the priesthood, to make the fireworks you see at festivals."

Arran Green was not impressed. "What of it?"

"Well, imagine what would happen if I ignited fireworks inside . . . the stables, say."

"You'd certainly spook the horses," Liam said dryly.

"Not to mention blow the walls out," Rig added.

"Exactly," said Gwylim. "And maybe even more than that. The priestly orders have been trying to outdo each other at festivals for years, so they've been experimenting with the formula, trying to make it more potent. When I left the priesthood, the Order of Rahl was boasting of a concentrated form that was five times as strong as the ordinary blend. With enough of it, we might even be able to blast stone apart."

Erik leaned over the map, his gaze fixed on the Elders' Gate. "You think such a blast might bring down the tower?"

"I'm not sure, but we could test it on something and see what happens."

"We have little to lose by trying," Erik said. "How long will it take you to make the powder?"

"Too long," said Gwylim. "I don't have the ingredients, but the priests should have plenty of it ready-made. They stockpile it in barrels under the temples—which, by the way, you may want to consider outlawing, Your Majesty, unless you're keen to remodel the temple road."

Erik smiled. "The priesthood's loss is our gain. You are a good man to have about." Gwylim bowed, and it was the first time Alix had ever seen him blush. "I will pen you a royal decree," Erik said. "Take as many men as you need and bring the powder back here. We will reconvene in three hours. In the meantime, I'm sure Lord Black will be pleased to find you something suitable to blow up."

Rig rolled his eyes, but he did, in fact, look pleased.

Erik gave Alix leave to find something to eat, so she filed out of the study along with the others. She found her brother waiting for her, and when he judged there was no one within earshot, he said, "I saw that, you know."

"Saw what?"

"You, looking over His Highness like he was a five-course meal. Very disturbing, from a brother's point of view."

Alix couldn't hide a smile. "Yes, well, we're—"

"Allie, please, I really don't need to hear the rest of that sentence. Just be careful, all right? I'm not the most observant chap in the world, and if I've noticed, you can bet someone else will too."

She had no doubt which *someone* he was worried about, but thankfully, he didn't press the point. He trusted she would do the right thing. That almost certainly meant talking to Erik, a conversation the king would relish no more than she. Liam had assured her that he and Erik had reached an understanding, but he'd refused to go into details, terming it "private brother stuff." Even so, Alix and Erik needed to reach an understanding of their own. She owed him that much.

The elder Black and the younger went together to the kitchens, where Alix dined on some cold chicken and a hard-boiled egg, and Rig ate half a boar. He was still at it when she left him to head back to her room in the royal suites. She was making her way past Liam's door when it swung open suddenly, and she was seized by the wrist and dragged inside.

She laughed. "What is that, some kind of sixth sense?"

"I know the sound of your footsteps. I know *everything* about you now." He looked well pleased with himself, wearing that roguish grin that signalled a particularly mischievous mood. He pressed her bodily against the door and planted an equally demanding kiss on her mouth.

"Wait." She managed to break off long enough to say, "I have to tell you some—" before she was smothered again. He didn't seem to be very interested in what she had to say. A large and growing part of her wasn't very interested either. She got as far as, "We need to be careful, at least until I talk to—" before she gave up entirely, her words dissolving into a soft, hummed breath.

He was going after that delicate spot behind her ear, the one that liquefied her knees. It was the first weakness he'd discovered, and it was still his favourite. "Were you saying something?" His lips on her ear set the tiny hairs along her neck standing on end. She could hear his grin. Smug bastard. She didn't even bother to answer.

A sudden pounding at the door nearly stopped Alix's heart. Liam gave every sign of intending to ignore it, until an iron-hard voice called his name. He froze.

"Yes, General?" He tossed the words back over his

shoulder in an absurd attempt to sound as if he were somewhere other than right up against the door. Alix experienced a moment of sheer terror as she realised that they hadn't bolted the latch.

"I require your assistance," Arran Green said. The commander general apparently had no intention of treating Liam any differently now that he was a prince, which seemed to suit Liam just fine. "Gwylim will need help to gather the powder." There was a pause. "And if you should happen to see Alix, you might tell her the king is looking for her." The dryness of his tone left little doubt that he knew exactly where Alix was. She cringed into Liam's chest.

"Okay," he said.

The mood wasn't quite the same after that.

Liam poked his head above the low stone wall. "Nothing's happening. That's disappoint—" The word ended in a squawk as Gwylim grabbed his collar, yanking him down. Half a heartbeat later, the courtyard *roared*. The ground rolled beneath Alix's feet, and she let out a little yelp, in spite of herself. Gwylim threw his arms over his head, and Rig uttered a string of oaths that would have made their late mother faint. As for Erik, whatever he might have said or done was completely smothered beneath Arran Green's massive steel-banded shield. Even with a stone wall to protect them from the blast, the commander general was nervous about his king's safety. He'd practically begged Erik to leave the test explosions to the Kingswords, but Alix had never witnessed a more thorough waste of breath in all her days. The king shoved Green's shield aside, stood, and let out a cry of triumph.

Alix straightened. Dust drifted down like a light snowfall to settle in a fine blanket over the rubble that had been a warehouse only moments before. *Two feet thick of stone*, Alix thought, amazed. Two feet thick, and only a smoking crater remained. A single corner of the warehouse still stood, a jagged pyramid of broken, blackened rock. She pictured the Elders' Gate, and a slow smile spread over her, an expression she saw reflected on every face but Arran Green's. The commander general just frowned, as always.

"I think this will work." Gwylim sounded half surprised. "We'll get the Priest and his general all at once."

"There's just the small matter of getting it inside the gate," Rig said.

Alix's smile faded. *He's right. How will we ever get that stuff where it needs to be?*

"That's not the only problem," Gwylim said, and there was something in his voice that curdled Alix's stomach. "You saw how quickly I had to move to get behind the wall in time. We'll need a much bigger explosion than this to bring the gate down."

Erik was the first to grasp his meaning. "You'll never get clear."

Gwylim's only answer was a slow shake of his head.

Liam went pale. "Wait, are you saying . . . ?"

"It's a suicide mission," Rig said grimly.

"There must be some other way," Alix said. "A fire arrow, or—"

Gwylim shook his head again. "There's no other way. The powder needs to be stashed inside the gate tower itself, or the enemy will see it. Someone has to sneak inside and lay it somewhere out of sight, and then it has to be lit. Even a blood-bow can't send an arrow through walls."

"You could leave a thin line of powder," Liam said, "like you did just now, only longer."

Gwylim smiled. "All the way out the gate and across the temple road, without being seen? I don't think so, Liam."

"Gwylim is right," Arran Green said. "There is no other way. Whoever lights the powder will be killed in the explosion." He turned to Erik and bowed. "I will see to it personally, Your Majesty."

Erik looked a little queasy, but before he could reply, Gwylim said, "Let me do it, General. This was my idea, it's only right that I should take responsibility for it myself. Besides, with all due respect, you're no scout."

The commander general seemed caught between anger at Gwylim's insolence and admiration for his sense of duty. "I cannot permit it. The task is too important for me to leave to anyone else."

"But you're commander general. You're too valuable . . ."

"No one is too valuable to do his duty."

"You have a wife," Gwylim said stubbornly. "Sons . . ."

"*Enough.*"

Gwylim subsided.

Erik watched the exchange with a grim expression. Alix could see he was torn, but what choice did he have? *We have to unbind the thralls, and to do that, we have to kill the Priest. This is the only way to get to him. It's the only way.* Erik reached the same conclusion. "Very well, General. It grieves me that it has come to this, but it seems we have no choice. Your courage will not be forgotten, I swear it."

"One man can't do it alone, Your Majesty," Gwylim said. "Even a man as strong as General Green can't carry enough powder on his own. Someone needs to go with him, to bring a second pack."

Erik frowned. "You would have me send a second man to his death?"

"No, sire. General Green can wait until the second man gets clear before he lights the powder."

"Very well," Erik said. "I presume you wish to be appointed to that task?"

Alix bit her lip. *Gwylim is right. Green is no scout. He'll need help to sneak in without getting caught.* Gwylim was good, but she was better. The thought terrified her, and for a moment she couldn't find her tongue. Then she felt Green's eyes on her, and she knew he was thinking the same thing. *You know what you must do*, his pale gaze seemed to say.

She cleared her throat. "Your Majesty, I should be the one to go. I'm . . ." *A born thief.* She half expected Rig to say it, but he was only staring at her in horror. "I'm the best," she finished miserably.

"Agreed," Arran Green said, looking well satisfied.

"No!" Liam stepped between her and Green. "I mean, you are, but . . . you *can't.* Allie, you . . ." But there was nothing he could say, nothing that could measure up to the enormity of what lay before them. For a moment, he looked lost. Then his jaw set, and he said, "I'll come too."

That was too much for Erik; he gave a wild little laugh and

ran his hands over his face. "No, I think not. This plan sounds less attractive with every passing moment. The cost is too high. We should think of something else."

"There is nothing else, Your Majesty," Arran Green said. "I have done everything I can to keep His Highness out of danger until now, but we no longer have that luxury. At the gate or on the walls, we must all fight, and many of us will die. Liam would be a welcome addition to our party. He is an experienced scout, and he is strong. He can carry more of the powder than any of the others. We will be sure of having enough to do the job. With the captain scouting ahead, and Liam and me carrying the powder, we have the greatest chance of success."

Erik turned away from them all, shaking his head. Alix felt for him. It was a terrible choice to have to make, but she did not doubt for a moment what his decision would be. A few months ago, Erik would never have considered it, but he was a different man now. A different king. "As you will, then," he said quietly. "Make your preparations, Green. Lord Black will assume command of the Kingswords."

"It is the right choice, Your Majesty."

Erik shook his head again and stalked off toward his horse. Alix started to go after him, but Gwylim said, "Wait." When she gave him an impatient look, he added, "It's important, Alix." He drew something from his pocket that looked like a sewing needle. "Each of you should take some of these, just in case."

"What is it?" Liam asked warily.

"It's just a needle, but it's been dipped in *hrak* venom, and it can be fletched to make a blow dart."

Hrak. The word was Harrami and sounded familiar. "Isn't that a kind of spider?" Alix asked.

"A deadly spider. Its bite will kill a man in less than half an hour. Scratching a man with a needle dipped in *hrak* venom will paralyse him before you can count to ten, and knock him out cold soon after that. The mountain tribes of Harram use it to make poisoned darts for hunting."

Liam whistled, impressed. "We should have the archers dip their arrows in that stuff!"

"You'd need one hell of a lot of spiders," Rig said.

Gwylim smiled wanly. "You would, and the Order of Hew

has only a handful. But I can make a few darts out of them, and you can use them to knock out some of the guards around the gate. You'll have to be careful—they'll have time enough to call for help if they figure out what's going on, so it's better to do it the old-fashioned way if you can." He drew a thumb across his throat, in case anyone had missed his meaning. "But if you can't get close enough, this is better than trying to throw a knife, and you won't be able to carry bows if you're loaded down with powder."

Rig clapped Gwylim's shoulder. "The king is right— you're just full of useful tricks."

"Very useful," Arran Green agreed. "Well done."

The praise only made Gwylim look uncomfortable. "I should be going with you, General," he said one last time.

"Your place is with the scouts," Green said.

They made their way back to the palace in silence. Alix couldn't bring herself to look at Liam, even though she felt his eyes on her. She knew he was furious with her for offering to go with Green. He understood why she'd done it, but that didn't mean he had to like it, and Alix had no doubt he was just itching to have it out with her. For the first time, she dreaded being alone with him.

As they mounted the steps to the First Keep, Green said, "A word, Captain?"

Alix and Liam exchanged a look. *This can't be good.* Warily, Alix followed the commander general into a small sitting room. He closed the door behind her and stood with his hands folded behind his back, his pale gaze pinning her. "You did well to volunteer for this mission," Green said. "I will need your stealth, and Liam's strength. Your participation guaranteed his."

Alix dropped her gaze, embarrassed. They hadn't discussed her relationship with Liam since that day at Greenhold, so long ago. It was not a conversation she was anxious to repeat.

"It would have been preferable to avoid putting the prince in danger," Green went on, "but he is uniquely suited to the task. He is nearly as stealthy as he is strong, and for all his faults, he is one of the most reliable soldiers I have ever commanded."

"You might consider telling him so yourself." It was impudent, even for her, but such worries seemed insignificant now.

Green only grunted. "Perhaps I shall. In any case, as vital as Liam's participation in this mission is, he is a prince now, and he must be kept safe to the extent possible. That means no heroics."

Alix wasn't sure where he was going with this. "I won't goad him into doing anything stupid, if that's what you're getting at. I've learned my lesson."

Green's mouth twisted wryly. "I doubt that, but no—that is not my point. Let me be direct. My part in this is to sacrifice myself to light the powder and destroy the Priest. However, should I fail, the task must fall to another, and that other must not be the prince."

Alix felt the blood drain from her face.

"I very much hope it will not come to that," Green said. "I will do everything in my power to see that it does not. But I am fallible, like anyone else. We must have a contingency plan, and that contingency plan must be you."

She swallowed hard. "I . . . I understand."

There was a long silence. When Alix looked up, she found Green regarding her with something like sadness. It was the most emotion she had seen from him in a long time, and it frightened her. "Fate can be cruel," he said, sounding suddenly weary. "I have lived a long life, and have sons to carry on my legacy. But you and Liam . . . you are young. You have had little time in this world, still less of it together. I am sorry for the part I played in that."

For a moment, Alix was too stunned to speak. "I thought you didn't approve?"

"My approval was never at issue. I take no pleasure in keeping young people apart. As things stood at the time, your involvement with Liam was unwise and inappropriate, for both of you. My personal feelings did not enter into the matter."

"And if they had?" She wasn't sure why she asked.

Green shrugged. "I am no expert on matters of the heart. What I will say is that you do Liam an ill service by allowing him to abide in your shadow. He must learn to be a leader, and he cannot do that if he follows you about like a puppy."

Alix's skin grew warm. "He does not."

"Of course he does. But he is every bit as much a White as his brothers, and he has the potential to be a great leader, if you let him. Use your strength to support him, not to over-power him."

She opened her mouth to deliver a sharp reply, but instead, she found herself saying, "I will."

"Good." Green's gaze took on a faraway look. "I have served the Whites all my life. Those brothers have been like sons to me, each in his own way. One of them betrayed himself, but the other two are becoming the men I have always known they could be. I leave them in your hands, Alix. Do not disappoint me."

"I won't, General," Alix swore, and she prayed to the gods it was the truth.

Alix returned to the study, where she knew the king would be waiting. She moved in half a daze, her mind churning over her conversation with Arran Green. Fear scratched at her belly with cold claws—fear for herself, for Liam, and for Green. If all went to plan, Green would die. *That* was their best-case scenario. And if things didn't go to plan . . .

She found Erik at the window, looking out over the rose gardens. He turned as he heard her approach. "Care for a drink, Captain? I daresay we need it." A servant appeared as if from nowhere to pour them some wine. Erik sat, motioning for Alix to do the same. She obeyed mechanically. Her fingers curled around the cup, but she wasn't feeling very thirsty. In the low light, the wine looked like blood.

Silence hovered over them. Erik sipped his wine. Alix tried to think of something to say, something that might re-assure him. Instead, she blurted, "Liam and I are together." She didn't know what made her say it, now of all moments. Maybe it was a simple desire to get it over with. Or maybe she'd decided they were both already so numb that it was a good time to broach an otherwise painful subject.

"You don't say." Erik made a dismissive gesture. "Let's not do this, Alix, not now. Liam and I have already spoken about it, as I'm sure he told you."

"But I know how you must feel, and I owe it to you—"

"You don't owe me anything." Erik fixed her with that determined stare of his, the one that brooked no argument. "None of us was responsible for the situation we found ourselves in. All that was left to us was to decide what to do, and I for one have no regrets about the choices I made. As for what I feel, I don't think you do know, but I can say this: however unpleasant this may be, it's a lot better than how I would feel if I came between my brother and the woman he loves. I've been down that road once. Never again. You have my blessing, Alix, both of you."

Alix's heart flooded with ache, and she reached across the desk to take his hand. "How do you manage to always be so *good*?"

His only answer was a sad smile.

There was something in that look that overwhelmed her. The tears finally broke free, spilling warm over her cheeks and spattering the surface of Erik's desk. She tried to stand, to escape, but he kept a tight grip on her hand.

"Please tell me this isn't for me," he said gently.

"I'm so sorry. I've made such a wreck of everything, and now . . ."

"Alix." He came around the desk and drew her up out of her chair. "Please don't."

She swiped her face with the back of her hand, angry with herself. *What must he think of me? I'm supposed to be apologising, and instead I'm blubbering like a scared little girl.* "I'm sorry." She drew a shaking breath. "I shouldn't have let myself go like that. It's just . . . This feels like good-bye."

"It is, of a sort."

"It's just so bitterly unfair. For all this to be happening now, when you and Liam are just getting to know each other . . . If something happens to him because of me . . ."

"If something happens to Liam, it won't be because of you."

"He's only coming on this mission because he wants to protect me. And what if Green falls, Erik? What then? One of us will have to light the powder . . ."

Erik blanched. He hadn't thought of that. "It won't come to that," he said in a voice like stone. "It can't." *I won't let it,* she could almost hear him say, as if there were a damned thing he could do about it. He threw his arms around her, and for a moment Alix feared she would break down again. But she didn't. Instead, she allowed herself to be comforted by her friend and king. Or maybe she was the one comforting him.

Good-bye, of a sort. Or maybe just good-bye.

THIRTY-THREE

† "I hate this plan," Erik said. That did not mean he would change his mind—it was too late to back out now—but he wondered what sort of madness had led him to agree to this. *My brother, my dearest friend, and the man my father trusted above all others. I'm sending one of them to die. Or maybe all of them.* It felt like a betrayal.

"Oddly enough, I'm not wild about it myself." Liam leaned out over the parapet. The wind that reached up to riffle his dark hair carried the smell of smoke.

They stood together on the ramparts, gazing out over the city—what was left of it, at least. Most of the populace had either fled or gone to ground. The lucky ones hunkered down in the catacombs beneath the temples, and the truly privileged sheltered in the Three Keeps on the palace compound. The rest gathered in cellars, warehouses—anywhere they could find. For all the good it would do them. Erroman was left hollow, like a discarded seashell on the shore of a dark and swelling tide.

Erik squinted into the distance beyond the city walls. Campfires glittered in the pre-dawn light, blanketing the landscape in tiny dots of flame. He had never seen so many.

They covered the horizon, like so many stars on a clear night. It was almost beautiful. In their midst, great hulking shadows began to take shape, wooden giants with broad shoulders and mighty fists. Siege towers and trebuchets. Erik counted half a dozen of them near the south gate alone, their grim forms sharpening against the slowly blooming sky.

"I guess it'll be over soon, one way or another." Liam sounded more pensive than afraid. He lapsed into silence for a moment, then asked, "Have you ever wondered where you'll go when you die?"

"What Domain, you mean?" Erik shook his head. "Not since I was a boy."

"I've always figured myself for a Hew man."

Erik smiled. "That sounds about right. What do you suppose his Domain is like?"

"Hell is full of crows that peck at your eyes, and heaven is an everlasting tournament of verbal jousting and improvised comedy. You never stumble over your words, and everyone laughs at your jokes."

"You've thought a lot about this."

"Boring childhood." Liam's grin was short-lived. "Actually, my mother was quite devout."

Most common folk are, Erik almost said, but he caught himself in time.

"What about you? Eldora, I suppose."

Erik grimaced. "I don't feel very wise just now. Just as well, really. I can't imagine spending eternity with Albern Highmount."

Liam managed a brief laugh, but it died almost as soon as it left his lips. Very quietly, he said, "I know where Arran Green will go."

"Destan," Erik said without hesitation. Somehow, that made him feel a little better.

"A more honourable man never lived," Liam agreed.

Erik flicked him an uncomfortable glance. "Honourable, to be sure, but hard."

His guilt must have shown on his face, because Liam said, "I know what you're thinking, and you needn't. I couldn't have asked for a better mentor. You chose well."

"So you know about that." For some reason, that only shamed him more. "I suppose Alix told you?"

"Give me some credit. A banner knight doesn't just show up in Lower Town looking for a squire. Who else would have sent him?"

Erik sighed. "Yes, I sent him. But it was too little, too late."

"You wouldn't think so if you were in my boots."

And you wouldn't be so forgiving if you knew that everything you went through was my fault. Erik resolved to tell Liam the truth one day, if they lived long enough.

"Anyway," Liam said, "all that's in the past. I have a brother now, and I'm in love with an incredible woman. I actually feel pretty blessed. You're the one who showed me that."

And what if it's all gone tomorrow? Will you still feel blessed then? Erik kept the bitter thought to himself.

A slash of dawn appeared on the horizon, low and bloody. Against its glow, Erik could see the enemy camp stirring, tiny dark specks swarming like flies around a wound. "Are you a praying man, Liam?"

"Sometimes. Are you?"

A trumpet sounded in the distance, as cold and sharp as a blade through the heart.

"I am today."

Erik covered his head with his arms, throwing himself against the parapet as stone rained down around him. The noise was deafening, drowning out even the screams of the archers who tumbled off the ramparts to spatter sickeningly onto the pavement below. A second missile followed hard upon the first; a slab of stone the size of an ox shattered the wall walk not ten paces away, sending a shower of flagstones in all directions. A royal guardsman huddling nearby took one in the head; warm blood sprayed across Erik's face. He snapped his visor down. It would do little to protect him from the trebuchets, but he did not want the men to see him bloodied.

"Sire, we must move!" Rona Brown reached for him. "It's too dangerous!"

Erik ignored her. Leaning down into the courtyard, he called to the men operating the onager. "You're nearly there! Ten paces to the right!"

Below, a Kingsword cracked his whip, and the oxen began to pull, rotating the great wooden platform beneath the onager. They had scarcely begun before the Kingsword hauled back on the reins, drawing them up short. The mechanism shuddered to a halt, and the men scrambled to load up another clay ball. Erik closed his eyes and said a silent prayer as the great arm snapped to and flung a missile over the wall. He followed its arc through the sky, fearing they had overcorrected, but no—the clay ball struck the axle of the trebuchet and exploded, sending pitch tumbling down over the frame. "That's it!" Erik cried. Fire arrows retraced the onager's trajectory, and the pitch burst into flame, setting the trebuchet alight. Erik was just about to give the command to fire at will when someone screamed, *"Take cover!"* and he dropped to his haunches as the trebuchet answered, slamming another massive rock into the wall. The world shook under Erik's feet, and one of the merlons crumbled behind him, but the blow left the wall walk mercifully untouched.

He waited until the second trebuchet had spent its load before uncoiling from his crouch to look over the parapet. The siege towers were drawing relentlessly closer. At their feet, thralls swarmed like angry ants, ready to clamber up the moment the towers touched the walls. The battering ram was afire, but only on one side, and the thralls operating it scarcely seemed to notice. They continued to heave even as their flesh withered in the heat. The ram pounded the gates with a steady, thunderous *boom*, like the heartbeat of some dark god, but so far, the iron-plated oak held. *We still have time*, Erik told himself. Time was the prize they sought, time for Arran Green to light the black powder and bring down the Elders' Gate. It was a poor reward for so much blood, but it would have to serve.

The sky bristled with a steady thrum of arrows in both directions. A few of the thralls took cover beneath their shields, but most fought on, undaunted, though some of them were as feathered as any bird. Only a fatal shot—throat, heart, head—would drop them, and even the famed female archers of the Kingswords were hard-pressed to find their marks through visor slats and chinks in armour. *It takes a woman to thread a needle*, the Kingswords were fond of saying, but this was like trying to thread a needle while breaking in a stallion on the deck of a heaving ship. *We need more oil and pitch*, Erik thought, but he had spent most of it on the battering ram and the trebuchet, and he knew he could not replenish their stock—not without robbing one of the other gates. Assuming the banner lords had any left, they surely needed it more than he, for the gates they manned were of far more modest make, with only bands of iron to gird them.

Yet even metal plating was not indestructible. A terrible screech rent the air, as if some great bird had been wounded, and for a moment the pounding stopped. Erik leaned out between the merlons, already knowing what he would find. The point of the battering ram had punched through the iron plate at last; the screech sounded again as ragged edges of metal scraped against the ram. Another thrust sent wood chips flying. The ram continued to burn, but slowly, so slowly. It was soaked in something that seemed to quell the spread of the flames. *They're going to get through*, Erik realised with dull certainty. *It's too soon. Too soon . . .*

"Archers! Two bands, with me!" He raced for the tower and the stairs that would take him down to the gates, archers and royal guardsmen following close behind. The gates continued their steady thunder, each blow answered by an echoing shudder.

By the time Erik reached the gates, the enemy was almost through. The terrible drumbeat had gone from *boom* to *crack*, a split working its way up the grain of the wood. "I want every bow trained on that split! The moment you see daylight, *thread the needle!*" The archers answered with a stout *"Aye!"* Bows creaked. "Infantry, form up!" The order echoed down the lines. The Kingswords tightened their ranks and waited.

And waited.

Crack, went the gates. *Crack*. The split widened and lengthened.

The gates finally gave way in a shower of splinters, five inches of sharpened log poking through. The point withdrew, leaving a hole no more than a handspan wide, but it was enough. Arrows hissed through the air, stuffing the hole and fringing it with feathers, so many at once that they bounced off each other midflight. There were no screams on the other side of the gates. Thralls never screamed.

The ram blasted through a second time, sending more splinters flying. Slowly, resignedly, Erik swung his shield down and slipped his arm through the straps. He reached across his body and drew his bloodblade, its steel whisper louder to his ears than the pounding on the gates. He could feel the men's eyes on him, could smell their fear. He licked his lips, tasted sweat. He closed his eyes for one brief moment, but it was not the gods he prayed to.

Hurry, Green. By all the Virtues, please hurry.

Alix jerked her blade across the Oridian's throat, quick enough to avoid the wash of warm blood that gushed from the wound. She caught him under the armpits as he sagged, one hand clamped awkwardly over his mouth in case he tried to scream. He didn't.

Four down, fifty thousand to go. She glanced back over her shoulder and waved, bringing Liam and Arran Green out from behind a mound of grass-flecked rubble.

Things had gone smoothly so far. They'd stolen out through the north gate, giving the city walls a wide berth until they were well clear of the south gate. From there, the ruins of the old imperial walls made for good cover; even Arran Green managed to stay hidden, provided Alix prowled ahead to deal with any stray Oridians. There hadn't been many. The enemy hadn't bothered with sentries, and why would he? Who would expect anything as suicidal and point-less as three stray Kingswords on the wrong side of the city walls? The four Oridians they'd encountered so far were no more than strays, drunk or relieving themselves or simply looking for a place to hide while their comrades took care of the fighting and dying. Alix hadn't even needed Gwylim's poisoned darts to deal with them. Better still, their corpses had provided her small party with Oridian bucklers, a useful bit of costume that would allow them to pass for enemy men-at-arms. Only once had she feared they'd been discovered, and that was only paranoia; a flicker of movement in the corner of her eye had proved to be nothing more than a shadow.

Liam shifted his pack awkwardly. Of the three of them, he bore the heaviest load of powder, and it was starting to wear him down. "Are we there yet?"

They weren't far. Alix could see the top of the gate tower poking up from behind the rubble. They were at the edge of the southern fortifications, where seemingly random piles of stone began to assume man-made shapes. Before them, the wall climbed gradually up from the grass, only to crumble away again, looking like a stairway to nowhere. Beyond the gap, the wall remained intact right up to the Elders' Gate.

Alix chewed her lip. "Maybe we should just walk up to the gate like we belong there. No one could possibly recognise us."

"Perhaps not," said Green, "but I doubt they will permit us inside without express orders from an officer. We could try to trick our way in, but my Oridian is not good enough to pass for a native speaker. Is yours?"

Her mother must be smirking in her grave. "Er, not quite."

"Anyway, there are no women in the Oridian army," Liam said.

Green grunted. "True. I had forgotten how backward they are."

So says General One-Light-One-Heavy. Alix took a moment to soak in the irony before pointing at the sway-backed stretch of wall before them. "Let me climb up there and a take a look." She slipped her arms out from the pack and left it at Liam's feet. Then she scrambled up the loose rock and flattened herself against the top of the wall.

The sight that greeted her was an ugly one. The Elders' Gate, a great square hulk with rounded towers for corners, overlooked the rear ranks of the entire Oridian host. South of the gate, the sloping fields were sprinkled with tents and the ash of campfires. Only a few men milled about, presumably healers or smiths or those too injured to fight. Inside the gate, about a furlong up the temple road, a wide column of soldiers stood in loose ranks, waiting. They stretched for half a mile, almost all the way to the city proper, ready to charge as soon as their enthralled prisoners breached the walls. *So many*, Alix thought, *and all of them just waiting in safety while the thralls do their dirty work. Cowards.*

She scanned the tower. A handful of guards prowled the ramparts between pointed merlons capped with fearsome iron spikes. She saw movement through a high window, but lower down, the arrow slits were dark and empty. From this angle, she could see nothing of the entrance.

She rejoined the others. "There's no way to get near the gate without being seen. If we go along the top of the walls, we'll be spotted from the ramparts. We might sneak in from the south, but then we'd have to explain what we were doing on the wrong side of the gate. And if we keep to the northern side, the rear lines will spot us and wonder what we're doing scurrying like rats."

Green didn't like what he was hearing. His customary frown darkened into a scowl. "What do you propose, then?"

"I have an idea, but we'll have to double back to where I killed that last soldier . . ."

It was a nasty bit of business, but Alix didn't see any alternative, so she squeezed her eyes shut and did her best not to retch. By the time they were done, she was so covered in gore that her own brother wouldn't have recognised her. They hid her hair under the dead man's helm, her shape under his too-big cuirass. She draped an arm over Liam's shoulders, another over Green's, and they were off.

Alix played the part from a long way out, in case any stray eyes should see. Liam and Green half dragged, half carried her toward the old temple road, moving as quickly as the deception would allow, and it wasn't long before they came within sight of the enemy lines. *This is it*, Alix thought. Her guts squirmed, and her tongue was dry and bitter in her mouth. If this didn't work . . . *Fifty thousand to three. Awfully long odds.*

Heads started to turn as they reached the old temple road, but the sight of a mangled soldier being dragged back toward camp did not arouse suspicion. Most spared them only a cursory glance before turning their attention back to the smoke and thunder in the near distance, where the thralls and their siege engines battered the city walls. A few more soldiers were coming up the road in twos and threes—officers, presumably—but most paid them no more attention than the rank and file. Only one called out a question, but he sounded more curious than suspicious, and Arran Green's curt response of "Flying rock" seemed to satisfy him; he just nodded and continued on his way. It was almost enough to make Alix believe in the gods.

But the real test was only just beginning. The gate loomed over them now, spilling a broad shadow over the flagstones. They could see little beyond the mouth of the tunnel. The imperial walls had been built at the top of an incline, the better to defend against invaders, so the tunnel beneath sloped quickly out of view. That made it impossible for Alix and the others to see what they were about to walk into, but on the plus side, it also shielded them from prying eyes on the temple road.

"Here we go," Liam said in an undertone as they started down the slope.

The tunnel was empty, thank the Virtues, except for a pair of guards flanking the door to the tower. Unlike the others, however, these men were immediately suspicious; Alix saw them poise their spears before she let her head loll forward, playing up her injuries.

One of the guards barked out a question. Arran Green kept his answer terse, so they wouldn't notice his accent. "Need help," he said, gesturing at the tower. "The priests." The guard wasn't impressed. He said something harsh and pointed down the road with his spear. "Need help," Green repeated, dragging Alix right up to the door, one hand surreptitiously reaching for the dagger at his belt. The guard started to say something else (probably "Are you deaf?") but it ended in a wet gurgle. A heartbeat later, the second guard met the same fate on the point of Liam's dagger. Alix shouldered her way between the dying men and barged through the door. Inside, a young soldier lounged at the foot of the stairs. He barely had time to scramble to his feet before he found a sword in his belly.

"Hurry." Green dragged one of the bodies inside, Liam the other. Alix shut the door behind them.

Shadows enfolded them, pierced only by a single torch in a sconce near the stairs. *The Priest is up there*, Alix thought, shivering. *Along with his general, and gods know how many dozens of guards.*

Green started toward a dim archway along the back wall, motioning for Alix and Liam to follow. The shadows deepened as they ducked through, but there was just enough light to glimpse a short passageway and a ladder, presumably leading up to a murder hole. *This is perfect*, Alix thought. No one had any reason to come back here, and it was too dark to see from the entryway. Green obviously agreed, for he shrugged out of his pack.

Alix's hands shook as she unlaced her own pack and upended it, the powder sliding out with a soft *hiss*. By the time all three of them were done, they had a pile thigh high. They packed it down the way Gwylim had showed them. And then it was time.

Liam opened his mouth to say something, but Arran Green silenced him with a gesture and jerked his head toward the archway. Liam hesitated. He pursed his lips and shifted from foot to foot, a look of pure anguish in his eyes. Then he flung his arms around the commander general. Green stood stiff as a board, stunned and annoyed and apparently at a loss. He extricated himself after a moment, but even as one hand shoved Liam away, the other clapped him on the shoulder in what was, for Green, an effusive gesture of affection. For Alix he had only a grave nod. Then he pointed at the door, his eyes every bit as commanding as his voice. Liam might have hesitated longer, but Alix grabbed his hand and pulled. They had to get out before they were discovered. Every moment they lost put the mission in jeopardy, cost Kingsword lives.

No one troubled them on the far side of the tunnel. The few Oridians they passed took one look at Alix's bloodied form and concluded that Liam was bringing her to the healers. It was easy to lose themselves among the deserted tents and slip back through the ruins of the imperial wall. They followed it all the way to the crumbling stair to nowhere before Alix said, "Stop. We can watch from here."

They climbed up and flattened themselves along the top of the wall. Alix watched the guards on the tower ramparts for any sign of alarm, but they moved casually, as if nothing were amiss. She breathed a sigh of relief.

They waited. Alix burned with impatience. Every moment seemed like hours. She wasn't the only one: Liam scratched at the rock under his fingers, his jaw twitching. "Is it me, or is this taking too long?"

More time passed. *What is he waiting for? He was only supposed to count to five hundred . . .*

"What's that?" Liam raised himself up on his elbows. "What are they doing?"

Something was happening on the ramparts. The guards clustered together, jostling excitedly. Between them, Alix caught a glimpse of a figure with his arms wrenched behind his back.

Merciful gods.

Liam made a strangled sound and started to rise, but Alix clutched at his tunic. "We can't help him." Liam subsided, gripping the stone wall so hard that his knuckles went white.

The gatehouse guards marched Arran Green to the edge of the ramparts. For a horrible moment, Alix feared they meant to fling him through the crenels, but instead they held him there, facing him out toward the city, toward the carnage. *They know who he is.* The Oridians had the enemy general in their clutches, and they wanted him to watch his men being slaughtered. Green stood straight and stoic, his head tilted proudly as though the sight gave him courage.

One of the guards drew his blade. Someone grabbed Green by the hair, jerking his head back to expose his throat. Alix started to look away, but it happened too fast—the blade flashed, and a gout of blood erupted from Green's throat. His knees buckled, and he sank out of view.

Liam scrambled to his feet. Alix started to reach for him, but she froze, transfixed. The guards weren't finished yet. The sword flashed again. It came down in a bloody arc, once, twice, each blow exciting a cheer from the enemy soldiers gathered around. The executioner stooped, vanishing behind the ramparts, only to reappear with a severed head dripping with gore. *Not Green's,* Alix thought, irrationally. *It can't be*

Green's. But there was no mistaking the meticulously close-cropped beard, even at this distance. The guard climbed up between the merlons and mounted the head on one of the iron spikes, twisting it to face the city walls in the distance.

"No!"

Liam's cry went unheard amid the cheers of the tower guards. Alix grabbed his tunic and yanked him back down. They couldn't be seen. Not now.

They had work to do.

THIRTY-FOUR

Erik tried not to think. He let his limbs move automatically, lunging and blocking, slashing and parrying, keeping light on his feet to cope with the chaos around him. He had long since lost track of Rona Brown, not to mention most of his knights. They had fallen back almost to the river by now, and their ranks grew more and more disorganised. It was all Erik could do to have his commands heard. Not that he had given many since the gates fell; it was every man for himself now.

He threw his shield up to block an incoming blow, answering with a cut that crashed through helm and bone and brain. No sooner had the thrall gone down than two more stepped in to take his place, closing in from either side. Erik coiled and waited. Both of them lunged at once, and Erik sprang back, letting their blades cross before he dove back in. He hacked an arm off at the shoulder, relieving one thrall of his sword before turning his attention to the other. He kept the one-armed thrall at bay with his shield while he drove at the more dangerous foe, battering away until he found the soft space between cuirass and spaulder. Chain mail parted before his bloodblade, and he gave the weapon a sharp twist before withdrawing it, just to be sure. After that, the one-armed thrall was easy. Erik felled him with a single blow.

He paused, his gaze flitting over the scene. For the moment, they were holding off the enemy advance; only a trickle of white-hairs made it through the front lines, and they did not make it far. Erik slung his sword back in its scabbard and propped his hands on his thighs, grateful for the chance to catch his breath.

"Your Majesty!" A runner appeared, shoving his way through the men.

Thank the gods. It had been too long since Erik had news of the other gates. "Tell me."

"Lord Black reports that the east gate is holding, sire."

"Good. And the others?"

"I'm sorry, sire, I don't know."

Erik nodded, dismissing him. The ranks were tightening up again, under the instruction of Rona Brown, who had somehow reappeared. Erik weaved his way through them, heading for the riverbank and a look at the north gate. He reached the foot of the bridge and peered across. The view was not as clear as he had hoped; smoke smudged the skyline on the right bank. He could see movement, but little else. *I should dispatch a runner . . .*

Screams sounded from the ramparts. Erik whipped around. *"They're over the walls!"* someone cried. Erik saw them now: white-hairs flowing between the merlons and hacking their way through the archers. The siege towers had made it to the walls. Swearing viciously, Erik drew his sword and rushed forward.

He had scarcely made it through the rear lines before more shouts sounded, this time from the river. He lost a moment to indecision before running back the way he had come.

Please, don't let it be . . .

But it was. Thralls were flooding across the bridge. *The north gate is down. Dear gods, the city is falling, and I am outflanked.* He struggled to suppress the dread rising inside him. He had to stay strong for the men.

"Your Majesty!" Another runner appeared, eyes wild with fear. "Terrible news!"

"I can see that," Erik snapped. "Brown's lines are overrun."

The runner shook his head frantically. "I've not come from Lord Brown. I've come from the watchtower!"

The watchtower, where Erik had posted men to keep an eye on the Elders' Gate. He sucked in a breath. "Does the Elders' Gate still stand?"

"Yes, sire."

"Then *what*?"

"We saw . . . with the longlens . . ." The boy swallowed hard.

Erik's heart fluttered like a weak, wounded thing. He knew, somehow, what the runner was going to say, knew it with the certainty of a man living out his own nightmares.

"General Green is dead."

Erik squeezed his eyes shut. For a brief moment he was back at Boswyck, watching helplessly as his army was butchered while they waited for reinforcements that would never come. He could smell the snow, feel the icy sting of the wind against his skin. He prayed that it would make him numb. Then the shouts of his men wrenched him back to the present, to his duty. His moment of self-indulgence was over. It was time to lead.

"To the bridge!" He pointed with his sword. "Five bands!" Fifty men ought to be enough. The bridge was barely wide enough to permit a pair of oxcarts to pass one another. All they had to do was choke off the foot of the bridge and pin the enemy out over the water, where they would be easy prey for the archers. Erik still had three companies of longbows waiting in reserve, and they would do more good at the bridge than on the walls, where they were little more than fodder for enemy swords and spears. He called to their commander, and she shouted out an order he could not hear. Her archers moved as one.

"Shield wall!" Erik cried. "They must not cross the bridge!"

Infantry formed up shoulder to shoulder at the foot of the bridge, hunkering low with their shields overlapping like the scales of some great wooden reptile. The tactic was better suited for pikemen, but Erik needed to keep his pikes in reserve for the Oridian cavalry. The enemy horse had not yet charged the gates, but it was only a matter of time.

The first wave of thralls had reached the foot of the bridge. They crashed into the shield wall and broke apart like so much human shrapnel. Some were shoved into the water, while others fell to Kingsword blades darting out between gaps. "Forward!" Erik ordered. "Drive them back!" If they could keep the wall tight enough, they could turn a swordfight into a shoving match, and let the river do the rest.

The Kingswords leaned into their shields and scuttled slowly forward, inch by agonising inch. Behind them, a second line began to form up, in case the first should be breached. Meanwhile, thralls continued to surge across the bridge. A knot of them heaved against the shield wall, so many that those at the edges spilled into the rushing waters below. The white-hairs wore too much armour to keep afloat; most did not even try, sinking passively to their doom without so much as a gasp. A crowd piled up, several score deep, stretching back nearly to the half span. As Erik had predicted, they made an easy target for the archers. Volley after volley of arrows arced over the shield wall to slam into the thicket of thralls. The bridge soon grew cluttered with their dead.

Erik ordered a third shield wall to form up behind the second. *That ought to keep them busy for a while.* Satisfied that the line would hold, he handed over command of the bridge and raced back to the walls.

The ramparts were a maelstrom of swords and arrows and death. The archers had fallen back to the towers, from whence they continued to pepper the siege towers and the thralls teeming outside the gates. Kingsword infantry choked the stairs and the wall walk, trying to keep those thralls that had gained the walls from making it down to the courtyard. Below, Kingsword cavalry hacked at the enemy foot soldiers, keeping the bulk of them at bay.

Erik tightened his grip on his sword and squared his shoulders. He did not dare to think about Arran Green, what his fate meant for Liam and Alix, and for all of them. For now, there was only this battle, these gates, this one duty that lay in his charge. As always, he knew his part, and he would play it.

A thrall was bearing down on him, its dead eyes fixed on

him with singular focus. Calmly, Erik turned to face his enemy.

Alix darted through a gap in the rubble to where Liam waited, crouched behind the remains of the imperial wall. "They're moving out," she said between short breaths. "I think they've breached the gates."

Liam just nodded. He hadn't said a word since they had seen Arran Green's head mounted on a spike, his face turned toward the city walls so the defenders might see what had become of their mighty general. He followed Alix's lead efficiently enough, but he seemed half in a daze, his eyes as expressionless as a thrall's. Alix wasn't faring much better. Her head buzzed and throbbed as though a swarm of stinging wasps had been set loose inside her skull, but she did her best to keep going, putting one foot in front of the other as they weaved their way back through the ruins toward the Elders' Gate.

She slipped back through the gap and along the inside of the wall, scurrying in fits and starts like a mouse trying to avoid the keen eyes of a hawk. The enemy column had moved up the road, but there might be other eyes about, and without Green, they were more vulnerable than ever. If they failed, there would be no one to take their place, no one to light the powder and bring down the gate . . .

I can't do this, she thought as they moved through the shattered bones of the ancient city. *I don't want to die. But if I don't . . .*

That was the thought that kept her going, that drove her steps in a determined, if unsteady, rhythm. If she had been on her own, she might not have found the strength to walk willingly to her doom. But she wasn't on her own. Liam was here, and if she didn't do this thing, he would. He would do it, and he would die, and then she would have to live with the knowledge that her cowardice had killed him. Better to die a hundred deaths than suffer that fate.

They could see the old temple road now, and the dwindling shapes of the rear lines as the enemy advanced toward the broken city gates. The wind carried a distant song of steel and screams. Just ahead, the Elders' Gate loomed. Alix could almost feel Arran Green's gaze upon them.

It's time.

She crouched behind a low ridge of stone that might once have been the wall of a temple. Liam tucked in beside her. Alix swallowed the quivering knot in her throat and said, "You stay here."

That punctured through the haze quickly enough. "No," Liam said, so harshly that Alix winced. "I'm the one who's going."

She'd known he would protest, and she was ready for it. "I'm more likely to get in without being seen, and besides, I—"

"*No.* You can stop right now, Allie, because you're not going to talk your way around me. Not this time."

"Liam, please. This is bigger than us. They found Green, which means they've probably posted more guards. They probably found the powder too. I doubt they'll know what to make of it, but still . . ."

His jaw set in that stubborn cast that reminded her of Erik. "If they've set more guards, then you'll have no chance of getting in there unseen. In which case it's fighting we'll need, and I'm the better fighter."

That sounded perilously logical, but Alix ploughed on regardless. "We don't have time to argue about this. I'm going. I have Gwylim's darts, remember?" She showed him one of the tiny needles resting in the moist hollow of her palm. She hoped he didn't notice her shaking.

Liam slipped a hand around the back of her head and pulled her close, resting his forehead against hers. She felt the warmth of his skin, the whisper of his breath on her lips. *Never again . . .* Her chest clenched so tightly that it was all she could do to breathe.

"For once in your life, listen to me," he said. "I can do this. I *have* to do this. I could never live with myself if—"

"And you think I could?"

"You'll be all right. Erik will . . . He'll take care of you."

"I don't need Erik to take care of me. I need you."

He sighed. "Well, that's not going to happen, is it? I'm sorry, Allie. For everything. Just promise me . . . Promise me you won't forget."

He's not going to let me go. Not unless . . .

"All right." She spoke in a whisper so he wouldn't hear the sob battering at her ribs, trying to break through. "There's no more time to argue . . ."

He pulled back, his gaze soft with regret. "Time. We wasted so much of it. I should have told you every moment of every day . . ."

"Just go, before I change my mind." Her fingers curled around the dart, moving it subtly into position. *All he has to do is look away* . . . The fear drained from her then, replaced by a strange calm. He would hate her for this, but one day, when the war was over and he had a wife and children and a long and happy life before him, he would forgive her, and that would be enough.

He smiled. Tears shone in his eyes. "You didn't really think I was going to fall for that, did you?" He brushed her face gently, and suddenly she realised that his other hand was tucked into the pouch at his belt. She read it in his eyes a moment before he struck.

They lunged at the same time. Only one of them drew blood.

Erik fell back again. The thralls were everywhere, swarming over the Kingsword ranks in a relentless tide. His arm ached, and his grip was slick with blood. His shield was splintered almost beyond use. There were so many bodies in the street—Aldenian, Andithyrian, Oridian—that he stumbled as he fought. It would not be long now. There was no place for tactics anymore, no prospect of retreat. It ended here, one way or another. Erik could sense despair descending on the men, slowing their hearts and weakening their limbs.

He was about to call for a new shield when a strange *crack* sounded in the distance. Erik barely registered it, but a heartbeat later, it was followed by an earthy rumbling sound, a low, steady thunder unlike anything he had ever heard. On and on it went, like the pounding of a hundred thousand hooves, and then abruptly it was gone. Erik paused, his mind groping through the fog of battle. Something important had just happened, but for a moment it eluded him, as though he were grasping at the fading wisps of a half-remembered dream.

Someone bumped his shoulder. A thrall. Erik raised his blade, but the man had already moved beyond his reach, heading for the gates at a flat-out run. He did not make it far; one of Erik's knights cut him down. Others were running too, Erik saw. Dozens of them. More. All around him, thralls were scattering, in every direction at once. *Retreating*, Erik thought, but no—this was not organised enough to be a retreat. They were *fleeing*. Those that were not running just stood there, stunned, blinking in confusion as though they did not even know where they were. Some threw their weapons down. Others began to scream and clutch at wounds as though they had only just discovered the pain. Still, it took Erik a moment to process what was happening.

Then he saw the cloud of dust rising in the near distance, and he understood. The fear he had locked away tore free, for its time had come at last.

With a broken cry, the King of Alden fell to his knees.

THIRTY-FIVE

E rik stared, unseeing, at the bloodied flagstones. His ears rang. His thoughts were thin and watery. He could not feel his heart beat in the cold hollow of his breast. Vaguely, as from a great distance, he heard voices calling him. Someone put a hand on his shoulder.

Breathe.

He looked up. Soldiers were gathering around him. "Are you hurt, sire?" "Someone fetch a healer!" "Look to the king!"

Get up.

Leaning heavily on his sword, Erik pushed himself to his feet. He stood on an island of stillness in the midst of a raging river of thralls, a small crowd of Kingswords standing around him in a protective perimeter. The sight of the enemy fleeing inspired no emotion; Erik merely registered the fact as he would the direction of the wind, or the course of the tides.

Focus.

The Andithyrians could be left alone. They had never been the enemy. But the Oridians themselves had started to trickle through the shattered gates, and twenty thousand more stood outside the city walls. They were still a danger. Erik drew a long, steadying breath. Then he started giving orders.

Many of the men had paused to celebrate, but they moved back onto the attack with little prompting. They fought with renewed energy, their blood spiked with triumph and the intoxicating fear of the enemy. Erik was fuelled by a different fire. Grief and rage mingled to form a powerful alloy, and he hacked through his enemies with a strength he had never known.

"Your Majesty!"

A wall of Kingswords closed in around him, and Raibert Green appeared, bloodied but seemingly unharmed. Grateful as he was to see Green alive and well, Erik did not understand what he was doing here. "Who commands the west gate?"

"Commander Ibon, though there's little enough for him to do. We've got the enemy pinned to the south, just outside your gates. Those that aren't running will be crushed soon enough. I'm here to relieve you."

"The battle is not over . . ."

"It will be soon enough. Lord Black ordered the cavalry onto the field, all three battalions of them. The enemy ranks have scattered. We'll ride them down and butcher them like sheep."

"They're retreating?"

"Their Trion and their general have fallen, and their thralls have deserted them. They're disorganised and confused. Easy prey. I can take it from here. Go find Prince Liam."

Hearing the name unleashed a fresh wave of grief. *There may be nothing to find*, a treacherous voice within him whispered.

Seeing Erik hesitate, Green grabbed his shoulder. "This isn't a battle anymore, Your Majesty. The men no longer need their king. Go find your brother."

A moment more was all it took to decide. "Thank you," Erik said, and he called for a horse.

He did not dare ride out the south gate, where the fighting was heaviest. He headed east, clattering through empty cobbled streets with a half-dozen knights in tow. He flew past bolted doors and shuttered windows, empty livestock pens and boarded-up warehouses, scarcely conscious of the twists and turns he navigated through. An ache was welling up in his chest, rising steadily to his throat, as though he were slowly drowning. He welcomed it. The pain he could endure—it was the fear that tortured him. He did not want to face it, to know its shape. *How shall I pray to you, Virtues? Shall I ask to see my brother again, or the woman dearest to my heart? Have you not yet tired of making me choose between them?* He didn't care that the thought was blasphemous. There could be no punishment greater than this.

When he reached the east gate, he saw that it had not been breached. The ramparts looked a wreck, with shattered merlons and heaps of broken corpses littering the wall walk, but Rig had obviously managed to hold off the bulk of the assault. Lord Black himself was nowhere to be seen. His second, Commander Morris, presided over the gates, and he hesitated when Erik demanded passage.

"But, sire, there's still fighting out there."

"Where is Lord Black?"

"Outside, Your Majesty, looking for his sister."

"And I am looking for my brother. Now open these gates."

Commander Morris obeyed unhappily, and Erik and his retinue rode out. It was quiet outside the walls, but Erik could hear the sounds of battle from the south. He rode flat out, following the city walls until he reached the southeast corner, where he drew up to take in the scene.

Disorganised and confused, Raibert Green had said, but that did not begin to describe the state of the enemy ranks. Hemmed in on both sides by Kingsword cavalry, some were still trying to fight, but most were fleeing, pouring through every gap in the crumbling imperial walls. The Elders' Gate was a ruin of rubble, completely impassable. It forced the tide of fleeing Oridians west, where the old walls were weakest. The gate itself seemed to have been cleansed of enemy soldiers. Erik could see at least a score of Kingswords gathered at the foot of the old temple road, standing guard. *Rig's men*, he realised. With his heart in his throat, he kicked his horse into action.

He did not draw up until he reached the gate, and even then, the animal had barely slowed before he swept down from the saddle, stumbling a little as he started toward the shattered pile of rubble. The gate tower had collapsed northward, spilling itself over the walls and leaving only a ragged crescent of masonry on the southwest corner. The air was still choked with dust; men coughed and rubbed their eyes, and the horses twitched their ears. Erik's gaze raked over the scene, but he saw no sign of Rig.

"Where is Lord Black?" he demanded of everyone and no one.

"Here."

Erik spun to find Rig walking toward him, cradling a limp and bloodied form in his arms. A tattered braid of copper hair dangled at his elbow, swaying with each step. Erik's breath failed.

Her skin was white as alabaster, and her lips were blue. Blood caked her body from her greaves to her hairline. "She's alive," Rig said in a voice like shattered stone.

Erik reeled against a rush of nausea, relief crashing against despair as his prayers were answered and his hopes destroyed in a single breath. He could only nod weakly as Riggard Black carried his sister off the field.

Erik lingered, unable to move, staring at the ruin of the ancient Elders' Gate. The hurt was worse than he could have imagined. He felt small and broken in its grip. Around him, the air crackled with latent energy. Soon, joy would overcome weariness and fear, and the men would rejoice. A good king would rejoice with them, thanking the gods for sparing his city. But Erik was not that king. He was only a man who had lost his brother.

Both of my brothers, gone. The last of my family, gone. One I killed, and the other I sent to die. The pain clutched at him, tightening its grip, squeezing the air from his lungs. He felt himself cracking. The scene swam before him, and he sucked in a sharp breath, blinking furiously.

He tried to distract himself, to focus on the happenings around him. He spotted his brother's former comrades, the little blond scout and her tall, lanky friend. The blond girl was sobbing, and the other looked red-eyed and miserable. *They weep for Liam. As I must.*

"Erik."

He turned. The face that stared back at him was spackled in dried blood, but he would know it anywhere. Erik could not even speak, for there was no breath in his body. All he could do was throw his arms around his brother.

Liam returned his embrace warmly. "I'm so glad you're safe, Your Majesty."

"*You're alive*. Both of you. How is that possible? They told me Green was taken!"

"He was."

"But then who . . . ?"

"Blew the gate?" Liam smiled sadly. "Gwylim."

Erik stared. "Gwylim? The scout? He was with you?"

"No." Liam looked over at his friends with a sigh. "He followed us. I should have known he would. He was so adamant that Green bring him along . . . When Kerta realised he was gone, she knew what he'd done. She and Ide came looking for him, but by then it was too late. I don't know what he meant to do if everything went according to plan. I guess we never will. But when he saw what happened to Green, he took matters into his own hands."

"What about Alix? What happened to her?"

"Oh. That." Liam winced. "We couldn't exactly agree on who should light the powder, so . . . I may have . . . er . . . You know Gwylim's darts?"

Erik's mouth fell open. "You poisoned her? On *purpose*?"

"She would have done the same if I'd let her. She almost got me." He looked over his shoulder to where one of Rig's knights was helping him gather his sister onto his saddle. "She'll be all right, won't she?"

Erik let out a laugh that sounded half manic. It was all too much—he could not hope to process it, not until the fear and grief and rush of battle had faded. For now, all that mattered was that his loved ones were safe. "Don't worry," he said, putting his hand on Liam's arm. He could not help squeezing it, just to reassure himself it was really there. "She'll be fine. Everything will be fine."

For the first time in a very long time, he truly believed it.

Alix's eyes flew open. She lay still, letting her surroundings sink in. She recognised the panelled ceiling of her bedchamber in the palace, and for half a heartbeat, she sagged with relief. Then she *remembered*. The look in Liam's eyes the moment before he struck. The strength of his grip on her wrist. The prick of the needle, the sigh of the grass under his boots as he left her. And later, as darkness took her, the deep, slow rumble of a dying tower. Her heart had screamed at the sound.

Despair flooded in. It pooled in her chest, into her throat and her eyes, until tears ran hot down the sides of her face. The Elders' Gate had come down, and she had not been the one to do it. That could only mean one thing.

"Allie."

The voice was like a spear in her guts. She froze, her whole frame rattling with unspent sobs. She didn't dare to move, afraid to disturb the vision that knelt beside her like a visitation from beyond.

"Don't cry, love. I'm here. We're safe." Warm fingers gently brushed the hair from her eyes. His breath caressed her cheek. Hesitantly, her arm trembling, Alix reached for him. She rested a hand against his face. He met her searching gaze with silence. As the moments crawled past, amusement warmed his eyes, and a corner of his mouth curled into a grin. "Yes, I'm real. You can stop looking at me like that."

She flung her arms around his neck. In that moment, she didn't care if he was real. She didn't care if she was dead, or in some hell. All that mattered was his warmth, the strength of his arms. Real or not, he was *here*.

"Gwylim did it," he said. "He blew up the gate. He'd been following us, and when he saw what happened to Green . . . While you and I were arguing about who would do it, he got on with the business."

"You pricked me with a dart." Or had he? It all felt like a dream.

"Yeah, about that . . . how are you feeling?"

"Gwylim blew the gate."

"Right."

"You're alive."

He grinned. "Seriously, are you all right? Didn't hit your head or anything? You seem a little slow."

She clutched at him again, so tightly it hurt. "You're alive!"

"Not for long, if you keep that up. You're choking me, Allie."

Abruptly, Alix realised that her head hurt. A lot. Until this moment, she hadn't even noticed. "I think I'm going to be sick . . ."

The door opened, and Rig appeared. He paused at the threshold, his brow crumpling in a mock scowl. "Honestly, Allie, I've been gone for less than a quarter hour. You just had to wake up at exactly the moment I stepped out?"

"While we're on the subject," said Erik, poking his head in the door, "it's wretchedly bad protocol not to wait for the king."

Without thinking, Alix rolled out of bed to greet them. The impulse was rewarded with a wave of dizziness that left her staggering.

"Are you insane?" said Liam.

"Careful," said Erik.

Rig just rolled his eyes.

Alix paused to let the blood return to her aching brain. "I'm fine." She resisted the urge to cradle her head in her hands.

Liam gave her a flat look. "Yeah. Just so you know, that was—"

"—completely unconvincing," Erik said.

Alix glared at the brothers. "You're finishing each other's sentences now? Well, isn't that touching."

Rig snorted. "See? Didn't she say she was fine?"

She ignored him. "The city . . . it's safe?"

"For now," Erik said. "The Oridians have scattered to the four winds. No doubt they will regroup in time, and the Warlord is still perched at our border. But with the Priest gone, Sadik will think twice before marching on us again. We have time."

She tried to understand, but her mind felt sluggish. Liam's earlier words were only now starting to sink in. "Gwylim . . ."

"His memory will be honoured for as long as a White wears the crown," Erik said.

It's true, then. Gwylim did it. He saved us. Liam, me, the whole city . . . He'd sacrificed himself for all of them. What could they possibly do to honour something like that? An image flashed into her mind, a vision of a small stone man with kind eyes presiding over the Gallery of Heroes, and she almost laughed. *He would have laughed too.*

"I'm starved," Rig announced, drawing her out of her reverie.

"You're always starved," she said with a tired smile. Her brother only shrugged.

Liam put a hand on her arm. "Are you sure you're okay to be out of bed?"

"Fine. You go ahead—I'll catch up."

The men filed out of her room. Erik was last, and before he could leave, Alix grabbed his hand and gave it a tug. No words were needed. He threw his arms around her and held her close. They stayed like that for long moments, content in their stillness. He planted a gentle kiss on her forehead. Then he smiled, as bright and golden as the dawn.

They left together.

EPILOGUE

L iam stared at himself in the mirror. The tailor hovered by nervously, awaiting the verdict. The man was very old, very proud, and very Andithyrian—in other words, he was not at all disposed to criticism of any sort. Anything less than wild enthusiasm for his creations could trigger an extended sulk, and with the wedding two days away, there was simply no time for that. Erik prayed that a month at court had been enough to teach his brother a modicum of tact. He prayed, but he feared.

Rig leaned against the table beside Erik, arms folded. "Gods' balls, Liam, I've seen noblewomen who primp less than you do."

Then again, perhaps tact is not a function of time spent at court. "You look very well," Erik assured him.

"Easy for you to say. You're not the one getting married."

Rig winced. Liam flushed and looked guiltily in the mirror. Erik watched it all from behind the wooden screen of his smile. "Perhaps not," he said smoothly, "but I have rather a lot of experience being at the centre of official functions, and I can assure you that you look the part."

"That's what I'm afraid of," Liam said. "Are you sure I can't convince you to let me wear ceremonial armour?"

"Armour!" The tailor was visibly aghast. "How *vulgar*! Surely His Highness jests!"

Erik arched an eyebrow and gave Liam a significant look in the mirror. "He does."

"Thanks be to the gods." The tailor fluttered his pale little hand as though shooing a fly. "Really, Your Highness, you must put me out of my misery. Does the doublet please you or not?"

Liam cocked his head, considering. Rig groaned and rolled his eyes. Finally, Liam said, "I think it will be fine."

"Fine." The tailor's colour heightened. "His Highness *thinks* it will be *fine*. I can hardly express how deeply gratified I am that my work should be so appreciated! *Stezaan!*" His assistant rushed over and held out a box, and the tailor threw a fistful of pins inside with such vigour that they stuck to the bottom like tiny spears. The tailor grabbed the box, snapped the lid shut, and stalked from the room, Stezaan scurrying behind.

Liam watched him go in the mirror. "I think he was being a bit sarcastic with me at the end there."

"You could have humoured the man a little," Erik said. "You know how he gets."

Liam at least had the grace to look sheepish. "This just isn't me, is all."

"You'll have to get used to it." Erik put just enough edge in his voice to make it clear that he meant it.

"I don't know what you're grousing about anyway," Rig said. "It's just one day out of your life. You'll be spending plenty of time in armour, *Commander*."

"Speaking of which, *General*, when do I get to start recruiting?"

Rig shrugged. "Don't worry, you'll have plenty of good men to choose from. The White Wolves are still the most prestigious posting in the Kingswords."

A knock sounded, and a servant entered bearing a package wrapped in silk. "As you requested, Your Majesty."

"Ah, excellent. Look here, Liam, your gift has arrived."

Liam cocked an eyebrow as he took the package from the servant. "My gift?"

"An early wedding present. Open it."

Cautiously, Liam untied the cord and swept the fabric aside. "Silk wrapped in silk?"

Erik flicked his eyes skyward. "Take it out, Liam."

Liam drew out the long, shining garment, his eyes widening as it fell loose. "Is this . . . a *cape*?" he asked in horror.

Erik frowned. "Of course it is. Look, I don't like them any better than you, but it's a wedding."

"You didn't think you were going to get away with not wearing a cape?" Rig said. "Gods' blood, man, you're a *prince*!"

Liam stared dumbly at both of them. The dreaded cape drooped in his hands.

"Oh, here, give it to me." Erik grabbed the cape and swept it grandly around Liam's shoulders, affixing it in place before standing back to admire his handiwork. "There."

Liam gazed at his reflection in a state of mute disbelief. The fabric itself was bad enough, a deep purple silk so shiny that it almost looked metallic. It was trimmed in white lace, as elaborate as any ball gown, and amethysts glittered along the hem. But it was the collar that really made it: six inches high and ruffled, threaded with whalebone to make it stand straight up. It was the most dreadful thing Erik had ever seen.

Liam's expression was one of such perfect misery that Rig could no longer hold it together; he started sniggering into his beard. Erik made the mistake of looking over at him, and Rig lost it completely, nearly choking with laughter. Erik broke after that. "Gods, Black, you never could keep a straight face."

"I'm sorry." Rig swiped at his eyes. "The *look* on him, though . . ."

"Wait . . ." Liam looked from Rig to Erik and back. "Is this . . . ? This is a joke, isn't it? You're *joking*!" He scowled and fumbled with the clasp, tearing the cape off with such alacrity that Erik and Rig nearly doubled over with laughter.

Liam folded his arms, looking for all the world like a petulant two-year-old. "So this is what it means to have brothers, huh? Lucky me."

"Oh, quit sulking," Rig said. "Believe me, the prank I suggested was a lot worse."

"It involved the Maiden's Pearl."

Liam gave him a wary look. "The what?"

Rig started laughing again. Erik said, "I'll tell you when you're older."

"Oh, Alix, it's fabulous!" Kerta clapped her hands together and held them to her lips as she struggled not to cry. "How I love weddings!"

Alix did a little pirouette, enjoying the way the gown flared at her ankles. It seemed like an eternity since she had worn a dress. She felt young and beautiful and *female*. She hadn't realised how much she missed it. "I just hope I remember how to walk in heels."

"Don't worry, a lady never forgets how to walk in heels. We'll practice here in your room, just to be sure."

Alix smiled over her shoulder. She had grown rather fond of Kerta in recent weeks. Gwylim's death had brought them together in a way she wouldn't have thought possible. In her grief, Alix no longer found Kerta's effusions to be cloying. Gwylim deserved every tear, every sigh, every fond memory. And if she could still be a little sickly sweet for Alix's taste, at least Kerta was genuine. That was more than could be said of most people, especially at court. Alix had never met someone with a more generous heart, and she cringed to recall every petty, unkind thought she had ever had about Kerta Middlemarch. "Thank you for your help with the dress," she said. "I'm so fortunate to be able to call upon your impeccable taste. You do your family credit."

"Listen to you. I'd almost think you were trying to flatter me."

Alix felt herself flush. "Maybe I feel like I have something to make up for. I haven't exactly been . . ." *Kind? Fair? In any way pleasant?* ". . . the easiest to get along with."

Kerta shrugged. "You had a lot on your mind." Coming from anyone else, it would have sounded sarcastic, but Alix didn't doubt for a moment that she was sincere.

"Actually," Alix said, sweeping the dress aside so she

could perch on the bed beside Kerta, "I had only one thing on my mind: Liam. I had no right to be jealous. I'm sorry about that."

Kerta blinked, momentarily confused. Then she burst into laughter. "Alix, you can't be serious! Surely you didn't think there was something between Liam and me?"

Alix stirred uncomfortably. "Well . . . yes, actually, at least a little."

"What in the world gave you that idea?"

"Liam, for one. I practically confronted him with it, and he didn't deny it . . ."

Kerta smiled. "Well, it wouldn't be the first time a spurned heart tried to make his ex-lover jealous."

"I never spurned him," Alix said quietly.

Kerta gathered Alix's hands in her own. "Liam has been yours since the moment he met you. We all saw it. Gwylim used to say . . . Well, never mind." She smiled a secret smile. "Anyway, that's why it was so hard to see things going badly between you. Liam was a mess. You have never seen such brooding, Alix, I promise you. It was awful."

Alix squirmed. She couldn't help wondering if Arran Green had been half as perceptive as Kerta. What must he have thought of her?

"I tried to be there for him," Kerta said. "I listened, but that's all I could really do." She gave Alix's hands a little tug. "Anyway, that's all in the past. It doesn't matter how you got here. What's important is that you're here now, and you're getting married."

"In the middle of a war." Not exactly ideal, but they'd wasted enough time, and after coming so close to losing one another . . . Besides, maybe Erik was right, and a royal wedding was just what the kingdom needed. There would be few enough bright spots in this season of gloom.

Kerta sobered. "You must be worried, now that he's commander of the Pack."

"I'm not thrilled about it. But he's a prince now, and we're at war. He has duties. Besides, this is what he's always wanted, and it's not as though I'll be in the safest of places, either. Erik has no shortage of enemies."

"In that case, it's a good thing he has you."

"Kerta . . ." Alix's gaze dropped to her lap as a familiar ache tightened her chest. It was gentler these days, its edges smoothed by hours of endless worrying, but it was there all the same. It always would be. "When Liam was confiding in you, did he tell you . . . ?" She trailed off, unsure how to finish.

"About the king?" She squeezed Alix's hands gently. "What a pity that love can't be simple. The heart is a miraculous thing, isn't it? It can be completely full of love for one person, yet still find room for another."

Alix smiled sadly. "How did you get to be so wise?"

"By observing the folly of others," she said, and they both laughed.

A knock at the door, and Ide entered. She was dressed in her scouting leathers, as always, and her hair had been sawed off yet again. She looked like a teenaged boy. *However are we going to get her ready for the wedding?* Alix thought ruefully.

Oddly, Kerta didn't seem worried. "Oh, good, you're here! Show her the dress, Alix!"

Alix rose obligingly and gave a twirl, sending the silken folds swirling. The plunging back was exactly one half inch north of scandalous, which was sure to tax Liam's discipline for the many long hours of public pageantry ahead of them. It was a little bit of revenge for his constant teasing, especially in the bedroom.

"And the chain! Let's show her the chain!" Kerta handed over the marriage links, beaming.

Ide turned the necklace over in her hands. "Leather? Would've thought you'd have gold."

"Liam insisted." Alix didn't mind. Some would no doubt disapprove of the prince and his bride having their marriage links bound in leather like common peasants, but it suited them, and she liked the way the two gold loops contrasted with the dark leather thong. The only concession Liam had made to their station was to have a master goldsmith fashion the loops in the shape of two sprigs of ivy, just like the ring Alix wore on her little finger.

Ide held the chain up to Alix's throat, admiring it in the mirror. "Looks good."

"It's *perfect*," Kerta declared. "But you must give it to Rig right away. It's bad luck for the bride and groom to handle their chains too close to the ceremony."

"Where's Liam's?" Ide asked.

"Erik has it."

Kerta gave a sad little sigh. "It should be Arran Green."

She was right. Arran Green was the closest thing to a father Liam had ever known. Liam would be missing him on their wedding day, Alix knew. They both would.

So many lost. Gwylim. Arran Green. Adelbard Brown. Thousands more whose names she would never know. And still more war on the horizon . . . But not today, and not tomorrow, and that would have to be good enough for now.

They stayed silent for a moment, each lost in her own thoughts. Then Kerta swept to her feet and clapped her hands. "And now, my dear Alix, what shall we do with your hair?"

Erik was headed for the courtyard when he came across Alix. She was hurrying down the corridor on her tiptoes, as though she were afraid to be caught. Her attempts to be quiet were somewhat frustrated by the clack of high heels and the rustle of raw silk.

"Why, Captain, exactly whom do you intend to sneak up on in that magnificent dress?"

"Bugger and *damn!*" Alix fairly threw down the hem of her gown in frustration.

He laughed. "Charming. Your King's Service has not tarnished your courtly polish, I see."

"You weren't supposed to see me! Nobody was!"

"Did you imagine yourself invisible?"

She scowled. "I imagined that I was only going to be out here for a few seconds. I'm just going to fetch . . . Oh, never mind! I've got to hurry before Liam sees me! It's terribly bad luck for the groom to see the dress. Maybe it's even bad luck for the groom's brother to see the dress, and *what are you grinning at?*"

"Nothing at all, Captain. Except that I got my wish."

"Your wish?"

"To see you in a gown. I had quite forgotten." On cue, she

flushed from head to toe, offsetting her dress in a most becoming fashion. It was really too easy. "Now if we can minimise the cursing, we'll be getting somewhere. I'm not hopeful, mind you. You Blacks really are an uncouth lot." So saying, he flashed her a wink and continued on his way, perfectly aware of the smirk she directed at his retreating back.

He made his way into the courtyard and from there to the rose garden, where he wended his way through the maze. When he came to the duck pond, he nearly bumped into a figure harvesting a rose with his dagger.

His good mood evaporated immediately. "What are *you* doing here?"

"Stealing your roses, Your Majesty," the spy said. "But I assure you, it is for a good cause. I find myself unaccountably overlooked for an invitation to the upcoming nuptials, so I must content myself with a bouquet of flowers for the lovely bride-to-be."

"How did you get in here?"

"By sneaking, but that is only because I have a reputation to maintain. Our mutual friend the captain has graciously accorded me free movement privileges throughout the grounds. She has uses for me yet, it seems." He cut another stem, brought it to his nose, and breathed deeply. "You should be careful, Your Majesty, wandering about alone. It's not safe. The White Ravens may be spent, but there are others who would gladly see you fall."

"You sound like Alix."

"Or she sounds like me. Either way, it's sound advice." He considered his rose, twirling it in his fingers. "I hear Onnan has declared war on Oridia."

"They have. Our example served as a warning, it seems." Erik tried not to sound bitter, just as he had when the Onnani ambassador had informed him of the Republicana's decision. It had taken Onnan far too long to reach the inevitable conclusion. But at least they had reached it—which was more than he could say for Harram.

"I'm sure the Trions are duly terrified. The two that remain, in any case."

"Onnan may be small, but her people are fierce fighters. Just ask the old empire."

"It has been centuries since their revolt, and they have not known war since. You will not find many battle-tested generals there, I fear."

"They may surprise you." Erik wanted to believe that.

The spy shrugged. "We'll see. In the meanwhile, I will ply my contacts in the Republicana. We must know what our ally's leaders are thinking."

"*We*, is it? So I'm to suffer a spy in my midst?"

"A great many, I should think. Be thankful you know what this one looks like."

He has me there. "Very well. But if we're to make common cause, you should know that you're wasting your time infiltrating the Republicana. The speakers are just puppets; the real power lies with the secret societies. The Shield, especially. I have it on good authority that the first speaker himself is a member."

"First Speaker Kar is with the Sons of the Revolution," the spy said, "as is his second. Perhaps you are thinking of the chairman. He is a Shield."

"You are well informed."

"It is my trade, Your Majesty."

"In that case, perhaps you'll find a way to put that knowledge to work for the good of your country, instead of just your coin purse."

The spy smiled. "Perhaps."

"Just so we're clear, this doesn't mean we're friends." In fact, Erik would just as soon have nothing to do with him, but his country was at war, and even he could not deny that spies had their uses.

"I shall try to control my disappointment, Your Majesty." He spoke the words with such masterful sincerity that Erik could not help smiling. *I'll bet he's a bloody good spy at that.*

The man bowed low, and was gone.

Erik pulled his own dagger from his belt and cut a particularly splendid rose. This he laid at the foot of a jade obelisk, the newest monument to grace the royal gardens. It was beautifully crafted, its polished facets reflecting the fluid dance of the duck pond. But it was not here for decoration; it marked the place where Arran Green's bloodblade had been buried. It was all they could find of the commander general after the explosion, though perhaps that was a mercy. The mangled corpses of the Priest and his men had been terrible to look upon.

Erik cut another rose, and this he set at the foot of a second obelisk, the identical twin of Green's monument, save that it was made of quartz. Gwylim had no family name, nor a banner colour to guide them, so Alix had suggested they use the native crystal of the Blackland foothills, where Gwylim had been born. It made a beautiful pillar, flecked with cloudy swirls of white and silver, like a snowstorm frozen in time. It marked only a memory. Of Gwylim, they had found nothing at all.

Erik knelt between the obelisks commemorating the two heroes. One he had known all his life, the other he had only just met, but he owed them both more than he could say. "Thank you, my friends," he whispered. "For everything." He closed his eyes and bowed his head in a silent prayer. Then he rose, dusted his knees, and headed back to the palace with a brisk step.

There was still so much to do.

Erin Lindsey is on a quest to write the perfect summer vacation novel, with just the right blend of action, heartbreak, and triumph. *The Bloodbound* is her first effort. She lives and works in Bujumbura, Burundi, with her husband and a pair of half-domesticated cats. Visit her online at erin-lindsey.com.

Want to connect with fellow science fiction and fantasy fans?

For news on all your favorite Ace and Roc authors, sneak peeks into the newest releases, book giveaways, and much more—

"Like" Ace and Roc Books on Facebook!

facebook.com/AceRocBooks